Cry Republic

KIRK MITCHELL

ACE BOOKS, NEW YORK

This book is an Ace original edition,
and has never been previously published.

CRY REPUBLIC

An Ace Book / published by arrangement with
the author

PRINTING HISTORY
Ace edition / August 1989

ISBN: 0-441-12389-9

Ace Books are published by
The Berkley Publishing Group,
200 Madison Avenue, New York, New York 10016.
The name "ACE" and the "A" logo are
trademarks belonging to Charter Communications, Inc.

PRINTED IN THE UNITED STATES OF AMERICA

10 9 8 7 6 5 4 3 2 1

Ace Books by Kirk Mitchell

PROCURATOR
NEW BARBARIANS
CRY REPUBLIC

Now at the feast the governor was accustomed to release for the crowd any one prisoner whom they wanted. And they had then a notorious prisoner called Barabbas. So when they had gathered, Pilate said to them, "Whom do you want me to release for you, Barabbas or Joshua Bar Joseph, who is called Christ by you Hellenes?" While he was sitting on the judgment seat, his wife sent word to him, "Have nothing to do with that righteous man, for I have suffered much over him today in a dream."

Now the chief priests and the elders persuaded the people to ask for Barabbas and destroy Joshua. The governor again said to them, "Which of the two do you want me to release to you?" And they said, "Barabbas." Pilate said to them, "Then what shall I do with Joshua who is called Christ?" They all said, "Let him be crucified."

Now, with a troubled face, the governor sank into thought. And when Pilate awoke from it, he doubled the guard at the feast and then ordered Joshua Bar Joseph to be released. There was a great cry from the crowd against him. But Pilate was adamant.

The governor honored his wife for her dreams.

> —From an ancient Perushim scroll found near Lake Asphaltitis during the imperium of Caesar Fabius

CODEX I

CLAUDIA

1

FAR BELOW THE sparse layer of morning clouds, deep within the verdant cone that was Mount Vesuvius, Vulcan was fanning the coals of his forge.

For weeks now, the smith god had been hammering Campania and Latium with temblors felt as far north as the town of Forum Appii, although some sensitives as distant as Rome claimed to have been made queasy by his mischief. On a moonlit night with the stench of sulfur hanging in the air, the waters amid Puteoli's harbor had suddenly boiled, and when dawn at last broke, it was seen that the ancient mole had risen a full six inches above the level of the Tyrrhenian. A senator who owned a villa at Baiae had written Caesar Germanicus that his spring, once the coolest and sweetest in the region, had been corrupted by heat and the taste of rotten eggs. The Emperor should exercise care in all matters, the patrician had insisted, as evil and detestable things were on the way. Had not a pig with claws been born in Moguntiacum, the birthplace of Germanicus Julius Agricola? And wasn't there news of a woman in Pannonia bearing half-bestial twins? Hadn't it always been thus when Vesuvius shook off its slumber?

Poppycock.

Yet, it was this latest dispatch of a spring suddenly turning hot that had hastened Tora to Campania from his apartments in Caesar's palace on the Palatine. He knew from experience in his own country, which was peaked with many abodes of Vulcan, that this signaled the change Italia had been trying to ward off with votive offerings and animal sacrifices.

He banked his cloud-galley to soar around the summit once more, and the Gulf of Neapolis sprawled in gleaming tilt below. A spangle of sunlight rolled across the sea, its distant end seemingly anchored to the mist-shrouded isle of Capreae.

He was taking a headwind in the face now. The shape of his

5

eyes grew more tapered than usual, and his straight, jet-colored hair bristled up off his brow.

"Poppycock," he muttered to himself, thinking again of Lord Vulcan.

Tora was not a Roman, so he put no faith in offerings to the Jovian gods, as did the Italian masses. But it was much the same in his country, Nihonia, a crescent of wooded islands far to the east and under vassalage to the Makers of Silk—or the Sericans, as the Romans insisted on calling the Xing. In his homeland, however, bribes were made to the *kami*, the holy spirits dwelling atop such violent mountains. But he had no more faith in the efficacy of the *kami* than he did in the House of Jupiter. That hundreds of millions the world over bowed and sacrificed to such "powers" made them no less imaginary.

He was a *machinator*, a man devoted to machines and the principles that made them possible. But more importantly, he was an adherent to *Yinshaya*, a philosophy and way of life he'd been able to explain to narrow-channeled Latin ears only as *a complete submission to reason*. And it was because this obedience to *Yinshaya* superseded all other obligations in his life had he taken leave of his increasingly troubled emperor and lorried his craft south to prove to the Romans it was not the labors of any god but rather the superheated interplay of gases, silica, and water that was the cause of Vesuvius' restiveness. Only Caesar Germanicus, a Roman with a surprising affinity for reason, seemed open to the suggestion that this was the cause of Vulcan's mounting frenzy. He had even gone so far as to ask aloud how Lord Vulcan, whose original abode had been inside Mount Aetna on the island of Sicilia, had moved his huge forge north to Vesuvius, particularly in light of the fact established by the *pontifex maximus*, or chief priest, that the Cyclopes, the smith god's gigantic one-eyed minions, were dead—thanks to a spat with their mother, Terra.

Rome was the most superstitious great power in the history of the world, Tora was convinced of it. That her legions had managed to hold sway over half the globe for more than two thousand years was the only genuine miracle he could think of. But this miracle was now leaking from a thousand wormholes; it would not hold water much longer.

He leaned on his yaw regulator and veered toward Vesuvius' simmering crown.

A small plume of steam had just spurted out of a fumarole. Earlier, during dawn's twilight, he had seen an unearthly blue glow inside one of these natural vents, and he now wanted to capture some of the escaping gases in a glass vial. In such wispy discharges he expected to find traces of sulfur dioxide—one more sign that Vulcan might soon clear his clogged throat.

The air, even that which was rubbing up against the flanks of the mountain, was calm, and his cloud-galley glided toward the already fading spew.

"Cloud-galley," he said, shaking his head. Annoying—this insistence of the Romans to describe anything mobile in relation to their ancient sea craft, but as usual he'd bowed to their predilection. He had traded a Xing master for a Roman one, but knew it would dishonor him to be anything but loyal. "So cloud-galley it is . . ." Affectionately, he glanced roundabout his frail-looking device: gull-winged, spindly, a thorax of aluminum tubes and copper skeins enclosing a dense little iron heart chugging on an elixir of petrol and oil.

Vague movement drew his eye toward Vesuvius again. "What thing here?" he asked himself. It appeared as if the outwardly deformed and heavily cracked slope surrounding the fumarole had shuddered out of focus. And then this fleeting impression gave way to another—that the bulge was growing, trembling up curtains of dust as it swelled. But this too was short-lived, for after only a split second the entire declivity began to crumble in on itself, disintegrating into a chasm that hadn't existed moments before.

"No!" he cried, finding the presence of mind to shove the twin pitch regulators all the way forward. "Too soon!"

Diving when his terror begged him to climb, he resolutely fixed his eyes on the isle of Aenaria due west, waiting for Vulcan's hot fist to smash his cloud-galley from behind.

A lateral blast—he knew now it would be this rather than a less dangerous vertical explosion. The force of the eruption would reach directly out for him. It was only seconds away.

I never thought it could come with so little warning. It should have been heralded by swarms of temblors. Then a sudden absence of temblors. And even had these signals been lacking, the emissions of sulfur dioxide should have increased thirtyfold during these past hours!

Then it hit him, a roaring buffet that nearly tore the Aegyptian muslin off the wings.

He gnashed his teeth and squeezed shut his eyes.

As the shock passed through his cloud-galley he felt the craft jounce, float for a deceptively placid moment, and then cartwheel into a languid spin. Around and around he was jinked between two dizzying views: one of the sea, sunlit with the hope he might yet survive; the other of Vesuvius being ravaged by a huge pall of curdled ash.

Fighting the urge to pull back on the pitch regulators as if they were reins, he dove ever steeper in order to gather the speed he would need to break free of the vortex—even though the super-heated upheaval was creating a draft contrary to itself, which was howling down the flanks of the ruptured mountain and carrying along the tiny craft in its raucous wake.

He could feel the blood rush to his head. The congestion was excruciating, and he screamed to relieve it.

Finally, he was able to stop the wild spinning, but found it impossible to coax the craft out of its dive.

He continued to hurtle toward the ground at a speed certain to shake the cloud-galley apart.

From the corner of his eye he could see the plume burgeoning skyward. It was now taller than any mountain on earth, a dark gray mushroom stitched by strangely delicate lightning. Hoary godheads materialized and then vanished in the ever-shifting convulsion, Vulcan and his retinue triumphant. Phantasms, certainly—but still with the power to terrify him.

Bellowing again to lessen the pressure inside his head, he switched tactics and pulled back on the pitch regulators with both hands.

The vineyards at the foot of the mountain were coming up at him swiftly, altogether too swiftly.

On the verge of crashing, he purposely abstracted his thoughts. It was the way of the warrior class to which he'd been born: to couch indifference to one's own death in a final sensibility for the beauty of the world. The vines below had been lit vivid green by the warmth of early summer. And some said that beneath these vineyards an ancient city lay entombed in volcanic ash and mud. Perhaps that was the underworld to which Tora would now go, although a Nihonian looked to the sun in the moment of his death.

He supposed that these thoughts constituted his death poem.

But then the earth announced its threshold in a sensation of thicker air. The tips of the cloud-galley's bent wings were almost touching, but enough muslin was presented to this sterner layer of atmosphere to slow his dive—and he felt the blood drain back into his torso and legs as the craft cleared the vinous rows by mere feet and arced back up into the sky.

When he had recovered a bit, his first thought concerned the direction of the wind. It was out of the south—and driving the plume north toward Rome at a fast rate.

Exhausted, he flew along the northern rim of the bay, avoiding the cluttered center of Neapolis should any part of his machine suddenly fail and necessitate a landing, and finally descended to the pasture near Puteoli. There, the five praetorian guardsmen who'd escorted him down the Via Appia last night now sat on the cedar bed of their boar-prowed lorry, unmindful of his hard bouncing across the rutted meadow. They were gaping up at the eruption.

Yet, keeping their own company was another contingent of praetorians. These members of the imperial bodyguard seemed to have little interest in Vesuvius, and they gazed at Tora with such ruthlessness he immediately thought of his *katana*, or long sword, which was snugged in the storage area behind his seat.

Their centurion approached. "A word, Tora-*san*," he said over the last mutterings of the cloud-galley engine before Tora silenced it with the snap of a lever.

"Yes?"

"We're to escort you back to Rome at once."

"On whose authority?"

"Why—Caesar's, of course." The look in the centurion's eyes said otherwise.

"Then I shall go directly to the Campus Martius."

"How, sir?"

"In this machine."

The man smiled away his sudden annoyance. "If you do so, you countermand the wishes of Antonius Nepos."

"Then it is the praetorian prefect, not the Emperor, who orders me back to Rome."

"When you've been in our country longer, Lord Tora, you will appreciate how the prefect's and the Emperor's orders are most often one and the same."

"But not always . . ."

The centurion gave the same irritable smile. "No, and I see now what they say is true—your wit is as keen as your Latin." Unconsciously perhaps, the centurion gripped the hilt of his short sword, rattled the blade in its scabbard. "By your leave, will you follow me to the prefect's sand-galley?"

"Yes, if you will permit me to convey my machine over to its lorry for loading."

"By all means." Lighting some lungweed and exhaling a stream of smoke, the centurion inclined his silvered helmet toward Vesuvius: "Some stew, what?"

"Indeed . . . some stew." Tora restarted the engine and inched the cloud-galley forward. But instead of turning toward the lorry, where two praetorians were already readying the tie-downs, he accelerated out into the meadow and—after a short, jarring run with the guardsmen shouting and waving their arms in pursuit— lofted into the dark noon sky. It was spitting a pithy volcanic hail, so he turned out to sea.

Down they trooped from their brick bastion of the Castra Praetoria—a thousand strong, a full cohort of guardsmen resplendent in their burnished cuirasses and red capes. At their van marched Decimus Antonius Nepos, the foremost of their number and, by a tradition that went back nearly two millennia to Caesar Tiberius, the chief partner of the Emperor's laborers, the man who never lifted his finger off Rome's erratic pulse.

"Wheel right!" his first centurion bawled, turning the column at a dogleg in the street.

A conspicuously handsome man, Nepos had fine, well-balanced features any Italian patrician would have been proud to put to the test of physiognomy, although he was as Lusitanian as common cork. His heritage was something no one dared broach in his otherwise confident and easy presence.

"Quickstep now, First Centurion."

"Aye, Prefect. Lads, to the quick—*march*!"

No steam-spewing rattly vehicles slowed the progress of the praetorians. By ancient edict, none was permitted on Rome's narrow streets during the first ten hours of the day. So, within minutes, the cohort was being arrayed by the first centurion into a double file that completely encircled the Curia.

Nepos continued on alone into the Senate house, whose paunchy aristocrats rose from their curved stone benches to applaud his entrance. Patricians who only a year ago would have shunned shaking the hand of this son of a cork merchant, he reminded himself with a wry smile.

He acknowledged their noisy approval with a military salute, then eased down into a seat at the rear of the Curia.

The president of the Senate—a dotard who would have been fit only for the fuller's occupation, wallowing away his days in a vat of piss had he not been born to an ancient and venerable family—rose with cracking knees from his curule chair on the low dais at the front of the chamber. As he rocked unsteadily on his feet, the hem of his toga flowed around his swollen ankles like a purple wave. "Conscript Fathers," he began in his obnoxiously feeble voice, "those of us enrolled in the College of Pontifices are convened today at the summons of the *pontifex maximus* . . ." Assiduously, Nepos showed no emotion at mention of the chief priest, nor did he trade glances with the forbidding-looking man, who himself had been plucked out of obscurity when Germanicus declined the highest religious office as a means of streamlining his own. Caesar had also recently divested himself of the post of censor, thus legally denying himself supreme authority over the Senate—a curious thing for a Julian emperor to do, a most curious thing indeed . . . "to investigate a matter of potentially divine relevance"—the president squinted at a wax tablet held up to him by one of his child slaves—"which—which occurred or did not occur within the Sanctuary of Helios at Augusta Treverorum on the *kalends* of last month—or was it the ides? Damn you, lad, hold the bloody tablet still!"

Whatever—Nepos recalled the day in Belgica perfectly, although what had or had not actually happened would have little bearing on what was decided here today. What mattered was the impression that would be planted in these fallow wine-soaked brains.

Frowning, the president suddenly brushed aside the tablet. "Well, the noble *pontifex maximus* will clarify matters."

Yes, indeed, Nepos murmured inwardly.

Then a hundred men who'd been found too dull by their own fathers even for military service came to their feet in deference to the equally useless head of their useless college of myth-tenders and hairsplitters. *Did the Trojan horse exist as an historical object or was it Homer's symbol for Poseidon's divine intervention in the form of an earthquake that shook down Troy's walls?* From this very chair Nepos had watched in disbelief as a week of debate was wasted on that vital question.

Two slaves placed a curule in the middle of the marble semicircle formed by the curvature of the benches, yet the *pontifex* did not take it. Instead, he called for Antonius Nepos to come forth for questioning.

His expression properly grave, Nepos descended the broad steps and, at the *pontifex's* bidding, sat in the chair, leaning forward slightly to give an attentive appearance. Men often make up their minds because of such small gestures.

The *pontifex* hooked his forefinger across the bridge of his nose—a gesture of extreme pensiveness. In this way he remained silent for several moments, then said to Nepos, "Encounters of the sort purported here are serious affairs. Very serious indeed— particularly when they involve great personages. For if such an encounter is genuine, we mortals are given a glimpse of celestial favor or disfavor. Empires can be raised up or destroyed on the turn of such auguries. For this reason, any inquiry into an event like this must be incisive beyond customary propriety. Can you, Decimus Antonius Nepos, understand this need for frankness in regards even to the first citizen of Rome? You, the man who is charged with the greatest loyalty of that citizen?"

Nepos paused, artfully. "I believe I can."

"Very well. Before we delve into what happened at Augusta Treverorum, I would like to establish certain facts which might prove pertinent to the event. First, your relationship to Germanicus Julius Agricola. Are you a member of the Julian gens?"

"I am no blood relative to Caesar, Lord *Pontifex*."

"But you *are* related to Claudia Nero, mother to young Quintus Agricola, Caesar's adopted son."

"That is true."

"Would you say that this fact was material in your being appointed praetorian prefect?"

Nepos' eyes flashed with anger, but he quickly recovered himself. "No—for two reasons," he went on evenly. "First, my cousin Claudia Antonius was married to the late Gaius Nero, whose treason is the most notorious betrayal of Rome since Coriolanus'. For this cause alone, Caesar might well have nominated another. Yet, he did not. This leads me to give credence to my second reason—that Caesar looked not at my lineage, for which I am helpless, but to my valor during the siege of the Aztecan capital of Tenochtitlan last year. It is said within the Tenth Legion that none was braver than Decimus Antonius Nepos on that final day." He smiled as if realizing he'd over-stepped decorum. "You must excuse my immodest words, but there is a greater virtue than humility at work in them. To deny fame is to deny goodness itself. And I cannot turn a blind eye on my own goodness any more than I can on Caesar's . . . or *Rome's*."

There were several grunts of approval—more for Nepos than for Germanicus, the praetorian prefect felt sure. Lately, in many circles, Caesar's natural humility was held to be false.

"Very well then," the *pontifex* said. "Turning to that final day at Tenochtitlan—was Caesar wounded?"

"He was, in severalty."

"And the nature of those wounds?"

Nepos hesitated, looking uncomfortable again. "Well, his legs were broken . . ."

"And was he not alternately insensible or delusional for some days?"

Nepos tightened his lips, then finally nodded.

"And was it not the opinion of Caesar's physician, the Greek Epizelus, that the head injury he sustained at Tenochtitlan inflamed an older one Caesar had suffered during the Anatolian revolt?"

"I wasn't aware of this prognosis. At the time I had my hands full with the Aztecan eagle knights."

"But were you aware of a report that, for several days after being wounded by sword in Agri Dagi, Germanicus Agricola, then procurator of Anatolia, carried on conversations with the likes of the deified Gaius Julius Caesar?"

Nepos let his silence speak for him.

"Then let us turn to more recent events," the *pontifex* said curtly. "What business brought the Emperor to Augusta Treverorum, if you're at liberty to say?"

"Yes, I may—the coming transfer of the province from imperial to senatorial control . . ." This reminder was enough to make several senators glower. While Caesar's plan would give the senators wider latitude, it also promised to distrupt their idle and gouty status quo. But more importantly, as Nepos knew all too well, it was a hint of something ominous in the future of the imperial apparatus on which they all staked their comfort and prosperity.

"And what reason did Caesar give for going to the Temple of Helios?"

"Long ago, his father had given thanks there after a victory over the Germans. It was my impression that Caesar wished to relive that day."

"So you and the Emperor entered the sanctuary together—"

"No—pardons, Lord *Pontifex*, but Caesar commanded his guard to remain outside. He went in alone."

"But what of his German legionary, who reportedly never leaves his side?"

"The centurion Rolf stayed with us in the courtyard."

"I see . . . I see . . ." The *pontifex* tapped his lower lip with a knuckle. "How would you describe Caesar's mood on this day?"

"Prior to entering the sanctuary?"

"Yes, Prefect."

"Well . . . a bit distracted, I'd say. He's had much to occupy his mind since returning from his exhausting campaign against the Aztecae."

"And his mood after coming out of the sanctuary?"

Nepos sighed. "Shaken. I suppose I can think of no better word than shaken."

"Was his complexion ashen?"

"To the lips."

"Was his speech coherent?"

"Yes, but rapid and breathless. I couldn't quite catch everything he said."

"But that which you did catch, Prefect—please tell us."

Nepos gazed up at the aperture in the roof, then followed the stream of light down to where it glanced off the bald pates of the senators. "He said he had been praying before the bronze effigy of Helios when it suddenly stirred to life . . ." He paused; it was so still in the Curia he could hear the scuffling of sandals in the Forum Romanum outside. "And when Caesar turned to flee he found Victoria standing in his way, holding a laureled crown she promised to bestow on him if only he would shed his purple mantle, forever—" The gasps and murmurs that followed made it hard for Nepos not to smile. This show of dismay among the old men fulfilled his expectations.

The *pontifex maximus* met his eyes and held them. He started to ask another question but at that instant a praetorian colonel burst inside and cried: "Vesuvius erupts!"

To a man, the senators hiked up the hems of their togas and hobbled outside to peer south at the dark brown smudge riding the south wind toward Rome.

But the prefect and the *pontifex* remained inside.

They had known about the eruption for over an hour—but had not wished to spoil the surprise for the others. The world often hinges on surprises.

2

THE CORRIDORS HE prowled were forlorn of window and atrium. But for an occasional oil lamp bracketed to a clammy wall, it was the lightless heart of the Palatine.

Outside, he'd been told, the first soot from Vesuvius was dimming Rome's afternoon sky. A portent, perhaps. Yet he felt too weary in mind and body to be much alarmed by omens.

A stocky man with a slight limp from an injury received at the final battle for Tenochtitlan, he hurried from door to door, testing the locks, questioning the braces of bored praetorians he sprang upon in the vestibules between the various apartments of the imperial household: "Have you seen the child, my men? Where now is young Quintus . . . ?"

No one claimed to know.

Shortly before the eighth hour of the day, with a scorched smell wafting into the palace, he gave up the direct approach to finding his adopted son and instead resorted to old-fashioned Latin cunning. Recalling a hypocaust flue from the explorations of his youth in this, the ancestral home of his gens, he bent double and stole down the summer-cool heating pipe that ran beneath the widow Claudia Nero's sumptuous apartments—every wall and column embellished with erotica, no doubt—to the furnace room of a small bath which had once served the more sordid revels of the late Emperor Fabius.

At least Claudia had chosen her surroundings with tradition in mind, albeit a perverse tradition—of which this gilded hill had many.

There, the limping man used his powerful arms to wrench an iron grate out of its rusted casing. Then, grunting, he crawled through this opening into the *tepidarium*, only to be challenged by a thoroughly confused guardsman: "*Caesar Germanicus*?"

"Uncle!" Quintus cried from the lukewarm pool, not yet

versant with the fact that he was the Emperor's one and only heir, the *imperator designatus* as most saw it—a glimpse of innocence that tore at Germanicus' heart. "Bathe with me!"

"A moment, my boy." Germanicus turned to the praetorian: "Retire to the *frigidarium*."

"But, Caesar, the dowager has given—"

"There is no dowager on the Palatine. The dowage-*what*?"

"But I have my—"

"Orders from me! And if you tell anyone of this, I'll cuff you with my own hand! Do you understand?!"

The man saluted and withdrew. There was no worse indignity for a citizen than to be struck by hand—even a sword blow was preferred to being slapped. In a better hour, Germanicus might have regretted threatening such a powerful insult. But this was not a better hour.

He dropped his simple linen tunic to the tiles and slipped nude into the pool. The boy stared fascinated at the middle-aged soldier's scars, some bleached white by the years, others still purple with the freshness of pain. And with equal captivation Germanicus regarded the boy's pale, unblemished skin. Had he himself ever been so flawless? Did the rancorous human spirit eventually corrupt the body as well? "Are you ill, my child?"

"No, Uncle."

Another of Claudia's lies then, but Germanicus said nothing about it. "I've missed you, Quintus."

"And I you, Caesar. Mother says you haven't been"—his bright gaze foundered in search of the word— "*right*."

Germanicus cupped his hand and lapped water over a shoulder cratered decades before by Anatolian shot.

"Have *you* been sick?" the boy went on, innocently enough it seemed.

"I suppose . . ."

"From what?"

Germanicus tried not to sound too bitter; however, his own son deserved the truth about his innermost feelings. "I have the sickness that comes from seeing the labors of a lifetime take on the stink of futility."

"I don't understand."

"You will soon enough, I fear. Sooner than later, the mighty as well as the powerless—we're all acquainted with this sickness. Some say the gods infect us with it."

"Why?"

"To prepare us for death." Then he smiled sadly and stroked the child's wet straw-colored hair. In light of what he had in mind, it had been mad to adopt Quintus; yet, there are so few ways in which an emperor of Rome might manifest his love for anyone. The citizens of the Empire required good government of Caesar, not love, and the love they offered in return was as hollow as reeds, as brackish as a stagnant pond. Inescapably, the adoption had contained a political as well as a personal motive: Germanicus had wanted it known that the perfidy of Quintus' late father, Gaius Nero, with the Aztecae, didn't jeopardize the safety of his family and clients, as had been the custom with convicted traitors all too often in the past.

However, Claudia Nero—Gaius' cunning harlot of a widow— had seen more in the adoption than a lonely man's devotion to a child who so closely resembled the natural son he had lost to war. It seemed only logical to her that Caesar's adoption of her son would inevitably lead to herself becoming empress. And not one to let matters meander down their own course, she had chosen a propitious night—when the moon was full and the arteries of a man supposedly gorged with passion—to steal into Germanicus' apartments and await him in his military-style pallet, her flesh glistening with unguents and her dyed blonde hair undone around her shoulders. Germanicus Agricola was not in the habit of bedding the widows of his dead adopted nephews—and had calmly told her so.

After that ghastly night, she began keeping Quintus from his daily tutorial with Germanicus on transparent excuses of illness. He had lived too long on the Palatine not to realize that Claudia's wrath might go beyond putting the boy under wraps. She was already calling herself the dowager, based on some spurious claim Gaius Nero had once made to the purple.

But more disturbing than any menace Claudia could concoct against him was a rumor that the first cohort of praetorians, the very one safeguarding his person at this moment, was on the verge of mutiny.

At noon Germanicus had sent his personal bodyguard, the centurion Rolf, to the Castra Praetoria to sniff out any truth in this report. As usual, the German veteran had groused at leaving Caesar's side, but in the end had obeyed his orders.

"Are you tired, Uncle?" Quintus now asked precociously.

"Yes, my boy. Very."

"Why are you always so tired these days?"

Germanicus paused, carefully composing the words in his head before saying them. This child, who was now sealing his palms together to squirt little jets of water across the pool, might well be his only apologist to a future that would question why he had risked civil war in order to restore the Republic. "Over the centuries," he said finally, "we Romans have done something very foolish . . ."

"How can true Romans be foolish, Uncle?"

He smiled again. "On a grand scale—believe me. But whatever the case, we Romans invested all of the power to do things, even quite ordinary things, in one man. And it often seems to this solitary man that the instant he turns his back his subjects change to stone on the spot."

Quintus was eyeing him carefully; it was unsettling, for his eyes resembled his mother's. "Is this man the Emperor, Uncle?"

"What do you think?"

"I think so." He wiped his sweat-pearled face on his arm. "Then we shouldn't have an emperor?"

An innocuous enough question—yet one that could demolish both peace and prosperity for half the world. Germanicus hadn't enjoyed a decent night's sleep in months.

"Long ago," he went on in the same schoolmasterish tone of voice, "in the good, brave time after we Romans had thrown off our last king, it was believed that men of good character and breeding should share equally in this burden we now place on one man . . ." And to resuscitate this ideal in the hearts of modern Romans was about as easy as persuading today's Aegyptians to build pyramids.

"Are you a *republican*, Uncle?"

Good Jupiter—had Claudia put him up to this one? "I'm a cranky old man of fifty-three summers who's boiling hot to think that you've not lifted a *codex* since our last lesson!"

"This isn't true. I finished all of Dio Cassius, as Caesar commanded."

Germanicus' eyes softened. "Thank you, Quintus—Caesar apologizes. You have no idea what that means to him. Especially now . . . especially now." Then, dripping, he rose from the pool and donned his tunic, which clung to his body. "Are you worthy of a confidence?"

"Yes, of course!"

"This is deadly serious, I fear."

"Anything, Uncle!"

Germanicus lowered his voice: "Should a stranger come to you and say: *Son, bestir yourself, call up the Zephyrs, take to your wings and glide*—you must go with that man. You must go even against the wishes of your mother. Can you promise me that?"

Quintus' face was agonizingly grave for a few moments. "Yes, Caesar."

Germanicus nodded. "And for a sesterce—the source of the quotation?"

"The *Aeneid*."

"Well done." Then Germanicus suddenly realized that he had no coins on his person, but Quintus looked preoccupied with something more than sesterces.

"Uncle . . . ?"

"Yes?"

"Did you *really* see Helios and Victoria?"

Germanicus touched his hand to his brow as if it had begun to ache. "I don't know what I saw. The sun was very hot, very bright that day. And a man often sees what he needs to see in order to carry on. Farewell for now—and say nothing of this meeting."

"I promise, Uncle."

Midway between the Castra Praetoria and the tumbledown Baths of Diocletian, on a sidestreet too narrow for all but handcarts, stood a wineshop known as the Red Cape. It was unlike other wineshops of the city in that its tables were never thronged by Tiber bargemen, runaway slaves, and the usual provincial riffraff. The Red Cape had a select clientele. It was the favorite haunt of off-duty praetorians.

However, the tall and powerfully built German in the coarse woolen wrap who marched inside out of the light ash fall found only a handful of guardsmen.

They scowled up from their cups, but it took them only a glimpse to recognize the German's martial bearing—if not the barely perceptible bulge of a short sword beneath his civilian traveling cloak. Satisfied that no one unacceptable had invaded the quiet gloom of the Red Cape, they turned again to the fussy Roman ritual of mixing wine with up to eight times its volume in water. Only a barbarian would take his satisfaction undiluted, a barbarian like the German who now took a scarred table bench, keeping his broad back to the wall and his gaze fixed on the scallop of arches that opened the shop to the street.

Awaiting refreshment, he began stroking his blond mustaches. He was also doing some addition in his head concerning the nine cohorts of the praetorian guard quartered in the city:

One cohort, as always, was in service on the Palatine. A thousand men clicking back and forth across the priceless mosaics in their hobnailed sandals.

Five cohorts were being held in active reserve inside their brick fortress, ready at a moment's notice to race down the smoky funnel of tenements between the Viminal and Esquiline hills to preserve the Emperor's life.

That left another three cohorts at leisure, either in their barracks or out and about the neighboring ward in patronage of its many brothels and wineshops. Yet the German had already determined that these three thousand guardsmen were not in their barracks, and now it was apparent they weren't to be found in any numbers outside the Castra Praetoria as well.

For storms building at sea, one watched the horizons. For storms brewing in Rome, one kept an eye on the praetorian guard. Something was wrong.

The owner of the Red Cape finally noticed him and hobbled over to the table, carrying a wine jar and two small bowls. Like the German, he was a man with a long skull, reddish blond hair, and freckles from years of service under the blistering sun of the Mare Nostrum. He tossed down the bowls, waited for them to stop wobbling, then poured. Not only did he disdain to cut the drink with water, as did these prissy peninsular folk, he forwent wine altogether in favor of *met*, stronger fare made from honey and malt. "You shit for that old man too, now?"

The German at the table growled back at him: "I shit for no man."

"Not even yourself? Then that be why you be surly, Rolf of the brainless Marcomanni."

He smiled a little. "Enough of this fine Cherusci welcome—I be thirsty."

"That be nothing new."

They drank, then the owner poured again. This round they savored at a pace Romans would have still found reckless.

Like Rolf, who'd quit the guard for a legion posting closer to his dying father, the owner had once been a praetorian—until a Parthian warrior lanced him through the hips. As gangly youths fresh from the forests of Germania, the two had served the

Emperor Fabius together in a callower world they now recalled in a moment of silent longing.

"To Caesar Germanicus' health," Rolf said, hoisting his bowl.

"Aye, to good Germanicus," the owner responded without hesitation.

Rolf's eyes narrowed. "To Prefect Nepos' health."

The owner paused for a split second, but then said offhand, "Aye, to the prefect then."

And from this Rolf realized that the owner had no special affection for Decimus Antonius Nepos, that he probably thought of him as a latecomer to the brotherhood of the red cape.

Lapsing into silence again, they drank broodingly.

Rolf was tempted to switch to the Gothic tongue for what he needed to ask next. But he was Marcoman and the owner Cheruscan, and the dialects of the two tribes were distinct enough to make Latin necessary in a matter this delicate—and explosive. Besides, Gothic whisperings aroused fear in most Romans, who saw an uprising of the long-skulled tribes at every turn, even though most Germans had been reasonably Romanized for nearly two thousand years.

Rolf flicked his chin toward the empty tables. "Business be poor, aye?"

"Since last eve . . . aye."

"Vesuvius, maybe?"

"Nay, they drink more when Vulcan blows. Not Vesuvius."

"Discipline then—the lads be kept to barracks?"

"Nay, nay . . ." The owner poured again. "Three cohorts be gone to Etruria last night."

"Etruria?" Rolf echoed in confusion. "Where they be garrisoned there?"

"No garrison. Afield, I hear—the sad lot barter for sleep with the crickets."

"Which cohorts be so lucky?"

The owner told him. And if Rolf had been forced at that moment to wager which three cohorts of the nine were most loyal to Caesar, he would have been naming those sent by their prefect to the countryside north of Rome.

The owner obviously smelled something too, although his expression remained bland. "I hear the brainless Marcomanni gather for Assembly soon."

Rolf shrugged. "Aye, sooner than usual."

"You be going then?"

"Nay, I be busy here."

The owner's eyes were hard on his. "How soon to retirement?"

"For me?

"Aye, for Caesar's own bodyguard."

Rolf didn't answer.

"Go home to the Wald, Rolf of the Marcomanni. Be quick and go home." The owner got up and tended to some other customers, even though they hadn't called for service.

By the tenth hour, Rome lay under a bronze-colored pall. It had been ferried all the way from Vesuvius to the Tiber by a south wind that had died suddenly in the past few minutes, leaving curtains of ash to waffle down through the thick silence. The city's millions had withdrawn into their houses and tenements. Shops were tightly shuttered, their awnings struck; the unaccustomed vacancy of streets broken only by the raised stepping-stones at the intersections, each so roundly heaped with ash, it appeared to be an enormous mushroom.

One dwelling in the whole of Rome, it seemed, had a window open to the dusky sky. Beneath that window reclined Antonius Nepos, abed with his first cousin, the self-proclaimed dowager Claudia Nero.

They were both spent by lovemaking, but too wary of each other to luxuriate in it.

Still, his heavy-lidded eyes watched Vesuvius' silica glitter down as if this cinched the best possible omen in his behalf. He failed to wipe away the gray dust that had collected across his cheekbones and in the pronounced cleft of his chin. "What hour is it?" he asked, refusing to lower his gaze from the sky for even a moment.

Half-rising, she glanced at the antique water clock across the room, her heavy breasts lolling back and forth as she lay down again: "A bit past the tenth."

"Good—your son's out of the palace by now. In another hour the object of our future regency will be tucked away safely in the garrison up at Fidenae." He sighed. "I'm dying for news out of the south. Are the bastards marching? I've never trusted the Third Augusta. Now give me the lads of the Seventh Geminia and—"

"I do so wish Quintus could have left with me in my litter. The curtains were drawn—"

"No, it just wasn't possible. The old republican bastard has all his antennae up. One whiff of danger—and he'll try to rally the guard around him."

"What good would that do him?" Her bejeweled hand left his bare chest and tenderly brushed the ashes off his face. "The guard is yours."

He laughed as contemptuously as he dared—he still needed her. "*Some* of it is mine. And a man in my position is seldom sure which *some* is entirely his. It's bold enough to even think about killing Caesar. I feel no need to be reckless." He turned back to the ash fall, and satisfaction washed over his features again. "His world is going up in smoke. That's what this means, truly. His imperium is disintegrating . . ."

It was too warm for the damask coverlet, and he kicked it down around his ankles. When Claudia, as cold-blooded as an asp, reached down to bring it up again, he stayed her with a glare. "Even as a child you were cold to the touch."

"Was I?"

"Yes, but I hope no offense is taken."

"Oh, none is." Stone-faced suddenly, she began stroking his chest, but then seized a fistful of hair and yanked as hard as she could. Unclenching her fingers, she watched the dark brown tuft float down to the sheet.

He slapped her. She answered the blow with only a smarting grin.

But then he kissed her, his passion lit again. And she returned his fervor as if no anger had just passed between them.

"Tell me something . . ."

Her breath was cold on his cheek. "What, my love?"

"Honestly now, could you have let the old bastard touch you?"

She backed away from him a few inches and said nothing.

"Could you have become his empress at that price?"

Again, the smarting but childishly triumphant grin. "He has a grave virility I find attractive."

"Good Mars, he's old enough to be your father."

"I loved my father," she said a bit ambiguously. Her hand brushed the hair off her brow, revealing a mole beneath her arm. Disliking imperfections of any kind in a woman, he glanced away. "Besides, one thing can't be denied—Germanicus is highborn, more so than anyone alive. Wouldn't you say?"

His confident look faded for an instant, revealing a vague uncertainty of self he carefully masked from the world. It was the same inner gnawing that sets men of humble birth down the path of unbridled ambition—and even highborn conquerors off to foreign lands in search of an exalted destiny. He and Claudia had hostaged each other to a shared past: Her uncle, his own father, had exported Lusitanian cork to Rome—a bung peddler, as Claudia described him with a sneer; and his uncle, her father, had enjoyed only a slightly more elevated status, having won the tax collection contract for the down-at-heel district surrounding Olisipo.

Nepos realized that if she felt sure of her power to do so, she would have him murdered. And he would certainly attempt to murder her—by strangulation with his own hands, he sometimes fancied with relish—but for Quintus. He required her son to gain the purple. And of all the men in Rome, Decimus Antonius Nepos deserved the imperium.

By rigorous drill in his personal habits—when licentiousness was more to his taste—he had acquired a certain graciousness that passed most patrician tests. By utter ruthlessness in battle he had won a reputation for fearlessness and martial prowess; no one questioned that he was a soldier to be reckoned with. Yet Claudia Nero was now telling him none of this mattered, that he was still the son of a cork merchant.

True to her patient brand of anger, she had returned his slap. Claudia seldom struck when first incited; she waited for a moment of flawless advantage before baring her fangs.

However, she knew him well, he admitted to himself. And he in turn knew her just as fully, just as unsympathetically—the two views were unavoidably one and the same in his mind, for to have intimate knowledge of another human being was to detest and distrust him. By clinging to this mental outlook in his dealings with others, he had survived a long time for a man in the thick of Roman politics.

He was twenty-nine.

Leaving Puteoli, Tora had flown twenty Roman miles out to sea and then north in keeping with the Campanian coast, a course that put him on the outer edge of the rapidly advancing pall. In the time since he'd soared away from the meadow and his praetorian escort, the color of the plume disgorging from Vesuvius' summit had changed from dark gray to almost black and finally to a rich umber—signs that fresh magma was worming its way toward the surface.

Eventually, a bank of fog curling around the isle of Pontia forced him back over the mainland and into the wispy fringes of the volcanic cloud. Even this light concentration of ash stung his eyes and seared his lungs—each particle was in fact like a minute shard of glass, seemingly ripping tissue with each blink and breath he took.

He was almost to Tarracina when his engine began coughing. The exhaust flowing back over him stank of vaporous oil, and no amount of tampering with the flux lever quieted the loud sputtering.

Listening to the clattering of the pistons with a keener ear now, he worried that they might freeze suddenly in midstroke, leaving his craft to spiral down like a dry leaf.

Rome. He had to get back to the capital.

He had glimpsed it in the brittle courtesy of the centurion sent by Antonius Nepos to Puteoli: Something was about to explode in Rome.

Reaching overhead, he gave a steady tug on a copper skein. As he banked back toward Vesuvius, the countryside tilted away toward the yet bright sea and then the tendril of fog over Pontia. The ever-growing plume was hooded now like a king cobra's head, sprawling north over Campania into Latium as the stiff southerly wind pushed it on toward Rome.

In three hours the skies above the Forum Romanum would be dark and cindery, he was sure of it. But long before that, the worst of the ash would overtake him and make flight impossible—unless he could tap out his air strainers somehow and be on his way again quickly.

Swooping over a windbreak of olive trees, he began to descend on a field of spelt, but had to pull up for a feathery row of asparagus marking a hidden canal. At last he bounced down—his engine dying before he could shut it off—into the ripe winter wheat, and the cloud-galley rustled to a halt near a dozen slaves bundling straw in the dusty wake of a steam-driven threshing lorry.

At first, their leathery faces showed no emotion, then fear twisted them. Some of the men tried to fend off the sight of the strange machine by holding their hands out in front of them. One by one, they began plodding off for the windbreak, phlegmatically, as if they'd never run before.

"Stop!" Tora cried. "In the name of the Emperor!"

One man, who'd been hobbling arthritically, gave up and turned back to face the Nihonian.

"Who are you, lord?" he asked. Perhaps he believed Tora and his machine to be a single monster unleashed from the fiery gorge of Vesuvius. His undershot jaw was trembling as he bowed from the waist. "Have I sacrificed to you in the past, lord?"

"I'm no god—but a legionary on Caesar's business. Tell the operator to bring his lorry over here!"

"Anon."

While this was being done, Tora unhitched his air strainers and examined them. As suspected, the silk-weave screens were clogged.

Where was that bloody lorry?

Glowering, he saw once again why Rome, which had stood countless times on the brink of invention, had never lofted a cloud-galley until his arrival: Even in terror, the Roman slave was as lethargic as a domesticated water buffalo—and here was the very person on whom the patrician class, ever disdainful of the work of the mechanic, had sloughed off the skills necessary for the development of even the simplest contraption.

Finally, the lorry chugged over, its cowlings aswarm with slaves who were now more curious than afraid.

"Stop there and touch nothing!" Tora ordered the operator, a Nubian youth with a fine musculature showing through his tatters of a *tunica*. The labors of the field would soon waste away such audacious health. Or even worse, the young slave would be carted off to a gladiatorial school.

Tora found the boiler petcock and bled a jet of rusty-smelling steam onto each of the strainers, then knocked off the excess moisture against the cleated treads of the vehicle.

"Take me with thee, lord . . . or I die."

Tora looked up in surprise. The slave with the undershot jaw had spoken. He averted the man's moribund eyes. "I cannot break Caesar's law."

"Then have Caesar break his own law . . . I beg thee . . ."

Tora strapped himself back into his cloud-galley. The engine fired without hesitation. He would have smiled to himself but for the pleading of the slave, which he now drowned out with a surge of the throttle. Long ago in the empire of the Sericans, Tora had suffered the life of a slave. It had been far more comfortable than the existence of these wretches, but it was still a time he tried to forget.

He rolled away from the lorry and gained speed across a strip of wheat that had already been cut and threshed. As always, he savored the thrill that came from suddenly slipping into the air. The slaves fell away as if the ground on which they stood was being lowered into the underworld.

The sky was like midnight's under the thickening pall—another minute or two and he would have been forced to remain in the spelt field.

Southeast of Tarracina he veered away from the Via Appia, which heretofore had served as his guide, and cut twenty miles off his course by not following the road's bend through that industrialized city. When he rejoined the cobbled trace near Forum Appii, a way station fifty miles south of the capital, he was surprised to see a horde of women and children streaming toward Rome.

Why refugees here, when the roads closer to Vesuvius had been clear?

Diving to have a closer look, he saw that they weren't moving in panic but with an unruffled confidence that was partly explained by the military freight lorries Tora sailed over next. So, the women and their offspring were camp followers to a legionary column which was filling the Via Appia as far north as he could see. The cargo lorries gave way to wolf-prowed craft, lumbering sand-galleys bristling with huge siege weapons called *ballistae*, the iron decks taken by officers too proud to walk. In front of the armored units, setting the pace, marched cohort after cohort of legionaries, helmets and breastplates in the soot-dimmed sunlight a burnished color instead of their usual silver. And at the head of the column Tora saw the gleaming standard of the legion known as the Third Augusta.

A legion was marching on Rome—in violation of a decree as old as the Senate, one most famously challenged at the River Rubicon by a balding upstart named Gaius Julius Caesar. Tora knew enough of the history of these strange and obstinate people to realize that Germanicus Agricola's power was about to be challenged.

Then the road was empty.

As he sped north he expected to spot some indication of praetorian opposition to the Third Augusta's affront to the Emperor. Surely, with his vast network of spies, Prefect Nepos knew something of what was boiling up the Via Appia.

But in all that countryside—the clutter of ancient tombs flanking the road, the wooded estates of the bloated rich and the tenement enclaves carved off the edges of those patrician holdings by Caesar Germanicus in behalf of the veterans who'd served with him—between the advance of the Third Augusta and the Porta Capena, Tora didn't see a single praetorian guardsman.

The road was open all the way to the foot of Palatine Hill.

3

BEFORE HASTENING BACK to Caesar's side, the centurion Rolf reluctantly decided on one more undertaking.

Putting the battlements of the Castra Praetoria to his back, he strode down the Via Nomentana, past the Baths of Diocletian and, a half mile later, the Baths of Constantine—both apparently forsaken by the usual late afternoon crowds because of the ash fall. From there he negotiated the seedy, plebeian lanes of the Quirinal to a piss-stained archway through the Virgo aqueduct, where he paused to look over the Campus Martius, the academy for imperial officers and, with its modern glass-and-iron basilica dedicated to Mars, the spiritual center of the far-flung legions.

Here, as at the praetorian fortress, all was calm. No future tribunes huffed in drill around the broad field where in antiquity thousands had huddled and wept during the great conflagration while Nero, reminded of the burning of Troy, recited from the *Aeneid*. Rolf had seen this reenacted in a command play at the palace. It had been based on the ancient sources, mostly a fellow named Tacitus. He had read little of Tacitus—only those writings about his native land of Germania. Other than military orders, which followed a strict form, he didn't understand written Latin very well. Besides, too many books could ruin a good soldier. Vigilance and reading didn't mix.

He squinted up: Fine ash was trickling down from the woolly sky, drifting across the paving stones.

His face grew even more somber than usual.

What inroads had the conspirators made into the cadet corps? Could Caesar rely on these recruits to counterbalance the loss of the loyal praetorian cohorts Prefect Nepos had so conveniently dispatched to the hinterlands of Etruria?

He rushed on, passing the mausoleum of the deified Augustus, Conqueror of Germania. The tomb looked hunched and neglected

29

today, its dignity smutted by Vulcan. But Augustus had been no
fool, and Rolf had often begged Germanicus to do as the first
emperor had so cleverly done: to cloak the raw might of the
imperium in republican trappings, to flatter those swag-bellied
senators, but then do as he bloody well pleased—the only sensible
approach to Roman politics, as far as the Marcoman legionary
could see. But Caesar was a headstrong man, brimming with
needless principles. "No man on earth but you, Germanicus Julius
Agricola, be worthy of the purple," Rolf had argued in one of
their private discussions, which were always marked by the
utmost frankness. "So why give it up to the rabble?"

"The Senate and People of Rome are hardly a rabble."

"Caesar be inside the Curia or down to Subura ward of late?"

Germanicus came close to smiling. "No, my friend—I won't
carry on Augustus' shopworn ruse, no matter how agreeable its
expediency. The Senate must stand on its own, and I can't nurture
that independence with blandishments. You see, Augustus was
promoting his own ends—the subjugation of the senatorial class,
his recent enemies in the civil war—just as today I am serving
mine."

"Which be?"

"The elevation of that class, my class really, to the full
responsibility of statecraft . . ."

Rolf had only shaken his head. Surely Germanicus had great
faith in the gods, for only such faith explained his willingness to
burn Rome's strongest bridge to her past—the two-millennia-old
principate, the unquestioned authority of her first citizen—behind
him. But he also trusted that Caesar knew what he was doing. Had
it not always been so? The fierce and zealous Anatolians and
later the blood-glutting Aztecae had antagonized Germanicus
Agricola—and suffered mightily for it. Perhaps as the ancients of
Sumer had believed, this man had a private god, one who
unbeknownst to him lit his way through the dark passageways of
this world.

Now as he turned and stamped down the pathway atop the
Fabian levee, which held back the Tiber's yellowish tide in flood,
he suddenly stopped to gape at the Nihonian's wizardly machine.
It was limping across the Campus Martius' parade ground like a
bird with a broken wing. Nevertheless, the cloud-galley eventually built speed, its little engine screaming, and then at the last
possible instant rose off the field within feet of smashing against
the stone embankment of the Via Flaminia.

"Ach!" Rolf cried, bewildered. Was the Nihonian out of his mind to fly so?

The flimsy-looking craft sputtered overhead—engine racked by dangerous-sounding hesitations—then moved across the outer wall of the city before turning back over the river.

"What deviltry now?" the German muttered, for the craft had abruptly vanished behind the Vatican hill, half convincing him that it had crashed somewhere on the far side of the Tiber. He would have thought little of all this—the curiosity surrounding Tora's cloud-galley had paled considerably since its maiden flight at Ostia—except for the crack of *pili* he had heard punctuating the sounds of the liftoff.

Legionaries had been discharging their niter pieces at the Nihonian.

It had been an escape then, Rolf realized. But who would dare do such a thing to one of Caesar's adjutants? This angered him more than the act itself.

Drawing his sword and breaking into a trot, he ignored the city watchmen who thought to detain him on the Aelian bridge but quickly decided they had no stomach to cross blades with the towering and burly barbarian. They let him pass over into the Trans Tiberim, a ward of brothels, wine stalls, and tawdry shops owned by men with eastern surnames; of beatings and robberies after nightfall; of shattered *electricus* fixtures dripping sparks onto the lanes.

Rolf, like many at first, had been wary of the lemon-complected man with tapered eyes. For one thing, Tora, once a minion of the devious Sericans, had served with the Aztecan fleet as a *machinator,* a fixer of the wizardly things that enable a bireme to do away with its twin banks of oars and still shove through the deep faster than a Hibernian pony can thrash through the surf. Tora had fallen into Germanicus' hands when imperial marines boarded his strange, jaguar-prowed ship during the Battle of the Mare Aztecum. Yet, in the year since, Tora had proved himself to be a loyal aide to Caesar—enough so that, when the imperial standard was safely returned to Rome, Tora was made Germanicus' agent of matters so dark and wizardly Rolf's soldierly mind could not grasp them. Previously, this post had been held by Epizelus, Caesar's Greek physician, but poor old prissy Epizelus, weakened and half-deranged by months of captivity on the bloodstained island capital of the Aztecae, waiting each and every moment to be pressed down on their high altar to have his heart ripped from his chest by their murderous priests—he had retired to his native Achaea to recover his health.

"Peace be his," Rolf muttered, halting to scan the smirched sky for the cloud-galley.

A whorl of ash danced in front of him like one of the ecstatics to be found in the streets of eastern cities of the Empire. It then vanished, leaving behind as much substance as one of the daft wrapheads. Sometimes he missed Anatolia. But not often.

He moved forward again.

He had just rounded the tidy ruin of the Circus of Nero when he saw the Nihonian shambling toward him. Tora's small hands were fisted; but not only was he without sword, his long and curved scabbard was missing as well. He was wary of the tall figure in the traveling cloak until he recognized him. "Rolf!"

"Aye." He put away his short sword. "What be this mischief at Campus Martius?"

The Nihonian visibly tried to gain control of emotions. "They surrounded my cloud-galley as soon as I set down—"

"Legionary instructors?"

"No, not legionaries—though the swine dressed thusly!" Tora seethed. His mastery of common Latin in so short a time shamed Rolf, who after a lifetime of hearing *nova lingua vulgata* still stumbled through it like a drunk barbarian on his first night in Rome. These Nihonians might one day prove formidable enough to make Romans grateful they lived a far ways off. "Not cadets either, Rolf."

"Aye?"

Tora stabbed his forefinger toward the distant Castra Praetoria: "*Guardsmen* dressed as legionaries. They relieved me of my sword. But I relieved their suboptio of his *pilum*."

Rolf gave him a grudging smile. "This corporal be slain then?"

"Aye—and two more while I ran for my cloud-galley."

"Where be this machine of yours now? Broke upon the earth?"

"No, I hid it in the courtyard of . . ." For once, Tora's Latin seemed to fail him, and he appeared to blush, if the deepening of his sallowness could be called a blush. "How is it said? A house of ten thousand pleasures?"

"Ten thousand . . . ?" For a long moment, Rolf stared at him, mystified, but then a knowing smile lifted his mustaches. "I never count."

"Where is Caesar?"

"In palace, of course."

Tora started back toward the Tiber.

Despite his longer legs, the German had to trot to keep up. "What be the reason for your hurry?"

"As far as you know—is any of the guard deployed to the south of the city?"

"Nay, but three cohorts be in Etruria, stroking their virility and smoking up their lungweed ration. All thanks be to Antonius Nepos."

Tora cursed. Rolf did not know the Nihonian word, but recognized it by tone to be a curse.

"The Third Augusta is marching up the Via Appia at this very hour, centurion."

Rolf seized the man by the tunic and swung him to a halt. "*What!* Third Augusta be forbidden to cross north of the River Volturnus!"

"I know. But this entire legion, even its camp followers, is now less than forty miles from the Porta Capena. They intend to enter Rome fully armed—and *stay.*"

The German began running for the Palatine, and now it was the Nihonian's turn to try to keep pace.

He had been reared in one of Rome's scabrous tenements.

Insufferably hot in summer, chilly even in the mild Italian winter, the thousand-year-old, five-story structure had been propped up with pine beams on its street-facing side to keep it from tumbling onto the heads of pedestrians. Once in the sweet coolness of a spring evening, a balcony had given way, carrying an entire family screaming to its death against the moldy paving stones of the interior courtyard. Even to this day, he couldn't smell charcoal smoke without thinking of that grimy building, for long after the Emperor Fabius had piped oil to Rome most women persisted in cooking with charcoal. The small apartments were unvented, so over the centuries the ceilings had grown as black as the night sky. His mother, in the only artistic expression of her brief life, had stuck up bits of broken glazing to represent stars and make the ceiling seem more like the pitchy vault he'd seen only once through the crystalline air of the Appeninus. He had gone up into the oak-clad range with his father to gather acorns in a pig fodder enterprise that later failed. All his father's enterprises had failed sooner or later, and he could still close his eyes and hear the superintendent's slave, the detestable *insularius,* looming at the open door to the sweltering cubicle and bawling for the rent like the crass, ill-tempered Gaul he was.

But there had also been the joys of the Circus Maximus. He had lived for those holidays spent in the brave dust rising off the enormous elliptical track. And from the plebeian benches he had gazed up at the palace, a vast complex of soaring golden-and-white buildings, never dreaming he would one day serve inside that glory of glories as a praetorian guard, provided with a handsome Attic crest and glistening short sword—never dreaming he would one day kill the most powerful man in the world with that sword.

But that is what the guardsman Terence would do in the coming minutes.

Not that he had anything personal against Germanicus Agricola, but it had been carefully explained to him that Caesar had grand and reckless ideas. And the most dire consequence of these ideas would be the *dissolution* of the imperium. That, in a nutshell, meant the *dissolution* of the guard. This was a word he hadn't understood at first, but then Prefect Nepos had taken him down into that dark and unspoken of portion of the Castra Praetoria and shown him an enemy to Rome chained to a stone vat. The enemy's right arm was shoved into a kind of iron brace and then submersed to the wrist in the foul, coppery liquid steaming within the vat. The enemy's caterwauling was fearful, but Terence revealed no weakness of spirit in such noble company—even when the brace was cranked up out of the liquid and he saw that the enemy's right hand was missing. It had suffered *dissolution*, Prefect Nepos explained with a wry kind of grin; and this is what would happen to the entire praetorian guard if the dotard presently on the throne had his way. It would vanish completely.

From that moment on, Terence had seen it all clearly: He could afford a good drunk and a whore whenever he desired; his tunics and capes were of the finest wool, fullered weekly at no expense to him; and in the rowdy good humor of the mess, he ate meat or fish daily, while his kin at home settled for spelt soup, and he drank the same vintages downed by the couch-cuddling patricians. *Better* vintages, if the wine merchants knew what was good for them.

Terence had no intention of going back to the hopeless life of the tenements. Nor could he envision himself finding a home with one of the legions, as even the Italian-based legionaries spent much of the year in the field with sixty pounds of gear strapped to their backs, repairing roads and fortifications, enduring discomforts and indignities Terence knew he would find unbearable after four years on the Palatine.

Germanicus Agricola had to die.

But before this could be accomplished, Terence would have to kill the guardsman standing at attention beside him in the last vestibule before Caesar's most private quarters.

The bearded youth was German and, by the gullible looks of him, fresh out of the Wald, an outland of virgin forest in southern Germania. He could be counted on to obey Caesar even if commanded to slit his own throat. Such was the mindless loyalty of German praetorians who, long ago, had carried out Caligula's insane edicts without so much as a shrug. And even Germanicus relied on a long-skulled barbarian, Rolf, to guard his person.

Fortunately, at this moment the centurion was not on the hill.

Terence had practiced what he was about to do now on living subjects: three runaway slaves from Nepos' household, who'd had the misfortune of being recaptured. In all three cases, the bolters had died instantly, physically prevented from crying out by a most gruesome application of the blade. And the *gladius,* the Iberian short sword carried by guardsman and legionary alike, proved perfect for the coming task.

Terence checked the corridors, fortified himself with a deep breath, then whispered, "You hear something inside, mate?"

The German shifted his head to the side to listen to anything coming from Caesar's apartments. "Nay, I be—"

Those were the only words he got out before Terence's sword flew from its scabbard and pierced the soft tissues between his chin and throat, pinning the man's lower jaw to the roof of his mouth as the point slid up into his brain.

Terence supported the German's weight so his armor wouldn't clatter as he slumped against the tiles.

Then he wrenched free his sword, cleaned the tip on his already blood-colored cape—before stealing through the door he had guarded with his life until this moment.

The palace gate facing the Flavian amphitheater was flanked by a pair of winged demons with the bodies of lions and the heads of men, *cherubim* of the ancient Jews, which Titus had carted back from Jerusalem as token tribute after sparing the rebellious mountain town. This was the entrance used by Caesar's retinue, and its proximity to the Colosseum gave Rolf an idea. He gestured for the Nihonian to follow him.

They swept past the gargantuan statue of Nero, his head and shoulders blanketed with ash, and into one of the seventy-four arcaded entrances to the amphitheater, eventually making their way out onto the wooden floor of the ellipse. The great bowl echoed with the voices of laborers, who were up on the rim scaffolding, striking the great, brightly colored awnings before the growing weight of the ash might collapse them.

"Come," Rolf grunted.

With Tora on his heels, he bolted up the steps to the topmost story, which was walled in but had glazed openings. From here he could peer down upon the courtyard inside that was called the Jewish portal because of its *cherubim*. "Well, well," he said in a low voice, "the bloody traitors be bright with welcome for us . . ." There in trim ranks stood what he quickly counted to be a full century of guardsmen, waiting to arrest any of Germanicus' followers so witless as to stroll into the palace in the first hours of the mutiny.

The Nihonian understood at once. "They intend to kill us on the spot."

"Aye." Rolf began kneading one of his mustaches with his fingers. "And toss our flesh to the imperial zoo."

"Should we go back for the cloud-galley?"

"Nay, no time. Come—there be another way. Maybe."

What, truly, had happened that afternoon in Augusta Treverorum?

He could not surmise.

He begged the gods—the once-vigorous gods of his forefathers, who'd grown so somnolent over the centuries they could be stirred no longer even to their favorite habits of irascibility and caprice— for an insight into what had happened to him that searing day in Belgica. But instead of clarification he was given confusion and weariness, and the sense was growing in his heart that even these frustrations were not bestowed but simply *occurred* without reason like most everything else in this god-empty universe.

But this much Germanicus could reconstruct while he lay on his couch in his Palatine library:

After a galling audience for a sleepy-eyed senator and his

equally drowsy provincial subordinates—who'd shown nothing but yawns at the prospect of Belgica passing from imperial to senatorial control—Germanicus had felt a desire for cool air and open spaces. He told his sand-galley crew to take him south along the River Mosella, hoping for the moist and green countryside to act upon him as a calmative. Yet the day was so breathlessly hot, the leaves hung limply off their branches and the sun ironed the Mosella's riffles into glass. His head began to ache as if Athena were straining against the vault of his cranium—to be born fullblown and armed as from the brow of Zeus. *As if such an absurd thing could have ever happened, even in dim and primeval Greece.* It had been a day heavy and listless with doubts.

He hadn't been thinking of the Sanctuary of Helios when he set out, but when the temple coasted into view he bid Antonius Nepos to halt—it would be cool within its thick granite walls.

"But, Lord Caesar," the praetorian prefect said, "the attendants won't be prepared for a state visit."

"No matter . . ." Germanicus was already descending the chain ladder down the hull of the craft, having slapped away the eager hands that tried to assist him. "I'd like to come upon it as my father did long go."

"When was that, Caesar?"

"After putting down the final German revolt at Aquae Mattiacae."

"Of course—forgive my lapse of memory." Nepos turned to the colonel at his side. "Go in advance and clear the sanctuary."

But Germanicus countermanded the order. He wished to go inside alone, excluding even Rolf, who had clambered down from the main deck onto one of the tracks and fumed until Caesar repeated in a harsher voice: "I go *alone*."

So he marched up the stone path to the temple, the sun beating down on his pate, and the steam of the dank earth curling up around his face. The sensation was dreadful. His blood seemed to be expanding his arteries to the point of bursting his entire head. Glare tormented his eyes until he stumbled into the abrupt shadow of the portico, whose attendant cried out when he recognized the regal suppliant—the price one pays for having his profile on the coinage of half the world: "Caesar Germanicus!"

"Yes, yes—where may I wash?"

"This way, *Imperator*! Someone—wine and incense!" He spun around in the midst of his thrall and bowed deeply. "Does Caesar wish to see one of our augurs?"

"No." The last soothsayer he'd bothered to consult had mumbled some nonsense about the fate of the Empire now resting on three women, none known to the other and none a true lover to the great man under her spell. When Germanicus had asked if these mysterious women should then be considered faithless, the old Chaldean had only smiled. "I wish to be left alone in the shrine."

"Of course, Caesar." The robed man sprinted ahead, his sandals clapping against his heels, to make sure the chamber was empty.

Germanicus paused to let a sudden spell of dizziness dissipate, then stepped inside the shrine.

The green copper-plated doors eased shut behind him.

Except for the guttering of a few votive candles, it was quite dark and he could scarcely make out the silhouette of the life-sized statue of Helios. Fumbling for the stone bench found in all such places, he slumped down and closed his eyes.

The room was indeed cool, but altogether too tomblike to feel comfortable.

And he had a strange impression that the colonnaded walls were clicking away from him as if on clawed toes, leaving a limitless expanse, inconsolably dim, where the slightest presumption of hope remained inchoate.

He mourned the loss of his son.

He mourned all the other losses of his life, the three extraordinary women he had loved and lost to the underworld: Virgilia, his wife, who had died by the thimbleful over bedridden years. Crispa, whom he'd had executed—and had it been only for the offense of loving two men at once? And finally Alope, the new barbarian woman, who had used love to lure him and his legions down to Tenochtitlan so he might destroy the Aztecae and save her people. Gone. Were these the three women the old Chaldean had alluded to? No—he had said, "the fate of the Empire *now*."

Had he not been so weary, he would have fled right then; for seldom did he find solace in prayer—and grief, once again, was coming at him with its scalding knives.

Then his heart began racing.

The artery along his right temple began hammering wildly— and when he brought up a finger to try to still it, the chamber exploded into a molten dazzle in whose midst the bronze effigy of Helios appeared to slowly rotate. However, and this was the thing he later told no man: The suddenly animate god was not the Lord of the Sun, but rather a faceless being who muttered on a blast of icy wind, "In one you shall become many again."

When he spun around to flee, he stumbled into what was undeniably a female presence, something diaphanous and cold, but nothing as definable as Victoria or any other goddess he could name. He passed through this presence as if it were a patch of fog, yet in its midst he felt a fleeting joy that died as soon as he slammed the doors behind him.

That, as well as he understood it, is what had happened within the Sanctuary of Helios. Others had embellished these facts to suit their own needs, but Germanicus could no longer name his own needs, so he had failed at each attempt to decipher what had truly occurred.

Now, he glanced up as hobnailed sandals tapped on the tiles at the far end of his library. A young guardsman, the plebeian one who was refreshingly less obsequious than the others, was standing at attention, touching his right fist to his left shoulder.

"Yes, lad, what is it?"

"I have a message for Caesar . . ."

"Yes, yes—from whom?"

"Why, the great dog Cerberus, lord—who barks you down to Hades."

And with that, the praetorian drew his short sword.

4

THEY WERE RUNNING across the Forum Boarium, their sandals raising clouds of ash on what had once been the city's cattle market, when Rolf suddenly seized Tora by the scruff of his tunic, turned him around and half dragged him down a twisting side street. The lane narrowed and soon ended at arched double doors shut against the gray blizzard still swirling down upon the deserted-looking city.

Tora pulled the lower half of his face down into his tunic collar when he noticed the embossment of the fuller's guild in the capstone.

But the German threw open one of the doors and entered without hesitation, leaving Tora with no choice other than to brave the unclean odors and follow.

"Hurry," Rolf said, racing down a long line of knee-high stone tubs, each occupied by a fuller-slave treading with Sisyphean montony, his puckered hands grasping the wooden supports as he slopped a wet garment under his feet. The slaves paid the German no attention—he had bolted through these works on other occasions, perhaps—and went on stamping in their foul brew. The excess dribbled down the sides of the vats and was carried off by a shallow culvert running down the middle of the chamber. Overhead, from the tiers of drying racks came a warm rain that stank of wet wool; each drop on the back of his neck made Tora flinch, but he kept up with the German.

Rolf made directly for the grate at the far end of the culvert and, with a grunt, pried it out of the floor. Then, turning to remove a pine-pitch torch from its wall bracket, he smiled at Tora's sour expression. "You be first?"

The Nihonian was already thoroughly disgusted by the gurgling of the mustard-colored stream as it cascaded away into the darkness. "No, with thanks—after you, centurion."

"Aye . . . take this then."

Accepting the torch from Rolf, Tora shook his head at its bickering flame. Reduced to a symbol, here was the contradiction that was imperial Rome: *Electricus* motive had come to the Eternal City decades before, yet all but the most exclusive wards were still illuminated by pitch, tallow, and olive oil, simply because the slave labor force charged with stringing and repairing wires did so at a snail's pace. The freeman guilds that indentured these poor drudges in behalf of owners who'd wearied of their faces around the household did nothing to assure the slaves that their efforts might one day bring about an improvement in their lot.

Holding onto the rim with his hands, Rolf lowered himself into the opening, then let go. The soles of his sandals slapped wetly against a flooded concrete surface. He reached up for the torch, and Tora saw that the German was crouching in a drainpipe with a circumference a foot less than his height.

Cringing from the sensation of dirty, lukewarm water twining down the backs of his thighs, the Nihonian dropped, landing harder than Rolf had, because his legs were shorter.

"Take the light—and *hurry*!" Then the German led the way down the drain.

"Where does this go?" Tora asked, his voice echoing.

Rolf ignored him.

On they sloshed through the polluted flow, which became deeper as the flushings of more fuller shops, public baths, and latrines foamed into the pipe out of algaed spouts. Tora wanted to retch: Never before had he been exposed to such rank corruption. He ached for *ofuro*, the leisurely and thorough bath of his homeland—almost as much as he desired to save Caesar Germanicus from assassination.

Then, abruptly—given his prior urgency—Rolf crept to a halt and scraped his sword out of its scabbard as quietly as he could.

Instinctively, Tora's right hand darted for his own hilt, but came up empty. Once again, he smarted from the shame visited on him by the disguised praetorians at the Campus Martius. They would suffer greatly for having stolen one of his proudest possessions. The only possession he was prouder of was the unquestioned fealty he gave to the temperate and courageous shogun of the Romans. And this he had retained.

Rolf motioned for Tora to stop well behind him. From this same gesture the Nihonian also understood that the German wanted him to do something about the glow of the torch. He shielded it as best he could with his torso.

He could see where the drain joined a larger tunnel, whose dimensions were spacious enough to be lost in a gloaming. And whatever flowed through this great channel, it murmured as profoundly as the Tiber itself. Then, without warning, Rolf sprang around the corner and out of sight. The faint spill of the torch caught only his elbow as he cocked it back and delivered what obviously was a quick sword thrust.

A scream followed, and then a loud splash bespoke waters of considerable depth.

As if nothing had happened, the German motioned for Tora to follow again.

"What wonder?" the Nihonian asked in a hush, stepping out onto a timber parapet lashed to a brick wall that curved out of sight. The torch brought a portion of the long vault into definition. At its downstream end a corpse could be seen bobbing away on the broad tide. "What place is this?"

"*Cloaca*," Rolf said with no breathiness in his voice to indicate that he'd just killed a man. The effortless violence in his nature reminded Tora of the bear-slaying aborigines of the northernmost island of his homeland, a wild people who never gave a second thought to their tempestuous urges, whereas a true Nihonian struggled all his days to find gentleness and beauty in the crevices of his own hostility. "This here be the *cloaca maxima*."

The Great Sewer of Rome.

In the distant past it had been a rude ditch to drain the swamp that meandered between the Seven Hills; but at the dawn of the imperial age it had been covered and sufficiently expanded to admit a rowed war galley—and win a rather ostentatious bet that such a pointless thing could be done.

"Was it a praetorian you slew?"

The German made a huffing sound deep in his throat, leaving Tora to wonder if it had been a laugh. "No guardsman come here." Then he turned and shouted into the darkness: "*Rex Subter!*"

Tora was confused. The German had just dubbed this unknown king with a Latin word that meant either *below* or *underneath*. His bewilderment only increased his anxiety. "Shouldn't we be on our way?" he urged.

"This *be* the only way."

"Then let us go!"

"Nay—the walkway."

"What of it?"

"Breached in a dozen places. They tear at it for cooking fires."

"*Who*, centurion?"

"You see." Scabbarding his sword, he cupped his hands around his mouth: "*Rex Subter*, come forth!"

"Who so bloody demands!" a deep, raspy voice echoed down the *cloaca* from far upstream.

"You know well, *Rex Subter*."

"Is it me rosy red Goth?"

"Aye."

The voice began rumbling with laughter. "And what of me sentry?"

"Dead—he be dead."

"Why?"

"He make no challenge—except with his spear. This be no way to welcome me."

Tora expected some nastiness over Rolf's killing of the man, but the raw voice went on laughingly. "So bloody be it. Death's a diddle what when one lives on the very banks of the Styx. And if me mate will not challenge thee, I shall. What is the password, Rolf of the Flaming Locks, if I say now to thee: *In the end . . .* ?"

"*. . . Orcus— he rule all above and below, even the mighty Rex Supra.*"

"Excellent, my rosy red Goth. Stand as thee and thy mate are . . ."

At first Tora could make no sense of the dark objects which filed out of a kind of cove in the *cloaca* and spilled one by one into the turbid stream. Briefly, he even imagined them to be upside down mushrooms—until the upturned stems were transformed into the shapes of men, scruffy men poling the small, round wicker boats in which they stood. One of these tublike craft held both a poler and a passenger. The former drew in his pole, then threw a ragged hemp line to Rolf, who tied it to the parapet railing.

"Bow," the German said out of the corner of his mouth.

"*What?*" Tora was amazed by the command. The passenger in the round boat was the most disreputable-looking man he'd seen in all of Italia.

But Rolf insisted: "This be *Rex Subter*—bow, or we die down here. And Caesar—he die above."

The King of Below wore a soiled toga so shabbily wrapped around his person that the crack between his buttocks was revealed when he turned to slap his poler, who'd dared to belch on so august an occasion. The monarch was gaptoothed, and his hair afflicted with a kind of mange Tora had seen heretofore only on Umbrian cattle. Yet the king and his entire host were armed with niter pieces and cold steel in every imaginable fashion of blade.

Tora bowed.

"How fares *Rex Supra*?" the filthy man asked with a polite smile, obviously inquiring about Caesar Germanicus—as if the two of them were equals with neighboring realms.

"He be strong as ever," Rolf said. "But he needs must leave the Golden House for a time."

"What does Rolf bloody say?" *Rex Subter* seemed genuinely taken aback. "Is there some godly ruin about?"

"Aye, Vesuvius blows—"

Loud murmuring arose among the boatmen, and Tora whispered to Rolf, "Don't they ever leave this place?"

"Nay, they be of no need."

"How is that possible?"

Quickly, in a low voice, the German explained how these sewer-dwellers extorted a living from Rome's houses and shops by stopping up the drains feeding into the *cloaca*—unless baskets filled with food, wine, and sesterces were regularly dangled from the grates. Then he again faced the gently bobbing throng. "As I say, Vesuvius blows and the ash madness be on the land. Some of *Rex Supra's* guards be mutinous with such lunacy—so he go to his villa in Ostia until the skies be clear and all his subjects be sane again."

Rex Subter then proved himself as much a businessman as a sovereign. "Then what does my brother, the Lord Overhead, need of me? And what price will he pay?"

"He be wanting this in the hour—safe passage down the *cloaca* . . ." Rolf paused.

"And *what* price?"

"Above the grate of the *cloaca palatina* there be a corridor . . ." Again the studied pause.

"Yes, yes?" A fluttering of *Rex Subter's* stained fingers told the German to go on.

"My comrade and me, we needs must go right down that corridor to seek *Rex Supra*. You and your lads go left—"

"No, oh bloody no, no, no." The king chuckled. "Never in all the days since Great Augustus have we diddled the Palatine. We live in darkness, Rolf of the Long Skull, but we *see* perfect. One diddle into the palace—and what? Why, the praetories will have every barge on the Tiber putt-putting up these freshets. And then what would become of us, Orcus' poor lot?"

"Down left of that corridor in the Palatine," Rolf went on, adamantly, "there is a treasure room. One guarded only by mutinous red capes who be on sentence of death anyways—"

"How does me fair Goth know that?" *Rex Subter* interrupted.

"If you still doubt, let it be *Rex Supra* to tell you himself."

The master of the *cloaca maxima* fell silent. He began rolling his pallid underlip between his fingers.

"Will you at least give me the parting courtesy of telling me who sent you on this errand?" Germanicus asked, slowly backing up to the floor-to-ceiling library shelves. The cautious advance of the praetorian had already cut him off from the bronze figurines of Minerva and the Muses flanking the door.

"To air the names?"

"Yes, if you will." With a sinking feeling, he realized that he'd left his wax tablet kit—and its dirklike silver stylus—in his bedchamber. "One has an overwhelming curiosity at a moment such as this."

The guardsman smiled slyly over the tip of his short sword. "I'm sorry to disappoint Caesar—but it would be stupid of me to divulge anything when I need not."

"I see." Germanicus felt the shelves bump against his back. "We must exercise caution in even the most convulsive moments of our brief sojourn. Aurelius would have approved, I'm sure."

The praetorian tried to blink away the sweat that was trickling into his eyes. "Who?"

"It doesn't matter . . . someone whose private meditations will outlive us both."

The youth crimped short a laugh. "You sooner than I, Germanicus Julius."

"Yes, so be it." Never once did it occur to him to shout. The guardsman's audacity meant only that the praetorians on duty were either allied with the young man or already dead. "Is it too much to ask—Terence, isn't it?—why you do this?"

"Nothing personal, Caesar." He flicked his damp head to the side, thinking perhaps that he could hear approaching footfalls, but then gave his attention back to Germanicus. "I bear you, the man, no malice."

"Then that makes your reason all the more interesting."

The young man smiled, tenderly almost. "Does it really?"

Germanicus nodded, scanning from the corner of his eye for a weapon, anything like a weapon.

"Well, it's your world or mine, isn't it . . . ?" Terence stopped in the middle of library to sort his thoughts; it was not often one got the chance to lecture a Julian emperor, and the last one at that. "I mean, time was when our worlds were one and the same. Everything was all right then, truly. Especially for a lad like me brought up lean. No country villa on Ostia's fair shore for me and my ilk. Just a stinking tenement to go back to. But I did fine for myself, what? I won the right to wear this red cape. And everything was lovely, what? Then you got a notion lodged in your head, and any fool in the ranks could see what it meant plain and simple—the end of the guard . . ."

Here it was in the open at long last—the revelation he had feared but expected all along. However, like Medusa's leering eyes, it still had the power to petrify him for several seconds. So then, this attack on his person wasn't the gambit of some power-lusting praetorian colonel or bored legion commander—it was a manifold reaction to his secret efforts to restore the Republic.

The die had been cast.

And had the moment not been filled with such peril, he might have felt relief. The terrible pretense of these past months had been lifted at last, but lifted only in time for him to perish.

"There will always be a praetorian guard, my boy. I say this a bit sadly as one who has known no privacy since taking up the purple. The guard, of all our ancient institutions, is the most indestructible."

Terence shifted his sword to his left hand. His grip had been too tight and had probably caused a cramp, which he now tried to shake out. "What d'you mean?"

"If my notion—as you call it—comes to light, I see two, three, perhaps even four times the number of cohorts we have now."

The praetorian smirked. "How can that be?"

"Why, you'll be protecting the authority of the Senate, whose members are ten times as numerous as the provinces—" Germanicus appeared to fold his hands behind him, but he was actually slipping two scrolls off a waist-high shelf, "—as opposed to that of the Julian clan, whose lineage has come down to one old man in dire need of rest."

Terence looked uncertain, but only for an instant. Then he closed on Germanicus once again. "Well, a man facing death will say anything."

"True enough." From afar in the cavernous palace came a rattle of *pili* fire. The mutineers were being resisted, he realized with a bit of satisfaction.

The guardsman fixed his gaze on Germanicus' neck. With the slow deliberation of a Roman who knows what a momentous thing it is to murder his Caesar, he once again transferred his *gladius* to his stronger, right hand. He lifted the blade, and it flashed lamplit at the top of its arc.

Unseen by Terence, Germanicus was now firmly clutching a scroll in each hand. And at the center of each parchment bundle was an oaken dowel onto which the sheets were rolled after the reader had finished with them.

"Hail Caesar!" the guardsman cried, bringing down his sword.

Germanicus met the blade in midflight with the scroll in his right fist. Terence's steel slashed through the parchment, but the dowel slewed the blow—and nearly cost him his balance as well. He was shuffling backwards to recover his stance when Germanicus brought up the second scroll, striking the praetorian squarely in the throat with one of the gilded knobs capping the ends of the dowel.

The sword spun out of Terence's grasp, but it was some moments before he sensed the awful damage that had been done to his larynx. Then he began gagging, suffocating to death.

Germanicus seized him by the chains that fastened his cape to his breastplate, vainly trying to keep the young man on his feet for a purpose he could not name. Perhaps he wanted to see some hint of forgiveness in the vitrifying eyes, but the light went out of them without emotion, only a frantic bulging that abruptly went flat.

Then it occurred to him that the first battle of the new civil war had been fought in his library. It felt nothing like a victory.

The chamber whose riches Rolf had promised to *Rex Subter* was not so much a treasure room as a small bank from which Germanicus made disbursements to his *clientela*.

A Goth, Rolf found it difficult to see the virtue in an arrangement by which the pudgy descendants of free retainers, who'd tilled the lands of the Julian Agricolas in antiquity, would show up at the palace once a week to receive Caesar's counsel in even the most trivial matters, representation in the courts if needed, and—of course—enough gold coinage to see their worthless kin through another seven days of dinner parties and public games. Professional toadies—and Rolf hadn't been afraid to call them that to Caesar's face. But Germanicus insisted that the clientage was a good tradition; it reinforced the ultimate responsibility of the patrician class for the less fortunate plebeians.

But Rolf didn't see it that way, and as far as he was concerned, *Rex Subter* could do just as well with the money as Caesar's *clientela*—not a single member of which, incidentally, had shown up for the weekly dole this morning. But as soon as the last grate to the *cloaca palatina* was removed, the Lord Below turned reluctant again to steal into the palace. Like most sewer-dwellers, his nightmares were probably filled with praetorians. So with Tora shouldering a borrowed *pilum* as tall as himself, Rolf and the Nihonian had to lead the motley horde down the corridor toward the clientage vault—while Caesar waited somewhere, in the opposite direction, probably imperiled.

When they came upon the first brace of guardsmen, Rolf cried: "I come in Germanicus' name!"

Both praetorians went for their swords, which was good enough for Tora, who shot them dead.

And this was good enough for *Rex Subter*.

At the van of his men and waving a pry bar over his head, he charged toward the treasure room—and the intervening guard-mount room of the praetorians on this level, whose guardsmen they soon engaged with *pili*.

But Rolf and Tora didn't join them in this clash, for they were racing the other way for Caesar's apartments.

In the vestibule, a young German praetorian lay dead on the tiles, apparently spiked through the underside of his chin.

Growling with rage, slashing his sword back and forth before him, Rolf leaped over the corpse and began tearing through the maze of rooms: the small chapel confusingly dense with human-sized effigies of the gods; the private banquet hall, his own reflection giving him a start as it rippled over the mirrorlike gold leaf of the interior colonnade; the atrium, once open to the sun but now—for reasons of security—closed off and lit by *electricus* motive; and, finally, the slave annex, which gave every indication of having been vacated in great haste. No slave, even a blameless one, could hope to survive the death of the master of the house. Particularly Caesar's house.

Standing in the midst of a slave kitchen littered with dropped crockery, Rolf heard Tora cry out from the direction of the library.

"I come!" he answered.

There among the scrolls he found Germanicus, sprawled on the floor with a dead praetorian clasped in his arms.

"What be—?"

But Tora quieted him with a gesture. It was then Rolf understood that Caesar had slain the guardsman. Such was the nature Germanicus had revealed to his bodyguard over the years: a most ready violence, always followed by remorse. Secretly, this was a tender-hearted man. But then he let go of the body and came to his feet, his eyes suddenly determined. "Which cohorts of the guard can we still rely on?"

"None what be here on the Palatine, or those at the Castra Praetoria too," Rolf said.

"*What?*"

"Prefect Nepos—he send the best lads to Etruria. We needs must go *now.*"

Germanicus bent to take the dead man's sword, then froze as he began to straighten up again. "*Antonius Nepos . . . ?*"

Rolf scowled: "Aye."

"Then we must be doubly quick." Caesar started for the door. "We'll find Quintus and take him out with us. Hurry!"

Rolf and the Nihonian caught up with him in the vestibule. "No, Caesar," Tora said, boldly stopping him by the elbow, "I am sure young Quintus cannot be found here."

"What makes you say so?"

"From such things in my own country. This blow against you has been well planned. And these rebels would not risk it unless they held the princeling in some hidden place. He gives weight to their claim to the purple. So, your adopted son will not be found on the Palatine."

Briefly, Germanicus closed his eyes. "Good Jupiter." Then he said between clenched teeth: "We shall retire to the south and rally the Third Augusta around us—this mutiny can be nipped in the bud by tomorrow's eve."

"No . . ." Sadly, Tora shook his head. "As I flew back to Rome this afternoon, I saw the Third marching up the Via Appia."

"Marching on *Rome!*"

It troubled Rolf how stunned Caesar looked. For the first time it struck the German that they might have already lost.

"Is Gessius Pansa still in command?"

"We hear no different," Rolf said, checking the next bend in the corridor for praetorians.

"I hatched that asp out of obscurity!" Germanicus cried. "And this is how he thanks me?"

"Come," Rolf said in a commanding tone of voice. "Others be of the same mind to thank you."

This was it, then.

Wrapped in a filthy traveling cloak begged off a *cloaca* denizen. Conveyed down the foul stream in a wattle boat. The last of the Julian emperors expelled from power via the Great Sewer.

How fitting.

The torches of the little armada winked around Germanicus, reflected in wan rays across the black waters but scarcely grazed the brick vault overhead. He might have said yes to despair but for one thought: the three loyal cohorts of praetorians encamped in the Etrurian highlands. These he would fire with the ideal of a new republic and then unleash them on Rome and its greedy conspirators.

The polers began skidding their staffs along the bottom as the boats neared the outlet of the *cloaca maxima* on the Tiber.

"Now, guvnor," the chief of this squalid tribe said, tying up his boat to the wooden parapet as all the others were doing, "there won't be a row about the *denarii* we diddled, will there?"

Germanicus cleared the hoarseness out of his throat; his heart couldn't have felt heavier. "No, my friend—consider it a reward for your patriotism."

"Me what?" The grubby chieftain chortled. "Why, there's one to be scribbled in charcoal on our bloody archive wall! Me *patriotism!*"

Rolf and Tora had poled across the river to check out the Aemilian quay. It was usually guarded only when Caesar embarked for Ostia from it, but the centurion refused to take any chances.

Either the wind had shifted or Vesuvius had stopped spewing, for a thin swatch of stars was visible, bending all the way down to the long shadowy hump of the Janiculum hill. The darkness on those heights made him realize that the conspirators had cut the power to the city. How many disruptions of normal life would follow this first one?

He burrowed deeper into his smelly cloak.

Having installed Tora on the quay, Rolf returned. "It be clear," he whispered, helping Germanicus into his boat. "But the *vigiles* make a round up and down the Via Portuensis on the hour."

"Do you think the city watchmen have thrown in with the bastards?"

The German's torchlit eyes were disconsolate. "I know nothing no more."

In silence, Caesar was poled across the Tiber.

Crouching as they ran, the three men came down the north slope of the Janiculum, intending to skirt the Vatican hill and join the Via Clodia in order to continue north out of the greater city. Suddenly they spied a lone guardsman making for the Pons Neronianus. That the praetorian was suspiciously alone persuaded Germanicus to let Rolf waylay him before he reached the bridge.

The man was terrified, and the centurion's short sword resting against his jugular did little to allay his fears. "What cohort be yours?"

"What do you think you're—"

"Tell what I ask!"

A nudge of the blade made him answer promptly.

Rolf grunted and lowered his sword. It was one of the loyal praetorian units. "Where be the rest of your lads?"

The man's lips trembled, but no words came forth.

Germanicus stepped out of the shadows. "Please, my boy, we need to know these things. . . ." Despite the tattered cloak he was wearing, Caesar was instantly recognizable to the praetorian, who fell to his greaves and clasped Germanicus around the knees. He began to weep.

Germanicus gently touched the back of the praetorian's head, but said, "Stand and report—I command it."

Choking down a sob, the man rose. "I ran . . . I ran far . . . and caught a vegetable lorry on the road to old Norchia—"

"Yes, my boy—but what happened before that?"

He stared vapidly at Caesar for a long moment, then an eerie monotone crept into his speech. "At noon, our colonels ordered us into the amphitheater at Tuscania. All three cohorts. Our arms stayed back at our bivouac, stacked. We expected a speech, but got wine in skins instead. We should have known . . . we should have bloody well known then. . . ."

Germanicus' mouth had gone dry. "Go on."

"We drank, we smoked, we made jokes—and not a handful of us noticed when our tribunes and centurions lined the uppermost tier with *pili* at hand. I was already running when the first shot was fired. That's the only reason I made it. I was already running. . . ." He began to weep again.

Germanicus drifted off a short distance to gaze at the benighted city.

After a while, Rolf approached and asked quietly, "The lad—what be done with him?"

Germanicus' voice was croak: "Where was he bound?"

"Home—to Samnium."

"Then let him go home. And tell him to give thanks that he still has a home."

Rolf was silent for a moment. "What of us?"

"I don't know," Germanicus said without looking at the centurion. "I just don't know."

While Rolf went to tell the praetorian to go on his way, Tora begged a word with Caesar.

"Speak, Tora-*san*."

"Believe me when I say that I have lived through an hour such as this. I see but one thing for you to do. Is there not one subordinate you can trust with your life?"

Germanicus thought briefly, then said, "Gnaeus Salvidienus!"

"Aye, a good man." Rolf had rejoined them, his voice suddenly bright. "General of the Illyrian legions—he be a rock of a man."

"Then Caesar must fly to him. A shogun in peril must hasten to the castle of his closest ally."

"Good Jupiter—do you mean you can take us all to Illyricum in that little craft of yours?"

Tora glanced down, then looked inquiringly at Rolf, who nodded. Despite the weak starshine in which they all stood, Germanicus sensed that an understanding of some sort had just passed between the two men.

"Yes, Lord Caesar, it can be done," Tora said. "I will have to buy some petrol from the place I have hidden my cloud-galley. But all these things can be done. . . ."

"Then we go." Rolf seemed strangely cheerful all at once.

• • •

The men dragged the cloud-galley out of the courtyard of a brothel near the Vatican hill, the prostitutes in their bright gossamer gowns, watching and giggling from the portal.

Germanicus shook his head: *Discharged down a sewer, seen off by a delegation of whores—yes, all perfectly fitting for a fool who'd never seen the disaster cresting over his head. And yet had I rid myself of everyone I distrusted, even slightly, I would have inaugurated nothing but a bloodbath with my imperium.*

As Tora nursed the engine to smoothness, Rolf helped Germanicus squeeze into the narrow confines behind the Nihonian's seat. It was only then, with the engine wailing at its highest pitch, that Caesar shook off his heavy distraction of the past hour and saw there was no room left for his bodyguard.

"Wait!" he shouted. "This won't work! Stop, Tora! There's not space for Rolf!"

"Aye, no space." The German's look seemed evasive. "I be all right."

"How? What will you do!"

"I be of a mind to keep the long-skulled tribes loyal until I hear again from you."

"No! Stop the engine! We all go on foot!"

"Nay, Germanicus Julius Agricola—hail and farewell." Rolf stepped back and saluted. "*Ave* Caesar!" Then he motioned for Tora to proceed.

The cloud-galley began bouncing down the broad, sloping street.

"No!" Germanicus bellowed. "How can you survive? Where can you go!"

Rolf's words faded in the sudden rush of air as the craft sprang free of the ground; however, Germanicus had understood the first of them: *A Marcoman always be with a home.* . . .

An hour later, miles out over the Adriaticum, with a light rain stinging the side of his face, Germanicus was still peering back toward Italia. The very presence he had so often resented as an infringement on his privacy, he was now missing, achingly. "I should have made you a king while I had the power," he said to himself.

5

JUST WHEN THE night seemed eternal, the sky backdropping the coastal firs glowed cinereously. Yet it was a half hour more before Germanicus could make out the offshore boulders against which the surf had been thrashing in the darkness. At last, the shingly beach brightened; across it were strewn tattered swatches of muslin, little twists of aluminum tubing, tangles of copper skeins, and—at the farthest point that debris had been hurled from the impact—the cloud-galley's engine had gouged out a place for itself in the barnacled stones.

Tora huddled beside him, the Nihonian's broken left wrist swaddled in a piece of Caesar's tunic. Both men were shivering, gazing out across the sea as if some hope might suddenly materialize there.

"I feeling nothing but shame, Lord Caesar. I trusted my *index* to deliver us to Salona—"

Germanicus cut short the man's apology by clasping his sinewy shoulder. "The storm wasn't your fault. And perhaps it was best not to fly directly into the provincial capital. This gives us a chance to look things over."

Tora nodded, miserably. "Does Caesar know where we are?"

"I would guess quite a ways down the Dalmatian coast. No islands to the west of us, so we must be north of Epidaurum." Germanicus came to his feet, tried to stretch a kink out of his sore back. "From the garrison at Epidaurum we can send word to Gnaeus Salvidienus."

"Pardons, Caesar, but I have already failed you once—"

"Nonsense, man."

"It is a wonder you survived my inexpert alighting on this beach. Let me restore my honor."

"In what way?"

54

"By going alone into Epidaurum to make sure no treachery awaits you there."

"But your wrist—"

Tora smiled through his pain. "It is indeed fortunate I will not have to walk on it. . . ." And with that, he started walking south along the shore, looking back once to wave encouragingly.

While Germanicus awaited his return, a sour-smelling mist rose out of the forest and blocked the warming rays of the sun. He salvaged some petrol from the engine and was finally able to ignite it with a spark off two flinty pebbles, then began feeding damp driftwood into the flames. The time passed more comfortably, but still his eyes were moist and seemed shrunken in his face. He supposed that the civil war he had always dreaded was already lost, that the oppressive and cumbersome imperial apparatus would go on forever.

But then again, there was Aufidius Gnaeus Salvidienus. If a solitary loyal general could turn things around—it was he.

Friends since their cadet days together at the Campus Martius, both from patrician families with ancient pedigrees, Gnaeus and Germanicus had entered imperial service in the waning days of the cavalry, and poor Salvidienus might have been more highly regarded by his mentors had *machinalis scientia* not supplanted horsemanship at the top of the curriculum. However, it was on this brambly coast that the young tribune Salvidienus had won the first of the peculiar accolades that would come to typify him: He successfully resisted the pirate siege of his garrison on the island of Arba; and the brigand chieftain, during crucifixion, had complained, "Can I be blamed if this Roman was too stupid to know he was beaten?"

Germanicus chuckled to himself as he held his palms close to the feeble flames.

In the Novo Provinces, Salvidienus had held back an Aztecan horde from the gates of the provincial capital at Otacilium while his entire staff counseled withdrawal. That vicious war won, Germanicus had rewarded his unflapple old friend with the quietest command he could think of—Illyricum, where Gnaeus might once again delight in spurring his favorite Andalusian mount through the labyrinthine trails in the thorn copses of Dalmatia's rocky coast.

He closed his eyes on the thought: Some quiet this reluctant Caesar had given his old friend, all his old friends—a civil war to ravage their final years.

But no, he resolved not to wallow in despair. Salvidienus, like Cincinnatus of old, would be honored to put aside his peacetime pursuits and come to the aid of the Roman Republic in the hour of her genuine rebirth. He, too, had no fondness for mincing terms—Rome was either a bloody republic or she wasn't. And if not—why not?

With Gnaeus' unstinting support would come the cream of the legions within striking distance of Italia: the Thirteenth Gemina and the Fifteenth Apollinaris of Pannonia; the First Italica, Fifth Alaudae, Seventh Claudia Pia Fidelis and Fifth Macedonica of Moesia; and the mighty Fourth Flavia of Dalmatia. And now, in a buoyant frame of mind all at once, Germanicus was afraid only that the conspirators might be obliterated before they might be properly tried by a revitalized Senate. For if ever there was a Roman with the stolid, sensible, and unadorned temperament of the ancient republicans—he was Aufidius Gnaeus Salvidienus.

At the tenth hour of the day, with the sun four hands above the Adriaticum and sinking fast, some heretofore hidden shrikes were startled to wing, and Tora stumbled out of the woodlands, down a gorse slope and onto the beach, clutching a basket with his uninjured arm. "Lord Caesar!"

Germanicus helped him the last steps down to the smoldering fire. "Let me take that, lad."

"Forgive me . . ." His head bobbed; he was that exhausted. "It proved more than six of your miles into Epidaurum . . . and eight on my return . . . for I made sure I was not followed."

"Did you get in touch with Salvidienus?"

"Yes . . . a message was sent by wireless from the colonel of the garrison."

"And the name of that colonel?"

Tora told him, and Germanicus muttered: "I don't know him, but no matter. The important thing is this—did Salvidienus send a return?"

The Nihonian smiled, drowsily. "Yes, right away."

"Excellent!" But then Germanicus more carefully regarded the man. "Are you well?"

"Yes, Lord Caesar . . . except . . ."

"Except what, my friend?"

"The light fades. . . ." He looked around him as if suddenly perplexed. "Strange, for such faintness often comes from not eating. And I have eaten . . . the colonel insisted I take victuals for the Emperor and myself with me. . . ."

It was no wonder the man was spent, what with an icy rain driving against his face most of the night while he strained below for a glimpse of the phosphorescence indicating waves breaking against the coast.

"You must sleep, Tora-*san*. But briefly, what did good old Gnaeus have to say?"

Again, the weary, sleepy smile. "He begs the most noble and reverend Caesar Germanicus to avail himself of the hospitality of Epidaurum's garrison until the proconsular sand-galley arrives from Aspalathos to convey him to more apt accommodations. . . ."

Germanicus' expectant grin vanished. "Were these the general's own words?"

"So I was assured, Lord Caesar."

He turned seaward so Tora wouldn't see the worry in his eyes. Everything about this wireless message was suspect: its tone, which was florid for a man who, in the past, had greeted Caesar with such blurtings as *Why, Germanicus Julius—you still have most your hair!*; its promise of borrowing the proconsul's ornate sand-galley from the civil administration at Aspalathos, whereas Gnaeus was familiar with Germanicus' penchant for transit without fanfare; and lastly, its faint echo of a threat that Caesar take advantage of the garrison's "hospitality."

The truth was hidden within the wording of the dispatch, and it brought a burning sensation to Germanicus' already salt-stung eyes: Salvidienus was dead. What a strange new source of melancholy—to have both failed and outlived the best men of one's own generation. And yet it was not the hoary-headed general Germanicus now recalled with self-reproach; it was the thickset child-soldier with brows beetling over eyes so mild and kindly they didn't become a legionary.

Motionless, he watched the sun decline. The disk was split evenly by the horizon when a clatter of shingle made him turn—Tora had toppled over. He was scarcely breathing. "Tora-*san!*"

When the words failed to rouse the man, Germanicus tried gentle slaps, but this brought no reaction, either.

It was then that he examined the contents of the basket.

The roast capon, from which Tora had torn off a wing, seemed wholesome enough, although one could never be sure; but the wine gave off the unmistakable miasma of mandrake root. The list of poisons swifter and surer than mandrake was long, so Germanicus surmised that the colonel at Epidaurum had intended only to narcotize Caesar and his adjutant long enough for one of his patrols to discover and bind them.

And then what for the last of the Julians? A long march in chains back to Rome? A month or two in the Mamertine prison before the final heir of Augustus would be stripped naked, his head thrust between the tines of a wooden fork, and—with all Rome howling for his blood—flogged to death with rods? He felt certain the conspirators would come up with something traditional like this, the ancient punishment for treason. New tyrants always adhered to tradition at first.

Meanwhile, there was only one thing to do.

He hoisted the unconscious Tora onto his back and, turning away from the sea, started limping up into the forest. He came upon a stream and followed it, keeping to its stony shallows in order to leave no tracks for the legionaries who most certainly at this moment were scouring the Dalmatian coast for him.

Highest among their priorities was the restoration of gaiety to Rome. So all within the same flawlessly blue morning one week after the flight of the despot Germanicus, Antonius Nepos and his cousin Claudia Nero were married in a state ceremony by the *pontifex maximus*. Then they jointly presided over a weak-kneed Senate who tried Germanicus Julius Agricola, *in absentia*, convicted him of high treason and nullified his adoption of Caesar Quintus Nero, both the Curia and the praetorian guard had already confirmed the boy as emperor-designate with Nepos and Claudia as his regents. Finally, they convened the games in the Flavian amphitheater at noon.

That Nepos chose to hold this celebration in Vespasian's nineteen hundred-year-old Colosseum, instead of the more modern and commodious Circus Fabius, sent a clear message to those who still pined for Germanicus: Flavius Vespasianus, a simple and parsimonious soldier without a drop of patrician blood in his veins, had been proclaimed Emperor by the military. Only later had his brutal son Domitian—after murdering his wife Domitia before she could surprise him in the same way—wedded a surviving cow of the Julio-Claudian house, a near simpleton with eyes as vapid as the brain behind them. In this way Domitian had connived to suffuse his own lackluster bloodlines with a tinge of purple. It was only by this tenuous link that Germanicus was related to Caesar Augustus, Nepos reminded everyone.

And it was in Domitian's fashion he intended to use young Quintus, in whose veins swished an echo of the daft emperor Nero, to legitimize his own ambitions.

He laughed quietly as something occurred to him: Had Domitia succeeded in murdering Domitian, instead of the other way around—thanks to the warning given the Emperor by a Jewish spy and longtime toady to the Flavians named Josephus—old Germanicus might have found himself in humiliating straits long before now. He might have been born the son of a cork merchant.

Enough ruminating, Nepos decided with the abrupt and complete shift of mind that was his habit. The present was the proper arena for a vigorous man.

He found it keenly arousing to stroke Claudia's thigh with the eyes of all Rome upon them. The people liked a leader with a vigorous sexual aspect—it augured fecundity for the entire Empire, didn't it? So he continued to sip wine with one hand and caress his bride with the other. The rays of the sun showered down on their gallery like gold coins; he could not have felt better. Well, one thing would have improved the day—he himself being named Caesar on Quintus' inexplicably early death.

But that too would come in time.

Below, on the sands already bloodied by the first gladiatorial combats, a herd of aged men, each stripped down to his soiled loincloth, was being dragged by ropes and prodded with javelins toward the restraining posts which had just been erected at the center of the arena. These sniveling old poops were the city magistrates appointed by Germanicus "for the ripeness of their sagacity."

It had been inspired for Claudia to suggest their execution in so public a way, for the judges had always been detested by the rabble. And really, whose entertainment did it serve by strangling the bastards in the seclusion of the Mamertine prison?

The gigantic humpbacked bears imported from the Novo Provinces were already snapping at the bars of their cages. They were as naturally surly as German recruits—and smelled little better, come to think about it.

Again, he chortled to himself. *Good Mars, what a day to seize!*

Claudia suddenly gripped his hand passionately.

He felt a thrill akin to those he'd savored when his infidelity—

Nepos had had in those days a properly dull little Etruscan-blooded wife—was as fresh as dawn at sea.

The crowd bellowed for the cage doors to be sprung.

But laughing, Antonius said to the praetorian colonel standing at the edge of the gallery: "Let their passion marinate a bit more, Lucius. These swine would wolf down everything raw."

"Very good, Lord Regent."

Quintus was reading again, which annoyed Nepos. Bookishness bespoke an effete nature. But he wasn't in mood for another quarrel with Claudia over the boy's less than manly habits.

He noticed a tribune, dusty from the roads and with a dispatch packet in hand, whispering to the colonel. Waving the young officer up, he accepted the message, then tossed the man a leather purse bulging with gold coins: "Spend this foolishly, tribune. It won't be long before you're saddled with a big house and a demanding family as I am."

Claudia gave him a mock slap, which the patricians in the adjoining galleries enjoyed. "See how she henpecks me already!" he cried to them happily.

In the lulls between the roars of the crowd, he could hear the condemned magistrates pleading for their lives. Ignoring them, he scanned the message, then read it more carefully—before suddenly guffawing.

Claudia asked him what news had arrived, but he winked at her and rose to share the dispatch with the seated patricians: "Friends, Matrons of Rome, Conscript Fathers—I have here a missive from Illyricum. . . ." He could not help but grin, although he'd intended to remain deadpan. "It seems that in a mountain village of Moesia Superior a man of regal bearing accompanied by a jaundiced barbarian was nearly caught by the *vigiles*, stealing chickens from a coop! So the old traitor has gone from usurping the imperium to filching his supper!" He cut short the howls of laughter by scooping Quintus up off his couch. "Now, my beloved son, order the gamemaster to let go the bears!"

"No," the child said obstinately.

Nepos gripped the small arms more tightly—painfully, he hoped.

Quintus resisted a moment longer, but then shrilled: "Let go the bears!"

For five minutes the ill-tempered beasts slashed and gutted the screaming magistrates. A swipe of claws accidentally freed one old man, who hobbled toward the ten-foot parapet surrounding the arena, dragging his severed rope behind him. His race for life incited all the bears to give chase at an amazingly swift lope. They caught up with him at the section of wall directly below the gallery of the Vestal Virgins.

Screaming, he vanished beneath a huge mound of fur and clicking jaws.

Yet this climax to the magistrates event had an unforeseen consequence, for no one had correctly estimated the prowess of these bears, and one of them leaped off the top of the swarm into the gallery above—and had a vestal before the praetorians could lance it to a roaring death.

Some said that this was the worst possible omen at the advent of a new imperial order.

But Antonius Nepos saw it as a sign of a new vigor in the world, and so proclaimed at his banquets of the next week that his regency had now been anointed with the blood of a virgin.

For nine miles east of the garrison city of Augusta Rauricorum it remained a proper Roman road, as straight as an arrow's flight. But then the first buckling of the Alps took its toll on the Roman obsession with the most direct route possible, and the Via Germania Superior began zigzagging as if the *architectus* had been unsure precisely where ahead Vindonissa lay, or had sprawled drunk in his tent all day. However, the ribbon of paving stones eventually wound down into this last Roman outpost before the frontier.

Here, the tall pilgrim in the common cloack refreshed himself at an inn.

Inquiring if there was any news about the deposed Emperor, he was dished up the same rumors he'd heard at every way station along the Rhondanus and Arar rivers since he'd stolen out of the port of Massilia two weeks before: Germanicus had raised a loyal army in Dacia and was marching on Rome; Germanicus was dead and rotting in Moesia, the victim of brigands; Germanicus was nowhere to be found—that was the most likely of the crop.

At the eighth hour of the day, with the sun poised midway between its zenith and the hilly horizon, the pilgrim set out again.

After Vindonissa only foot traffic was allowed, so there was no choking dust from passing freight lorries. He slogged up the long inclines as if in a trance. The soles of his sandals were almost worn through, the hobnails dropping off like ripe seeds, and his cloak was the same earthen color as the road cuts.

At a spring he met an old man of the Chatti tribe, a white-haired scribe for the Roman government in Jura, and decided to walk with him a while.

"With each step now I shed a bit of purple," the old one said in Gothic, huffing for breath. "How long for you, my son?"

The tall pilgrim was silent for a moment, ashamed he'd grown rusty in his mother tongue. He had always passed back and forth between two worlds and had never been completely comfortable in either. When Rolf finally spoke, it was in his awkward Latin: "Ten years, grandfather, last I come."

The old man correctly guessed that he was a legionary. "Many in imperial service are coming home now instead of later."

This was true: The crush of pilgrims would not begin until August, when they would leave off their Roman occupations for a month and hike up into the Wald, but most of Rolf's fellow travelers were what he once might have described as deserters—had he not agreed with their refusal to serve the likes of Antonius Nepos and Claudia Nero. Yet, no soldier had boasted of his allegiance to Germanicus, or to any other *imperator* for that matter, and the wiser of them sneaked through the garrison towns after nightfall or avoided them altogether.

The arrests had begun in earnest. The new rulers were mopping up the opposition. Rolf had seen it before, when Fabius had snatched the imperium away from his older brother. Only Germanicus had swept into power on the wings of a general amnesty.

"Are you a thane of your people, my son? You carry yourself thusly."

"Aye, a *thegan* of the Marcomanni."

"Oh, then you've returned for the Marcoman Assembly."

He shrugged noncommittally.

"The Romans have always been so clever," the old man went on blithely when Rolf declined to talk about the affairs of his tribe. "So very clever."

"How be that, grandfather?"

"Indeed—clever little men, the Romans. When their general Varus vanquished our dear Arminius up in the dark thick of the Teutoburg Wald, did Caesar Augustus take everything of our past away from us? No, he let us keep one forest as it was, the most scared of our walds, and let no Roman come into it. Augustus was no fool. Oh, yes indeed, he knew that the driest tinder for war is resentment smoldering in the German heart. We do not take well to resentment."

"Aye, grandfather, the walls of our hearts to be too thin to trap despair. . . ." In decades past, a rock slide had reduced the road to a footpath, and now Rolf fell in behind the old man. He began to repeat something Caesar Germanicus had said, that if the Germans rather than the Romans had triumphed at Teutoburg forest, the world would be vastly different today, that Rome itself might not even exist, and that the Empire would be reduced to a gaggle of warring nations with none adept enough at government to establish universal peace and prosperity. Also, Caesar had recited a hard-to-understand sibylline poem revealing how the Marcomanni would have been driven southwest toward Pannonia—had Arminius *not* been vanquished by the legionaries. This had made no sense, for why would his people, the fiercest German tribe, have been forced out of their ancestral lands if their Cherusci ally had *won*? The outcome of history always seemed to him a riddle, even with Germanicus patiently explaining the hidden meanings of ancient events to him.

But then Rolf realized with a start that he'd almost let slip his secret tie to the most hunted man in the Empire. He was more spent than he'd realized, beaten down by his escape through Italia and then his long trek through Gaul into Germania.

But now at last, his destination lay just beyond the mountain pass whose sharp vee dipped down to meet the rising of the trail a few miles ahead.

The old man suddenly stood aside. "Go ahead, my son. Your legs are longer and stronger than mine. And I have come back to the Wald each year for as long as I remember."

"*Ave atque vale*, grandfather."

"Hail and farewell?" He snorted. "The same to you then. But we have been among the Romans so long we even take our leave as they do!"

An hour later Rolf presented him self to the attendant in the wind-polished timber station at the pass. "I be Rolf, *thegan* of the Marcomanni."

"Welcome home, Lord Rolf." The unshorn man took his Roman-style clothes, his hobnailed military sandals, his short sword—all to be kept for him until he left the Wald—and exchanged them for a rough woolen cloak, which Rolf fastened at the shoulder with a large thorn. Now that all but the highest snows were gone, no footwear was worn in the Wald, and for this reason the first week of a Romanized German's return was called the *blister season.* "All the other Marcoman lords are already down at your lodge."

"Aye?" It surprised Rolf that this year's earlier-than-usual Assembly would be so heavily attended, but he accepted a cup of *met* without another word. Late, not early, summer was the time for the thanes of his tribe to come together. But, while afar in imperial service, he had missed ten of these gatherings, and perhaps much had changed during the decade. Also, there was bound to be consternation among his people because of Germanicus' fall from power. Still, he could not remember all the lords returning to the Wald on one occasion.

Outside, he made resolutely for the overlook on the lip of the pass.

The evening breeze was rushing down the slopes of the Alps, making the firs whisper roundabout his head. Below him lay forest and stone, and then beyond the stone, great rivers of ice—all unbroken by the lines of agriculture or roads or marble villas, an outland untouched by Rome. A lurer sounded in the distance.

He snapped off a sprig of fir, mashed the needles between his fingers and stroked the resin into his mustaches. He smiled: It was the sharp and wild spice of the Wald; it was the untamed forest itself.

Whatever had possessed him to leave? Of noble blood, he was one of the few entitled to make his permanent home here, although most Romans assumed all young Germans were "fresh from the Wald." But instead of remaining in the Marcoman village, he had put this windy pass—and all the privileges due him by noble tribal birth—to his back and descended into the arduous and disciplined life of a Roman soldier.

Well, it had seemed like a good solution at the time. And, undeniably, it had preserved his honor and that of a beautiful woman-child with amber eyes. But enough of the past—Rolf of the Marcomanni started down into the Wald. The mellow-throated lurer beckoned.

6

Segestias staggered up the earthen steps from his half-buried log-and-clay hut, spilling *met* over himself. As he emerged from the dimness and into the guttering of the portal torches, the honey-colored liquid sheened wetly on his bare chest. The stain had just begun to dry when he gasped, childlike, and saluted the evening star with his horn, slopping more of the sticky beverage on himself. He halted uncertainly on the final step before ground level and began milking the point of his beard as if it were an udder, eyes straining to bring the tall stranger into focus. "Do I know this pilgrim?"

"Maybe," Rolf said. "Maybe not. I be of no mind to know your mind."

"That be a Roman kind of answer. Aye, as Roman as Tiber mud . . . as Roman as burnt scones . . . as . . . as . . ." Running out of comparisons, he snuffled and tugged at his tight-fitting Gothic undergarment as if it were pinching his maleness, then eased his buttocks down onto the low edge of the steaming, manure-heaped roof. "Well . . . ?" His eyes, ordinarily a clear and arresting blue, were moist and runny with confusion. "You be fresh down off the pass?"

"Aye."

Segestias asked the same question once again, and Rolf calmly made the same reply as if for the first time. Then, unsteadily, Segestias handed him his horn of *met*. "Welcome, then."

"Your health." Rolf drank, then wiped his lips on the back of his forearm, which felt springy with hair—he had not done something this uncouth in a long time. Romans had devoted an entire branch of etiquette to napkins, and these fancy cloths were so prized that a dinner guest usually brought his own to carefully dab the corners of his mouth after each bite or sip.

"What be your lineage, pilgrim?"

Rolf decided in a blink that, in light of his cousin's present condition, the Long Account—a ritualistic boast of one's famous ancestors that could burble away an hour or two—would be wasted. He hiked a shoulder: "I be with some of old King Maroboduus' blood in my veins."

"Then we be kinsmen and fellow *thegans*," Segestias said, blandly, borrowing back the horn for a gulp. "Aye?"

Again, Rolf shrugged. A nobleman returning to the Wald could find peers in every hut or sleeping under the stars in the dank, meandering pastures. Roman rule, by denying the tribes real power, had held down the murderous and protracted rivalries of old to occasional fits of temper. Why kill off your siblings when none of you will ever wind up king?—this was how most thanes looked at it. And thus the sons of the German regal clans had multiplied like lemmings, safe from the plum of envy that had poisoned the entire Julian clan except for Germanicus Julius, who himself might now be dead of treachery within his own family. Until recent days at least, Roman rule had taken the malice out of German politics. But some said the *Pax Romana* had also castrated the Assemblies, turned the boldest of the barbarian races into sheep. A month ago, Rolf would have argued against this, but now he wasn't so sure. He feared what Antonius Nepos might do to his homeland; the lord regent might not honor the ancient Julian treaties.

At this moment, Segestias' wife came lithely up the steps with a wolf-fur cloak for her husband—Wald twilights were quick to grow chilly.

She stopped and regarded the stranger with suspicion for several moments. He scarcely breathed—so hard were her eyes on him. But then they softened and she cried, "Rolf!"

Although his pulse had quickened, he resisted giving her even a modest embrace. Segestias was deep in his cups, but jealousy is fueled, not dampened by *met*. "Glaesea."

Her name meant amber, for her eyes were the translucent brown of this gem that had been formed long ago when, for an awful instant, the sun turned black and its orphaned light crystallized the smoldering air into teardrops of a thousand shades—golden brown like Glaesea's eyes, saffron, dusky blue, Rhine-green, and all the other hues swirled in the fabric of that distant convulsion. The malevolent spirits which had attended that first death of the sun could be reawakened by rubbing a piece of *glaesum* against the fur of a hare, and their voices would then crackle and hiss once again with portents of doom. Inevitable doom for all men, good and bad, brave and cowardly—despite the friendly magic of the god-friend, who was Woden on some occasions, Donar on others, and even Mother Nerthus sometimes; but all powerless in the end to help mankind. Like the feather-clad Aztecae Rolf had so recently fought, the Germans believed in the ultimate destruction of all things. Yet, unlike the man-sacrificing Aztecae, his own people had little hope that the cataclysm could be forestalled by human entreaty. It would come, and violently too, whatever man did.

"Why have you missed so many Assemblies?" Glaesea asked, the edge to her voice reminding him how bitterly they had quarreled at times. Once, they had gone a winter without speaking to each other, and never had the snows lingered so long in the village. "Where have you been?"

"I be about the Empire."

"With the midget warriors?"

"Aye." This name for peninsular Romans was too timeworn to be considered an insult any longer. Besides, according to Caesar's physician, Epizelus, milk and cheese from Gaul and Jura had added a half foot to the height of the average Roman since olden days. "Always with the legions."

"Did you remember us . . . ?" The torchlight was giving that amber depth to her eyes he'd recalled so well in distant hellholes—but only briefly on each occasion. He had always reined in his recollections of her before they could turn him toward evil thoughts, before he could wish his cousin Segestias dead and Glaesea gentle and warm in his bed. A soldier's life was too precarious for him to glory in evil; he must gird himself with noble thoughts, or risk the retribution of the god-friend. "Did Rolf of the Marcomanni remember his Marcoman friends?"

"Nay," he said, carefully. "I be terrible busy."

"With the soldiering?"

"Aye, much soldiering."

In their youth, Rolf had been in love with Glaesea, and she with him. Even now, he could not swear that this love had faded—on either side. But he had masked his strong feelings for her in gruffness when his more prosperous cousin was first to present her family with an acceptable dowry. Contrary to the Roman custom, the German groom and not the bride brought the dowry to the marriage—and not baubles to please a girl's fancy, but sensible things such as a pair of oxen or a horse and bridle. The bride gave her husband only one kind of matrimonial gift: the arms with which to safeguard her virtue. German passion was honed by practicality, and in truth Rolf would have been comfortable with nothing less. Besides, Segestias had not gone the way of rape and purchase, which would have been in accordance with tribal law. He had not lain with Glaesea before purchasing her from her family. And for this, Rolf was still thankful. Had his beloved cousin taken her first, taken her as he himself had ached to do all of his feverish youth, he would have killed him.

Sighing, he peered up through the framing boughs of the larch pines at the icy glimmer in the sky.

"The evening star," she said, perhaps reading his thoughts as women inhabited by the god-friend can do. The better if she couldn't, he realized—she might see the pain Segestias and she had given him by settling into a contented marriage, the pain they were still giving him. For never once while afield with the legions in Germania Inferior, Mauretania, Hibernia, and Anatolia; while trying to forget his brief and turbulent marriage to a Bithynian woman; while haunting the corridors of Palatine as a praetorian during the reign of Fabius; or more recently while campaigning across the Oceanus Atlanticus with Caesar Germanicus—never once after leaving the Wald had he let himself dream of lying with Glaesea. The instant that remembrance of her stirred his loins, he had only to recall the punishment in the Wald for adultery: Her head would be shaved, then she would be stripped naked and— before the eyes of her family—flogged by her husband up and down the muddy lanes. After all that, if Segestias so desired, he could put her to death.

Something so pitiable could happen only here in the Marcoman village, for when the Assembly was concluded and Segestias and Glaesea again left the Wald, he to labor in the glazing factory at Augusta Rauricorum and she to her chores in their small atrium house on the outskirts of that sooty industrial city, they would take on all the trappings of Roman civilization again, including the equality of women under the Twelve Tables.

So it was for all but the few who remained here year-round under the old customs of the Marcomanni.

Segestias was now weeping drunkenly. "Rolf . . . my *Rolf*?"

"Aye."

"You be dead a thousand times in my fears!"

"Mine too. But fears be the thinnest kind of dreams. Come,

cousin." Rolf helped him to his feet, and together they descended into the smoky gloom of the hut.

Glaesea followed at a distance.

Rolf could feel her at his stooping back. He believed he could feel her eyes on his back.

"It be Estammic who call us together," Segestias said after an hour's nap. It had done much to clear his head but little to blanch the redness out of his eyes.

Rolf at once stopped chewing on the roasted horseflesh Glaesea had served him. He lowered the shank bone.

Estammic was a kinsman to Rolf, a warrior renowned for his fury in battle. But his name was also linked to the Gothic Revival, a cult on the fringe of brigandage that called for the annihilation of Rome. Yet, now that Germanicus was deposed and only the gods knew where, was the Revival such a bad thing?

His expression growing somber in the the fire light, Rolf realized that he might have to rethink all his former loyalties—and with no Germanicus at hand to explain the consequences.

"Why an Assembly now?" he asked Segestias, although he already had a few ideas.

"The Julians—they always be friends to Germania—"

"*Ja*," Glaesea murmured in Gothic as she patiently turned the spit, "Augustus Caesar—he gave us the Wald to come home to. He gave us *something* when he really had to give us nothing. He could have given us salt and ashes."

"And now," Segestias went on, frowning at her interruption, "the last of that great clan be gone."

"How be my cousin so sure?"

"Rolf has news we don't?" Glaesea asked.

He lowered his eyes from her face. "Nay, woman."

"We too be pleased to hear of Germanicus alive and back in Rome," Segestias said. "All Germania be pleased what if that be true. But to wish and to have be different things, aye?"

Rolf nodded morosely.

"So this be the business at hand, if Rolf be of a mind to ask me. . . ."

"Aye, tell me."

Segestias went on to explain that with Germanicus' imperium in shreds, Estammic and his most ardent followers intended to proclaim the existence of the Gothic Revival, which had been a tribal secret heretofore, and incite first the Marcomanni and then all the tribes to throw off Roman rule, forever. These were the reasons behind .tomorrow night's Assembly, which was being convened months ahead of schedule.

Rolf picked up the shank bone and began gnawing again, silent but for the champing of his teeth, deeply alone within his thoughts.

Germanicus had come down to Corinthus if only because there were numerous ways to flee the isthmus city. By sea, if the need arose, he and Tora could go westward through the Gulf of Corinthus and out into the Ionian Sea; or they could sail eastward into the island-strewn Aegean, and eventually find refuge in the Greek-speaking provinces to which he'd always afforded every possible benefaction. To the south of the bustling provincial capital lay the bulk of Achaea, the senior senatorial province, governed by a proconsul Germanicus had chosen because of his republican leanings, a man—if he were yet alive—who might be trusted to shelter Caesar and his Nihonian adjutant against Antonius Nepos' spies, at least until they could recover their strength.

Also here in Achaea, recuperating in his native village from his harrowing captivity by the Aztecae, was Epizelus, Caesar's longtime physician. But Germanicus was not eager to burden the frail man with hiding the most-sought-after fugitive in the Empire. In fact, he put Epizelus out of his mind—*let him heal in peace*.

From Corinthus, he was willing go in any direction except that from which Tora and he had just arrived emaciated and in rags—north. Behind them lay a month of hunger and mountain cold and the countless petty humiliations survival takes as its toll. Leaving the Dalamatian coast and Tora's shattered cloud-galley, they had trekked east into Moesia Superior, only to be shunted south toward Macedonia by an unseasonal snowfall in the foothills of the Dacian alps. Near Heraclea Lyncestis, while sleeping exhausted in a ditch beside the road, they were discovered by a band of Macedonian auxiliaries returning from a brothel. But for the disguise of his beard, the first of his life, Germanicus might have been captured then and there. However, the drunken soldiers were content just to rough the scruffy vagrants up a bit before kicking them on their way. Fortunately, the troops garrisoned at Dium were too busy with a riot over a grain shortage to pay much attention to transients. But the next morning, so defeated in spirit was Germanicus while skirting Mount Olympus, he was tempted to fall behind the plodding Tora and then make for the snowy wastes above, to take final residence with the gods. Had not the Senate, in better days, offered to deify him and thus ensure him a place on this very summit? He laughed grimly to himself all the way to the pass at Thermopylae, where the winds of twenty-four centuries had worn away nearly all the evidences of the Spartan sacrifice, leaving nothing but pyre-scorched stones and an atmosphere of futility. The world, really, was barren of nobility, and history was adventitious to the point of meaninglessness. How could it be otherwise if the likes of Claudia Nero and Antonius Nepos, who—according to the rumors of the road—spent their days indulging their most base desires, had been entrusted with the purple?

"Lord Caesar," Tora now whispered beside him in the shadowy lee of Corinthus' north market wall, "where do we proceed from here?"

A hard rain, attended by occasional lightning and thunder, was slanting across the torches set about the temple of Apollo. "A moment, Tora-*san*—"

It was well past midnight, and all of Corinthus but its canal district of wineshops was becalmed. The only legionary in sight was tramping indifferently down the length of the northwest stoa, passing in and out of view behind the long line of columns. His hobnailed sandals clipped echoes out across the night. Then he was gone, having turned up the Lechaeum Road toward the Baths of Eurycles.

Tora pointed at the rain-blurred outlines of the fortress perched atop the Acrocorinthus, a monolith rising nearly half a Roman mile above the level of the sea: "Are any praetorians garrisoned here?"

"Not during my imperium. This was entirely a senatorial province—no red capes on hand to intimidate the local curia . . ." And then Germanicus realized once again that his imperium was no more and that Nepos might well have barged a cohort of guardsmen up the Fabian canal to cow the civil administration. "But now . . . who knows?"

Tora was shivering. He appeared to have only enough flesh left to hold his protruding bones in place. Germanicus promised himself he would free Tora of this fatal obligation at the first opportunity and let him go home to his native land—the only trick was how to do this without offending the man's exquisite sense of honor.

"What of the proconsul here?" the Nihonian asked.

"Gessius Fadus? A modest man. But capable."

"It is his loyalty I ask about, Lord Caesar."

He sealed his cloak around his throat to keep the rainy wind from flowing down his tunic-front. "I know. And to that I have no answer. He was loyal once. Perhaps he remains so. Perhaps he doesn't. There's but one way to find out. Come . . ."

Rising stiffly, he led Tora across a balustraded gallery perched above the fountain-studded agora, the ancient marketplace of the city. This broad square was surrounded by the usual public buildings of a Roman provincial capital, plus a great basilica honoring the Julians of old. All this had been rebuilt a half dozen times since Nero had visited the venerable seat of the Achaean League on his famous Greek junket—the devastations of civil war and earthquake were no stranger to Corinthus.

Tora clutched his broken left wrist in his right armpit as he ran. Never once had he mentioned the pain of his injury, and this only heightened Germanicus' remorse that it had been incurred in his behalf. He no longer felt worthy of the sacrifices of others.

They halted on the steps of the local curia.

Germanicus was having difficulty recalling the way to the proconsul's house, although he'd been a guest there many times over the years. Shock and grief and hunger seemed to be effacing his most familiar memories. "I think . . . this way. Yes, I'm sure—the house was situated on a rise behind the south basilica."

If Tora had any doubts, he hid them well.

However, they soon glimpsed the grand atrium house, its portal guarded by a pair of legionaries. That these were soldiers of the legion rather than the praetorian guard did much to reassure Germanicus. Nevertheless, he gave them a wide berth and conducted Tora to the garden wall at the rear of the house.

There, they regarded the ten-foot barrier. In their present state it seemed as towering as the Acrocorinthus itself.

"Lord Caesar," Tora whispered, "can you bear my weight on your shoulders?"

He nodded, then bent over and braced his hands on his knees, feeling ridiculous, like a member of one of the tumbling and juggling troupes that had performed for him on the Palatine. Tora briefly gripped him around the throat with his good forearm, then clambered up Germanicus' back and planted his feet athwart

Caesar's broad shoulders. "Stand erect, sire," he hissed. Groaning under his breath, Germanicus struggled to his full height. Tora's weight was nothing, that of a child. But still it was enough to make him dizzy. He shut his eyes against the sensation, hoping it would subside before he fainted.

If Gessius Fadus refused him help, how many more days could he abide on reserves of strength so feeble he felt Tora's bulk as that of one of the Cyclopes? Should he surrender to the garrison here and accept whatever followed with the stoicism befitting a Roman patrician?

And then, suddenly, he was free of his burden.

Tora had leaped up and grasped the lip of the wall under his right arm. Grunting softly, he swung his left leg over the top, then straddled the wall with a triumphant grin, which was caught in the city's *electricus* reflected by the low rain clouds.

The Nihonian signaled that he would meet Germanicus at the gate in a section of the wall they'd just passed.

Then he dropped out of sight.

Germanicus made quietly for the gate, realizing that his limp was more pronounced than usual—the foul weather taunting him with wet and chill when the usual dry warmth of midsummer should have been salving his old battle wounds.

A frenzy of lightning fell behind the Acrocorinthus, bringing into black definition a wireless transmission tower of the newest type. If Fadus betrayed him, Rome would know of it within minutes.

He leaned heavily against the gatepost. *Instead of breaking into Fadus' house, I should be recounting those of my gens who fell upon their own swords rather than persist in a life of indignity—*

The rusted hinges behind him began screaking.

He stood aside as the gate slowly swung outward to form a gap no more than a foot and a half wide, revealing a garden courtyard within. He slipped through the opening, and Tora slid shut the gate again, but didn't latch it.

Turning toward him, Germanicus held the blade of his hand above his head as if it were the crest of a legionary's helmet— asking by this sign if Tora had seen any of the guard.

The Nihonian mouthed the word *no*.

Together they inched over the flagstones, deeper into the courtyard. It was enclosed by two-storied porticoes on three sides. The colonnades on the lower level were lined with the sleeping chambers of lesser relations and slaves—or a household contingent of the guard, if Fadus preferred to stable some of the men closer to him than the garrison atop the Acrocorinthus.

Pausing, Germanicus stayed Tora with a hand. He wanted to listen for a few moments.

The Nihonian dipped his head, then sat on his heels.

Over the prattling of the rain and a louder music of water trickling in the fountain at the center of the quadrangle came the blaring of a foghorn somewhere along the gulf. Germanicus sniffed deeply. From the blossoms of the miniature orange trees around him came a sweet, aromatic lie that all the civilized world was pleasant and harmless; that all men, by the grace of their fellow men, live out their natural lives in peace and dignity; that treachery and pride are the stuff only of Greek tragedy and Scandian epics.

He had once owned a garden much like this—at his procuratorial headquarters in Nova Antiochia. Another lifetime ago.

The household was dark, silent.

Fadus was not one to entertain late. And sooner or later, most eastern governors adopted the Greek habit of rising early if only to synchronize their workday to that of their constituency.

Then Germanicus caught a whiff of smoldering charcoal.

Fadus was plagued with a rheumy cough and could be expected to have his slaves set a brazier close to his sleeping couch on a night as dank as this one.

He led Tora the rest of the distance across the courtyard and up the marble steps to the folding doors which barred their entrance into the atrium, or great hall of the place.

These doors, as expected, were not locked. But there was also no way to go around them and avoid crossing the atrium. The design of the house was such that entry from the garden had to be made through them.

Taking a deep breath, he was preparing himself to go first and overpower whatever guard was stationed inside the atrium—when Tora stepped in front of him and barged through the doors.

Once inside, the Nihonian crouched in a fighting stance, his right hand formed into a claw.

Germanicus rushed to his side, wrapping the tail of his cloak around his forearm to lessen the effect of any sword blows.

But no legionaries awaited them on the glistening mosaic floor, and a search behind the statuary and drapery revealed that Fadus had gone to bed with no expectation of trouble.

Rain streaked down through the square opening in the ceiling and dimpled the pool that in ancient times had supplied the household with water. The slaves would have to lower its level with buckets in the morning, Germanicus thought idly. He was finding it hard to keep his mind on the task at hand.

Tora shrugged as if to ask where next.

Many Romans adorn the traditional small study off the atrium with trophies of war, but Fadus—as was proved by a scan of the room—was not a martial man. Only a fresco of the many-breasted goddess Astarte adorned his wall, and even this accentuated her romantic aspects more than her bellicose attributes.

By now, Germanicus' palm was aching for the heft of a good short sword.

"Come," he mouthed, taking a staircase that wound up to the second-story colonnade.

The preferred bedchambers in an atrium house were placed on the west side of the courtyard in order to catch the morning sunlight, and it was to these Germanicus went with Tora scurrying behind him.

He had only to follow his nose to the chamber leaking charcoal smoke from the space between the lintel and the top of the door.

There he sprung the latch and reached inside for the *electricus* lever.

In the sudden wash of glare, the proconsul blinked, then sprang up from his sleeping couch. "By the gods—!" he gasped.

Tora choked off the man's cry, keeping his hands around his throat until Fadus said with a roll of his eyes he understood that he was to keep silent. With effort, he suppressed the beginnings of a cough.

Germanicus shut the window, which had been cracked to admit a little night air. "Do you know me, Gessius Augustulus Fadus?"

Still unable to speak, the proconsul shook his head.

Germanicus drew his filthy, bearded face closer to the proconsul's. "Are you sure?"

Again, a mute denial.

Germanicus stared deeply into the terrified eyes, and in Fadus' panic he glimpsed something he had not believed true of the man before: The source of his modesty was timidity. Still, could the proconsul be counted on to keep his mouth shut until Germanicus and Tora could restore themselves before stealing out of Corinthus? "You honestly don't know me, Gessius? Why, I'm offended."

"I mean no offense," the proconsul croaked, "I keep no money in this chamber. None at all. Everything's locked away down in my *tablinum*. *Everything*. The strongbox is chained to the floor . . . and . . . and the key is kept up at the garrison until dawn!"

Germanicus chuckled sadly. "Would the man who gave you the signet ring you now wear sneak inside your house after midnight to rob you of your sesterces?"

The eyes widened a little. "*Germanicus Julius?*"

"Yes, in the weary flesh."

Fadus had to control a tremulous jaw before he could mutter: "Praise to the gods you're still alive!"

"And to whom do we give praise that you are still governor of Achaea?"

Fadus began coughing so violently, Tora covered the man's mouth with a corner of the bedding.

When he could speak again, the proconsul whispered, "These are dangerous and confusing times, Caesar. I expect a summons to Rome at any hour. . . ." Fadus did not have to explain what recall to the Palatine by the new imperium invariably meant to a governor. He then lowered his voice even more: "We mustn't talk here. There are visitors from Rome in the next chamber. Come, you can eat while we talk. . . ." Showing that he had no dagger concealed beneath his coverlet, Fadus rose and padded in his bare feet to the door. He checked the corridor. "It's clear."

"How is your household guard posted?" Tora asked.

"Two lads at the portal."

"That is all?"

"Yes. This is a tame province—ask Caesar."

Germanicus peered over Fadus' shoulder and down the shadowy corridor. "Has Nepos detached praetorians into Greece yet?"

"No, but that's coming . . . it's coming soon enough." Inclining his bald head for the two men to follow, Fadus crept out the door.

During the few minutes they'd spent inside the bedchamber, the rain had dwindled and a dense fog had infiltrated the city from the Ionian side of the isthmus. Germanicus tried to fight off a chill, but it racked him so hard his shoulders lurched. This cold, really nothing when compared to Scandia's in midwinter, was cutting through him. He hoped there was hot bread dipped in olive oil to be tasted in Fadus' kitchen—and chafed vinegar, if the gods were disposed to comfort an exhausted man who'd not had a decent meal in over a month.

Fadus halted them at the top of the stairs and motioned that he wished to go down first, alone, apparently to make sure no slaves—perhaps the bakers, who'd soon be at their work—were skulking around the atrium or the dining hall.

Germanicus hesitated, but then agreed with a nod.

Stifling a cough, Fadus crept down the steps, although as master of the house he had no need to creep.

After a moment, he could be heard opening and shutting doors. In all but the most modern Roman houses, there were six small chambers adjoining the atrium, including the study, and Fadus was carefully checking each of them before heading to the dining hall, which the two intruders had not entered.

Germanicus glanced at Tora. The Nihonian's eyes were so swollen with fatigue, they scarcely seemed open.

At last, Fadus' torchlit pate appeared at the foot of the stairs. He waved them down.

Only when Germanicus and Tora had set foot in the atrium were they able to see the two praetorian centurions looming with drawn swords at opposing ends of the chamber.

"Arrest these traitors," Gessius Fadus told them. "Arrest them in the name of the lord regent!"

7

THE SKEWERED HUNKS of horse meat sizzled and spat juice into the flames.

Standing just outside the firelight, concealed by the spring-lush bracken, Rolf watched the Marcoman women do the last-minute cooking for the nightlong revel their menfolk tried to dignify by calling it "an Assembly." Perhaps he had been among the midget warriors too long and now saw the customs of his own people through Roman eyes. If true, it was a curse that would bring loneliness without end.

Yet, he took heart form the sight of the Marcoman women. Faces framed by their long, swaying plaits—braids of blond, red, brown, auburn, and silver-gray—the women squinched down into the smoke while attending to their tasks. And as if not to annoy these somber-eyed women too much, the smoke spirits curled swiftly up into the wild indigo sky of the Wald. These were the makings of his earliest memories: women and smoke and a galloping black sky full of restless gods.

"Bring another platter," an old women snapped, her scrawny hands flitting in and out of the flames to retrieve the charred pieces of meat. "And someone—you there, girl—take over another amphora of curdled milk! At once now!"

He shouldered his *framea*, the short and narrow-bladed javelin Segestias had given him—for no Marcoman would think of letting his kin attend any gathering unarmed, and continued on toward the Lodge of Assembly. The torches set before the long structure were winking through the pale trunks of the birches. Overriding Segestias' protests, he had insisted on making his entry into the lodge alone. Of all the *thegans*, he was the one most closely linked to the midget warriors. He had, after all, been Caesar's right hand. And now he didn't want Segestias—the ranking member of his *sippe*, or clan—to suffer the wrath of the Gothic Revival because of his own allegiance to the Rome of Germanicus Agricola.

He had no doubt that he would be tested. And there would be trouble with Estammic. If not tonight, soon enough. He wanted to leave his cousin out of it. But this might prove hard. As the spiritual head of Rolf's clan, Segestias, more than the former centurion himself, would be targeted for vengeance in the event of bad blood—unless Rolf could forestall violence by a show of ferocity that would dismay all but the most rash of challengers.

He paused at the bearskin hung across the portal, sensing movement at the edge of his vision, something out in the darkness.

He grasped a torch to have a better look.

A young Marcoman warrior, having lost his shield on the field of battle against Gaulish brigands who'd ventured into the Wald on the day before Rolf's arrival, had hanged himself from a tree limb. Here in their sanctuary, Germans fought with archaic weapons and, more importantly, under the old code of courage.

The disgraced warrior had been dangling there a day and a half now, and no one dared cut him down.

Segestias had told Rolf all about it—and about another shirker who'd been condemned to death by the Assembly. This craven had not been given the choice of suicide: His arms pinioned behind him, he had been crammed inside a wicker hurdle, which was then pressed down into the ooze of a nearby bog.

Shame must always be buried out of sight.

Estammic had reportedly blamed this blight of cowardice on soft Roman living. But Rolf knew this to be claptrap. More than once he had stood knee-deep in slain legionaries who'd been too proud to give up. And there was no one alive more brave than Germanicus Agricola—and no one more Roman.

Estammic cared more for his hatred than the truth.

The night breeze rocked the youth on his rawhide tether. His blackened tongue had crept out between his front teeth as if to taunt all who would gaze upon his humiliation. "Aye, lad," Rolf sighed, "there be peril in coming home to the Wald. . . ." All decisions made by the Assembly were final. And thanks to Caesar Augustus' generous covenant with the tribes, a condemned man could not appeal in the last resort to the Emperor, as could every other citizen of the Empire. "A German be wise to know how German he be before coming back."

Then Rolf turned and whipped aside the bearskin.

What he did next he had planned from the moment Segestias

had told him about Estammic's growing rebelliousness. Circling his hands around his mouth, he loosed a deafening *baritus* into the crowded lodge. His war cry, deep and defiant and promising swift punishment to any insult, silenced the thanes and their retinues. The cry of a natural chieftain. It asserted everything, apologized for nothing.

All the men had shocked expressions—except Segestias, who looked amused.

"I be Rolf, son of the Marcomanni. . . ." And this time he went through the entire Long Account, beginning with King Maroboduus and continuing on for ten minutes until he had articulated the last syllable of his proud and bloody heritage. "And that be my lineage. No man here have a better one."

Only then did he march through the midst of the throng to the big copper vat of *met*. He ladled himself a hornful.

Standing on the far side of the vat, chewing on a chunk of meat stuck to the point of his double-edged sword, was Estammic. His bloodshot eyes betrayed the fact that, like most of the others, he had been drinking heavily since dusk. But ruddier than his eyes was his strange hair. It had been dyed a jolting red, greased and then twisted into seven spikes that jutted out from his head—a symbol of his desire to see the Seven Hills of Rome flow with blood, as Segestias had forewarned.

Estammic seemed aware that all in the lodge were waiting for him to answer Rolf's bold entry, but he looked to be in no haste to do so. Still ignoring Rolf, he took the last steaming bite off his sword, then stretched his arms in the air before giving the amber pendant dangling against his bare chest an idle turn with his greasy fingers. His unconcern was too overdone to be genuine, Rolf thought.

"It has been some long, long time," Estammic said at last, offhandedly.

Rolf glared at him across the lip of his horn. "Aye."

"And it must be said," Estammic spoke up so all could hear, his Gothic enunciation as sharp as sleet, "it is always good to have Rolf among us."

Several of the more affable lords lofted their horns. They were all too ready to cheer any boding of goodwill between Estammic and Rolf. But what Estammic said next made them lower their vessels: "We should rejoice that with his Roman master wandering the countryside a beggar Rolf comes home to be a Goth once again." He gave a mocking Roman salute, and a few men laughed.

Rolf's horn fell from his hand and thudded against the earthen floor.

He had been scorned, of course, but asked himself if the remark warranted bloodshed this soon. The *thegans* must not think him too quick to anger; but neither must they think him too tentative to save his own honor. There was a precise moment in which to answer such things, and he relied on his instincts, the voices of his ancestors singing in his arteries, to tell him when the moment had arrived. With luck, it might never come.

But Estammic went on in the same way, seemingly oblivious to the danger he was stirring: "And glad we must be that so brave a warrior has returned to us. For was not Rolf brave when he stood shoulder to shoulder with the legionaries of the Sixth Victrix, the legion that has oppressed Germania Inferior for two thousand years?"

Rolf saw that known members of the Gothic Revival were inching toward the vat, holding their weapons altogether too carelessly. Those lords who hadn't made up their minds as to whose part to take in the coming clash—they began making space for the fight. Most had already come to a decision and now sifted forward, some lining up behind Estammic, and others to Rolf's back. Many more declared for Estammic in this way than for the former centurion, but Rolf was not disheartened by this seeming disadvantage. If tribal law still held sway, the contest would be one-against-one. So what did it matter if all of Germania—except the fearless Segestias—lined up behind Estammic? This declaring for one man or the other was simply posturing, a way of voting on the issues that were still taking shape.

"Aye," he said when the *thegans* had finished shifting around the lodge. His voice was steady, his eyes locked on Estammic's. "I, like many here, be a veteran of the Sixth Victrix. And one thing always be said of the Conquering Sixth what *never* be said of the Gothic Revival—the Sixth never be of a heart to kill brother Germans over words."

This won several grunts of approval, and Estammic's eyes flickered roundabout for an instant. Then he grinned. But it was a stung grin, for no true German can mask his feelings. And whatever else could be said of him, Estammic was a true German.

"Well said—for the legionary who then shipped with the Third

Augusta to murder Hibernians. All for that whoremaster of an emperor, the late and glorious Fabius!"

"I care not what maiden the emperor bends low—as long as she be not Germania." Rolf realized with a bit of self-amusement that his hours of standing guard in the Roman Senate had taught him a thing or two about retorts.

The howls of laughter singed Estammic's cheeks, and the veins on his hand gripping the hilt were suddenly prominent.

Rolf thought the attack was coming then, but no—Estammic chuckled and accepted a horn of *met* from one of his young firebrands. "By Woden's hoary head, I hate all that stinks of Rome. Let me drink to that. All may join who will."

As bewildering as it would appear to a Roman senator, who carefully observed decorum in all disputes in order to stave off violence, this reckless quarrel didn't mark the collapse of protocol. It was the very means by which affairs were decided by the Assembly. A German's sincerity was measured by his willingness to back up his argument with arms. And the feasting and drinking that continued in the background were considered inducements for a man to blurt his innermost thoughts, as the real dangers to tribal peace were held to be cunning and secretiveness. Yet, Rolf had rubbed elbows with the Romans too long not to see wisdom in putting this issue aside for the time being. The state of the Empire at present was too confused for Germania to decide what course to take. But he also realized that such a sensible suggestion would be seen by the thanes as submissiveness. And he could never submit to a man who had just insulted him.

"And speaking of whore-maidens," Estammic went on blithely, although his eyes were pinched and damp with rage, "how did the brave Rolf serve Caesar Germanicus in Anatolia by lopping off the head of his Scandian mistress?"

Rolf's face flared and his hands tensed around his *framea*, but he held his tongue. The execution of Germanicus' Scandian adjutant for treason was something he detested even thinking about, let alone hearing it openly discussed among men who would never understand Caesar's pained relationship with that unfortunate daughter of Odin. "I be compelled that sad night to do my duty," Rolf seethed at last. "As now I be compelled to do my duty!"

"Duty? To an emperor most likely dead?"

"Nay, Estammic—for me, for Rolf of the Marcomanni!" He had had enough. However, he would not draw first blood, even though at this point no one would think less of him for it. Instead, he would insult Estammic in the fashion of the Romans. Nothing was more degrading to a Roman citizen than to be struck by hand. And even though Estammic was no Roman, he would know that he had been chastised.

The crack of the slap hung in the smoky air long after Rolf had lowered his hand to his side again.

Tears came to Estammic's eyes. But they were from neither pain nor humiliation. Rolf saw them for what they were—for he understood how strangely violence and sentimentality were swirled in the nature of his people. Estammic admired Rolf, and his tears were in regret for what must now follow. And Rolf, in turn, regretted that Estammic could not let a Romanized Marcoman become his rival for tribal leadership—not now, with the Empire on the verge of collapse.

Estammic's sword flashed down across Rolf's field of vision.

But he caught it at a glance on the fire-hardened haft of his *framea*. His parry was not completely spent, when he spun the javelin and smacked Estammic in the jaw with its butt. The man spat teeth, but advanced headlong, roaring at the top of his lungs. He overturned the vat as he came, loosing a flood of *met* against the forelegs of encircling lords, who cried out in boyish glee at the sight of the fulvous tide frothing around their feet.

Rolf forced Estammic to back off a pace by flicking the point of his javelin again and again at his eyes. Yet the man refused to flinch.

"Do you see any *idisi* yet, my brother?" Estammic spoke of the gracious minions of Woden who materialized to enroll a soon-to-be-slain warrior in the Army of the Disembodied.

"Nay, but I see Estammic's own blood on his lips."

"To bleed a jot makes me lighter on my feet!"

"Then be ready to dance in plenty!" Rolf charged but could deliver no final, piercing thrust—so furious were Estammic's counterblows. Wheeling, he prepared for the next onslaught by crouching into the stance he'd taken in drill ten thousand times as a legionary. He did it without thinking. Each and every move came automatically to him now.

Estammic unleashed an upward swing, hoping to cleave the haft of Rolf's *framea* in two. However, his blade sank into only the last foot of oak.

Rolf ignored the splintering sound as he drove the javelin point toward Estammic's throat. The man used his left forearm to shield himself against certain death, but the stone-sharpened steel of the *framea* split open both skin and dark red muscle all the way down to bone.

Estammic made no sound, although he cocked his head oddly to the side. After a few seconds, his eyelids began to flutter. "My arm," he tried to joke, but his voice was shrill. "No matter. I have another."

"Relent," Rolf croaked. "I be without hate for my brother Estammic."

"Relent!" others took up the cry. "It is decided!"

Estammic turned on them and bellowed: "Nothing is decided!" His blood was trickling down his arm and off his fingertips, pooling thickly on the dirt floor. "Will you be slaves to Rome forever!" He misstepped, then fully staggered. A comrade tried to help him, but he fended the youth off with the tip of his sword. "Do not think so little of me!"

"Relent, my son," the aged head of Estammic's *sippe* said gently. "Rolf is full of the god-friend tonight. No man could defeat him."

"No!" he howled, then lunged at Rolf in a move so decisive it was later said that Estammic's fate had been tossed like dice by the gods in this fleeting second. But long before the warrior with the flaming hair could rear back his sword, he found himself impaled on Rolf's javelin. Somehow he had known this would happen—the knowledge was etched in his eyes, briefly, before the brightness went out of them.

With a groan and a savage yank, Rolf retrieved his *framea* from the man's chest.

Estammic's sword tumbled to the *met*-sopped earth behind him. Clutching his wound, he eased down to his knees as if afraid the least jarring would finish him. He tried to laugh, but choked up blood instead. "So . . . so . . . " he gagged, unable to go on. At last, he crumpled to the dirt, his head slamming against the overturned vat. Then he moved no more.

"Brothers!" Segestias had rushed to the center of the lodge. Rolf tried to shove him into the background again, but his cousin bared a dagger at him—he was deadly earnest about this. "Be gone at once, Rolf! Back to my house!" he said in a low voice. "I be quick to offer payment to their *sippe*! Go!"

Rolf scowled at Estammic's hotheads, who were menacing him on all sides. But he elbowed his way through them without suffering any harm and went as Segestias had commanded. Such was the power of the head of a clan.

Now, before the bad blood could solidify like Roman concrete, the leaders of the two clans would try to come to terms over a price for Estammic's life, and further violence might well be avoided.

Rolf was almost to the portal when a messenger raced past him and into the lodge. He had probably come from the station at the pass, the closest wireless to the Wald. Rolf halted and turned to hear what urgent news he brought.

The messenger gawked at Estammic's corpse for a moment, but then remembered his duty: "A message from Rome to all stations."

"Go ahead, lad," Segestias said from a cluster of Estammic's grieving kin and followers.

"Germanicus Julius Agricola is dead."

"*Where*?!" another *thegan* asked.

"In Corinthus."

"How?!"

"Drowned while trying to escape the praetorian guard."

Before Rolf could absorb this, the worst news he'd ever heard in his life, he was distracted by something peculiar Segestias had suddenly done. He had reared up on his toes and gasped. For an instant Rolf thought that his cousin had been as shaken by the report as he—but then he saw the spreading red stain on the back of Segestias' cloak.

Estammic's men had taken their revenge while it was still hot.

Half smiling, Segestias, with a faint wave of his hand, besought Rolf's help, then pitched over dead.

For the second time that night Rolf let go with a *baritus*. But this one sounded as if it had been born in the fire and steam of Hades. Seizing a sword on the run and then another, he barreled into the midst of the Gothic Revival. He parried and hacked and raked and chopped until his arms grew too heavy to lift. Finally, with the screams of the dying at his back he kicked out the timber side wall of the lodge, caving in a portion of the bark roof behind him, and ran into the dark woodlands of the Wald. He did not feel the stones under his bare feet. Nor did he feel the branches flailing his face and arms.

Standing in Gessius Fadus' atrium, his wrists bound behind him with one of the proconsul's silk scarves, Tora saw clearly how at the conclusion of each leg of Caesar's ignoble return to Rome the strength of the prisoner escort would grow.

These two centurions, who had been snoozing half-drunk on Fadus' plush dining couches, too lazy following the banquet in their honor to hike back to their barracks, would be reinforced atop the Acrocorinthus with perhaps a maniple of fellow praetorians. Surely Antonius Nepos, with his widespread ambitions, could not afford to squander more than sixty of his precious guardsmen on such a lapdog of a province as Achaea.

For the voyage to Italia, this praetorian maniple would be augmented with a century of legionaries or, in a pinch, two centuries of Greek auxiliaries. According to the most unfathomable bias Tora had encountered in the Empire, one Roman was held to be worth two provincial citizens and three un-Romanized barbarians in *any* enterprise. However, what he had seen in the campaign against the Aztecae convinced him that some of the most skillful soldiers and sailors were of Iberian or German stock.

An entire cohort, one thousand praetorians in full regalia, would be lorried across the Appeninus mountains from the Castra Praetoria to greet the bireme at Ravenna, and this cohort would be joined by at least that many imperial marines from the great naval port to shepherd the once regal prisoner and his famished Nihonian aide back to Rome and the Mamertine prison.

Tora had to act in the coming minutes, or the chance to free his lord would vanish forever.

During the binding of the captives Fadus had averted his eyes from Germanicus'. Tora believed he had done this out of shame—and perhaps fear as well, for the proconsul seemed anxious for the guardsmen to rid his house of the prisoners. Was he afraid Nepos might ask him why, of all the dwellings that lay between Illyricum and the southernmost tip of Achaea, Germanicus Agricola had chosen this house to seek refuge? Was Fadus secretly a republican, after all?

No wonder the man was itching for Germanicus to be gone.

The senior centurion, on the other hand, wanted to send one of the two legionaries who'd been guarding the portal up to the Acrocorinthus for more troops to conduct the prisoner back to the garrison. A wise suggestion, Tora thought. But Fadus would hear none of it: "Be on your way—immediately!"

"What's a few minutes' more wait, noble consul?"

"Depart—I order it!"

The senior centurion sighed and motioned for the prisoners to follow him toward the front of the house. His comrade fell in behind them, tapping the flat of his short sword against the side of his leg as if to warn the prisoners against thoughts of bolting. Neither guardsman was armed with a niter piece, and the absence of *pili* encouraged Tora.

Germanicus turned to the proconsul and said with a remarkable lack of malice, "Hail and farewell, Gessius Fadus. I'm sorry we both belong to an empire that makes you think this necessary."

Fadus took one look at Caesar's benign expression and hastened to the privacy of his study.

"Pick up your feet there," the senior centurion said as if herding a petty criminal instead of the great lord he'd once been sworn to protect. Yet Caesar seemed to take no offense, and in this, Tora glimpsed an inner balance the Roman had brought to his moment of greatest degradation. Whatever came their way, Germanicus Agricola would be a fitting master for whom to die.

Outside, a luminous fog sifted over the city. The diffused light trapped within it was from the many torches and *electricus* fixtures set around the public buildings. The small and silent party was headed for the steep ramp of a road that wound up the flank of the Acrocorinthus to the garrison, whose battlements were misted over at present. But long before they started up the slope of the huge rock, Tora would have to surrender himself to the Way of the Warrior.

Losing his sword to the disguised praetorians at the Campus Martius had been galling enough, but even worse had been the loss of the scabbard. Its metal mounting had been fashioned by the great teacher Musashi four hundred years before Tora's birth, and the design depicted a monkey reaching out his long arm for the moon's reflection on a pond. With this simple ornament Musashi had been reminding the warrior to always ask himself what is possible and what is not. And Tora now admitted to himself that it was not possible for him to save both Caesar Germanicus and his own life. Unarmed, weakened by hunger, the bones of his left wrist still knitting, he might be able to slay one of the centurions— but never both.

Yet the killing of one would be enough of a diversion to allow Germanicus to run into the fog, to make his way to the Fabian canal on the northern limits of the city and perhaps find a small boat.

"Does Lord Caesar think we will leave this city by way of the canal?" he asked the weary-looking silhouette in front of him. "A boat of some sort, perhaps?"

"Yes, of course."

"Quiet there!" the centurion behind them barked.

Fortunately, it seemed to Tora that Germanicus had understood the hidden meaning in his words.

Then it occurred to him that he had been wrong, that his outlook had been too narrow: He did indeed have a weapon, one provided him from Proconsul Fadus' perfumed wardrobe. Smiling grimly to himself, he recalled what Musashi had written of a moment such as this: *When you lay down your life, you must make absolute use of your weaponry. It is false not to do so, and to die with a weapon yet undrawn. . . .*

Tora began to ready himself with deep, rhythmic breaths.

"Pick up the pace now," the senior centurion growled over his shoulder.

Tora waited until this praetorian looked forward again, then he sprang as high as he could—straight up.

At the split second in which his leap slowed and his body appeared to hang in the air, he doubled his knees under his chin and whipped his bound wrists from the small of his back, beneath his feet and around to his belly. He had not touched ground again when he wheeled and drove his legs like pistons against the shins of the centurion trailing him.

Upended, the praetorian dropped his sword. He was reaching for it when Tora closed the scarf around his throat and began garroting him. "Run, Caesar!" he cried. And when Germanicus hesitated, he shouted even louder: "As you live—so does my honor!"

Germanicus began hobbling into the fog.

The senior centurion started after him, but the terrible gurgling noises coming from his comrade made him turn back with the aim of dispatching Tora before giving chase to the middle-aged former emperor.

Tora felt the praetorian in his clutches go limp.

Then he prepared himself for the bite of steel and the good darkness all Nihonians covet as the capstone to valor. In the expectation of pain, oblivion is a sweet thing.

Germanicus took a dozen strides toward freedom, then halted. "No," he muttered. He began working his binding loose as he ran back toward the senior centurion, who was closing on Tora.

"I, First Centurion! It's this old fool you want!"

The scarf fell from Germanicus' wrists just as the praetorian turned with murder in his eyes.

Germanicus shucked off his traveling cloak and held it before him in the manner of a *retiarius*, a gladiator outfitted with a heavy net.

The centurion must have realized what Germanicus had in mind, for he said snidely, "Been to the circuses a few times in your day, what?"

"Far more often than I should've, lad."

The centurion closed on him, swinging widely from shoulder to shoulder.

Germanicus stumbled back a few paces, but was able to snag the short sword in the folds of his cloak. The centurion had to hang on dearly to keep the hilt from being yanked out of his grasp. And he had just freed it when the gleaming point of another blade sprouted out of his tunic front a few inches above his breastplate.

Tora had skewered him from behind with the strangled praetorian's sword.

A moment later, as Germanicus and Tora were retrieving the swords, the forelamps of a freight lorry flared over the grisly scene. The driver braked, then swiftly backed away from the carnage.

"Come, sire," Tora said, "before he reports this!"

However, they hadn't gone far through the northern wards of the city when their exhaustion overcame them. They sought a moment's rest in an alley between two Roman-style tenements, panting as if they'd sprinted from the plain of Marathon instead of trotting but a few blocks from the foot of the Acrocorinthus.

"If . . . if only . . ." Germanicus said, gasping, "we could get our hands on some decent nourishment."

Tora was staring at him as if confused about something.

"What is it?"

"I do not understand . . ." His voice trailed off as he was suddenly afflicted by a spasm of shivering.

"Understand what, my friend?"

"Why Lord Caesar would risk himself to come back for the sake of his least retainer." He seemed genuinely bewildered, offended even.

"And what would've been the case in Nihonia?"

"My lord and master would have kept running. Both he and I

would have understood why this had to be. We would have rejoiced together in his freedom."

Germanicus laughed sadly. "Well, I'm no longer Caesar, let alone your lord and master. We're equals now."

Tora looked stunned. "Under what authority are we equals?"

Cradling his head in his hands, Germanicus fell silent for a moment. "One I can't name. One that may not exist. Enough—I don't care much for putting too fine a point on things. Come, we can make the canal—"

The siren atop the Acrocorinthus began wailing.

"Damn." Germanicus came sorely to his feet.

"Should we hide here for a time?"

"No, soon all the cohorts of Greece will be flooding into this city in search of us. We must be gone before dawn, or not at all."

Tora rose and braced himself against the tenement wall for a few seconds. "It was not proper . . ."

"I beg your pardon?"

"It was not *correct* for Lord Caesar to rescue one as unworthy as myself." He dropped his eyes. "But I thank him."

Germanicus smiled. "Come . . ."

They smelled the late Emperor Fabius' great canal blocks before they came upon it—the waterway also served Corinthus as an open sewer. "We must be wary of the quaysides," Germanicus whispered. "They're sure to be guarded—"

Tora silenced him with a wave.

After a moment, Germanicus heard it as well: the unmistakable cadence of military sandals. "Where's it coming from?"

Tora shrugged; he too was confounded by the echoes skipping back and forth among the concrete warehouses of the district.

"Let's keep heading north."

The Nihonian nodded.

A block later, Attic-crested helmets began to take shape in the fog before them.

They reeled, only to glimpse more helmets behind.

Two praetorian patrols were converging on the small *agora* in which the two men stood. As luck would have it, the square was probably the place their officers had arranged for them to meet after a sweep of the northernmost wards.

From nearby, Germanicus could hear the hollow reverberation of wood knocking against stone—a hull riding against the masonry side of the canal.

He didn't think Tora and he could be seen through the scudding mists, but then a Roman voice shouted: "There, suboptio, two men!"

He felt Tora's hand clutch at his cloak to drag him toward the canal.

Within a few strides, he understood what the Nihonian intended, so it was no shock when the paving stones beneath his sandals suddenly fell away and he tumbled blindly, out and then down into the satiny fog.

The water was cold, but he paid it no mind as he broke to the surface. There were little spouts of *pili* fire all around him.

8

THE GRANITE PINNACLE rose sheerly out of the larches, almost high enough to pierce the shifting gray bellies of the thunderclouds. On a clear day its windswept summit afforded a view well beyond the forested limits of the Wald, beyond Germania Superior and into the tame, farm-checkered countryside of Belgica—nearly to a hazy suggestion of the plains of Germania Inferior. But this was not a clear day. It was an afternoon murky with cloud and fleet shards of mist riding north on the wind. An afternoon of celestial unrest.

Atop the pinnacle, his shoulders dusted with the snow that comes to such heights regardless of season, crouched the outcast warrior of the long-skulled people. He stared out into chaotic spaces of the storm, the heaving fields of moisture on which one could expect to see at any moment the Army of the Furious, a host of phantom warriors galloping toward horizons that no longer existed for them. Every few seconds lightning seemed to crack the strong blue of his unblinking eyes, shattering the irises like glass. The booming frenzies were heralded not only by yellow lightning, but by gold and orange, and even red—the rarest color with which Donor painted his bolts.

An auspicious color, the warrior realized, numbly. A sign of spiritual favor, many said. But he could no longer think of any divine favor that might stir his heart.

An hour or two before, he had watched an unworldly ball of fire waft through the fens far below, stitching in and out of the woolly fog before suddenly fading out. It might well have been Donar himself, god of thunder, prowling the twilight.

Once, Donar had been the most favored god of his people. But that had been in the remote days before the Roman conquest, a time when warriors of the long skull had bowed to no man—not even to their kings, whose office entitled them only to show more valor than any of their *thegans* on the field of battle; a time when courage and brute force had been more valued than cunning.

The Roman occupation had turned Germania toward a more hairsplitting god, Woden.

But maybe the hour had come to turn back to Donar.

No longer would the outcast warrior pay homage to the Roman gods, even though he had often sacrificed to them, especially on the eve of battle. These gods had perished in Corinthus with Germanicus Agricola. The House of Jupiter was vacant, roofless, and now only blizzards swept down its corridors, only stars whispered in its chambers.

He bowed his head and ran his hand over his stubbly scalp. He had cropped his hair three days before, and in all that time he'd had nothing to eat or drink. He would take nothing for another two days in the belief that sustenance would only feed the force of his grief. Long ago, he had read—with considerable effort—what Tacitus had written about the ways of the German tribes. What the Roman historian had recorded about mourning was largely true, although what he'd put down in the same, often careless *codex* about the tribes having no word for autumn was not true. A forest people like the Marcomanni have as many different words for this season as the Scandians do for snow and Mauretanians do for sand. Nevertheless, his passage about German mourning was close to the truth: *Weeping and wailing are soon abandoned, sorrow and mourning not so soon. A woman may decently express her grief; a man should nurse his in his heart. . . .*

So it was for Rolf of the Marcomanni—except that he had no need to nurse this pain. It raged inside him. And because of a belief he'd inherited from his father and he from his father, it burned more in the manner of fire than ice. This belief would not let go of him: *Even the most heroic life be lived and spent in vain.*

Futility was heaped upon futility—that was the be-all and end-all of life.

He had slain Estammic only to keep Germania open to the day Germanicus might return to power. Yet Caesar was drowned hours before Estammic had hung limp and bleeding on the point of Rolf's *framea*. Why, then, had the gods let this happen?

The cold winds blew harder than before, and he huddled deeper in his cloak. He folded the hem over his bare feet, tucked it under his toes.

Besides him, coated with pilled snow, was the remaining sword of the two he'd seized from the warriors of the Gothic Revival and carried away with him on his flight into the forest. He had broken the other blade against a boulder in his last raging act of that bloody night.

Never could he have been persuaded to kill a fellow thane except in behalf of Germanicus. He could think of no other Roman worth Estammic's life, for his kinsman had been more like the ancient Teutoni than any man in modern Germania, a warrior brimming with the furious spirit that had guided their forefathers. And Rolf had impaled him on a javelin to defend the authority of a dead Caesar.

There was no repayment he could make to Estammic's clan— except to take up the same cause the man had served.

But Rolf wasn't ready to do this; whenever he closed his eyes, he still saw Segestias beseeching him and then falling dead. Yet Estammic's men would have had no reason to murder his cousin had he agreed with Estammic, even in the least, that the present imperium was evil, an enemy to the good of Germania.

He pummeled his face with his fists and howled against the gale whipping snow around him: "*Why?*"

With Germanicus dead and Antonius Nepos and Claudia Nero defiling the Palatine, was the Gothic Revival such a terrible thing? Yet, even if it were the salvation of Germania, an instrument of the god-friend himself, what place could the slayer of Estammic have in it?

He suddenly wondered if Germanicus had drowned himself rather than be taken. *Aye . . . it be for dignity's sake then?* And from this another thought sprang: Would it be honorable for him to do the same, to end his own life? Although the messenger had brought no word of Tora's fate, Rolf trusted that if Caesar had perished, so had the Nihonian—if only to keep his honor. As goes a great man, so go his followers gladly. The notion was as old as the world.

He reached for the sword.

The brass hilt felt like ice.

His eyes turned deliberate and remained that way for a long time while a mixture of rain and hail danced on the rock around him.

"Aye, this be the way, Germanicus Julius," he finally murmured. "I be with regret this be not sooner . . . and done together. On the walls of Agri Dagi garrison, maybe—against the wrappies of the Great *Zaim*, who afterward who proud to call you his brother . . ." He smiled thinly. "Aye, those in Anatolia be days of heart and courage, Germanicus Julius. Or if not them—maybe across the great sea, afoot the mountain of the Indee with the conches of the Aztecae to bleat in our ears. Or on that drive to Tenochtitlan with Libitina's handmaiden, Alope, who be blessed to see the tilt of worlds in your nod. Those too be days of courage. . . ." The smile vanished as a blast of wind deepened the squint lines around his eyes. "At last all such bright days be dim. I be gone now to the Army of the Furious. I go to drill the bastards what things I learnt from the midget warriors, for you yourself say Germans fight like demons but march like drunkards. *Ave atque vale.* I be proud to say your name last of all words I say, Germanicus Julius Agricola."

He realized that here, on this exposed and barren outcropping, he couldn't fall on his sword in the Roman fashion. So he hoisted it above him, point downward, and looked off into the storm.

The message to plunge was jangling up the nerves of his arms, when he hesitated—not that he'd grown fainthearted at the instant of death. He had felt steel bite into his flesh and rake his bones before. No, it was something else that had stayed his hands: an amber pinprick rising out of the mists below.

His eyes grew wide.

Up it welled through the layers of clouds, ever larger, ever brighter.

Instinctively, he turned the blade outward to face this eerie threat.

The glowing sphere continued to rise until it was on the same level as his puzzled gaze, then drifted ten paces or so beyond the brink of the precipice. He would have to step off into oblivion in order to approach it. Was he being invited to tumble off the spire into the ranks of the Army of the Furious? No monstrous object, it was about the size of the air-filled ball used by the Romans to play their tedious, three-sided game of *trigon*. But unlike that leather globe, it possessed a luminous depth that, when not blinding Rolf with its surges of brilliance, revealed the image of a godhead with a great, flowing beard. The countenance regarded him, and his bowels went cold: Those rime-encrusted eyes had never been softened by pity. Then the sphere drifted closer, and he resisted the urge to withdraw. Its pulsing warmth touched his face like fire, but just when he thought the scintillant thing would scorch off his features it floated up and alighted on the tip of his sword. A force more jolting than *electricus* motive flashed down the length of the blade, into his body, into his heart.

"Lord Donar!" he roared, disintegrating, expanding outward on waves of delight. He was being taken away to join the disembodied; it was the true thing he'd always desired, he realized.

Spray burst over the bow of the coastal hauler and ran down its weather decks in sheets of foam. Once again, the white marble sarcophagi lashed to the planking were left glistening by the retreating waters. A Greek trading ship of ancient design, it was a square-rigger with a single mast. At the stern a small engine could be found attached to the post between the twin steering oars, but this modern addendum was powerful enough only to help the four-man crew moor without having to break out their twelve-foot oars.

Tora thought it fortunate that in the two days since departing Corinthus the wind had been out of the northwest—for southeast was the captain's course and, although he was too polite to ask, the Nihonian was sure the little hauler couldn't ply the seas except on a following wind. Because it was a square rig, the sail could be only slightly adjusted to catch the prevailing force of the wind. The Greek captain had half acknowledged this handicap by mentioning that it was profitable for him to trade only with the people of the Cycladic archipelago, whose numbers were too few and anchorages too confining to be of interest to the larger and swifter steam-driven cargo galleys that kept to the main sea lanes between Alexandria and the Roman ports of Ostia, Puteoli, and Ravenna.

The hauler had already tied up at Delos to offload ingots of Iberian lead. These would be melted down and reshaped into drinking vessels by the affable islanders, who seemed to have no idea that contact with this metal would slowly poison them—and even accused Tora of being an agent of the silver guild. From Delos the captain had steered across a glassy night sea to Naxos, where he parted with thirty large *amphorae* of Cretan olive oil in exchange for three female slaves. These poor creatures—plain of feature and lacking voluptuousness, and thus deemed fit only for service as scullions—wept the whole of the agonizingly slow day in which the captain labored at the tiller to tack due west athwart the wind and cross the narrow strait that separated Paros from Siphnos. Tora, having asked for a stylus and wax tablets, sketched obvious improvements to the hauler's rigging, although he knew he could never bring himself to tell the man who had just saved his life how to better his own craft, of which he seemed inordinately proud. Mostly, he sketched to keep his mind off the wailing of the unfortunate women, who were finally landed at Siphnos and led off in chains by their new mistress, who saw them up a steep, rocky lane from the comfort of a canopied litter.

Now, after a night's anchorage to rest the crew, it was on to Thera, where the captain would deliver the four sarcophagi to a wealthy family whose villa had been ravaged recently by pirates.

From this private misfortune of a Theran family, Tora got his first glimpse of what was happening to the entire Empire since Germanicus had been forced out of Rome. Lord Regent Nepos had drawn down the Aegean fleet to reinforce his invasion of Aegyptus—the governor there had been named Caesar by the legions under his command. The immediate consequence of civil war to the people of the Cyclades was that pirates were once again venturing from their strongholds along the precipitous, roadless coast of Lycia to plunder the eastern Empire.

Yet, had this family not suffered four deaths, Tora himself would now be either imprisoned or dead. And Germanicus, now quietly conversing with the captain on the stern gallery, would be on a far different voyage—one that would most certainly have ended at the gates to the Mamertine prison.

Fondly almost, Tora once more glanced at the four sarcophagi, glinting beneath the warm afternoon sun of the Aegean.

"Again, my friend, you must try to explain," Germanicus said to the captain, whose curly black beard and shrewd eyes suggested more Phoenician ancestry than Greek.

"And what must I explain to Caesar?"

"Why'd you help us?"

"Why, you ask—when betraying you would've sat me down in luxury and comfort for the rest of my days?" The captain chuckled, then rotated the tiller to adjust his heading on Thera's distant and jagged volcanic cone. "If luxury and comfort were my wants, I'd never have took to the sea." Still, his weathered face turned thoughtful. He was only recently retired as a common seaman from the imperial navy. In fact, he had last served aboard the *Romulus*. This bireme had taken Germanicus off the riddled hulk of the quinquereme *Aeneas* in the final minutes of the battle of the Mare Aztecum, something the captain had mentioned in passing and then let drop. It had been a bitter day for the Emperor and Roman sea power. Returning to his native Thessalonica, he had purchased this worn-out hauler with the bonus which Germanicus had paid to all who had taken part in the Aztecan campaign. However, gratitude was an unlikely reason for his having fished Caesar and his Nihonian adjutant out of the Fabian canal. Thousands who had been paid just as much or more had willingly betrayed the last of the Julian Caesars. "I asked myself the same question as we plied the canal, looking for you," the captain went on at last.

"Why were you searching for us?"

"Round midnight or so, the auxiliaries marched down to the quay. Uppity whoresons—not a one of them fit for real imperial service." He spat over the top of the nearest weather-cloth. "They ordered all us hauler captains, what was in our cups at that hour—I admit—to keep an eye open for two mangies seeking passage out of Corinthus. Well, it didn't take much wit to see the *auxilia* was on your trail. There were reports of you being almost nabbed here and there the whole of the way down from Illyricum. The other captains turned in, saying how you was dead and buried and whatnot, thanks to the brigands. But I knew you better. I knew a Caesar what led his lads over Tenochtitlan's walls—*personal* now—wouldn't fall to the brigands. And I figured you'd realize your best bet out of Achaea was along the canal. . . ." He shrugged, then glanced around his boat proudly. "You always treated the likes of me well enough. And you didn't lash out at us lads when we lost that first time in Mare Aztecum—like some in your sandals would've done. You thanked us for *our valor and our sacrifices*, and—well—words like that made us fight doubly hard when we got us a second go at the Aztecae *and* thrashed the feathered beggars, but sound. . . ."

"Indeed you did, Captain." Watching Thera loom ever higher out of the sea, Germanicus asked himself why he felt so unworthy of this humble man. Was it because the captain had done far more than just fish Tora and him out of the fog-clad waters? Knowing the praetorians would search the vessel at the canal's outlet on the Aegean, the captain had hidden the two shivering renegades in the hold, covering them with a dunnage of spoilt cotton. But then as they motored ever closer to this encounter with the guardsmen, he had changed his mind and instead concealed Germanicus and Tora in two of the sarcophagi tied to the deck. From beneath the marble lid Germanicus had heard the captain tell a praetorian, who'd just ordered the crew to pry open the stone coffins, that they contained the corpses of four victims of a virulent plague in Epirus. He was transporting them to their native isle of Tinos for burial and had no objection if the lord regent's noble guardsmen wished to inspect the decomposing bodies—but, as for himself and his crew, he wanted to be off the boat while this was done. The seconds passed in agony as Germanicus waited for the praetorian's answer. Then the seconds became minutes, and still no muffled words drifted through the lid. At last, Germanicus had realized the hauler was moving again—out into the dark freedom of the Aegean.

Now, standing beside the captain on the gallery, Germanicus felt the need to ask another question: "Have any of your crew served under me?"

"No, none."

"Then why did they put their own lives at risk to help me?"

"I'm their captain, and I ordered them. Is this so hard for a Caesar to understand?"

He didn't respond, for the man had sounded irritated.

The captain checked the ruffles on the water, then muttered, "Wind is shifting . . . bloody damn."

"I have failed you, haven't I?" Germanicus asked quietly, then answered himself before the man could speak. "I have failed you and every other citizen of the Empire."

"Aye," the captain said with the same resentful tone of the moment before. Tucking the tiller under his arm, he began counting off on his fingers: "The credit markets are blown right out the old *vomitorium*, what with the grain factors being betting lads and not one them willing now to gamble on anything in an empire turned on its ear. Next, I know your stay in Corinthus was brief, but did you gather it's sitting on only two weeks' ration of corn? Thessalonica's down to one week. Dium hasn't a kernel left. And why? Well, that dim-witted knight in Aegyptus who calls hisself Caesar is putting the granaries in Alexandria to the torch rather than have them fall into Nepos' hands. The whole African crop goes unharvested, eaten only by the birds and vermin. Here in Achaea the plebs are already going about with rumbling bellies, but—praise justice—soon the honorable folk will be fainting in the streets too. The brigands own the roads. And the Lycian pirates chase me wherever I sail. Neptune be thanked, they haven't caught me yet, but that's probably coming too. And all this bloody mess fell upon us in a bat of eyelash. How's that possible? Now it's your turn, Caesar—how'd this happen to us?"

Germanicus stared out to sea.

"Some say you tried to wreck the government with something called a republic, but Nepos and his harlot got wise to you before you could go all the away," the captain went on, shaking his head. "I don't even know what a republic is. But if this is what it takes to have one, you ask too much of little men like me, Germanicus Agricola. And the world is made of little men."

9

THAT THE CAPTAIN would spend the night ashore with neither of his passengers accompanying him disturbed Tora more than Germanicus. The Nihonian feared treachery and said so, but Germanicus realized, when the captain emerged from his small cabin with his beard trimmed and curly black locks anointed with perfume, that he had a woman on Thera. With no imperial ships riding at anchor in the harbor and a flat calm over the sea to discourage the progress of the pirates out of Lycia, he cheerfully took his leave of Caesar and was rowed ashore by one of his crewmen.

"Is Lord Caesar sure we can trust this Greek?" Tora asked quietly.

Germanicus said nothing for the moment.

"And what of his crew? Can we put our faith in men who could become wealthy by betraying us?"

"Absolutely, Tora-*san*." He smiled wanly as he watched the captain's launch slip across the waters toward a whitewashed city shining in the last light. "We should trust them because we have no other choice, my friend." Then, after patting Tora on the shoulder, he made known his wish to be alone by strolling forward.

The Nihonian bowed to Caesar's back.

Night came swiftly as soon as the sun dipped below the sea. The pinks and reds of the sheer cliffs surrounding the hauler faded to gray and finally black. The bay itself had been gouged out of the heart of the island by a volcanic explosion more than a thousand years before Plato had recounted the legend of Atlantis. Perhaps this truly was the pulverized remnant of that utopia of concentric arcadias. Who knew? There could be no better death than one that illuminated all mysteries, Germanicus reflected. Soon he might know everything. Or nothing. Either way, he could not be disappointed.

The modern city of Thera stood darkened on its bluff, perhaps to offer no invitation to pirates, and in this absence of light the stars winked on in clusters so dense they seemed to band the sky with white.

Where to from here? he asked himself.

Thera or any of the islands of the Cyclades offered a poor refuge. The population of the archipelago was so small and close-knit that no matter on which pumiceous speck the captain put them ashore, Tora and he could never hope to blend in. Inevitably, their presence on Thera or Melos or Siphnos would be reported to Nepos' men. In his haste to be out of Achaea, he hadn't foreseen the problem; the Greek isles had seemed comfortably remote, but in truth they were nothing of the sort for a fugitive emperor.

Where to, then?

There was Anatolia, of course.

He had been the province's military governor prior to being named Caesar and knew its arid wastes well. And ever since turning away from the Dalmation coast with the unconscious Tora on his back, he had been thinking in a vague way of the Purple Village. It was the high abode of his old enemy, a snowy redoubt hidden in a cleft near the summit of Agri Dagi, the tallest mountain in what long ago had been the kingdom of Armenia. Through his network of spies, local priests mostly, the Great *Zaim* knew within twenty-four hours who had arrived and who had departed from Anatolia's shores. He would know if Germanicus had returned to his old province. And, on the basis of friendship alone, he could be counted on to give Caesar safe-conduct across the inhospitable central plateau and then welcome him to the Purple Village, although many in his tribe would not be eager to have their former Roman conqueror making his retirement among them in the holiest of their sanctuaries. However, the Great *Zaim* would prevail in this argument, for he had always believed that Germanicus, despite his Roman birth, had been given a destiny by God, that singular and implacable deity shared somewhat uneasily by Anatolians and Jews.

But then, as Germanicus stood at the gunwale feeling the barely perceptible rocking of the hauler beneath his feet, he realized he had wearied of his own destiny, whatever it held in store for him. He didn't feel up to all the scheming and compromising that would be required of him to arrive safely in the wilderness of Agri Dagi; he had no energy left for such extravagant measures—and to preserve what? The crushing sadness he now staggered under? He'd been dogged by periodic bouts of melancholy all his adult life, but those episodes had been nothing when compared to the intensity of this depression. Each breath seemed an inordinate labor, and only a wistful kindness toward his companions came effortlessly to him. The kindness that flows from imminent departure.

Where then to die in peace and dignity?

After a long time in which the ship seemed to be floating between the stars and the lustrous bay, he whispered to himself, smiling, *"Brother Aeneas has been tossed from one coast to another on the tall seas by acrimonious Juno's hatred. . . ."*

He nodded as if he'd come to a decision that gave him a little relief from his sorrow. And indeed, the last Trojan king had thought of a home to which he might return, a ruin where he might close all the literary accounts and die in a manner worthy of Homer and Virgil.

When, during the third hour of the black morning which was announced by bells on Thera's quay, the wind rose out of the southwest instead of the northwest, he took it as a sign that his final enterprise had won the approval of his long absent gods.

His only remaining chore on this earth was to free Tora from fealty in such a way that disobedience would be impossible for the honorable Nihonian.

The captain was rowed back to his hauler just as dawn began to gray the east. He had no sooner climbed the rope ladder to the main deck than he ordered the youngest—and therefore most keen-eyed—member of his crew to go ashore and mount the highest point on the rim of the caldera. From there the lad was to keep watch for sails in combination with steam plumes, for the craft of the Lycian pirates were propelled in this twofold manner in order to outrun the imperial biremes that hunted them.

"Run back down if you see the bastards. I sniff a squall on the wind, but stay up there until you can't see anything, even our own ship, through the rain." Then he turned to greet Germanicus, "And how is Caesar this morning?" He seemed restored rather than dissipated. Quite a woman, Germanicus realized.

"I am without complaints, Captain."

"Do you have an appetite?"

"None, I'm afraid."

"Then what about you?" he asked Tora.

"I will try some food, thank you."

"That's the spirit—come."

In the captain's cabin, the table had been set with round loaves of bread, goat cheese, bowls filled with olives, dried figs, pistachio nuts, and a juglet of olive oil. When he invited his two guests to eat, Tora began to test everything first for poison, but Germanicus waved off the precaution and popped a fig into his mouth. He chewed without relish, swallowed, then leaned back against the splinter-rough bulkhead. His ravenous appetite of the first day aboard the hauler had vanished, and eating now seemed superfluous to him, a mere entertainment he no longer enjoyed. Poor Tora, on the other hand, had become seasick shortly after the ship cleared the Fabian canal and was only now regaining his taste for food. "I'm no mariner, Captain," Germanicus said. "Please confirm something for me. . . ."

"Anything, Caesar." Using his rigging knife, the man carved off a thick slice of cheese for Tora.

"Is this morning's wind steady out of the southwest?"

"Aye, and a most excellent one to weather here in Thera's harbor. It'll bring a hard rain with it."

"But also a most excellent wind to push us up the coast of Anatolia?"

His dark eyes musing, the captain tore off a hunk of bread, sprinkled it with olives and nuts, then finally dressed it with oil. "I've been up that coast only twice in this ship. And never by choice. Both times I was blown off course." He ate.

Germanicus sensed that this was not a man to be pushed into a corner. He decided to back off from this line of thought for a few minutes.

Tora was eagerly devouring everything except his portion of cheese—he had no taste for foods made from milk. "Did you hear any wireless news ashore, Captain?"

"Aye, a bit of this and that." He went on chewing for some time before realizing that he'd raised their curiosity. "Rome's put it out what Caesar drowned in the canal." He harrumphed at the notion, then wiped his oily fingers in his beard.

"That is good, isn't it?" Tora asked. "For them to think thusly?"

The captain nodded, although his face was worried. "Might buy us more time to do whatever. Might not. What if the praetorians know damned well the drowning's a lie? The whole thing stinks of a trap then. Something to make us careless, what?"

Germanicus took a deep breath. "Any other news, Captain?"

"Something boiling over in Britannia." He poured himself a cup of rich red wine; Germanicus' abstinence was so famous, the captain didn't offer him any, although Caesar was tempted to dull the pain in his heart with this rude vintage. "Or wait—maybe it was Nova Britannia. Right, that's it." He dug at his back teeth with a long nail he apparently kept unclipped for this purpose. "I remember now—an assassination in Tenochtitlan."

Germanicus closed his eyes. "Who?"

"Forget the name—that wrappie you made procurator."

"*Prince Khalid?*" Tora asked, looking stunned.

"That's him."

"Are you certain?"

Germanicus gripped Tora's arm. "I knew this would happen."

The Nihonian composed himself, then bowed his head. "Yes, we must expect many bad things to attend this war. Khalid was both brave and moderate in his habits. Death fancies these qualities in a warrior."

"I mean—it was predicted he would die like this."

"You *foresaw* such a thing, Lord Caesar?" he asked, incredulously.

"What? Oh no, dear friend, I can't even imagine how this day will end, let alone see the future. No, at the outset of the Aztecan campaign, Khalid's father, the Great *Zaim* of Agri Dagi, entrusted him with a letter for me. The prince was instructed not to read it under any circumstances, and then to hand it over to me at the end of the campaign. . . ." Germanicus' eyes, clouded over and once again, he scanned the *Zaim's* meticulous Greek letters as if they were set down on parchment before him; once again, he glanced up and beheld Khalid's trusting face over the top of the paper:

Germanicus Julius,
  Long ago, by the will of the Compassionate, the Merciful, you were my prisoner. My people cried for the blood of the Roman pasa, but I did not grant their desire for revenge. For the holiest of my holy, my blessed shaykh, had a vision of the conquest I trust you have now made. That night of rage, when you suddenly donned one of our soof robes, he

whispered to me alone: "So it is written: 'The son of the she-wolf will garb himself like the lamb of God. This man will secure a new land of fallow souls for the Compassionate, the Merciful.'" This is all I will tell you . . . except that I rely on you to value my son's services as you would mine. I now share the saddest secret of my heart: Khalid shall never return to me. He shall perish in your new province. So, as your brother, I beg that none of his light, so pure and honest, be wasted . . . Inshallah.

Germanicus shook off his distracted silence as if it had been a chill. Perhaps it had been—that of learning of his own son's death in battle all over again. "Forgive me, friends," he said at last, "memories swarm around one in a moment like this." He tried a bite of cheese, but quickly set the slice aside. Shaking his head, he tried to smile consolingly, but failed. "For his sake, I sincerely hope Khalid's god exists. He was deserving of nothing less than the paradise he spoke of with such delight." Then he carefully regarded the captain. Although the man's expression remained placid, his unease was revealed when he poured himself a second cup of wine. And Germanicus suddenly felt like a beggar. "Captain, I have no money, no power—"

"That makes two of us." He kept his gaze in his cup. "Caesar should tell me what he has in mind, direct-like. Then I can tell him if it's possible. I'll do my best. And so will my crew."

"Thank you."

The man shrugged. "There's no need to thank me for following orders."

"Yes," Germanicus said in a new, more decisive tone of voice—as if the captain's words had lit upon something significant he had in mind. They had indeed, and he stared at Tora, briefly. "If they are within the scope of what is possible for a mariner—these are my orders. Captain, today I wish to proceed north along the Anatolian coast."

"How far does—?"

Germanicus cut him off by raising a hand. "First, is that possible?"

"If the wind holds out of the southwest and we don't bash upon some island blind in the rain what's coming. Must we sail today?"

"Yes, each day that I linger aboard your ship the greater the risk to you and your crew. Is it possible to sail in the weather coming our way?"

"Aye, with Lady Fortuna on our side. But I must know Caesar's destination before I can plot a course."

"I want to be put ashore near Ilium."

The captain mulled this over for a moment. "All right. That means we can keep windward of Samos and Chios. What with this Aegyptian spat going, I don't know how much of the imperial fleet remains at Ephesus. But I sure as hades don't want some bireme chasing me down and planting its *corvus* in the middle of my foredeck." He spoke of the beaked ramp used by the marines of a Roman galley to board and seize another ship. "I have a mind to give Lesbos a wide berth too. The crew of the quinquereme *Scipio Africanus* went mutinous while she was being repaired in the port of Mytilene."

"In whose favor?" Tora asked hopefully.

The captain showed his palms to indicate he had no idea. "Loyalties change from day to day. But the point's this—the *Scipio Africanus* might be at sea trials in the channel. What with discipline the way it is, the bastards might blow us out of the water with their *ballistae*."

Tora looked taken aback. "Why your hauler?"

"We *move*. It's been happening all over the Mare Nostrum."

"You mean to say war galleys are destroying merchant shipping out of sheer mischief?"

The captain chuckled mirthlessly. "That's the word for it—mischief. An old Roman tradition. Go on a rampage and sack what you once defended. Bloody fine *mischief*." He reached behind him and removed a chart from a wooden tube, then spread the vellum over the crockery. "Ilium, Caesar says." With his forefinger he a traced a course up the middle of the Aegean to the Hellespontus. "And Ilium it will be for the two of you."

"No, you'll put only me ashore there. Tora shall continue on through the Propontis and out into the Pontus Euxinus."

The captain looked no less stunned than Tora at Germanicus' words. "I've never been in those waters. I've never been beyond the Hellespontus—even during my imperial service. And I doubt what my little ship could make it against the powerful current of the Golden Horn into the Pontus Euxinus."

"I understand," Germanicus said. "But can you go as far as the port of Cyzicus?"

"I suppose so."

"So be it. There, Tora-*san* can find passage to Colchis."

The Nihonian had not stirred for some moments when he bowed

his head. Kept by the captain's presence from questioning Caesar's command in the least—as Germanicus had intended—he asked only: "And where shall I go from Colchis?"

"East."

"*East?*" he echoed.

"Yes, overland, as you see fit, to the Serican Empire."

Tora hesitated, obviously concerned that too pointed an inquiry would make his master lose face. "Does Lord Caesar now discharge me from his noble service?"

This was the tricky part, and Germanicus was tempted to warm his severe tone with a smile. But he didn't. "Not at all. As soon as I wade ashore at Ilium, I'll be under the protection of the Great *Zaim*—"

"But Lord Caesar himself said this holy man lives in Agri Dagi—almost a thousand Roman miles east of Ilium!"

"The *Zaim* has a long reach," he said more severely, even though it pained him to see the the humiliation spread across Tora's face. "At any rate, I'll be entering into a kind of seclusion. A hiatus. Hopefully, not a long one. But I see no advantage in idling your energies at the same time, my friend. The Anatolians are distrustful of mechanized things, and I fear you'd be forbidden to tinker, as is your habit."

"If Lord Caesar commands me not to be a *machinator*, I shall cease being one."

"No, no—I have a far more important mission in mind for you than dazzling the Anatolians with your witchcraft." What he said next was like bile on his tongue: "The Roman Empire is at its worst state in centuries. Alone, I am to blame for this. Quite simply, I wasn't clever enough to hazard change without triggering catastrophe. Nevertheless, the Roman world, however governed, has no eyes and ears among the Sericans. And I greatly fear they will capitalize on our present misfortune, particularly in the Novo Provinces, where they have ambitions as keen as our own. So I send you east, Tora-*san*, to alert me if the Silk Makers conspire to move against us anywhere in the world."

Tora searched Germanicus' eyes for the truth. If the Nihonian sensed he was being sent away simply to save his life, he didn't reveal it. But he looked utterly miserable. "How could I send messages to Lord Caesar?"

"A trunk of the Silk Road passes through Agri Dagi. Any missive entrusted to the *Zaim* will be directed to me."

"I see." But then, when Tora brought up a personal concern to the captain, Germanicus knew that his own will had prevailed: "How much is passage from Cyzicus to Colchis? I have nothing."

"One hundred sesterces—well, if you help with the crewing, that is."

"I see." Absently, Tora began nursing his wrist, which was still mending.

Germanicus shifted uneasily on his bench. "Captain, I hate to ask—"

"Consider the money given. Say nothing more."

A cry came from the weather decks. Germanicus hadn't understood what the crewman had shouted, but the captain bolted from the table and started up the ladder two rungs at a time. Tora and Germanicus fell in behind him, climbing out onto the aft gallery, which was being swept by a stiff, moisture-laden wind.

The captain was already at the starboard weather-cloth, looking up at the cliffs.

For several seconds Germanicus could see nothing out of the ordinary, then he glimpsed a zigzag of dust rising off a talus slope that originated in a cleft near the crest and fanned out all the way down to the bay. The captain's lookout was racing down this rocktall, halting every so often to bellow something no one could make out for the echoes that bounced back and forth across the caldera.

A crewman stood waiting at the anchor rope, but the captain told him to stand by, explaining to Germanicus that he didn't want to be underway without knowing what the threat was—and from which direction it was coming. If it was an imperial craft he couldn't outrun, he might want to hide Caesar and Tora somewhere on board again, although the sarcophagi had been barged ashore yesterday afternoon and were now serving their intended purpose. If it was Lycian pirates, he might find it wiser to abandon his hauler and hide with the rest of the island's population in the ruins of the ancient city on the leeward shore.

The lookout had reached the launch and was untying it from a wooden piling.

"Come on, come on," the captain whispered to himself, "row like never before, my boy."

"Are Lycian sails square-rigged like yours?" Tora asked.

The captain must have found it a peculiar question, for he wrinkled his brow. "Of course."

Reaching midway between shore and the hauler, the lookout shipped oars, stood up and cried with his hands cowled around his mouth: "Sails with steam, Captain! I saw six sails with steam plumes flattened before them!"

"Damn the bloody Fates!" he growled. "From which point on your *index*, lad?"

"Southwest by south! Running fast before a squall! They came out of it sudden—otherwise I'd have seen them quicker!"

"How long do we have to get underway, Captain?" Germanicus asked.

He answered by gesturing at the first raindrops dimpling the waters of the bay. The squall was nearly upon them.

10

THE WORLD OF men was dissolving. All that remained of the Middle Abode, that which hovered in an illusion of permanence between the place of clouds and the land of fire, was a neverending mist that broke coolly against what still seemed to be his eyes and groping hands. His thoughts had grown as fragile as dreams, and of hope he knew nothing. Several times he resolved to halt and listen for the Army of the Furious galloping toward him on glacial white horses; yet, when he tried to stop, some undeniable force pushed him onward and downward. *Aye*, he was slowly descending. *Into what*? He had never put much stock in the underworld of the Greeks and Romans, for the boundless sky was clearly the province of the dead, but was he floating down from the summit of his last living day toward some grim encounter with Orcus?

"Aye, my woeful lord," Rolf suddenly whispered, "there be the torch set beside your portal!"

As he drifted closer, the bright speck swelled into a bonfire with a ruddy halo. A hunched figure was flitting in and out of the flames, dancing in the heart of the conflagration but not being consumed by it. But then he saw that this spirit was scuttling back and forth on the far side of the fire, feeding fagoted branches onto the whitely throbbing bed of coals. Whenever he might have had a glimpse of its form or features, the fire sent up spindles of blue and orange to conceal the aspects of this being.

"Who be—?"

Then, without the warning of a crackle from the resiny wood, sparks shot up like dead souls summoned by the god-friend. When Rolf looked down after this shower had jinked out, an old woman was standing gaunt beside him. The skin of her sunken cheeks was textured like dried apples, although her long braided hair seemed more silver than gray. While most German women wore a linen garment decorated with purple frets, she was clad in wolfskin like the fiercest warrior. One eye had a disconcerting skyward cast that made it appear she was both looking at him and not seeing him at all. Yet, he felt he could blurt anything to her and she would understand: "I be terrible weary, grandmother."

"That will soon pass." She handed him a horn of steaming *met*.

A scuffing of hooves on stony ground made him reel toward the sound. But other than a suspicion of treetops out in the mist, he saw nothing.

"You must drive my chariot for me," she said, then went back to feeding the fire.

For the first time, he had an inkling he might not be dead—perhaps it was the firmness of the ground beneath his torn and bloodied feet, or the feeling he had seen this woman long ago in the even more Gothic-mannered Wald of his childhood, for this was obviously a woman of the smoky past. This was a woman inhabited from head to toe by the god-friend, and no man could fully trust a female so possessed without placing his own fate in jeopardy—even if she spoke with his own mother's voice and stole confidences out of him as effortlessly as she might bone an eel.

Shuffling, he gazed about him, confused. "Where lie the Marcoman village from here, grandmother?"

"There is but one way for you to enter the village again."

He was watching her more carefully now. "What be that?"

"My chariot. My beautiful chariot and matched white horses will take you back to the Marcomanni."

"Are you Marcoman, grandmother?"

"I am of all the tribes. Perhaps my little finger or my big toe is Marcoman. I do not know. And what does it matter as long as my heart is German?" With a blackened stick she stirred some more sparks out of the fire. "Will you go with me, my son? I have grown too old to control such powerful horses."

He hesitated on the brink of saying yes.

Her words meant something more than a chariot ride across the fog-cooled morning, something that would bind him to an obligation. What that might be was beyond the horizon of his memory; however, he sensed that it was poised unseen to ensnare him.

Now, surely, he had returned to life, for his head was abuzz with fear. *Beware of this woman of the smoky past,* he warned himself, suddenly realizing that he was without the sword to which the orb of violet fire had attached itself. Was it still on the granite pinnacle above? His only defense was her eerie goodwill, and he had begun to question it. "Tell me, grandmother—I be in the sacred grove?"

"Oh, yes."

Dropping the horn to the ground, he took a half step away from her.

She cocked her small head to the side. "You *know* now?"

"Aye. And I be not fit."

"We will see who is fit and who is not. But I can say even now, without watching the reins in your burnt hands, you shine with the grace of Donar. Did you come face to face with him?"

Rolf examined his hands—they were indeed singed. "Face to face with something."

"Oh that I had a mirror to show you how your eyes shine!"

"I be blinded the night through by that thing."

"By Lord Donar, then?"

He didn't answer.

"Can you see now?"

"Aye, but all be mist."

"All *is* mist. It rose out of the lakes and streams and willowy dark fens when the rain stopped at midnight. It rose out of Donar's gaping mouth."

"I go now." He strode into the fog, but quickly realized he had no idea which way to go, and being enveloped by the clammy stuff again was too much like dying. The warmth of the fire coaxed him to turn around and face her again. "You be kind enough to tell me the way?"

"Where are you bound?"

"The Marcoman village—as I say before."

She plucked at her hair with her fingers. "You will be slain on your arrival there unless you go in my chariot."

That was true—at least the part importing how Estammic's kin would set upon him with swords and javelins as soon as he showed his face in the Lodge of Assembly.

"Is there not the blood of kings in your veins?"

Again he was steadfast in his silence.

"Why not let it bubble up into the present?"

"I be a centurion, not a king." But now his eyes were quick with uncertainty.

"You *were* a centurion. You may yet become a king."

"How?"

"If I see the signs when you drive my chariot."

Aye—this is what he had been trying to recall: She was putting him to the ancient test.

"What else is left to you?"

"I be of a mind to go back among the midget warriors," he said, with little conviction in his voice. "Some distant legion, maybe."

"If not your own *thegans*, the legionaries will murder you—unless you help me yoke my beauties to the chariot. Then and only then can I tell you your destiny. What do you fear?"

His eyes blazed at her. "*Why*?"

"Why what, Rolf of the Marcomanni?"

"Why *me*?"

"The night you slew Estammic the bogs trembled and boiled and finally gave up their shameful dead, who then ran ashen and screaming through this grove, past my hut, reeking of corruption and again dropping their shields as they had in life. I knew at once—these pale cowards were fleeing the coming of a new king, Germania's first in a thousand years. But who? Who in a generation of slaves and toadies to Rome? Who else but the warrior mighty enough to kill Estammic!" She cackled knowingly. "I saw it long ago in the restlessness of the horses when poor Estammic neared them—he was not the king all have awaited. But it was too soon for me to say so. You, Rolf of the Marcomanni, had not returned to us."

He squinted at her. "You know even back then it be *me*?"

"No." She smiled. "I had a glimpse of red hair, of freckled hands. And even now I am not sure it is you—not until you drive."

"You speak of slaves and toadies to Rome. I be a citizen and a centurion. I own a toga."

"You *were* a citizen and a centurion. Now you wear a cloak held together with a thorn. Will you at least approach the horses with me?"

She reached for his arm with her frigid hands, and at last he did not resist. Out into the grayness they walked, the sudden neighing of the beasts rendered faint by the fog.

"See," he said, his voice full of relief, "they be nervous of me already."

"No, they simply think I'm bringing them oats."

Then, two pure white stallions materialized out of the mist. They had been hobbled to keep them from bolting, as uncastrated young horses were wont to do, and had nibbled down their pasture almost to the ground, leaving only the vines of nightshade untouched. They pricked their ears as they regarded Rolf, but then went back to grazing.

The old woman laughed. "Nervous, you say?" To her back, tilting on its wooden tongue against the earth, was a fighting chariot, the gleam of its gold leaf dulled by a coat of dew. "Help me yoke my beauties. I want to see what they do when you place your hands upon them." She took a breast-strap and girth harness from the open back of the chariot and gave them to him. "Hurry now!"

He hesitated, scowling, but then gently fitted the breast-strap over the steamy nostrils and down the damp neck of the nearest stallion. The horse remained still, not perfectly still, which might have betrayed alarm, but with no more motion than what was required to breathe.

She shrieked. "See! See!"

"I see only a beast with a calm heart."

Yet, its match showed an equal unconcern when Rolf harnessed it, and within moments both were quietly yoked to the chariot. "Poor Estammic did not get nearly this far along," she said, stepping inside. "By now he was chasing my beauties across the meadowlands, cursing me and all prophecy!" She held out the leather crop to Rolf. "Come, my son."

Taking the place beside her, he knotted the reins and finally closed his hand around the supple stock of the crop. "How can a man see in such thick air?"

"Ah," she rasped, "at long last you glimpse the true test."

"But I needs must drive blind!"

"Yes, we all must drive blind. It is the first rule of the world. Now, my beauties, fast!" She made a clucking sound with her tongue, and before Rolf could raise his whip they were off at a dead run into the fog.

The squall suddenly lowered the morning sky over the western entrance to Thera's bay. In advance of this bleared curtain of rain, seeming to fade in and out of the soft edges of the storm, sped six galleys. Tora recognized them to be Liburnians, once exclusively the raiding bireme of Illyrian pirates but now a design adopted by the sea-going brigands of the entire Roman world.

Fascinated, he watched them dash into the broad bay. Their sleek iron hulls had been cobbled with rusty patches, and the yellowed linen of their square rigs and topsils had seen better days. However, the steam venting from their fluted exhaust chimneys signified powerful engines below decks.

He could not quite make out the reportedly ruthless Lycians manning the Liburnians, but realized he would see them up close soon enough.

Meanwhile, the crew of the little hauler was still preparing to lower the sail off the yardarm, so the captain was relying on his feeble mooring engine to maneuver his craft toward the two small islands in the middle of the bay. Like a minnow pursued by sharks, he was hoping to find refuge in the crannies of this reef.

A *ballista* roared from the ship that had taken the van of the ragged battle line. The pirate chieftain's galley, Tora suspected. Although the shell was too swift to be seen, he followed its ripping noise across the harbor's sky to a fiery explosion on the slope above the city.

The hauler had not been the target, he realized.

Instead, the pirates had fired to discourage the flight of Thera's panicked citizens to the cindery palisades above their homes. However, the islanders kept streaming upward, clutching their most precious belongings as they ran.

"What do you intend, Captain?" Germanicus shouted. Tora thought there was a hint of fresh resolve in Caesar's voice. He wondered why. The pirates were giving every indication they were quite adept at raiding port cities—and would tolerate no interference. And this foe probably numbered in the hundreds, while Germanicus had a half dozen men in his retinue.

The captain refused to flinch as an entire volley of *ballista* shells warbled overhead; he was obviously familiar with the sound. "It's up to Neptune, Caesar—but I'm going to try for the north opening to the sea!"

"Can we outrun them?"

"Never!"

Ignoring the pain caused him by his left wrist, Tora helped the pair of crewmen unfurling the sail. Big raindrops began to spangle the deck. Briefly but sharply, the wind veered, and in that instant the temperature plummeted. With this, the squall was fully upon the hauler and Tora was soon soaked to the skin. Shivering, he inspected the stays that helped hold the mast in place: Both ropes were badly frayed. On board this ship things were apparently fixed only when they broke, and occasionally not even then.

"Sail's set, Captain!" a crewman bellowed above the moaning of the gale in the rigging.

Morosely, Tora shook his head at the sail's inefficient square shape and its even more inefficient stationary attachment to the mast. While the captain could never hope to sail faster than even the slowest Liburnian—not with the wind out of the southwest and his only channel of escape lying to the northwest—he might, by gaining a bit more speed, confront the pirate chieftain with a difficult choice: Should the Lycians give chase to a decrepit cargo galley, or straightway steam on and tie up to Thera's quay before the islanders could carry off and hide the choicest plunder? A little more speed from the hauler's sail would pit the chieftain's greed against itself.

Germanicus was tugging at his elbow. His rain-wet face was animated, and some strange cheer seemed to be lighting his eyes. Tora had to conceal his surprise at this change in the man's appearance. "Yes, Lord Caesar?"

"I've asked the captain to beach this ship!"

It had not been an order; apparently Germanicus still did not feel up to giving orders. Tora tried to fathom the reasoning behind this request made to the captain, but couldn't. However, he would not question his master's authority. So as not to shout, he drew closer to Germanicus: "Did the captain agree?"

Caesar shrugged irritably. "He didn't say. He must be considering it."

Tora was studying the man's hazel eyes for an insight into his state of mind, when a *ballista* shell stitched through the sail forty feet above the deck. Fortunately, it exploded only on glancing impact with the water. A huge geyser of foam washed over the prow, knocking a crewman to his knees. Tora rushed to his aid.

But Germanicus followed and, from this, the Nihonian realized he was seeking approval of some kind.

It was unnerving—how far this powerful man had fallen in a few short weeks. What forces were so relentlessly humbling him? Would they be satisfied only by his complete destruction?

The crewman retched on salt water, but then nodded that he was well enough to resume his duties.

The hauler was now gliding slowly between the islands.

Ahead five miles, the open sea shone in the rapidly fading sunlight.

"Tora-*san*," Germanicus almost pleaded, "I think we should land to organize the resistance against this rabble."

Tora gazed at him for an extended moment, then bowed deeply. "If Caesar Germanicus means to go ashore and die the good death of a warrior, I will follow him. But if he hopes to find some resistance to these pirates, he will be disappointed." To bolster his point, he gestured toward the thousands of white-robed Therans scattering like goats into the heights. "And even if Caesar is victorious against this Lycian horde, how can he be sure that one of the grateful Therans will not be less grateful than the others—and betray him to Antonius Nepos and Claudia Nero? These are the things troubling me, sire. But I am troubled in your behalf, so I beg that you forgive me my impertinence. I will accept any punishment you deem fitting for these words."

Tora bowed again, then turned away, for he couldn't bear to see the anguished look in Germanicus' eyes.

Obviously, Caesar had decided on an honorable death, and now he was being denied even that. But Tora believed it the first obligation of a subordinate to spare his master a useless death. Death acquired beauty only when it was unavoidable, and he could never sanction a squalid end like this for a man who'd once ruled half the world.

"A ship follows!"

The frantic cry sent Tora astern, where, peering out beside the captain, he saw that the Liburnian on the left flank of the pirate battle-line had turned north to give chase.

Leaning over the weather-cloth, Tora thought he could see bottom through the clear water; here between the islands it was shallower than it was in the rest of the bay. "What of the Liburnian's draft, Captain?"

"The bastard draws even less water than this old turtle."

"Do you have any weapons aboard?"

"A few niter pieces—nothing to pester the likes of these wolves." The captain gave a brave laugh. "I won't be taken, you know."

"Nor I. But we speak of such things too soon as long as you still have a rigging knife."

Confusion screwed up the man's face. "My knife?"

"Please—if I might borrow it."

"Well, better for whatever you have in mind than me cutting my own throat with it." Laughing again, he tossed it over.

Tora leaped off the gallery onto the main deck and ran forward to the anchor, which was still covered with mud after its hasty weighing. With a crewman gasping at his back, he severed the

anchor rope a foot above the ring, then coiled off twenty feet of
line before cutting it again.

"What thing do you do!"

"Come please, I require your help," he said to the astonished
sailor, leading him to the starboard underside of the yardarm. He
began at the mast and sidestepped all the way to the gunwale,
slashing each of the buntlines that enabled the crew to furl the
sail—all except the last of these hemp brails, which he left intact
until the could tie an end of the anchor rope around the outer
corner of the sail. In his youth, he had served aboard a Serican
coastal hauler rigged much like this one.

Then, after handing the knife to the crewman and taking as firm
a grip as he could on the rope, he dipped his head for the sailor to
cut the buntline.

"Are you sure?" the man implored, casting a glance aft toward
the rapidly closing Liburian.

"Yes! Do it or we all die!"

The knife flashed down through the rain.

Immediately, the loosened half of the sail began flapping
around in the wind, whipping Tora around with it—until Germanicus rushed over from the other side of the ship and added his
surprising strength to the effort it required to hold the anchor rope
steady.

Tora's sandals touched down once again.

"What must we do now?" Caesar cried.

"Pull back even more!" Tora cried. "Give more sail to the
wind!"

Inch by inch, carefully planting each step on the slick deck, the
three men began hauling on the rope.

"Like this?"

"Yes, Lord Caesar!"

The starboard half of the sail was slowly transformed into a
funnel, curving the blasts of stinging rain down into their
eyes—but also catching the force of the wind instead of letting it
ripple uselessly across the expanse of linen.

"That's it!" the captain hollered. "We're picking up a bit!
More, men!"

Germanicus must have been bearing the brunt of the strain, for
his face had turned red. "Don't think . . . I can hold it much
longer!"

"We must! Another foot and I can tie it off!"

"More, men! Give me more speed!"

Just as they had begun to slip forward again, another crewman bounded up the ladder from the tiny engine hold and added his weight to the rope.

Quickly, Tora twice looped his section of line around a wooden deadeye. "Let go!"

The rope visibly thinned under the strain, but the tie held.

Then, as if of the same mind, all four men peered south toward the Liburnian.

On and on the pirate galley came through the hazy sheet of rain, although it had fallen behind the hauler perhaps a quarter mile since Tora's last sighting. It was passing between the islands now and, as the captain had predicted, was encountering no problems with the shallows. Like the shark, the Liburnian was perfectly adapted to its arena.

The *ballista* mount on its foredeck flashed.

Three heartbeats later the water erupted beside the hauler, rocking its hull nearly to the point of capsizing it. The two crewmen bracing themselves besides Tora began praying aloud—one to Poseidon and one to Isis. But Tora was encouraged that the Lycians had felt the need to shoot at the small galley. It might well have been a parting shot. And this hope was realized a few seconds later when, firing again without damaging effect on the hauler, the Liburnian turned northeast, first to clear the promontory on the larger of the two islands, and then due east to converge with other biremes on the city's waterfront.

Gabbling in Greek, the crewmen clapped Tora around the shoulders, embraced him and kissed his cheeks.

Laughing as his bow began bouncing against the rollers of the open sea, the captain called down from his gallery: "Are you in need of a job, my friend?!"

Only Germanicus failed to approach and thank him.

Hands clasped behind him, Caesar had strolled forward out of the meager shelter offered by the sail, to stand exposed on the prow. The waves broke across his shins, but he seemed not to notice.

The white horses halted before the Lodge of Assembly as if of their own accord, although Rolf suspected that the old woman had again worked her magic on them. Never once in the blind, headlong drive through the misty forest had they faltered, although at times the chariot wheels had cleared the tree trunks only by inches.

He returned the reins and crop to her. "Once be enough in a life for such a ride, grandmother."

"And once is all you shall have to do it!" Her wrinkled face was jubilant.

Marcomans were running from their huts for the muddy common before the lodge—among them Estammic's kinsmen. Rolf braced himself for the coming fight. First he would have to overpower someone and seize a weapon.

"Are you seeking this, my son?"

Turning, he was amazed to see a sword in her grasp, for none had been in the chariot before. Even more amazing was to realize that it was the sword he had carried up to the pinnacle. Several inches of its taper below the point had been burned an iridescent blue. "By Donar's blazing touch," she insisted.

When he reached for the hilt, she covered his hand with hers and held fast.

"Even with this in your grasp, you shall perish in this hour unless . . ." Her cast eye seemed to consult the murky heavens while her normal eye continued to bore through him.

"Unless what, grandmother?" He turned to watch the Gothic Revivalists, who were grumbling and beginning to threaten him with gestures.

"*Unless* Rolf of the Marcomanni *believes* himself to be the one chosen for this hour."

"I be no king."

She sighed dejectedly. "Then go and be finished with yourself." However, she refused to let go of him, and suddenly her lips grew thin with cunning. "What better way to avenge Caesar Germanicus than to lead your people against his enemies?"

Briefly, Rolf glanced away from the snarling Revivalists. A pale sun had burned through the fog. It was tossing vague shadows around the bare and filthy feet of the Marcomans ringing the chariot. The ruts in the unpaved lanes had turned to mud during the night's rain, and he realized he could never hope to outrun any javelins thrown after him if he chose to flee again.

"A king be king only as long as there be war, aye?" he asked.

"Yes, he is king no more as soon as the peace is restored. That is our ancient way. That is why we Germans are free and the rest of the world is self-enslaved."

He lowered his voice and asked, as if he found it hard not to believe that some terrible mistake had been made, "And it truly be me now? Me, *Rolf*, after all these centuries with no king?"

"I have never been more certain of anything."

He chewed on the tip of one of his mustaches for a moment. "Then so be it."

She freed his sword hand, and he leaped to the soggy earth.

He didn't have to wait long for the first challenge to his return. Two of Estammic's young but strapping cousins were waiting for him, swords drawn, at the portal to the lodge. The one to speak kept a white, two-handed grip on the hilt of his broadsword. "Hail, Rolf—the outcast!"

"Stand aside, brother," he said.

"I will kill you first, and rightly too, for you are banished!"

The old woman's cackle echoed across the common: "Then you fools have banished your own king!"

"*What?*"

"You heard me well—for aught I care."

The man's jaw went slack. "You chose this Roman dog over Estammic?"

"I chose no one. Lord Donar does the choosing. Now stand aside, as your king commands!"

And then she departed. The hooves of her stallions flung divots of mud across the air as her chariot careered into the mists.

Her departure was followed by a silence that suggested she had never been. But Rolf trusted otherwise, for he now growled over the point of his sword to Estammic's kinsmen: "Tell the *thegans* one and all, I, Rolf of the Marcomanni, be back. I be back as their *herzog*. . . ." The ancient word for king was so rarely uttered in this kingless age, it took a moment for the two young men to realize what he was asserting with its use; Caesar Augustus, in his efforts to further tame an already vanquished Germania, had tried to denigrate the title to one for a position of lesser nobility, but the Germans had subverted his intent by dropping it from common usage. "I call the Assembly *now*."

The two men did nothing but gape at him.

"The choice be yours, lads—fly like Mercury or fight like Mars!"

Stirring, the youths backed their way through the gathering throng and then took to their long legs—most likely to find the head of their *sippe*.

Inside the lodge Rolf found only the stale gloom of mid-morning. He went by the vat of *met* without pouring himself a horn, but pried a leg of mutton out of the grasp of an unconscious reveler, the only man besides himself in the shadowy hall. "Enjoy, brother, this be the last time a German lord nap in his own vomit."

Finishing his breakfast, he rubbed the mutton grease into scorched hands, which surprisingly caused him no pain.

Within minutes, the thanes began arriving in twos and threes, breathless with expectation, incredulous at the news.

He stood with his arms folded across his chest, the sword buried in the earthen floor before him as a challenge.

The head of Estammic's clan looked to be the most disbelieving nobleman of all: "My sons say the prophetess of the sacred grove brought you here in her chariot. Is this true?"

"You be of such a low opinion of your own issue, you believe me over them?"

"The sword!" another lord cried, unable to contain himself. "Show us the point of the sword!"

Rolf drew it out of the dirt, and another man rushed forward with a torch to inspect the blade. "What unearthly thing marred it so?"

"A great light, a great heat—together as one they come upon me in the storm." He lofted the sword so all could see the strange sear, then dropped it to his side. "Enough of such questions. They be insulting to Lord Donar who be of the mind to press this kingship on me. For I be sick at heart when I think upon my task. This be nothing I covet."

"But why?" an old man asked, twirling a lock of his white beard around a trembly finger. "Many have lusted to be our king, and generation after generation of prophetesses have found none worthy."

"*Why*, my lords?" Pushing through them, he seized the passed-out drunkard by the cloak and dragged him through the portal to deposit him, still unconscious, into the mud of the common. Raging back inside, he kicked over the vat, glaring at the *thegans* when they began carping because a day's worth of *met* was sweeping into the earth like dishwater. "The morn Arminius hand over Germania forever, he be so drunk even a sisterly general like Quintilius Varus beat him with enough time left for a long lunch! His legionaries burn Marcomans and Cheruscans in a pile one mile long, six bodies high! No more *met*—until we be victorious and safe from counterattack at the same time!"

Sheepishly, the men began taking their hands off the hafts of their weapons.

Rolf stepped squarely in front of the head of Estammic's clan. "I mourn Segestias, who be my dearest blood. But I mourn Estammic too." Turning away from the man's dumbstruck face, he said to all: "For that sad night I be blind to the treachery what soon marches out of Gaul on us. These new rulers of Rome be not honorable like the Julians. I be familiar with them. Nepos and Claudia be hungry for open places like the Wald—to pay their lickspittles with parcels of land."

"I will gladly die first!" a young voice cried.

"No, fight first—then gladly die if you needs must."

A few grunts of approval were sounded.

"*Herzog* Rolf . . ." A silence hung over the lords from this first use of the title, but after an awkward moment the speaker went on: "When you talk of victory and counterattack, who will we be fighting?"

He met each gaze in the lodge before saying, "All the praetorian garrisons of Germania Superior and Alpes Graiae et Poeninae be loyal to Nepos. And these be from where the invasion on the Wald will come—" He paused, realizing that the members of the Gothic Revival were saluting him with their swords and javelins.

However, someone wailed, "All of us have work and homes outside the Wald. If we make war on the midget warriors, what will become of us?"

"We will become Marcomans again," the head of Estammic's *sippe* said. He too had hoisted his sword in salute.

CODEX II

MARA

11

As HOMER HAD sung, it was a windy place, this ridge at the mouth of the Hellespontus.

The wind blew down off the riffled wastes of the Pontus Euxinus, over the Propontis and onto the plain that prior to silting up in the time of the first Caesars, had been the wide and sandy bay on which the thousand ships of the long-haired Achaeans had been beached and propped for the duration of their campaign against the Trojans.

And where Germanicus now sat on a slab of white marble, watching the wind press down the golden summer grass and tussle the boughs of the holly oaks, had once stood the Tower of Ilium, or perhaps not.

Nearby was the remnant of a fine and angled wall of dressed limestone, the very one brave Patroclus had thrice scaled only to be battered down by Apollo. Or perhaps it was not that famous barrier at all. Who could say after thirty centuries? And after thirty centuries more, who could say with certainty that it had been Germanicus Julius Agricola to surmount Tenochtitlan's circuit wall, only to be swatted down by the vengeful Aztecan gods and given a limp, as Zeus had maimed poor Hephaestus by hurling him off Olympus?

He had only to close his eyes against the drowsy heat of late afternoon to be filled with the truest and most enduring bardic rendition of all human history: *chirp . . . chirp . . . chirp . . .* To extrapolate more from the dim and contradictory past was to somehow spoil the warm tranquillity offered by the columnless pedestal on which he rested. It was a consolation, this cadence of hidden insects, for the most galling thing about being deposed was not so much the loss of his throne as the certain knowledge that Antonius Nepos and Claudia Nero would obliterate his legend and leave him a cranky buffoon in the eyes of history. Even rulers who secretly doubt the existence of the gods will often trust in a personal eternity as long as their countrymen remember them and make sacrifices in their honor. Why else had Nero erected his colossus, Vespasian his amphitheater, Titus his arch celebrating peace with the Jews? Although he himself was far from immune to this troubling desire, Germanicus smiled sadly at his own vanity: as if a man can cheat death with edifices of stone. But the crickets were reminding him—*it is nothing . . . it is nothing . . . it is nothing. . . .*

He lay back across the pedestal.

When he awoke, it was fully night, and the Trojan stars were jewel-like enough to make him think upon Helen for a long while.

Had she made love to Paris under such a sky, with Hector and his adjutant Aeneas, the father of Rome, standing guard at the portal? Are men and women ultimately so fragile they can survive only as echoes in hexameter? Or had these children of the gods ever lived at all? Had Homer only invented them to show a world benumbed by daily adversity the true magnitude of its inevitable destruction?

Chirp . . . chirp . . . chirp . . .

Thirty miles to the north a string of lights trickled across the land: a rail-galley headed for the bridge between Callipolis on the Thracian side of the Hellespontus and Lampsacus on the Anatolian shore. The glittering string was broken here and there along its length; these dark interruptions were unlit *ballista* cars, armored concessions to the civil war. So once again it was necessary to arm the rail-galleys for their dashes across the plateau and over the mountains of Agri Dagi into Parthia and Mesopotamia.

He wondered if the Great *Zaim* had been persuaded by the firebrands in his own family to resume attacks on the Great Artery, Rome's link to the far eastern provinces. It consisted of a rail trestlework straddling an oil pipeline—and had always been the favorite target of native mischief.

But then he put these things out of mind. They no longer mattered. The world would go on, regardless.

Burrowing deep into his shabby cloak, he again slept.

But he awoke sometime before dawn, his head full of torment and confusion. The disturbing image that had haunted his rest would not dissipate with consciousness, and again he was being rowed ashore with Tora glaring down at him from the deck of the hauler. At last the Nihonian had seemed to realize he was being dismissed in order that his life might be spared. And he had taken only humiliation from Caesar's parting gift. With the moment somehow stripped of its solicitous pretense of a spy mission on the Sericans, Germanicus had shouted, "Go home then to Nihonia— live long and be well!"

Tora had tossed him a forlorn wave, then turned away.

The captain had given him a week's worth of provisions, what Germanicus had told him he'd need to sustain himself while he hiked east across central Anatolia toward Agri Dagi. Doubtless, he could forage along the way, and he had every expectation that the Great *Zaim's* followers would meet up with him long before his rations were exhausted. But, in truth, he had intended to go no farther than Troy's ruins, ever.

Now it occurred to him with a mild shock that a week had passed, for his canvas pack was empty and he was still alive—not that he had grown fainthearted about falling on the unadorned mariner's sword the captain had presented him. However, on that first night ashore, he had found the mild warmth and the solitude of the place so consoling, the way in which the echoes of his scraping footfalls died among the tumbled walls so plaintive and suggestive of ghostly whispers, he saw no harm in a modest postponement of his final hour.

The urgency had dribbled out of his life like wine from a ruptured goatskin.

One day flowed into the next, and he thought little of his own disembodiment if only because he already felt like a ghost— Hector's perhaps, wandering the shattered parapets and towers, asking himself how the devastation encircling him could have sprung from loyalty to one's own brother. Perhaps only Zeus, god of the Black Cloud, son of Cronos of the Crooked Ways, could understand how selfless good could result in universal evil. It made no more sense than how profligates like Antonius Nepos and Claudia Nero could be allowed to demolish the restoration of a just and equitable republic. Was not even one of the gods—Athene of the Luminous Eyes, Here of the Bovine Eyes, or even Apollo of the Bow—moved by Germanicus' cause?

No—Germanicus again smiled to himself. And the only plausible explanation was that the gods were as dead as the ashes that encased Pompeii, as dead as things that had never lived.

Chirp . . . chirp . . . chirp . . .

Yet, despite the shadows cast by these thoughts, now was the first time in his life he'd been free of crushing obligations, of vapid rituals on drawn-out holidays, of all the other *pro forma* to-dos that so trivialized Roman life. Still, no matter what kind of life it was or wasn't, it had to be sustained. And unless he meant to get on with his suicide without delay, he knew that he'd better find some food, or at the very least fill his canteen in the spring-fed pool at the base of the mound.

"*Inshallah,*" he greeted the half-dozen field workers lying on the banks of the pool. At the sun's zenith, he had watched them trudge in from the cultivated plain on which Agamemnon, Odysseus, and Achilles had encamped for ten long years.

"As God wills," the peasants repeated the intonation.

Most Anatolians were pious, and those who weren't, were most likely brigands. Some of his worst battles as a legionary had been against these courteous and seemingly docile people.

He tossed his canteen into the water, let it gurgle and sink.

The Anatolians were watching him closely.

He trusted he was sufficiently bearded and grime-covered to pass the test of their curiosity, although there was another part of his mind that didn't care if they found out who he was.

"Where are you bound?" asked a man with not more than five teeth to call his own.

"Nowhere."

"How is that?"

"I am just staying here for a while."

"To dig at the infidel ruins?"

"No."

"To pray, then?"

For a moment, Germanicus stared at this man whose head was wrapped in a soiled *jamadani*. "Yes . . . this is a fine place to pray."

Instantly, the men turned more gracious. The eldest among them smiled as he said, "It is too soon in the season for the apricots we are tending. But we have cucumbers and onions. Will you have some?"

"Thank you—I will, after I have prepared myself."

Recalling the habits of these people, he carefully washed, remembering to rinse his mouth and nostrils. Then he bowed his head and appeared to pray. During those moments he thought only of the cucumbers and onions, which were floating in the pond to cool. However, the Anatolians seemed pleased by the God-respecting ways of this stranger, the effect Germanicus had desired. He had rubbed elbows with these people long enough to know what abraded them and what earned their affability—and theirs could be an appealing hospitality, full of gentle humor and small kindnesses.

The onions were sweet, and Germanicus told them so.

"Yes," the old man said, "the nights are still cool, so the onions will be sweet for a while longer. But soon they will be fit only for cooking, unless one likes them with tears. Try the cucumber, I beg you."

"Yes . . . delicious." He fetched his canteen from the shallows and drank.

"Are you the man who came ashore from the galley?" a youth asked.

The old man censured him with a sideward glance, but Germanicus murmured that he didn't find the question impolite. "Yes, my boy, I arrived on that ship. It was a long and difficult journey. But now that I am here, I am content. Thank you for your generosity. It has proved as sweet as your onions." With that, he began limping up the slope toward the top of the ridge. "*Inshallah.*"

"*Inshallah,*" they said in unison to his back.

The next forenoon, as he was reclining in the sunlight on the ramp that led up to what had once been the Scaean Gate, he sensed he was being observed. For a man whose every move had been scrutinized by praetorian guardsmen, the sensation was too familiar to be alarming.

Nevertheless, he inched toward his sword, which he had concealed in the shadow at the base of the collapsed Tower of Ilium.

A gerbil, its instincts more finely tuned to danger than his, bounded for its lair.

Then Germanicus heard it too: the clopping of hooves over stone.

A moment later, a robed man leading a donkey on a tether crested the ridge, noticed Germanicus, then touched the fingertips of his right hand to his forehead in greeting.

Leaving the sword where it lay, Germanicus stood and returned the gesture.

The panniers harnessed to the donkey were brimming with wild herbs and flowers: coriander, wormwood, chicory, dandelion, watercress, and sprigs of willow.

"It looks as if you have much healing to do, *zaim*," Germanicus said when the man had halted beside him.

"There is always much healing to do in a world full of corruption. *Inshallah*."

"*Inshallah*."

Although the robed figure had only a hint of the formidable majesty of the Great *Zaim*, he was no doubt the local holy man, charged by his distant superior in the Purple Village to investigate this intruder on the northwest coast of Anatolia. "Some plants thrive on the dust of infidel ruins," he said, his eyes hard on Germanicus'.

"But which ruins are most fertile? I understand from the authorities on such matters there are eight or nine cities here, one heaped on top of the other."

"Two thousands years ago a Roman city stood here."

"New Ilium?"

"Yes, I believe that is what the place was called."

"No." Germanicus smiled. "I haven't come here to see the Roman ruins. I have put all things Roman behind me."

"I see." Now the *zaim* was half smiling. "Then truly, you stand on the threshold of the East. How far toward the dawn sun do you intend to journey?"

"I have no idea. I haven't even decided on a journey. I may remain here."

"For how long?—if I might ask and not offend."

Germanicus said nothing.

"I see. You are leaving your plans to the Compassionate, the Merciful."

"In a sense. I trust I have a friend in a lofty place."

The *zaim* looked puzzled for a moment, but then he frowned and pointed at the tiny, bent figures laboring in the fields and orchards of the plain below. "These people are my own. I am responsible for them. If you make this place your home, you must do something. . . ."

"And what is that?"

"You must tell them you are not an angel of God. They are

convinced of it. They talk all night of you, and their work is falling off."

Then he gave a sharp tug on the donkey's tether and continued down the ramp, to disappear a few minutes later among the scrub oaks.

Germanicus suspected that his own words had been recorded as precisely as if a scribe had set them down in wax. And now they would be transmitted on the tongues of holy men across the parched and windswept length of Anatolia.

Chirp . . . chirp . . . chirp . . .

Night, and another rail-galley glittered soundlessly in the distant north. Each infinitesimal scintillation was a window, and—unless brigandage was scaring off the travel trade—behind each window sat a Roman, stinking of lungweed and the cheap vintages of the poorer provinces. An imperial paymaster returning with empty purses from the flea-bitten legions of Mesopotamia. A corn factor smiling over a lapful of signed contracts. A praetorian tribune on leave from Ecbatana or Seleucia or Ctesiphon or only the lesser gods knew where, with a Parthian mistress to his back and a Roman wife twenty hours ahead of him.

So, except for the isolated flash points of the civil war, the Empire and its citizens seemed to be plodding along as usual.

How could things have been different? he asked himself for the thousandth time—and not just in relation to him, but *fundamentally*.

He looked up. From where King Priam had once gazed out across the fires of the long-haired Achaeans, mystified at how vehemence of such duration could be possible, bats flitted and spiraled in search of prey.

How could the world have been different?

Hadn't he tried to put this question to rest only a few years before?

"Yes," he murmured to himself, pausing to listen to the wings of the bats beating against the night air, "and I dispatched an agent, a former priest of Isis who was well versed in most religious matters, to Alexandria on a mission of utmost secrecy. I told him Caesar couldn't openly consult any of the ten Sibyls without creating a crisis in confidence. . . ." His voice trailed off, and he found himself wondering for how many days he'd been woolgathering aloud like this.

"No matter . . . where was I?" He had been recalling the legend of Joshua Bar Joseph, hadn't he? "Yes, yes . . ."

He had first become aware of it while bound for the remote garrison at Agri Dagi on a rail-galley, perhaps the very one he watched speeding westward at this moment. "No, wait—I'm seeing the southern trunk. I was on the main Bosporus-to-Parthia line that night. . . ." At any rate, a tragedian whose little troupe was playing the backwater garrisons related a vision he claimed to have heard from the Sibyl at Alexandria, an unlikely story the Procurator Germanicus had dismissed as nonsense—but had not been able to banish from his mind. Only later, as Emperor, had he been able to send an agent, an Isiac priest, to Aegyptus to question the old woman and authenticate the actor's fantastic tale.

"Indeed, Caesar," the freshly returned agent had reported, "the Sibyl maintains that during the reign of Tiberius the procurator of Judea freed a Galilean holy man from crucifixion, thus saving the Empire from division and, ultimately, collapse at the hands of the Gothic factions."

"How can that be possible? She *must* have explained."

"I'm sorry, Caesar, she grew impatient with my questions."

"The gist of it, man—surely you have some intuition!"

The agent had chewed on the inside of his cheek for a moment. Why was it impossible to get a man consecrated to the truth to ever speak it? "I believe this Cult of Joshua could have gained impetus from the dramatic manner of his death. It could've gained a foothold in the resurrectionist cults of the Oriental provinces—and rippled across racial lines, perhaps to Italia itself."

"And she perceives that this cult would have caused our division?"

"I believe so." The man then lowered his gaze to the mosaic floor of the palace. "Caesar, I fear the Sibyl knew who sent me."

"Did you tell her?"

"No, never! But, in parting, she said to me: 'Caesar dreams of Arminius' deed, but only in dreams his scouts Varus does not heed!' "

The color had drained out of Germanicus' face. An amateur historian, he'd often pondered the fate of the Empire had Augustus' general, Quintilius Varus, not thrashed Arminius and his German confederation at the battle of Teutoburg Wald. The most renowned of the Sibyls was confirming the importance he had always placed on that distant clash. Victorious, Augustus' legions had—with the exception of a tract of virgin forest given over to the Germans for the pacifying illusion that their barbarous culture survived—secured the borders of the Empire all the way to the River Vistula and put Germania firmly on the path to Romanization.

So, in a nutshell, the Sibyl had suggested that the cancer of a new cult within the Empire and the threat of Gothic arms without could have combined to smash the Roman dream of universal peace and prosperity. "But Rome did indeed survive," Germanicus had muttered, and the travertine walls of the Palatine had multiplied his words into pompous echoes that now made him squeeze shut his eyes in the stillness of Troy's ruin.

"Indeed," the agent had repeated with a smirk. "Indeed, Caesar. And she said one more thing you may find of interest, but I fear I can't recall her exact versification. I never developed an ear for—"

Impatiently, Germanicus motioned for the man to continue as best he could.

"Well, it had something to do with Titus and Jerusalem."

"Titus as general or emperor?"

"As general I believe, for she said something like this—had not the best legions been freed by Quintilius Varus' victory earlier in that century from picket duty along the Rhine, the procurator of Judea would have had only Syrian auxiliaries with which to tame the Jews. As it turned out, his Roman and German troops kept the surly Jews well in hand. And the sack of Jerusalem which so brightly fires her dreams . . . well, it never came to pass."

"Came to pass . . ." Germanicus murmured, drowsy at last, snugging his malodorous cloak around him as he tried to get comfortable on the pedestal of a column Agamemnon might well have pulled down. Or might well have not.

Tomorrow he would wash his cloak in the sea and dry it in the north wind.

He would see how the world looked from a clean cloak.

12

ANOTHER WEEK SLIPPED away on Ilium's warm breeze.

Germanicus marked the passing of the days only by a steady decrease in the number of the sesterces given to him by the hauler captain. He was using the coins to buy vegetables and fruit from the Anatolians working the plain below. In deference to the wishes of the local *zaim*, he had informed the laborers that he was not a messenger from God but simply a tired foreigner in search of peace. They had been sorely disappointed, yet remained courteous toward him.

Then one dawn when his pouch of sesterces was almost empty, he arose to discover a small tent pitched at the base of the leeward slope of the mound. Near it was a cooking fire, sending a blue twine of smoke skyward. He could see no one in or around the encampment, so he went back to dozing atop the pedestal.

At noon, he strolled down to the pool to purchase his daily food, hoping the Anatolians would be able to explain the presence of the new visitor. They seemed genuinely unaware of the tent, as it was on the side of the ridge facing away from the plain, but agreed among themselves that it was another infidel come to root feverishly for treasure, which invariably turned out to be pottery little different from what they used in their own impoverished homes. Most of this old crockery, their elder noted with a bewildered shake of his beard, was broken. "Why are some men so taken with the godless past?" he asked.

"Because it appeals to them more than the godless present, my friend. *Inshallah . . .*"

The sun had just cast a bronze fan out across the waters of the Hellespontus when he heard the distinct clink of a hammer striking stone.

The sound had come from the direction of the tent.

Rousing himself after a long afternoon of reflection amid

occasional naps, he hiked over the top of the ridge and halted a few yards down the westward-facing slope. Again, no one was to be seen near the tent. However, along a section of the circuit wall exposed by a previous excavation, a gray-haired man was squatting to the depth of his shoulders, digging in a hole ringed with fresh dirt.

Approaching, Germanicus cleared his throat so as not to startle him.

The man didn't glance up from his labors.

Definitely not an Anatolian, he was perhaps ten years Germanicus' senior, although his arms and shoulders were still thickly muscled, and his movements were vigorous. His balding pate was deeply burnished by the sun, so Germanicus surmised he was no stranger to work under the open sky.

Stepping up to the lip of the hole, Germanicus asked in Greek, the common tongue of the eastern provinces, "Are you finding anything?"

"I always find something," the man answered in Latin tinged with an Aramaic lilt. Still, he refused to meet Germanicus' eyes. "Most of it is unimportant. Pure rubbish, regardless of its antiquity." Setting aside the small spade with which he'd been digging, he now took up a hammer and began pounding at a stone, trying to loosen it from the band of charred debris that was apparently the object of his interest. "That something is good simply because it is old is a Roman prejudice." The stone suddenly tumbled down around his ankles, and behind it skipped a shard. "Like this, for instance."

Germanicus bent lower to examine the fragment. His late brother Manlius had been Prefect of Antiquities, and a casual call on him had invariably turned into an afternoon-long tutorial, with Manlius dragging him by the arm around the musty imperial museum, illustrating his lecture by excitedly pointing to this Cretan urn or that Assyrian cachet cylinder. So it took only a glimpse for him to identify the pattern on the shard as being Hittite.

"Early Mycenean," the man declared, standing momentarily for the sake of his back.

He was as tall as himself, Germanicus surmised, although the man remained waist-deep in his pit.

"But we have already established trade links between the Peloponnesus and this coast. We did that last summer, conclusively."

Germanicus struggled to keep the skepticism out of his voice. "And who are *we*?"

"My daughter and I." The man went back to spading, grunting softly with each shovelful he hurled behind him, narrowly missing Germanicus' sandals with the sprays of dirt.

"My name is Julius," Germanicus said—a partial truth. "And yours, if I may ask?"

"Dathan . . . Dathan of Alexandria."

A Jew then, Germanicus realized.

At last, the man glanced up, but only briefly—as if he were reluctant to look too carefully at the bearded Roman.

"Then you, Dathan, must be with one of the fine academies in that city."

"Yes."

"And you come to Ilium each summer to dig."

"Yes."

Germanicus began looking around for the daughter Dathan claimed to have. This daughter might prove to be an armed accomplice, for the man had already falsely represented himself on two counts. Firstly, he knew nothing about ancient pottery. Secondly, any academician who had only recently forsaken his dark library for sunny Anatolia would now find himself possessed of a painful sunburn. Scholarship was, after all, a pale occupation. But this man had a skin well-seasoned by the elements.

Backing away from the hole, he said, "I must go now . . . hail and farewell."

Dathan did not answer.

Before first light, Germanicus found concealment among the uppermost ruins. It afforded him an unobstructed view of the tent and the oak-dotted hills beyond.

Gradually, as the blush in the east grew in intensity, the trees went from black to dark green, and finally the grasses were lit the golden color they would wear until sundown dimmed them again. At this moment, as the sun breasted the horizon, one of the flaps to the tent was tossed back, and a woman stepped outside into the dawn's coolness. Craning the night's stiffness out of her back, she surveyed the sky, yawned, then busied herself with restarting the cooking fire.

Dathan emerged from the tent, and it was only then that Germanicus realized how tall the woman was, for prior to this comparison she hadn't given the appearance of being gangly or clumsy. She refused to stand round-shouldered, as do some tall women to mitigate what they secretly believe to be their deformity. This woman was comfortable with her stature, and—in return—it became her.

They breakfasted. Then she slung two waterskins over each shoulder and, without farewelling her father, began skirting the base of the mound toward the pond. But she hadn't gone far when she hid the skins in a stand of acacia and struck off across the grassland toward the southeast, using the first dry watercourse she came upon as if to conceal her progress.

He lost sight of her for two hours.

He was on the verge of falling asleep when he noticed her in the shade of the acacias again, recovering her four waterskins.

"Well, my dear," he whispered to himself, "where have we been all morning? Meeting with the commander of the local auxiliaries? Or perhaps a praetorian colonel in a sand-galley just over that first line of hills?"

He decided to overtake her on the path to the spring.

She betrayed no alarm when he stepped out from a broken wall in front of her. "*Shlomo*," he said in Aramaic.

"Good morning," she repeated. But then, as had her father in conversing with Germanicus, she immediately switched to Latin: "You frightened me."

"You don't look frightened." There was accusation in his voice, and she frowned. He realized that their eyes were on the same level. "And have you forgotten your Greek?"

"I don't understand." She was raven-haired and, except for a smattering of dark freckles across her cheekbones, flawlessly olive-complected.

"Why do you speak Latin instead of Greek?"

"You look Roman to me."

"I appear to be stateless to anyone who looks carefully—a vagrant."

"*Shlomo*," she said brusquely, elbowing past him and continuing on toward the spring.

But he followed close on her heels. He wasn't going to let her get out of his sight again. Like her father, she had not—even by means of polite conversation—asked him to account for his presence here. This guarded lack of curiosity disturbed him more than pointed questions might have. "Your father tells me you're from Judaea."

She started to toss a scowl over her shoulder, but then checked the impulse. "No— Alexandria."

"Then I must have heard him wrong. Does he spend most his days shut up in libraries?"

"Yes, he is always with his scrolls and trays of artifacts." Although of a build more voluptuous than stout, she had thick calves, the kind that come from constant hiking on steep trails. "Why do you ask?"

"Well then, he takes the sun well for a scholar, doesn't he?"

"Yes." Almost imperceptibly, her pace had slowed, but then she resumed the same tireless stride. "And you spin webs well for one who is not a spider." She dropped her skins into the pond and, one by one, pulled out their bungs, holding the corks in a depression she formed by spreading her knees beneath her short linen skirt. "You do not look as if you eat well . . . or regularly."

Germanicus chuckled despite himself, recalling how Tora and he had nearly starved to death on the road to Corinthus. "I'm a glutton freed from Hades to make amends for a prior life of excess."

"You don't seem a man who is fond of excess." She had a determined-looking jaw, but also an upward curve to the corners of her full lips, which Germanicus' mother would have said indicated impetuosity. It was not a bad quality in a woman, his mother had insisted, for it prevented her from being taken for granted by her husband. "Will you take the evening meal with my father and me, Julius?"

"Will I be the only guest? Or are others presently on the way?"

"Again, I don't understand. Your speech is as full of riddles as a Chaldean's."

"Then let me put it plainly—I will dine with you on one condition. . . ." He paused, finding her look of expectation quite arresting, yet by no reckoning was she what he would consider a beautiful woman. He knelt beside her.

"Yes, Julius?"

"You must tell me—where did you go this morning?"

She corked the first skin that had filled. "I went out into the hills."

"Why?"

"To walk, to sing to myself—and I like to search the dunes for projectile points."

Again, suspicion lit his eyes. "Did you find any?"

She wriggled two fingers behind her thick rawhide waist belt and came out with a bronze arrowhead. Smiling, she pressed it on him. "Keep it."

"No, I—"

"Keep it, so if ever you doubt me again . . ." Purposely, she didn't finish, but continued to smile at him. Darts of sunlight reflecting off the pool danced on the underside of her chin.

"What's your name?"

"Mara."

"Hebrew?"

"Yes."

"What does it mean?"

"Sad, bitter."

He cupped his palm in the water and drank from it. "Then it doesn't suit you."

"Not this morning. But from time to time it does. Life is not a level journey."

"No, it isn't," he said more severely than he'd intended. Abruptly, he rose to go.

"And what does *Julius* mean?"

"Nothing." He started limping up the ridge toward his empty pedestal. "It means nothing anymore."

Set before his place at the makeshift table were two bowls, one filled with wine and the other with vinegar. Germanicus was careful to show no reaction to the little snare Mara and Dathan had seemingly rigged for him. Both his abstinence of spirits and his fondness for vinegar were well known across the Empire. As much as he now craved a sip of vinegar to rinse his palate before eating, he asked for plain water.

Smiling faintly, Mara rose from the drum of a broken column shaft that served as her chair and fetched him one of the coolly sweating skins.

"I apologize that we have no couch for you to recline upon, Julius," Dathan said, giving Mara and then the platter of tunny fish an impatient glance.

Germanicus asked himself if they actually knew his identity or were stumbling around for confirmation. If they recognized him to be Caesar and meant him harm, they were certainly taking their time about it. Jews were notorious to Romans for their circuity, but this was taking the habit to extraordinary lengths. Was he being fattened only for slaughter? He didn't believe so, but had no idea what the twosome had in mind for him.

Mara emptied his wine bowl into the stone jar, rinsed it, then filled the vessel with water. "Do you decline vinegar as well?"

"I've never liked vinegar."

He saw the urge to contradict him flash across her eyes, but she said nothing more about it.

Grunting under his breath for attention, Dathan then blessed the meal, most likely in the name of his nameless god. The meaning of the liturgical Hebrew was lost on Germanicus, and he didn't lower his head and join them. Unlike Anatolians, Jews were distrustful of nonbelievers who went through the motions of respecting their traditions. Instead of praying, he used the moment to study Mara. Face downcast, she seemed more handsome in the twilight than she had under the full brunt of the sun, and the olive tones of her skin were now kindled a soft gold by the saffron robe she was wearing. She blinked more often than normal—a sign, he felt, that she knew she was being examined by her guest.

At last, Dathan ratified his interminable supplication with an *amen* and seized the loaf of flat bread—it was flecked with chaff—and broke off a chunk, offering it to Germanicus with a sullen roll of his eyes.

"Thank you," Germanicus said.

"It is nothing."

"It is bread, correct?"

Dathan shrugged, and Mara shot Germanicus a defensive look.

"Your bread looks good," he quickly added.

Using a wooden spatula, she began serving the fish to the men.

"Mara," Germanicus said to Dathan around a bite of the coarse bread, "doesn't seem to be pleased by her name."

Her eyes blazed at him.

"It is not a name meant to please." Dathan went on eating, licking the fish oil off his fingers and smacking his shiny lips. "She knows that."

"But why a female name evocative of sadness and bitterness?"

"It is written." He held out his empty wine bowl for Mara to fill.

"What is written?"

Irritably, Dathan motioned with his free hand for Mara to explain so he could go on with his meal in peace. He dealt with questions as if they were hornets.

She folded her hands beneath her chin and gazed directly at

Germanicus. Her voice was nearly a whisper: *"Do not call me Naomi, call me Mara, for the Almighty has dealt very bitterly with me. I went away full and the Lord has brought me back empty. Why call me Naomi, when the Lord has afflicted me and the Almighty has brought calamity upon me?"*

"And how has your god afflicted you? I see only a woman in the bloom of good health."

She said nothing. For a few moments of her silence, Germanicus thought that she was framing an answer, but then she went back to her tunny fish without another word.

"Yes, well, that clears everything up. And what of Dathan?"

The man stared at him.

"What does your name mean?"

His words were muffled by a mouthful of bread.

"Forgive me," Germanicus said, "but I could have sworn you said Dathan means *of the fountain*."

He nodded *yes*, then peered over his shoulder as if he'd heard something approaching.

"Well," Germanicus said blandly, "it certainly can't mean *student of antiquities*."

Dathan stopped chewing. "What do you say?"

"I'm saying that you don't know Early Mycenaean from Hittite potsherds, that you spend most of the year out in the sun, and—unlike the Jews of Alexandria who speak Hebrew when among themselves—Aramaic is your native tongue . . ." Germanicus expected some kind of response to these accusations, but Dathan's eyes seemed to blear out of focus and then fix on a point above and beyond the Roman's head.

Germancius was tempted to turn around and have a look—before he suspected this to be a feint intended to make him do just that.

But then a voice said in peasanty Greek from the slope behind him: *"Pasa*, a word if you please?"

"What do you want?" Dathan barked at the Anatolian in the dark flowing *haik* who stood above them, imploring favor with the usual obsequious gestures.

"I seek a commission."

"I have no need of you."

"I am a most excellent hauler of wood and drawer of water."

"Go away!" Dathan then ignored him. He asked Mara for another helping of fish, although Germanicus caught him giving her a glance more meaningful than that required for a serving of more tunny.

A horse nickered on the far side of the mound.

Mara gave a slight start. But other than that, her eyes remained indifferent as the Anatolian went on describing what a fine servant he would make. He stressed that in the past he had attended to three diggers of treasure, and, if it were possible for any of those three to be present now, each would doubtlessly bear out what he had to say about his own worthiness. Germanicus wondered if the party around the table been composed of four instead of three diners, the Anatolian would have loudly claimed prior service to *four* diggers of treasure.

In his mind, he began counting the paces back to the pedestal—and his sword, which he'd left there in the belief that a show of steel would have forced the hands of his hosts before he could discover what they were really up to. Could he count on their help in a fight? Perhaps—the unease Mara and Dathan were displaying in the unconscious fisting of their hands convinced him that they weren't in collusion with this persistent Anatolian. But he had been wrong about people before. Antonius Nepos and Gessius Fadus, for instance. Did the constant fear of intrigue and assassination under which an emperor lived eventually erode his ability to judge human character?

From a holly oak atop the mound, a raven spooked up into the dusky sky, then winged away in haste.

"I beg you, *Pasa*—there is no work in this land. I rely on the generosity of rich outlanders like you."

"Go—I say!" Dathan laid his forearm over the knife Mara had used to bone the fish. "I have nothing for you!"

"It is not good your woman draws water for you, *Pasa*." For the first time, a hint of menace came into the Anatolian's voice: "It is a long ways from here to the spring."

Picking up the platter, even though the fish was only half-consumed, Mara ducked inside the tent.

With a quick side-glance, Germanicus noted the locations of the approaches off the ridge, a few trails winding down through the debris. Whatever was coming, it would come off the high ground.

The twilight was failing fast, and the most prominent illumination was now coming from Mara's cooking fire. A few feet from the table a tasseled shawl of unbleached wool had been spread out over a cassis shrub to dry.

From the direction of the Scaean Gate came the sound of a

pebble clicking down the paved ramp, and then the susurration of numerous men or animals—or both—on the move.

"*Please*, my *Pasa*, will you think on this again? My children have open beaks like little sparrows!"

Dathan did not answer this time. By the shifting of the man's eyes, Germanicus could tell that he, too, was hearing things closing on the small encampment through the nightfall.

But then another look came into Dathan's eyes. It was fearless, predacious even.

All at once the Anatolian whipped an antique *pilum* out from under his billowing *haik* and hollered over his shoulder, "Brothers, now!" He was turning back to take aim at either Dathan or Germanicus, when an explosion ripped the evening calm and the air around the table suddenly stank of spent powder.

The Anatolian let go of his niter piece and clawed at his bloody chest. He started to scream, but then tumbled back dead before the sound could clear his fire-bright teeth.

Mara bolted from the tent and pitched the *pilum* she'd just fired to Dathan. Clutched beneath her arm was a second niter weapon, which she expertly charged with a loud clack.

Germanicus begged her for it, but she ignored him and began scanning the crest of the ridge for silhouettes on the run.

An Anatolian *pilum* flashed, and she answered it with a white blast of her own from the hip.

Alexandrian scholars, Germanicus thought dryly. Reeling, he grabbed the shawl and threw it over the flames.

"Not my *tallith*!" Dathan cried.

"What's wrong?" Germanicus had been sure the man would be grateful for the sudden darkness that now enveloped them.

"My prayer shawl!" Dathan was starting for the smoldering fire when the first horseman dashed down into the camp, whooshing a great scimitar from side to side. Dathan leapt aside and then rolled against the wall of the tent, discharging his *pilum* as soon as he came to rest.

The silhouette of the horse was suddenly riderless. Like the Roman-trained war steed it probably was, the animal crow-hopped to a halt, thinking that its master had alighted to fight on foot. Germanicus seized the bridle and led the mount a short distance away from the tent. He was pleased to find a *pilum* in a leather quiver attached to the saddle and quickly trained it on the next horseman to charge down the slope. The muzzle flash obliterated his view of the figure; but when his eyes had adjusted to the semidarkness again, another stallion was standing riderless. "I thought I'd forgotten how," he muttered.

Just as one of the Anatolians lofted a phosphorous flare to brighten the scene, Mara leaped up into this horse's saddle, cocked her knee with her foot resting on the pommel—and so braced her *pilum* to pick an Anatolian off the crown of the ridge.

"Well done!" Germanicus shouted.

But she hadn't heard him.

"Mara!" Dathan cried as he erupted from the tent and began running down his own mount. Germanicus was amazed that the sixty-year-old man was still on his feet, let alone jogging after a loose horse in the midst of a skirmish with Anatolian brigands. "Be away—I am done with it! Be away!"

Germanicus mounted his steed and trotted over to Mara. "I suggest we go separate ways."

"Why?"

"These Anatolians like to leave a contingent of lads in reserve to the finish off the job. They'll be along shortly."

"My father has already thought of that. Come."

"I think not."

"Come!"

"You bargain for more than you realize if I go with you. The local auxiliaries will certainly investigate this row."

"And what must we realize?" When Germanicus didn't answer, she turned abruptly and yelled in Greek: "But what of our *gold*, Father?!"

"Leave it! Quickly now—follow!"

Germanicus was sure Dathan had been chuckling as he raced past Mara and him, riding low with the horse's mane flowing into his face. He was wearing his scorched shawl around his shoulders.

"I'll go my own way," Germanicus said stubbornly.

Yet before he could give a tug on a rein and turn away from her, she said, smiling in the light of the dying flare, "We are your only way, Germanicus Julius Agricola."

She spurred the flanks of her horse with her heels and galloped after her father.

After a moment, with more and more Anatolians streaming down off Troy's heaped ruin, Germanicus followed her.

The brigands did not give immediate chase to the three diggers of treasure, and that proved a great miscalculation. Germanicus saw from afar how the darkly robed figures rooted around the campsite and rifled through the tent in search of the gold Mara had asked Dathan about. They were nicely concentrated around the fire, oblivious to the small wooden box smoking atop its coals, when suddenly the scene vanished in a crackling dazzle followed by a pall of niter smoke that hung over ancient Ilium in the starlight for as long as Germanicus looked back.

13

THE TALL CENTURION crossed the torchlit bridge. It arched over a defile of noisy cataracts and then delivered him into the central ward of Octodorum. A typical garrison town of the high Alps, it was built around a modest forum and consisted of a porticoed main street, a temple dedicated to some Romanized local deity, the public baths, the municipal curia, and—gouged into an encroaching hillside—an amphitheater with wooden seats.

On two sides of the town stood the ancient beginnings of a circuit wall. However, the defensive project had been abandoned when the Roman general Quintilius Varus defeated Arminius during the reign of Augustus and the threat posed by the German tribes was ended forever, as some still felt. These two stout walls that ran down the flanks of the sloping town—and failed to intersect—now served as the back partitions for twin arcades of small trading establishments, like sausage shops, one of which the ramrod centurion passed with a pang of longing as the odors of cooked pork and spices sifted out into the street.

He hadn't enjoyed a sausage in weeks, nor would he in the foreseeable future. It saved time to simply jerk meat over an open fire, and his men were busy enough learning how to use and repair their weapons, to accept orders without questioning them, and to savor the intoxication of victory without enhancing it with strong spirits.

He left the row of shops behind and cut across the town's burial ground toward the garrison. The steep-walled fortress stood well-lighted on a promontory that jutted out into River Rhodanus, making it unapproachable from three sides. But of more immediate interest to the centurion were the tents pitched in the grassy spaces between the funerary monuments, the only open land in town. The tents were empty; but, as dictated by some timeless regulation of the Roman army, a water barrel was positioned between every two shelters. These, too, were waiting to be filled. That would come soon enough, the centurion suspected.

He realized how he had missed the warmth of the legionary's woolen *sagum* on chilly mountain nights like this. The underlying linen tunic was a bit tight across his back and shoulders, but the loosely flowing cape was quite comfortable.

He was within hailing distance of the two praetorians guarding the portal to the garrison, when a rattly and badly smoking lorry careened around a corner, tottering under the weight of a score of German woodcutters returning from their day's labor in the nearby forest. The vehicle was so overloaded, its forelamps slanted up toward the sky and scarcely spilled their glow across the paving stones.

Reaching the straight section of road in front of the garrison, the operator increased his speed, so much so that the centurion—who was crossing to the other side at that moment—barely had time to leap aside.

"Halt!" he bellowed.

The operator, not foolish enough to ignore the command of an officer of the legion, glided to a stop, apparently without benefit of brakes.

His engine sputtered and died.

From the fortress gate the guardsmen watched with wry grins as the centurion bounded up to the lorry, tore the canvas door off its hinges, and dragged the operator out of his compartment with a twist in the collar of his cloak.

"Which demon of Hades be you?!"

The woodcutter began to stammer something, but the centurion cut him short with a cuff. "You stink of *met*!"

"But, lord centurion—"

"Come with me!" He spun on the the sheepish-looking men crammed together in the bed of the lorry: "All you!"

"But what will we do with out kits, centurion? If we leave them here, they will surely be stolen!"

"Bring them!"

Picking up the brine-stiffened leather cases that held their axes and petrol saws, the Germans began to pile off the bed of the lorry. Using the flat of his short sword as a club, the centurion herded them toward the portal, where the praetorians snapped to attention.

"One of you lads—be off to find the *praetor*."

"I beg your pardon, centurion?"

"These sausages be of a mind to assassinate me." He had used the Latinism for rustic Germans as if to make a distinction between himself, a Romanized German, and these barbarians with pine pitch and sawdust in their beards.

The senior guardsman was now simpering.

"You be tickled if I die?" the centurion roared.

"Sir, no sir! But these fools always come down off the mountain like that. We'd be suspicious if they didn't."

The officer wasn't about to be mollified. "I be in need of the *praetor—now!*"

"Sir, I'm sure the magistrate is too far along in his cups at this hour to be troubled with process. And it's a question of seriousness, isn't it, sir?" The guardsman was taking liberties with the centurion which he'd never take with an officer of his own praetorian guard. "Why, what with German hostiles beginning to raid up and down the old line of fortifications, who's to be bothered by a bit of reckless lorrying?"

"Me!" The centurion pushed past the now flustered praetorians into the courtyard beyond the portal. With his sword, he angrily waved for the prisoners to follow him. "To the stockade, march!"

"Sir, by your leave . . ." As expected, the senior guardsman left his post to implore the German centurion: "My colonel is . . . well, is indisposed . . . but at the very least let me clear this matter with my tribune."

"Go—while I be putting this rabble in the stockade."

"Well, there's a problem with that. See, the tribune will have to admit your prisoners into our stockade. I simply don't have the authority under the new crisis regulations."

No sound came from the centurion for a few seconds—except for his breath passing noisily through his nostrils. "I wait for your tribune. Go!"

"Very good, sir. Thank you, sir." Off he trotted toward the headquarters building, holding his *pilum* by the strap. Had he turned for even an instant toward the portal again, he might have seen the recumbent legs of his comrade being dragged out of sight.

"All right," the centurion said in a low voice to his prisoners, "be out with your arms—quick now."

Jumping to the command, the woodcutters cracked their cases, taking from them *pili*, swords, and small bombs of Greek fire.

Briefly, satisfaction lit the centurion's eyes.

These men were coming along well. They were the cream of his warriors. The bona fide woodcutters of Octodorum were tethered and gagged in a wald clearing outside town. As Germans who'd long suffered under Roman arrogance, they had fully endorsed the raid on the garrison, had even begged to take an active part, but the centurion didn't want the praetorian guard to take revenge on these simple woodsmen and their families after he and his warriors had melted into the Alps again.

Roman arrogance, he thought to himself, *a year ago I be unable to hitch the two words.*

"Ready, *Herzog* Rolf," his chieftain of the Cherusci said.

After Rolf's second stunning raid on the Romans—which had uncovered proof in the form of enormous piles of materiel that Antonius Nepos was indeed preparing to mount an invasion against the Wald—all the tribes had proclaimed the former centurion king. The vote of the Cherusci had been especially important, for they were the descendants of Hermann. They had even proposed that Rolf assume the mantle of this name, or at least its Roman corruption of *Arminius*—but Rolf gently reminded the entire Great Assembly that this ancient warlord had lost, not won his great opportunity, and Germans must now win battles routinely, not lose them magnificently.

"Very well"—he addressed the Cherusci as a separate unit, for he'd learned that his warriors fought better if they went into the confusion of battle beside their own kinsmen— "you be gone to the barracks. Kill all within."

The Cherusci stole off across the courtyard toward the long building where two hundred of the men who'd betrayed Caesar Germanicus for gold slept the sound sleep of the truly wicked. The Greek firebombs would make short work of them.

Rolf turned to the Helisii: "Take to the parapets. Be swift and sure with the sentries up top there."

"Aye, *Herzog*," their leader whispered, thumbing the edge of his dagger blade. "We be merciful swift."

The remaining fighters were Marcoman, and Rolf personally led them toward the headquarters, which more importantly was the wireless facility—a lofty limestone tower topped by another hundred feet of iron antennae. This was the main receiver station for dispatches sent from all over Germania and eastern Gaul; from here, coded messages went chattering over *impulsus*-wire, across the mountains and into Cisalpine Gaul for prompt relay to Rome. Without this aerie, Nepos would find it cumbersome to communicate with the far-flung units he soon hoped to loose against the Wald.

Rolf's *thegans* had argued in favor of targets rich in booty and captives who could be sold later into Sarmatian slavery. But he had sternly reminded them that in war no prize is more valuable than a befuddled enemy.

The senior guardsman from the portal was hastening out the door of the headquarters when Rolf cut him down with a single slash of his sword. "Never mind, I find your tribune myself. . . ."

The Germans burst into the first chamber, killing everyone there with massed *pili* fire. Not a single praetorian had been able to reach his weapon—but Rolf knew this gift of surprise would be short-lived. "Hurry—be done with all on this floor, then set the niter charges."

Motioning for one man to accompany him, he rushed up the spiraling flight of stairs to the next chamber.

It proved to be the frankincense-reeking quarters of the praetorian colonel, who regarded the intrusion of a German centurion and an unwashed Marcoman warrior with drunken indifference. He reached for his cup, missing it on the first try. "What in the name of Chaos is going on down there?"

"Someone be clumsy with his *pilum*," Rolf said, jerking his head for the warrior to be mindful of the open door behind them.

"Oh, centurion!" the colonel whined as if no one ever did what he told them to do. "Do you take me for a complete fool?!"

"Aye, Colonel."

Grunting, the man swung his pudgy legs over the side of his couch and sat as straight as he could to glare at Rolf, although his head rocked as he worked up a look of indignation. "*What!*"

"Any officer who betray the likes of Germanicus Agricola be a complete fool."

For the first time, fear penetrated the man's intoxication. His piggish eyes seemed to grow even smaller in his flushed face, but he decided on one more show of fulmination. "Who the bloody Mars do you think you are! And what are you saying to your superior officer!"

"I be Rolf of the Marcomanni, and here be the only profit in trading emperors like horses."

With that, he lunged forward and took the colonel's head off at the shoulders.

It had not quit rolling redly across the alabastrine floor when the warrior discharged his *pilum* out the door, and Rolf pivoted in time to see a bleeding tribune somersault past the opening on his pell-mell way down to the first story.

"Come, brother." He bolted from the colonel's chamber and mounted the steps three at a stride to the wireless transmission center. Across the breadth of the equipment-jammed rotunda, the operator sat urgently tapping out a message in the glare of his instrument array.

At Rolf's nod, the warrior shot him dead. He twisted up out of his chair, then fell sideways to the floor.

Stepping back from the blood that immediately flowed from the praetorian's tunic sleeve was a legionary courier, pale with terror, waiting speechlessly to die.

However, when the warrior swung his muzzle on the unarmed youth, Rolf batted it down. "Nay—a moment."

Keeping motionless, the legionary nonetheless tracked Rolf's every move.

"Your insignia . . ."

"Yes, centurion?"

"It say you be with the Sixth Legion Victrix."

"Yes, sir . . . seven months."

"A legion of great honor. So what business bring you to these traitorous praetorians?"

"I brought a dispatch from Moguntiacum. Two days on the rivers and roads."

"What manner of dispatch, legionary?"

"A request for rations and pay from our general. He said this would be the quickest way for Rome to receive our plea."

Rolf raised an eyebrow. "When be the last time the Sixth paid?"

"Two months, sir."

"And fed?"

"We've been without basic rations for three days. Five now, if none has arrived during my absence."

Rolf looked deep in thought for a several moments, then said, "You live . . ."

The young legionary leaned back his head and exhaled.

"You live to take this word to the commander, Sixth Legion Victrix—I, Rolf, king of Germania, make no war on the Sixth what if it cross not east of the Rivers Rhodanus and Rhenus. And I invite the Sixth, what once be my own noble and victorious legion, to join me against the traitors and emperor-killers Decimus Antonius Nepos and Claudia Nero." Then he had the legionary repeat the message to make certain fright hadn't purged his memory.

"Good lad." Rolf gripped the youth's slender shoulder.

"But, sir, do I remain here until you depart?"

Rolf chuckled for the first time in weeks. "Nay—if so, you soon be flying across the clouds with the Army of the Furious. I see you safely out of this snake pit."

Then he picked up the chair and heaved it against the instrument board. The gush of sparks and explosion of black smoke delighted the Marcoman warrior, who shouted a triumphant *baritus* and drilled a crystal-covered brass dial with two *pilum* rounds for good measure.

Outside, the clash with the few surviving praetorians was dying down. Hidden somewhere, a wounded guardsman was begging for the chance to slit open his own veins rather than be taken prisoner. He was ignored.

Rolf halted and took it all in:

From the shattered windows along the facing wall of the barracks tongues of flame throbbed and undulated skyward, unchecked. Only a handful of Nepos' men had made it out the smoky doorway and as far as the colonnaded porch before being scythed down by Rolf's marksmen. Peering up, he could count ten embrasures in the crenelated parapet looking down upon the inner courtyard, and over each of these crenels a guardsman was slumped with his red-crested helmet covering his bared buttocks. For all Rolf's days since that proud-hearted one in which he had straightened his right arm in salute to the Emperor and repeated the selfless words of the *sacramentum*, this had been the saddest sight he could imagine: imperial troops slain and then mocked by barbarian forces. Yet now it fired a satisfaction inside him that could not be denied.

The Helisii, who'd so ably handled the topside guard with the loss of only one of their own number, were now bundling captured rations and ammunition with warm praetorian-issue bedding. Each woolen blanket would be more precious than silk when the snows came to the Wald, and nearly half the summer pilgrims intended to stay and fight beside their new king, yet Rolf took one of the bundles that was filled only with food and tossed it to the courier: "This be for a few of your hungry comrades of the Sixth."

"Thank you, sir." The youth hesitated, then blurted, "I hope we never cross arms."

"Aye, me too—now go."

The legionary walked through the gate, but started running as soon as he reached the road.

The remainder of Rolf's Marcomans flew from the headquarters, one of them shouting in a jumble of Gothic and Latin, "All blows anon, *Herzog* Rolf!"

He ordered his men to run for cover, but he himself marched out of the garrison, refusing to break stride even when chunks of the disintegrating wireless tower bounced on the pavement around him like Titanic hail.

Some later said that his face had shone like Vesta's as he strode forth unconcerned, the last German warrior to leave Octodorum's fortress, the bravest of the brave casting his fate into the dark, starry lap of the gods. But others insisted—at the point of crossing broadswords, as was the German custom—that it had been Donar's lightning which rested upon Rolf's brow that chilly night in late July atop the Alps.

Slowly, Antonius Nepos disengaged himself from the mass of living but exhausted flesh. He lifted someone's thigh off his neck and tossed it aside. It had glistened with some nauseating unguent and been soft to the touch; female then, he supposed, although there was no way of telling for sure in the fetid gloaming of Claudia's private dining hall.

Naked, he staggered about the chamber, groans and complaints rising from the pile when he stepped upon an ankle or an arm. He was looking for some wine with which to rinse the foul taste out of his mouth, but all the tripod tables set up earlier that night with expensive vintages and exotic fruit had been overturned in the passionate fray Claudia had orchestrated on a drunken whim.

The evening had started decently enough, a dinner party of eighteen with some tremulous-jawed dotard singing the *Aeneid* to the accompaniment of a lyre. But as the evening wore on and the scarcely diluted wine flowed like the Tiber, the classical entertainment proved too tame to suit the noble bride of the lord regent and mother to the *imperator designatus*.

Vaguely, Nepos recalled the debaucheries being heralded by gales of brassy laughter. Claudia's. Had she used hilarity, then, to warm the climate of the gathering to her own purposes? Whatever expedient she'd used to break the icy patrician demeanor that so offended her, none of the nobles present had declined to participate. Perhaps each guest had rightfully understood that any show of rectitude would have singled him or her out for one of Claudia's cheeky little murders.

Through his own informers, Nepos now had proof of it: She had mustered the late Emperor Fabius' *delatoris* from the cracks into which they'd scuttled after the late Emperor Germanicus had summarily dismissed them, and put these combination spies and inquisitors to work ridding her of any company she found objectionable—in a manner alluding to the specific behavior of the senator or matron she'd found irritating. The carved-up corpse of a Conscript Father notorious for his public bouts of flatulence was discovered by the city watchmen in a bordello with a pig's anus sewn over his mouth. A matron of the illustrious Gracchi family, who was partial to deep purplish hues of makeup and had once dared to sink one of her clawed witticisms into Claudia's thin plebeian skin, was found strangled in her bath with hundreds of magenta-colored crabs sharing the pool with her.

So no one had dared appeal to old Roman morality when Claudia began pairing off unlikely couples—old men to shy maidens, fat matrons to other fat matrons; even a Vestal Virgin was compelled to shuck her white veil and take a partner.

It had all been ghastly—but uproariously erotic, Nepos now admitted to himself. But for the first time, publicly at least, Claudia and he had betrayed each other, and the realization left him with a hollow feeling. His head was also pounding from too much drink and too little sleep. Perhaps his sudden depression came more from these causes than the indelible image of Claudia coupling on the floor with a hirsute knight she said she detested as much for his coarse jokes as his coarse body hair.

He staggered toward the vestibule and the figure of the praetorian tribune who now followed him everywhere. The girlish-complected officer waited for him at the portal with a military cape spread wide.

"You know what I like about you, Marcus?"

"Sir?"

"Your eyes."

The young man looked unduly flattered until Nepos added: "They're uncanny. They are both vigilant and totally unseeing." He steadied himself by grasping one of the tribune's leather shoulder straps. "Come . . . right now I would take eight hours of oblivion over a crack at the holy vulva of Aphrodite herself."

"Sir—your wife beckons."

Turning, he squinted back into the gloom. "So she does, Marcus . . . so she does."

The unbridled gratifications of the past few months were already showing on her. Her facial powder had been washed away by perspiration, showing crescents as dark as bruises under her eyes. Her once jaunty breasts had gone pendant, and her belly bulged beyond the curvaceous degree he found pleasing in the female form.

Truly, he thought, *what a cow.*

She slipped on her gown as unself-consciously as if she had just stepped out of her bath instead of a heap of insufferable patricians with whom she'd rutted the sweaty night away. Scowling, she crooked her finger for Nepos to come, but he ignored her and started for his apartments.

A few moments later he could hear her bare feet slapping the tiles in the corridor behind him. "Stop!" she shrieked hysterically.

"Lower your voice, for the love of Mars!" he hissed, spinning on her, his eyes widening at the repulsive apparition that had once been his sensuous paramour. He had been raised in a shabby household full of shrill female voices, and despised caterwauling as the essence of plebeian vulgarity.

"I'm sorry, Decimus Antonius. I was frightened you were angry with me."

His contempt for her might have been softened by this pathetic entreaty had he not known that in a blink her self-loathing could be replaced by a bottomless rage for everyone around her. Even the stone presences. Much of the statuary on the Palatine had already fallen victim to her wild outbursts, and Nepos had come close to snapping her wrist after she had bloodied his face with a jagged piece of marble. Whatever had happened to the cold quality to her anger? Did she no longer feel any inhibitions at all?

"I don't want to be alone," she went on in the same self-pitying vein.

"You were far from alone, my dear."

"No, please, I had a nightmare—"

"Oh, the gods spare me." He sighed.

"And in it Germanicus came to the surface of that canal as white as new cheese. He opened his lips to speak, but blood instead of words poured out—"

"Enough," Nepos said, relenting with a frown. He motioned for her to follow Marcus and him inside his apartments. He was uncomfortable with her being here; it was the one wing of the

Palatine in which he felt safely beyond her machinations. "Do you want some more wine?" he asked, flopping onto his couch.

"No, it will only further sink my spirits. Do you have some hemp?"

With a weary flick of his hand, Nepos signaled Marcus to go after some.

She sat on the end of the couch and pummeled out a nest for herself in the deep cushions. "What's the latest report from your men in Corinthus?"

He sighed. "Nothing."

"What do you mean *nothing*?"

"I mean I've ordered a cessation to the search. How many times must we argue about this?"

Her eyes flared. "On what grounds did you order the search stopped?"

He came close to striking her. She must have sensed it, for she abruptly changed her approach. With a pouty lower lip, she whimpered: "Don't you realize what a relief it will be to me to hold his severed head in my hands? To know at last he's truly dead?"

"He *is* truly dead. With a million sesterces offered for either his capture or the discovery of his remains, don't you think someone in Achaea would have turned him over long before now? His body sank into the canal mud or flowed out into the sea for the mullet to devour. That's all there is to it. I refuse to have my men drag the waterway with hooks one more time. It's pointless. And even worse than the futility of it—this obsession of yours makes us look like cowards, like we're in desperate fear of a dead man. I didn't fear Germanicus Agricola when he breathed. So why should I now?"

"But these reports . . . these sightings all over the Empire, Decimus Antonius."

He laughed. "One hundred years from now there will still be reports of him cropping up here and there. The superstitious plebs will build shrines to him wherever some shepherd or addlebrained slave saw him floating through the dusk with Jove at his side. It has to do with his manner of death. It was mysterious, you see. And people are stimulated by mysteries of this sort. Well, they can believe whatever nonsense they will—as long as they do what we tell them to do. Why," he said with a smug smile, "I've just defined the nature of Roman liberality, haven't I?"

Marcus returned with a hemp pipe for Claudia, lit it for her, then retired to the portal, where once again his watchful eyes tactfully bleared out of focus.

"This so-called German king sacking our outposts . . ." She inhaled deeply, holding the smoke in her lungs as long as she dared.

"What of him?"

A smoky breath burst out of her and she clasped her breast in a gesture she probably imagined to be demure. "Oh my!" Then she seemed to delve into her own sensations as if listening inwardly for the stirrings of the hemp's effect. "The general of the Sixth . . . now, what's his name?" Again, her lips closed around the stem of the pipe.

She knew as well as Nepos that the commander's name was Gaius Prudentius, so he ignored the question.

"Prudentius, isn't it?" She exhaled. "Well, didn't he say this king calls himself Rolf?"

"He may have. So what?"

"*Rolf*, my beloved! Remember the dullard Germanicus kept to guard his person? The centurion Rolf?"

"Every other Goth is called Rolf. It's as common a *praenomen* among them as Gaius is with us. And their lineages are too full of bastards for them to have much regard for surnames."

"No, no, no." She wagged her head obstinately. "Prudentius wired us that *this* Rolf was killing praetorians in the name of Germanicus." She giggled without cause, then snapped at Marcus to send for appetizers.

Nepos stared at her with disgust, but then his gaze turned thoughtful: Was it possible that Germanicus' Rolf was behind the current outrages?

"Now that Aegyptus is ours again," she continued as if enormously amused with herself, "and that weasel of a governor's in a sack at the bottom of Alexandria's harbor with an asp and crow and pig for companions"—she threw a fall of her blonde hair over her shoulder and chortled at the ancient manner of execution she herself had suggested—"we should send our spare legions to Germania and teach this King Rolf a thing or two."

"We have no spare legions."

"The Aegyptian weasel who turned on us is in a sack—"

"I know that!" he barked, giving her a start.

She consoled herself with the arrival of a tray of *antepast*. However, before she fell upon the first treats to catch her eye, the dormice tricked out with pearl-like dollops of roe, she had her female slave sample each offering—even the paste of peacock brains which had cost more than the Dacian girl herself—and then the obligatory wine that came with every repast, and finally, the water to be mixed with that wine.

Nepos turned away; he didn't care to watch her eat. She smacked her lips like a Lusitanian peasant after each bite.

And it also alarmed him—the extraordinary measures she was taking against poisoning; it only meant she herself was plying the herbalist's trade. Did that mean she might be familiar with the symptoms of toxicity in others? He prayed not.

"It's an unexpected consequence of taking up the purple, isn't it?" he asked, his anger under wraps again.

"What?" she asked with a full mouth.

"Facing each meal with a sense of trepidation. Always wondering if death is stealing inside you with your very sustenance?"

She quit chewing.

"No wonder Augustus eventually restricted himself to figs he picked with his own hands, what?"

And then it finally came, the sudden, reasonless explosion: "Why can't we send those legions to Germania!" A bit of peacock paste dribbled from the corner of her mouth.

"Which legions?"

"You heard me!"

She hurled a bowl—but wisely at the floor and not at him. "I say so be it—the legions march on Germania *now*! Five legions! No, make it six!"

"That's impossible." He kept a level voice he hoped would infuriate her. "The crisis in Aegyptus is far from over. While the rebellious legionaries are indeed mummifying on their crosses along the road to Memphis, you forget something—the grain that should be feeding Rome is rotting in the few Alexandrian storehouses not in ashes. The fields of Africa lie fallow, with no hands to plant the winter crop, as the wrapheads have run off into the desert for fear of being massacred by one group of Romans or another. So, the six legions you want to trundle off to Germania are more urgently needed elsewhere, my dear."

She wore a pigheaded grin he ached to bash in with the hilt of his sword. "Like where!"

"Like in Cyrenaica, Abyssinia, and Judaea, where they can impress the three hundred thousand laborers Rome will need to have bread next spring, *my dear*. Roman teeth must have bread. Without it, they'll eat you and me!"

She was rearing back her foot to kick over the small table supporting her tray of appetizers, when murmuring drew her attention to the portal.

Nepos saw that Claudia's personal physician was whispering to Marcus.

"What is it there?" she demanded.

The doctor frowned, then took two cautious steps inside the chamber. "Noble Claudia, I fear your son has taken a turn for the worse."

She screamed. The cry was so disingenuous and melodramatic, Nepos was tempted to cuff her. But, taking a deep breath, he restrained himself and, instead of thrashing the harlot with the back of his hand, cultivated a worried look. "Good Mars, man, what is it?"

He seemed on the verge of tears. "I don't know, Lord Regent. I've tried everything. *Everything*. At first I was sure it was some common ailment of childhood, and the vigor of his own youth would throw it off. But this colic persists and persists and—"

Claudia leaped from the foot of Nepos' couch and ran for the door. She turned her ankle mid-chamber and was sent sprawling. Beating her fists against the tiles, she wept.

It made Nepos want to smile, this tableau of an aggrieved mother in the consoling grasp of her son's effete healer. Quintus was nothing more to her than the excuse she needed to rule.

And the boy meant even less to Antonius Nepos, who believed he no longer needed an excuse to exercise imperial power, just some elbowroom here on the Palatine.

The physician helped her to her feet, and together they shuffled toward the corridor. Yet when they reached the vestibule, she turned back toward Nepos as if something had occurred to her, something chilling.

"Give Quintus my love," the lord regent said warmly.

14

"WAIT HERE," Dathan said, slinging his *pilum* over his shoulder. "In my absence, do as Mara tells you."

Then with arms outspread for balance, he swashed heel-and-toe down the narrow channel of water atop the aqueduct. Undaunted by the plunging darkness on either side of him, and the boulders certainly heaped below, he hurried across the dry gorge to check the far side for sentries.

"Doesn't he ever tire?" Germanicus softly asked Mara.

She was resting her chin on her niter piece, which she'd propped atop her doubled legs. "No, my father has never known dissipation."

"Not even in his youth?"

"I have heard he was even more unbending then." She must have felt that she had let slip a criticism of her father, for she quickly added: "Moderation is as natural to him as flight is to birds. This now tells in his vigor. Did you realize he is within a year of his seventh decade?"

"Good Jupiter."

"May you eventually see that there is nothing good about Jupiter."

Smiling, Germanicus shook his head, letting one more barb against his paganism pass unchallenged. And the minute before, he might have objected to Dathan's brusque manner of addressing him; however, in the five days since they'd fled Ilium, the man's orders had invariably proved sound, inspired even. After the threesome had pushed their captured stallions hard all that first night, Dathan insisted at first light that they abandon them. "The auxiliaries will be hunting for two men and a woman—all on horseback," he said, slapping his mount on the rump to send it cantering free into the sea of sun-scorched grass. "If they see two men and a woman afoot, they will believe us to be people different from those they seek. Who would be so stupid as to rid themselves of good horseflesh in trying to cross Anatolia? Now do as I say, quickly. . . ."

Four hours later, his peculiar but typically Eastern reasoning had been borne out when a file of rust-red sand-galleys, elephantine old rattletraps fobbed off on the Imperial Anatolian Militia by the Twelfth Armored Legion Fulminata, stirred the gravel on the highway between Cyzicus and Pergamum—and continued rattling and chittering on toward the coast, the topside troops paying no attention to the three figures plodding along the featureless plain within *pili* range of the road.

"See how God rests upon my father's brow?" she had whispered with a fervor that might have become tiresome over the miles but for the brightness that came into her face when she said such things.

Southeast of Sardis, the edge of the plateau had been folded by natural forces—Mara called them *antediluvian*, meaning before the flood—into a series of sheer basalt ridges, and Dathan had soon quit the tracks of the populated canyons in favor of a game trail too precipitous for horses, perhaps even too ruggedly steep for donkeys. In all those miles of stumbling up and down over an endless rubble of sharp black stones, Mara followed her father without complaint. If she suffered from sore ankles, as Germanicus did in tight-lipped excruciation, she kept it to herself, her calm expression changeless. She stood up to the rigors of the Anatolian wilderness better than most men could—better than Germanicus, certainly, who could go on putting one blistered foot in front of the other only by numbing his mind with the insoluble paradoxes of Zeno of Elea: *Why are motion and multiplicity impossible by virtue of logic? And why are change, generation and destruction illusory, mere tricks of the gullible senses?* But eventually he could distract himself from his pain and weariness only by studying Mara. He found something engrossing about her features; while she hadn't been blessed by Venus with any categorical beauty, her face was undeniably arresting. Perhaps it was those unapologetically bold eyes in combination with her full and sensuous lips. He had begun to suspect that he might never tire of her singular looks, unlike some forms of comeliness that with familiarity cloy rather than please the eye.

Now, waiting for Dathan to return across the aqueduct, he couldn't make out the cast to Mara's face.

What did this strange woman think about in these quiet moments?

He stared intently, but her features remained obscured by shadow. Although the night was moonlit, a thunderhead had drifted overhead out of the south. Its misty depths were restive with flickering spindles, yellow and white; thunder rumbled again and again, but not in predictable keeping with the lightning.

The couple continued to sit on their heels atop one of the aqueduct's buttresses. He flicked pebbles over the edge, down into the gorge.

Backdropping the outline of her head and shoulders was a dim smudge of *electricus*—Aphrodisias, once a city important enough to have been granted local autonomy by the emperors of antiquity, but now only a teamsters' way station of wineshops and brothels on the back road to Lycia. This afternoon, Dathan had announced they would skirt it—too many brigands and opportunistic idlers about, Mara had explained when her father didn't.

"Have I permission to speak in your father's absence?" he asked her, sounding a bit more resentful than he'd intended.

"Of course." She turned her face toward him; enough light from Aphrodisias glanced around her cheek to return the usual glints to the cores of her dark eyes. "You are not used to such a man, are you?"

"I am used to a people who are civil in their dealings with others."

"Ah," she said, "it was *civility* then that drove the legionaries and their *Zedukim* allies to murder all they could lay their hands on at En-Gedi."

"When was this?"

"When I was a young child . . ." Her speech faltered. "Among the slaughtered was my mother." Then, abruptly, the hurt left her voice and she calmly asked, "What did you wish to say to me?"

He paused, recalling the term *Zedukim* to be a variation of Sadducee, Judaea's Greek-speaking class to whom the priests, noblemen, and rich traders belonged. He had never heard of a place called En-Gedi, but what legitimate quarrel could its Jewish inhabitants have possibly had with their own patricians, whom Rome regarded as both sensible and accommodating? He suspected that the people of En-Gedi had done something blatantly rebellious to warrant the involvement of the Judaean-based legions, otherwise it would have remained a Jewish matter to be handled by the temple police.

But first another question to be answered, he reminded himself: "I've come this far with you and your father only because of what you said that first night as we rode away from Ilium. . . ."

"What did I say?"

"Don't you recall?" You promised me an explanation as soon as we were safely away from Ilium. Have you forgotten?"

"Of course not."

"Do you intend to go back on your word?"

"No."

"Well, *are* we safely away?"

"Perhaps."

"Then explain how it is that my friend in Agri Dagi sent you two to help me. Explain why an Anatolian *zaim* would enlist two Jews to help a Roman pagan."

"This is not the time. My father returns."

Dathan came plashing back across the aqueduct.

"So he does," Germanicus muttered.

Handing his *pilum* to his daughter, the man knelt, straddled the conduit, and drank directly from the cool flow. "No watch has been posted this far out from the city," he said when he'd had his fill.

"Do you intend for us to march until dawn again?" Germanicus asked.

"Yes. Are you up to it?"

"Quite."

"No time for Roman pride. I am older than you, but much stronger. And you were malnourished and exhausted when we came upon you."

"I agree—this is not time for any kind of pride. But I'll make it." The northern limits of the sky were free of the huge cloud, and Germanicus consulted the constellations for a few moments. "May I ask a purely geographical question? One I have shown much forbearance by not asking previous to now?"

"If you will be brief."

"As late as yesterday, when we passed within sight of Nysa, it would have made sense to turn up the river if . . ." Germanicus deliberately paused.

"If it were our intention to proceed across the central plateau to Agri Dagi?" Dathan finished the thought for him, sounding vaguely amused.

"Exactly. But now we're too far south and would be confronted by both the Lycian and Taurus ranges—*if* the Purple Village is our destination."

"Well, it is not." And with that, Dathan rose. "Come and mind your step—the conduit is slippery."

"Wait," Mara said. "it is time we told him *something*."

"No."

"Ignorance of his destination only makes a man's feet heavier."

Dathan snapped at her in Hebrew, of which Germanicus understood nothing. But then, surprisingly, she flew back at him in Latin, apparently so Germanicus would be privy to their quarrel: "At least let me tell him why we were sent!"

"Keep your voice down." Dathan's silhouette was motionless for a while—except for the fingers of his right hand, which were slowly raking his beard. The he relented as much as his nature would probably let him. "The next time we stop. Not until then."

Somehow, Germanicus could sense that Mara was smiling in the darkness.

The thundercloud sailed north without shedding rain on the three figures, and suddenly the full moon reappeared, although much lower in the western sky than before. Its light leached the dun color out of the ascending echelons of hills, leaving them pale and ghostly looking.

At last, Dathan called a halt, but didn't join Mara and Germanicus in sitting on the rocky ground. "There is a pass through a defile not far ahead. It is often used by brigands as a place of ambush. Remain here while I have a look." Then he left them alone.

She was regarding the moon, her face lucent but by no means dreamy. "How well do you know the Great *Zaim* of Agri Day?"

"I was his prisoner once."

"Ah . . ." She sounded surprised. "What came of that?"

"He spared my life. And later, he sent his last surviving son to campaign with me against the Aztecae. I named him the first procurator of the new province of Mexicae, and . . ."

"And," she said when he didn't finish, "Prince Khalid was assassinated in Mexicae for being loyal to your imperium."

Germanicus nodded, his head hanging between his arms.

"Then you should realize from this alone why we are not headed for the Purple Village."

"But woman," he protested, "the *Zaim* knows I took nothing but grief from his son's death. It was the last thing I wanted. I loved Khalid as if he'd been my own son!"

"The *Zaim* understands this. But his people do not." She smiled humorlessly through the moonlight. "Do you have any idea the problem your overthrow has given all the headsmen of the Empire?"

"Suffice it to say I've been out of communication with the Empire lately."

"Please—no anger, Germanicus Julius. I do not mock you."

"Is that so?"

"Yes, I am only telling you how these chieftains are under great pressure from their own subjects, who truly believe the *Pax Romana* is finally collapsing. But how can these lords be sure the death of Rome is at hand? Will they only bring a bloodbath upon their people by challenging Antonius Nepos now? Can't you see the struggle within their own hearts? So everything is in turmoil for lords and subjects alike. Agri Dagi is no different than Syria or Judaea or even Britannia, I suppose . . . although I have never been any farther west than the Hellespontus." She hunched her shoulders helplessly, as if dissatisfied with her remarkably cogent explanation of the situation in the Empire. "How, in such a mad time, can the *Zaim* open his door to the last Caesar? To the very Roman that his son, the heir apparent, perished defending? You must trust him to be your friend of friends, for it amazes my father and me how he jeopardizes his own rule to save your life. Every ruler has those beneath him who are jealous of his power. Did not Caesar? Now can you appreciate what the *Zaim* does for you?"

He kept silent.

"But the reason I asked you, Germanicus Julius, how well you know him is this; If you are acquainted with him at all, you must realize the Great *Zaim* to be a man with a generous mind."

"Indeed, a surprising liberality," Germanicus spoke at last. "While I was at the Purple Village, he was attended by an aged mentor who prodded him with the most improbable question to fall from the lips of an Anatolian holy man: *Is it possible God desires a Roman rule over us?* Any other chieftain of the East would have put such a wagging tongue to rest."

"Or chieftain of the *West*." She laughed softly. "Yes, his beloved and revered *shaykh*. He was a ray of light among the dark souls of this world, truly."

"Is he still alive?"

"No, but the *Zaim's* openness to such questions is very much alive. And perhaps that is why he takes such risks for you. I do not understand everything he does."

"But—for a second time I ask—why would he dispatch two Jews to help a pagan? Are you and your father secretly of his faith?"

"No, although as Jews we are People of the Codex—and he holds us in his esteem for that."

While Germanicus understood that Jews and Anatolians shared certain myths and biographies of sun-addled mystics, he was also of the opinion that they were more often in conflict than in accord over these writings. "I still don't grasp the reason binding you two and the *Zaim* in my behalf."

"Then let me repeat his own words as they were relayed to us: *The future is an ocean we drink from tiny cups, and it is enough for this time, this mote in the everlasting wonderment, that one proud and compelling man glimpses the Oneness of the Compassionate, the Merciful.*"

Germanicus wrapped himself tighter in his cloak, although he had felt no chill. "Then he still believes that I have a place in the future of the Empire."

"No, Germanicus Julius—he believes you are the very means to the future God desires."

"Good Jupiter, I don't know about that."

"Neither do I. But I listen when the *Zaim* of Agri Dagi speaks. So do all my people."

"What of the Sadducees?"

"They are not my people."

"You speak of them as if they're your mortal enemies."

"Yes," she said, simply.

"Then you must tell me about your tribe and the things in which they believe."

"I will. But first you must satisfy my curiosity about something. . . ."

"Very well."

"Why did you come away with my father and me? Especially when you gathered we knew who you are?"

He shrugged. "I had nothing better to do."

She sniggered unaccountably. "Is that *it*?"

"Yes."

"No, Germanicus Julius. You went to Ilium to die, and we were your alternative to death."

He was about to chuckle off her unsettling insight, when his right foreleg began to burn. His hand darted to the fiery spot and brushed a crusty thing that was trying to scamper away. Angrily, he crushed it under his sandal. "Damn!"

"What is it?"

"Scorpion."

"No!"

Stiff-kneed, he hobbled to his height, only to bend over and squeeze the wound with his fingers. Even under this pressure, it refused to excrete much poison-laden fluid. "Damn the bloody Fates!"

Without any further hesitation, Mara brought her lips to his shin and began sucking.—

"Please, woman—I'm fine. It's the African species that puts a man over the Styx in quick order. A bit of pain and more to come, but I'm fine."

She spat. "No, you are not. Stand still."

"As soon as we get moving again, I can sweat out the poison."

She spat again. "That is not possible."

A few minutes later, Dathan returned. He took the news with no visible emotion, but said, "He will be sick soon. His leg will swell twice its size, and he will not be able to walk."

"I know." She withdrew from them several yards and appeared to squat behind a boulder.

"We cannot camp at this place," Dathan went on. "In the defile I found a fire ring. The ashes were warm. Brigands. They can be counted on to come back to their roost at dawn. We must go higher into the mountains before we can safely camp."

"Then go we must," Germanicus said with what he knew to be an insipid grin. His lower leg now felt as if it had been run through with a javelin. The skin had already been pulled glossy by swelling. He closed his eyes against the agonizing throbs, which were crisping up his nerves to a create a dull ache inside his skull.

Then Mara was kneeling beside him, clasping a warm, moist cloth to his shin.

"What's that, woman?"

"Urine. The ammonia in it will help."

He laughed breathlessly. "Trust the noble lady to be plain-spoken."

"Would Caesar have me call it perfume even though it is piss?" Now she was laughing too, an earthy laugh he found appealing.

Dathan grunted. "You two idly jest while the brigands steel up on us."

Using her waist sash, she firmly tied the makeshift poultice to Germanicus' leg. "We can go now."

"Are you sure?"

"Yes, Father—this is a man. He has only to *believe* and he will become a great man."

They set off at pace he realized to be double time for legionaries on the march. Still, when Dathan asked him how he was doing, Germanicus said through clenched teeth, "Pick it up a bit, please."

For the longest while he couldn't make sense of the sky into which he gazed glassy-eyed. It was drab like dusty linen and seemed to be held up by a latticework of black snakes twisting around the pale sun. Once, when the fires inside his head began raging again and promised to consume him while he lay gasping, defenseless against them, his late wife, Virgilia, appeared on the edge of his vision, vanished briefly, then leaned overhead to rub his brow, cheeks, and neck with tepid water.

"Where have you *been*, my little mouse?" he croaked.

"*I arose to open to my beloved, and my hands dripped with myrrh . . .*"

"With . . . with what?"

"*. . . my fingers dripped with liquid myrrh, upon the handles of the bolt. I opened to my beloved, but my beloved had turned and gone. . . .*"

"What are you saying, Virgilia?"

"*I sought him, but found him not; I called him, but he gave no answer. . . .*"

Germanicus groaned. "Oh, yes . . . I let you die alone. A revolt in Anatolia prevented me from easing your last days. And then a campaign in the Novo Provinces kept me from properly mourning you. And now cowardice keeps me from joining you. . . ." Her powder-blanched visage dissolved in a blear of tears and when his eyes had cleared again a swarthy woman was leaning over him, her expression inquisitive.

What heretofore he'd believed to be the sky was actually her linen shawl spread translucently over the branches of an ebony-barked shrub.

"Who is Virgilia?" Mara asked.

"My wife."

"Dead, yes?"

"Yes, two years now."

"God give her peace," Mara said.

"If at all possible." He paused. "Did I say her name?"

"Again and again."

"Any others?"

"What do you mean?"

"Any other female names?"

"No, only hers." She paused, and he could hear the breeze whistling through the branches. It felt cool in his sweaty hair. "Have you had many women, Germanicus Julius?"

"Why do you ask such a thing?"

"Well, my father says Roman men are known for their promiscuity."

He began to chuckle, but stopped when it hurt the crown of his head. "Time was when Roman men were distinguished by their fidelity to their wives. And I mean one wife to a Roman. This was the same era when, I have it on good authority, your own kings were notorious for their many wives and concubines. For their . . ." His head was suddenly drained of thought and filled again with the feverish ache. "Oh, bloody hades . . ."

"Sleep," Mara said low. "Dream . . . you seem to be open now to dreams."

"Please remain by my side." He smiled thinly. "I fear I need a human voice to keep calling me back . . . lest I take Charon up on his infernal offer . . . and be ferried across . . . the Styx . . . before I know . . ."

"*How lonely sits the city that was full of people,*" he murmured, his right leg suddenly agonized by cold. Then his eyes snapped open, and he cried out, "Who dares—!"

He found himself blinking at Mara.

"My father went higher into the mountains," she said. "He found some snow in the shadows."

He lifted his monstrously heavy head and winced in the direction of his leg. It was packed in snow, which was rapidly melting.

"Are you up to answering something?"

He nodded, but continued to grimace.

"How does a Roman know the lamentations of our Jeremiah?"

"I don't understand what you're talking about."

"You just spoke the first line of this holy *codex*."

"I still don't know—"

She curved her palm against his cheek, checking for fever, then scooped up a handful of snow and applied it to his forehead. "Never mind. Your dreams are God-inspired, then. You must trust that this is so. What did you see?"

"Jerusalem being put to the torch. Soldiers—"

"Yes, it is written how General Nebuzaradan marched west and plundered the first temple of its riches, burned the city and carried off its people to—"

"No, I didn't see Babylonian troops."

"Whose then?"

"I saw *Roman* legionaries flinging torches into the Temple of Herod, the second edifice you Jews raised to your nameless God."

"But such a disaster never befell us. . . ." Then her eyes grew alarmed as if she'd realized his words to be an omen. "Tell me more, Germanicus Julius. Tell me everything."

"It was all so puzzling, all so—"

"Why were the legionaries doing this dreadful thing to a city that has never resisted them?"

"I have no idea. But like an eagle soaring above the siege, I saw the imperial forces circumventing Jerusalem. At least four Italian legions and their Syrian auxiliaries encamping under the mild sun of late spring. I saw this clearly."

"But there have been no Syrian soldiers in Judaea for nearly two thousand years!" She looked frantic with worry; he didn't understand why.

"I know. But I saw Syrians being slaughtered like sheep as they tried to storm the north wall. The legionaries stepped in only when the Jewish defenders were close to exhaustion. At great cost to themselves, they breached the wall and poured into the city."

"What do you mean—*at great cost*? What match are Jews with rusty *pili* to sand-galleys?"

"Oh, no. Didn't I mention this before? These legions were uniformed and equipped as in the reign of Flavius Vespasianus. The men fought with ancient weapons in the classical manner."

She sighed as if she'd been cheated of some urgent significance. "This makes no sense to me, then. What does your dream bode?"

"I have no idea. Perhaps it was just that—a *dream*."

"Never," she said obstinately. "How then could you recite the lamentations of Jeremiah?" When he gave no answer, she asked:

"Did it give you pleasure to witness this second destruction of Jerusalem?"

"No, the sight of a beautiful city dying has never pleased me. The majesty of the world is her cities." He thought she had come close to smiling as he said this.

"Jerusalem is the loveliest of cities."

He rose on his elbows. "At what lovely place do I find myself now?"

"Don't you recall arriving here?"

"No."

"But you spoke to us. You seemed in control of yourself."

"Those last hours were like walking through a fire."

She pressed more snow against his brow. "We are up on the crest of the mountains that lie between Aphrodisias and Comama."

"Oh, yes."

"Are you familiar with this country?"

"Somewhat. I chased a brigand or two up and down these ranges during my Anatolian service. Water, please."

She uncorked the neck of the waterskin and brought it to his lips. "My father keeps watch on the ridge above. So far, he has seen no one. We are miles distant from any road."

He held the liquid coolness in his mouth for a few moments, then swallowed, sorely. "How many days have I delayed you?"

"Three. But it is of no matter. It is safe here. We will stay until you are well again. As soon as we reach Attaleia, we will be helped by Perushim exiles, merchants mostly. The going will be easier from then on. These brothers and sisters will pass us from Attaleia to Traianopolis to Tarsus to Antiochia. They have lorries they use in their trades, so our walking is almost done. I am forbidden to tell you our final destination yet, but I can say that after Attaleia we will be there in but a few days."

"Good." Exhausted by only a few minutes of sitting halfway up, he eased down again. "Are you *Perushim*, as you say?"

"Yes."

"What does the word mean?"

"*To be apart.*"

He shook his head.

"Perhaps you have heard of us by our other name—the Pharisees?"

"Oh, yes. But I was under the impression there are but a few score of your sect scattered around the eastern empire."

"More score than the *Zedukim* care to admit." She whipped her face to the side and spat. Her eyes had turned venomous.

"Isn't the Great Temple in Jerusalem administered by the Sadducees?"

"Yes."

"Then why should it upset you in my dream that we Romans destroy the temple?"

"It is sacred to one and all. Even to the vile *Zedukim*."

"What has created such enmity between you two branches of Jews? Are you not of the same stalk?"

Ineffably, she smiled, then said, "Your lids are drooping midway down your eyes, Germanicus Julius. Rest, and later I will explain how the Perushim have suffered at the hands of Greek-speaking *Zedukim*."

He awoke in darkness, thinking that the whir was the breeze flowing through the shrub Mara had canopied for him with her shawl. But then he realized that the sound was a stream of soft words issuing from the woman's lips, which he saw moving in silhouette. It was an incantation of some sort, one she obviously held to be sacred. Each line was spoken in Hebrew and then translated into Latin for his benefit: ". . . *the Zedukim were quick to don the mantle of the Antiochene invaders, to utter Greek even in the temple and to contemplate God in the manner of the Hellenes, who worship their gods no differently than they do their earthly kings. And so it was at the festival of Sukkot that the holy rage of the Perushim boiled over and they pelted the high priest with citrons until his vestments dripped with the stinging juice. The temple police were summoned, but they were not sufficient to silence the scribe Eshek, who cried above the tumult: 'How can we agree—as the chief priest demands—that the Master of the Universe gave Mosheh only a written law for us to obey—and not an oral law as well? How can we sacrifice to the Lord with hands smirched by the plunder of our neighbors, hands bloodied by wars of conquest? Does He who lights our way lead us in such outrages? How then can we deny the resurrection of the dead and the coming of the Anointed Prince who will deliver us from the Hellenes, the One who will make us a light of the nations!' And the temple police answered by slaying him and many of the Perushim who followed him. Those not cut down at Sukkot-tide fled over the mountains to the steepest shore of the Sea of Salt, to dwell among*

the Hasidim for generations and take up all their ways but one.
For unlike their brothers the Hasidim, the Perushim took up the
sword to restore piety to Israel and the world beyond. . . ."

Just when he thought she was finished speaking, she drew so
close to his ear he could feel the warmth of her breath: "You must
not stray into fancy, Germanicus Julius. I will never be your wife.
Nor can I become your lover, for we Perushim lie only with our
spouses and then only as often as needed to beget children."

Then she brushed his lips with hers before rising. Her retreating
footfalls crunched over the hard ground.

At first he felt offended by her words and confused by her kiss.
But then he admitted to himself that he had been straying into such
a fancy over the long march. The kiss had pardoned his thoughts;
perhaps it had been a reminder as well that a man who wants a
woman, even in the privacy of himself, also wants to live.

Although it was yet night, Germanicus saw that the figure
before him was swathed in light—a luminosity seemingly of its
own inner origin. The radiance of its countenance forced him to
lower his gaze, although he had glimpsed enough of its molten
features to connect the bent nose and splayed teeth with the least
flattering statue on the Palatine, that of the deified Augustus,
commissioned by his stepson Tiberius.

Suddenly, the figure began to fade, and Germanicus cried,
"No! Please! Don't leave me!"

Augustus turned back. It was true what had been reported of
him: He had an engaging smile. But he said nothing.

Germanicus beseeched him with a hand. "Where did I err?"

Augustus gave a shrug.

"Please—you alone of our long and fallible lineage knew how
to juggle all the contradictions of this most wretched obligation—
and keep them *in motion*. And I—in all my wit and prudence—
I've simply ushered in a golden age for profligates, brigands, and
pirates. How'd this happen? And in the blink of my eye, too?
What did I do wrong?"

Again Augustus smiled and spoke at last. But, puzzlingly, he
sounded like Dathan: "You demolished one vision of the world
without replacing it with another. You insisted on actualizing the
Republic when most men were content to pretend it existed and
then go on with their little lives. So now you're committed, truly."

"Committed to what?"

"Why—to restoring your republic."

"But how!"

"You must come up with another vision, one that will capture the universal imagination—even if you yourself don't believe in that vision. Isn't that precisely what I did so long ago?"

"But—!" Germanicus fell silent.

It was first light, although the sun had wrapped itself in luminous clouds.

Dathan was standing with this chimera to his back, hands on his hips. "It is time to rise. I think you should try to walk some today."

15

Rolf DESCENDED INTO his late cousin's hut.

Following him at a short distance were two of his most trusted thanes, Marcomans and former legionaries like himself, men with sober eyes and hands ready upon the hilts of their swords. At his nod, they positioned themselves midway down the steps cut into the dank earth. There they remained, hidden from sight of the smoky living chamber but within earshot of all that would transpire between their *herzog* and Segestias' widow.

At the instrusion of footfalls, Glaesea eyes flickered up from the hearth. They were more golden than amber because of the firelight, and so moist that Rolf was tempted to put aside the reason behind his call. But that was not possible.

"*Rolf*," she said like someone who has been alone in a dark hut far too long. Then she remembered herself and serenely dipped her face. When she looked back up, her eyes were opaque. "You honor me with your presence, my *Herzog*."

"Aye . . ." Uncertain what to say, he carefully leaned his javelin against the log wall, readjusting its set twice, although there was little chance of it falling over.

"Will you have a horn of *met* and—?" She caught herself, and uncertainty made her suddenly curl her braid around her fist. On pain of execution by the king's own hand, no German warrior could now drink *met*, but the habits of hospitality were hard to break. "Will you have something to eat?"

"Nay, I be full of horseflesh. Every pot in every hut be bubbling with such stew."

"Indeed," she said with forced brightness, "the raid on Dibio has cheered everyone. Two thousand horses and that many panniers loaded with barley!"

"Nineteen hundred." He sat on a stool and twisted his hands together as if he didn't know what to do with them. His fingers itched to begin fidgeting with one of his mustaches, but long ago she had accused him of preening his first growth of facial hair, and that distant criticism still stung. "It be less two thousand Gaul mounts by a hundred. But they be fatted on summer grass. And this be enough meat to see us through winter. Maybe. If we take that many deer before they be migrating out of the Wald . . ."

"Does the war go well?"

He could see it in her smile—a growing sense of anticipation. Quickly now, he had to explain his purpose in coming, but he couldn't find the words, and plebeian Latin was not the tongue with which to express the Gothic sentiments that weighed on his heart. "This war, it just go and go . . ."

"What do you mean?"

He scratched his neck. "We be helpless to win."

"To win back our country then?"

"Aye. But the Romans be helpless to win too."

"Some say the Sixth Legion is crumbling like a rotten log."

"Who say this?" he demanded. How he hated rumors!

"I don't know. Just some talk in the village."

"Well, such talk be mad. The Sixth Victrix not be happy fighting us, but the lads do as ordered," he said with an echo of the old pride in his voice. Then, suddenly, his dark blue pupils shifted back and forth with confusion, and he realized that this mild boast was not in keeping with his present loyalties. Why did his Roman past refuse to let him go? Was it the buzzing that constantly sifted through the defensive perimeter he had set up around the Wald—that Germanicus had not been drowned in Corinthus, that he was hiding in Thrace, or Sarmatia, or was it Abyssinia this week? He tried to shrug off the troubled feelings this kind of speculation gave him. He was now too deep into the Gothic Revival to ever go back to the life of a legionary, and it was best not to dwell on his years in a wine-colored cape.

He caught Glaesea watching him.

She dropped her stare to her wind-chapped hands, which she had folded in her lap as if to conceal them from his view. Her hands were no longer young-looking, although he believed her face to be unchanged from the first day he had looked upon her with an inner gnawing he grudgingly realized to be love.

It was time, he decided. It would never be easy, and now was as good a moment as any.

He said her name to make her look directly at him, then: "I do miss my cousin."

She slowly exhaled as if suddenly she were very tired. "I too, Rolf."

"Segestias dead—because of me."

"Oh no, you must not think so—"

"Dead," he repeated adamantly, "because of me. My Roman stubbornness that night. So, I come this one last time to your hut and never again."

Her eyes began to glisten. "But *why*?" Her tone had been so strident with pleading, she immediately tried to salvage her dignity by saying, "You know you are always welcome here."

"Aye, and that welcome give me great joy. But I be of no heart to profit from Segestias' death."

"What profit, my *Herzog*?"

His chin sagged down against his chest. He knew his honor would never let him answer, that to form the words was to unleash the offense, to tempt the weakness within him.

She began to reach out for him, stopped, restrained herself by wrapping her arms about herself, then held out her hands to him again.

From that moment on, he could not trust himself to look at her.

He came to his feet and grasped his javelin. "Be of an open mind to other suitors, Glaesea."

"And you?" She had begun to weep. "Will you take another?"

He halted at the foot of the steps and said without turning, "Nay."

Then he rushed up the earthen flight, past his silent *thegans* and into the failing light of evening.

So this is it, Germanicus thought as he peered up at the monolith slowly taking shape in dawn's twilight, *this parched and vaulting spur of the mountains to the west of Lake Asphaltitis, or the Sea of Salt as Mara of the Long Gait insists on calling it.* This was the secret destination, the reason he had been led on foot across western Anatolia and then trundled from lorry to lorry—on whose jolting cedar beds he'd either been buried under a blanket of grain with only a hollow reed to breathe through, or jammed among piled bolts of tent canvas to sweat away a tenth of his weight—all the wearisome, sunbaked distance from Cilicia to the north shore of Lake Tiberias, not his favorite region of the Empire even under the best of circumstances. A Galilean fisherman, another clandestine Pharisee, had then boated the threesome across the lake to the village of Philoteria, which they hiked through in haste because it was "Greek-speaking." They headed south along a maze of trails stitching the dense undergrowth beside the River Jordan. This ribbon of vegetation, a cool and leafy corridor of dappled light, split an otherwise barren desert plain and concealed their progress all the way down to the swampy outlet of the river into Lake Asphaltitis.

Germanicus had expected the Perushim refuge to be in the vicinity of En-Gedi, where Mara claimed her mother had been slain by legionaries acting in concert with the *Zedukim*. However, in a desolate silence, unwilling or unable to look to either side of him at the fire-blackened building stones heaped everywhere, Dathan led them through the scorched ruin of En-Gedi, which stank of the sulfur rising off the hot springs there. Nor did he speak as they trudged another ten miles down the western shore of his Sea of Salt, through the sultry night, with the pebbles beneath Germanicus' sandals giving off such intense heat he could almost believe them to be embers.

What was this thankless country like at high noon? So far, by keeping to the shade of the Jordan's willowy banks and then traveling at night once beyond the river, they had escaped the brunt of Helios' dazzling fire. He had almost forgotten that such ferocious badlands existed, lands in which a legionary could be blistered by the heat of his own metal armor, or could suddenly die without any human enemy drawing a drop of his blood.

Finally, Dathan called a halt in the middle of nowhere, a wadi exactly like a hundred others they had slogged past without giving a second glance. Explaining nothing, as was his contemptible habit, he yawned widely, stretched, then sprawled atop an alkali dune and slept.

"Are we waiting for someone?" Germanicus eventually had to ask, realizing that Mara was about to volunteer nothing.

"No," she whispered, "only for first light."

"Why?"

"The trail up is steep and narrow."

"The trail up where?"

"You will see."

He began massaging the flesh around the scorpion bite, it was still sore. "I imagined your abode to be at En-Gedi or there-abouts."

"No. Long ago my people lived in peace at Mesad Hasidim, or Qumran as you Greeks and Romans call it. . . ."

He wondered what his Achaean physician, Epizelus, would think of Greeks and Romans being described as a single entity. The very suggestion would be enough to turn the man's stomach.

"But at Mesad Hasidim," she went on, "we were burned out by the pagans of Moab. Our forefathers led the people south to the oasis at En-Gedi, where we were safe from the raids of these Baal-worshipers. There we remained in peace for many generations. Safe until my lifetime, when the temple police and the legionaries came by darkness along the Hebron road and . . ." She could not finish. "My father took those of us who survived to a higher, safer place."

"Does this place have a name? Or, like your god, is it nameless?"

"Our Lord is not nameless. Why do you Romans persist in this misbelief? Every Roman I meet asks why it is our God is anonymous. It is simply that his name is too magnificent and holy to utter in our day-to-day lives, or in the presence of strangers."

With a flick of his beard Germanicus took in the starry night, the oily looking surface of the Sea of Salt, Mara's father laid out like a corpse across the sand. "This is hardly what I'd called day-to-day living. Nor would I consider us to be strangers, not after what we've been through together these past weeks. Won't you share that most thunderous name with me?"

"No."

Even in the faint starshine, he could tell she was smiling. "Then obviously you don't trust me."

"It is has nothing to do with trust. It is an affair of respect. And you are not a God-respecter."

"And what, may I ask, is a God-respecter? As a Roman, I quite naturally respect everyone's gods, even yours."

"Cleverly put, Germanicus Julius."

Once again he found himself captivated by her earthy laughter. What a peculiar ability she had—to discuss celestial matters with a worldly timbre to her voice as if she and her shy god had no secrets between them, and she felt no need to put on her best face when communicating with him.

"But you, like all Romans, are hopelessly confused."

"I've been told that by half of mankind, so how can I take offense from you?"

"True." She paused. "The only way I can explain is to show you a God-respecter, but you will have to be patient. However, I will tell you the name of this place. It is called Masada."

He had never heard of it and, on that basis, believed nothing noteworthy had happened here.

But Mara had then explained how, during the reign of Caesar Augustus, his vassal king of Judaea, Herod the Great, "a detestable Edomite"—she spat derisively—had fortified the rock that loomed in silhouette behind her. Herod had wanted a stronghold to which he could retreat in times of trouble, and so his artisans and laborers had hewed and erected a small but complete city atop the monolith. After Herod's death, the Romans had taken over the two lofty palaces, its storehouses, heated baths, and cisterns, and converted them into a garrison to defend the southern trade route to Petra. When the fabled "rose city" of the Nabataeans eventually declined in importance to Roman commercial interests, the garrison was abandoned. It remained unoccupied for a millennium and a half—until Dathan staggered here from En-Gedi with his half-starved band of Perushim, of whom Germanicus still knew precious little. When once again he had asked Mara to explain more about the beliefs and customs of her sect, she had said only that he would know everything soon enough.

"And when, woman, is *soon enough*?"

"If you must ask, then rest assured it has not yet arrived."

Now, with the rock citadel of Masada gradually pinking in the sunrise to his back, he heard Dathan snort. The man sat up, took stock of his surroundings—which appeared to please him—and said, "Let us go up. We can see our way now."

Germanicus found the serpentine footpath to the summit dangerously narrow. In some places there was scarcely the width on which to securely rest his sandal. What had looked from the salt-encrusted shore of Lake Asphaltitis to be a twenty-minute walk turned into an hour's climb, and all the while he was made uncomfortable by the sensation that he was locked in the dovetailed sights of someone's niter piece. Someone unseen. Someone with Mara's barely restrained loathing for Romans.

"Stay where you stand until I order otherwise," Dathan said, then gingerly negotiated his way up the zigzag directly above Germanicus and Mara. The reason for his sudden caution was revealed when his sandal dislodged a boulder the size of a man's skull, which skipped down the slope so near Germanicus he had to drop back on one knee in order to avoid injury.

Dathan frowned down at him. "You moved."

"Damnation I did!"

Shrugging, the Jew began picking his way up the bare suggestion of a trail again.

Germanicus let him get ahead some distance, even though to his back Mara was showing her impatience by shifting her weight from foot to foot. "Is it me, woman—or my race?"

"Don't fall behind." She gave him a gentle nudge between the shoulder blades. "And it's probably your race."

"Thank Jupiter. I was beginning to think your father disliked me personally."

"That too, perhaps." She chuckled.

Lake Asphaltitis seemed more expansive with each climbing step, although its north shore, where the Jordan joined its fresh waters to the brackish lake, was still lost in morning haze. It seemed a shame that every last drop of the river was not siphoned off for irrigation long before it could flow into the Sea of Salt, and Germanicus tried to keep his mind off the heat and exertion by applying the principles of Roman engineering to the challenge of damming the Jordan. The river flowed down a deep rift valley, and certainly at some point along its length a simple dam could be constructed. The Prosperina reservoir at Emerita Augusta in Iberia immediately came to mind as a model; such a project would require teeming manpower more than expertise, and the eastern provinces were certainly stronger in the former than in the latter. But then he reminded himself that this, after all, was Judaea and no project was easily accomplished, even a simple one. Titus, in order to keep the Jews from revolting had given their supreme council in Jerusalem, the Sanhedrin, plenary authority over most civil affairs. And in comparison, the Sanhedrin made the Roman Senate seem like the last bastion of reason and selflessness on earth. So, by the time the pompous, white-bearded Sadducees could be counted on to finally arrive at a consensus about such a massive irrigation project, the Jordan would probably have run dry.

"We lag behind my father," Mara said, not sounding winded in the least. "Please pick up your feet."

"If I pick them up any more than I am, you'll be picking my remains off the rocks at the base of this cliff."

"You exaggerate."

He cast a hard eye over his shoulder. "Do I now?"

"Indeed—such a soft body as yours wouldn't bounce all the way to the bottom."

He faced forward again so she wouldn't see his smile. Her company cheered him, and he hadn't been affected this way by a woman in a long time.

Then, without warning, a circle of earth beside the trail sprang back as if on hinges and a youth bolted upright out of the ground, brandishing a model of *pilum* Germanicus recognized as dating from his days as a teenager tribune.

"Good, Hanoch, good," Dathan said in Latin. "You're learning to use your imagination."

The Perushim sentry had been concealing himself in a pit covered by a wicker plate to which he'd somehow fastened gravel of hues that blended perfectly with the surrounding slope. Lean to the point of stringiness, tanned by the desert sun, he looked well-inured to life on this windswept outcropping.

"Dathan!" he exulted, then launched into an Aramaic greeting so reverent in tone, Germanicus suspected Mara's father to be some kind of royal personage to these people. Quietly, he asked, "Is your father king, then?"

For once, she didn't laugh at one of his gaffes. "We have no king but God."

The youth nodded attentively as Dathan explained something to him.

Germanicus knew, solely by rote, only a handful of Aramaic phrases, all of them related to urging some Aramaic-speaking recalcitrant to surrender on threat of being riddled with legionary *pili* shot.

"*Eques* Gutta," the youth said in stilted Latin, with Dathan smirking at his side, "I welcome thee to Masada. Mine and thine belong to thee."

"Thank you," Germanicus muttered, then began inching up the trail again at Dathan's terse beckon.

"And why," he asked Mara when they had gone on several yards, "do I require an assumed name here?"

"My father must prepare the people before telling them who you truly are. He told the guard you are a Roman knight who is on the path to becoming a God-respecter—and that you should be afforded every courtesy while you stay among us."

"Then why *that* name?"

"Don't you like it?"

"Oh, I'm absolutely taken with it. What knight wouldn't be?" *Gutta* was the Latin word for spot or speck.

At last, the trail wound up to a crude parapet of stacked stones. It was breached by a timber gate, which swung open for the threesome as if pulled by a spirit. They stepped out onto what could have passed for a parade ground if not for an ankle-deep detritus of broken crockery and dressed stone chips—remnants, no doubt, of the Roman occupation. Apparently, martial tidiness did not obsess the Perushim.

To the north across Masada's sloping tableland was a tumbledown complex, really just a roofless thicket of Corinthian columns.

Mara must have read the question in his eyes, for she said, "Herod's north palace." She slowly wheeled and pointed to a mound of rubble opposite the gate: "And the west palace."

"It served as the Roman garrison," Dathan said. "When the last legionary had gone, the local tribes tore it down with their bare hands." He had kinked his fingers into claws to make sure his point was not lost on Germanicus.

Ignoring one more vituperation against imperial authority, he surveyed the rest of the structures dotting the crown of the great rock. None looked in adequate repair to keep out the elements. "Don't tell me you house yourselves in any of these hovels?"

Dathan motioned for Mara to explain—as if it were beneath his dignity to play the guide.

"We live in caves cut into the banks of the north terraces."

"What's wrong with improving some of these buildings?"

"Improvements would draw attention to us. Make us appear more numerous and prosperous than we are. We are not strong enough yet to resist a siege by the *Zedukim*."

All at once, that trilled and hair-raising salutation of the desert peoples of the East was echoing among the ruins. Mara answered with her own shrill warble, and white-clad figures began racing out of hiding toward Dathan. His Perushim subjects were soon thronging him, dancing joyfully around his person as if he were a shrine.

"To what do you credit this adoration? Your father's lineage?"

"No, our leader is chosen by a general vote."

"For a life tenure?"

"No, just until the next vote," she said.

"And when does that come?"

"When it comes."

Sighing, Germanicus gave up.

His name was Shammai, and his chest was so widely muscled he walked with his massive arms splayed. He grunted in *pleb* Latin something to the effect that he'd once been with the finest gladiatorial "families" in Judaea and had killed fifty-three men in the arena at Caesarea, thirty-nine at Antiochia, and one at Ephesus. He would have had slain more at Ephesus, except that after the first brief but bloody combat no one else had been willing to take him on—or so he said.

"What name did you fight under?" Germanicus asked. "I recall no fighter named Shammai."

The man held his tongue as they emerged from the large cave in which the entire population of the settlement—Germanicus estimated the Perushim here to number more than a hundred—had taken the noon meal communally and in a silence violated only by the champing of teeth and an occasional belch.

"I have forgotten that Latin name," Shammai said at last. "Just as I have forgotten everything else you Romans gave me."

"Then, have you renounced killing?" Germanicus asked.

"Nay, just killing for sport."

"Good, that explains the Roman *pilum* you have strapped across your back." The sunlight that met them beyond the cave portal was blinding, and Germanicus begged a halt until his eyes could adjust to the glare. "Mara tells me there was a time when you Perushim refused to slay your fellow man under any circumstances."

"Aye, when we lived among the Hasidim after fleeing Jerusalem. But that was more their way than ours. Like not shitting on the Sabbath, it was a custom that did not suit us."

"What became of them?"

"Dead. The last one dead a thousand years now."

"How long after parting company with the Hasidim did you Perushim persist in this reverence for human life?"

"I do not know. A while." Then Shammai summed up with flawless common sense: "But those were days when there was many more Perushim. This country was thick with our holy men, three of them sitting cross-legged beneath each bush."

This sparked a sudden question: "Have you heard of a Pharisaic teacher named Joshua Bar Joseph?"

"The ancient *rabban*, you mean?"

"Yes, the fellow the procurator Pilate freed."

"I know nothing of this Pilate."

"But what do you know of Joshua?" Germanicus asked, growing impatient.

"This and that. Not much. I am no scholar like Dathan."

"Did Joshua live among you?"

"I think so. . . ." Shammai tugged at his lower lip with his calloused fingers for a moment. "Yes, I remember something like that. But I believe he was already hiding among the Hasidim when all us Perushim came from the city to the Sea of Salt. He was an old man by then. Sixty or seventy. And when your mad dog Titus Flavius threatened to burn the temple, all were willing to take up the sword to defend the Holy of Holies—all except Joshua Bar Joseph. He talked of peace even though the temple itself was threatened, and this made him many enemies. Titus backed off, and a treaty was made. Still, Joshua was ridiculed, forced out of Mesad Hasidim. He went north, far away north."

"To the Purple Village in Agri Dagi?"

"I do not know, Gutta." Shammai frowned as if all the talk had put him in a sour mood. "I have told you as much as I know. Why must Romans ask so many questions? And then ignore the answers?" Suddenly, he drew close to Germanicus and sniffed, only to steeple his beefy shoulders in confusion. "Are you sure you need a bath?"

"Absolutely."

"As you wish. But your own sweat will cleanse you well enough."

"I will test your theory some other time."

Again, Dathan's formidable adjutant shrugged. He seemed to be a man whose delight increases proportionate to the temperature. He probably shivered on days a less acclimated man would find withering. It was amazing to behold this paragon of flush health in a clime fit only for the mummification of human tissue.

They skirted the debris of the west palace and continued on toward the southern tip of the monolith.

When, at the conclusion of the somber meal, Dathan had mentioned the existence of a bathing pool near what he called the south stronghold, Germanicus had leaped at the chance to refresh himself, although it had briefly concerned him how much water the Perushim might have to spare for bathing. Mara reassured him that Herod, in keeping with his affection for Roman ingenuity, had commissioned imperial hydrological *machinators* to collect the rainwater that fell on Masada and siphon up all the subterranean flows in the area into twelve capacious cisterns. Amazingly, water was the one thing Masada did not lack.

"Now you tell me something, Gutta," Shammai asked, clapping his hands to shoo some small children out of their path, "What interests you in our God?"

Germanicus was taken aback by the question for a moment, but then said, "Perhaps because, like me, he finds himself alone."

"Where is your family?"

"All dead . . . except for my adopted son."

"And where is he? In Jerusalem now?"

"In Rome."

"Why have you come without him? Usually, God-respecters bring their families with them."

"Well, I couldn't bring the boy at this time. The adoption is being contested in the courts."

"Ah." Shammai nodded knowingly. "Roman magistrates. One of them condemned me to the life of the arena. They are all the same. Even the highest magistrate of the lot."

"You mean the Emperor?"

"Who else? He condemns the entire world to the life of the arena, doesn't he? He makes brother fight brother, doesn't he?"

"Who are you talking about? Germanicus or this pretender, Nepos?"

"They are all the same. All pretenders in the eyes of the Lord God."

"I see," Germanicus said, thankful they had arrived at the small pool. He dropped his filthy cloak onto the tiles of a sun-faded mosaic and waded in. The water was tepid and greenish, but still he found it pleasant.

Shammai took his leave by grumbling something in Aramaic that might have been a parting blessing, and Germanicus began floating on his back with his arms outstretched. He peered up into the cloudless blue, which was white with heat around the horizons.

He found it difficult to believe that only a few weeks ago he had welcomed death. Although his prospects at present were far from promising, he no longer wanted to die; and, while he entertained no hope of ever returning to power, he began thinking of some way to steal Quintus away to this desert aerie. What a tonic the child would be to him here! While this existence was inferior to the life of a young patrician in the most stimulating city in the world, it was to be preferred for the boy over a lascivious adolescence under the tutelage of Antonius Nepos and Claudia Nero. He hated to think what effect this unwholesome pair was having on Quintus' habits and outlook. No, perhaps coming of age among the pious and hardy Perushim would prove to be a most excellent preparation for a future leader of republican Rome.

"*Republican Rome* . . . " He chuckled sadly at the notion; the dream of a lifetime was hard to kill.

"What of it?" a voice said from the far side of the pool.

Startled, Germanicus stroked roundabout and beheld Dathan, who was sitting with his feet in the water.

"What of what?"

"Your republic."

"It's gone, I suppose. Stillborn." Germanicus swam to Dathan and hunched his arms over the tiled edge. After only a few moments the sun felt so hot on his shoulders he began cupping water over them.

"What would this republic have been like?"

Germanicus hesitated. It seemed strange and uncomfortable to openly discuss the very thing he had concealed within himself for years. "Do you really want to know?"

"Yes."

"Well, do you understand what the principate is?"

"Of course. A fancy name for the tyranny of the Emperor."

"I quite agree. And it would have been dismantled over a specified period of time, with all authority eventually invested in the Senate."

"With the principate gone, what would this first citizen of the state have done with himself?"

"Probably exactly what I'm doing right now—soaked away his aches in some desert pool."

Dathan smiled—an appealing smile if only for its rarity. "I will never understand the Roman penchant for bathing. Are you compelled thusly because your thoughts are so foul?"

"Oh, to lump together all Romans is like throwing together Perushim and *Zedukim*. A stoical and right-thinking Roman, of which I'm a poor example, bathes in the expectation his body will become as clean as his mind."

Dathan nodded, but looked preoccupied.

"What do you want from me?" Germanicus asked abruptly.

"I do not know yet."

"Then why all the trouble to bring me here?"

"I trust the *Zaim* of Agri Dagi." Then Dathan shook his head as if correcting himself: "I *almost* trust him. He is like a good horse broker, that cunning and holy man. Whenever he arranges a deal, both sides are satisfied. But neither side is as satisfied as he secretly is. I think this is one of those arrangements." Sullenly, he looked around Masada, then out across Lake Asphaltitis. "All I know is—we cannot continue to hang on to this rock by our fingernails. We must bring some changes to Judaea and quickly too."

"And I figure in these changes?"

"I pray so. Mara believes so."

"Then where do we begin? I am finished with running."

Again, Dathan smiled. "I suppose I must acquaint you with our options here, then see what you are willing to do to help us."

"How could I possibly help you?"

"Unless those scars on your flesh lie, you have had quite a life as a soldier. The Great *Zaim* says you are the most fearsome general in the Empire. As to me, I know how to lead raids. At this sort of fighting, I am the best in all the East. But I know nothing about telling large numbers of troops what to do."

"And where are we to find these large numbers of troops? You have fewer than forty fighting men."

"After a few days, when you are rested, I will show you."

"One night's sleep and I will be ready to go."

Dathan examined the Roman's eyes for a long moment, then said, "Very well. Tomorrow then. And please do not complete your bath by shaving. If you are recognized on our brief journey, we will die." He rose and shoved his glistening feet back into their sandals. "We will probably die anyway, but do not scrape off your whiskers—even though Mara is curious to see what you look like beardless."

After more than two thousand Roman miles had slipped past in a drowsy summer trance since leaving Germanicus at Ilium, Tora stopped counting them and began marking the distance in another way—the fading accuracy with which the Roman Empire was perceived by the people he met along his route, the Silk Road, which the mutual suspicion of two great empires had kept an indistinct and ever-shifting trace across the arid backside of the world.

The garrulous Bithynian sailors who had conveyed him across the Pontus Euxinus to the principality of Colchis repeated all the latest rumors about Antonius Nepos, Claudia Nero, and the "most likely rotting" Germanicus Agricola. But the taciturn muleteers who conducted him over the towering Caucasus Mountains seemed remarkably unaware of the turmoil in the empire on which they bordered, and one of them spoke for the first time in two days to ask: "Who be this Antun Neppo you revile?" To avoid any Roman agents in Parthia, Tora crossed the Hyrcanian Sea on a barge loaded to the gunwales with tin ore, and when he landed on that citiless shore claimed by no country, he no longer heard the word *Rome* in any variation. A week farther to the east, a holy man, who claimed to be the most widely traveled member of his impoverished tribe, admitted that he had never heard of Rome, but he was familiar with "the Empire of the Eagle," having met a ten-foot-tall stranger from that land. The caravanners Tora joined soon after were aware of the "Men of the Eagle" but had never heard of an empire by that name. However, these squat, sepia-complected men with slightly tapered eyes had been well-briefed about the latest happenings in the Serican Empire. They had even referred to it by its proper name: the Xing Dynasty.

At that moment, while lurching atop a musty-breathed camel with his and the beast's combined shadows stretching out across the late afternoon sands, Tora realized that he had turned the corner of the world.

And now on a breathlessly hot morning, departing on the back of a pony from the sprawling and fly-ridden mud city on the Xing frontier, he smiled at what the women of the shining black braids and joined eyebrows had told him: They had never heard of the Men of the Eagle, but they knew of beasts half-eagle and half-human who resided in the same nest the sun used at night. These beasts were called *Rumahn*.

He had laughed wearily, then spurred his pony east.

16

"THE PROBLEM AS I see it then, Procurator," Colonel Norbanus said after a long silence, "is to delay a tyrant who will not tolerate having his projects put aside, even briefly."

The Roman procurator continued to stare out the open window of his private quarters in Jerusalem. Aulus Valentinian was a thin man, ascetically so, with prominent veins twining down his arms. And had Norbanus not served with him fourteen years here in Judaea, he might have imagined the cast of Valentinian's face to betoken a nature too sensitive for this thorny post. But in those years, the man had proved himself as capable a military governor as a diplomat. After more than two millennia under Roman rule, Judaea was still a backwater adjunct to the full province of Syria, and the legate assigned by the Syrian proconsul to keep an eye on Jerusalem's contentious Sanhedrin was traditionally also given command of the legions in the district, just so the locals would make no mistake about the seriousness of his administration. In the eighteen centuries between the imperial reigns of Antoninus Pius and Fabius, the Tenth Fretensis and the Sixth Ferrata had pacified Judaea from the Caesarea and Jerusalem garrisons, but a decade ago the Tenth had been detached to the Novo Provinces, leaving the "Iron Sixth" to police all of Judaea alone.

This single legion had proved adequate to the job only because Valentinian enjoyed the trust of the sundry Jewish factions—something Lord Regent Antonius Nepos obviously didn't appreciate, Norbanus reflected.

"Well, friend," Valentinian said at last, "I have but a few days left to command here and would gladly postpone the lord regent's order until the arrival of the new procurator except . . ." Wearily, he shook his head, his watery eyes still fixed on the precinct of the Great Temple below his window. Jerusalem's garrison, the Fortress of Antonia, stood on the northwest corner of the holiest Jewish shrine, and Valentinian had taken as his own apartments the tower of the citadel's four which provided the best view of King Herod's grand edifice. His headquarters were technically in Caesarea on the coast, but he spent little time there. "Except that Procurator Hostilius will only think the Jews persuaded me to dawdle . . ."

"And then he'll double the levy to cow the Sanhedrin." Norbanus completed the worrisome thought for him.

"Precisely."

"*Hostilius*—what a name to assume!" the colonel said.

"Yes, his given one was Mucianus, as I recall. But he borrowed *Tullus Hostilius* from our despoiling third king as 'a warning to the lord regent's enemies.' "

"God in heaven, what does he think that sort of bluster will accomplish out here?"

"I have no idea. But at least we've been granted a few more days to consider the problem."

"How's that, sir?"

"Hostilius got so deathly drunk at the banquet in his honor at Corinthus, he'll be laying over a few days more at Proconsul Fadus' residence."

His spirits plummeting, Norbanus was again struck by the howling injustice that this profligate sycophant of Claudia Nero's would within the week be his new commanding officer. And what then would become of Aulus Valentinian?—a real soldier and, more importantly to the colonel these past several years, a man of spiritual sensibilities. Was the most skillful procurator in Judaea's often turbulent history being recalled to Rome only to have his intelligent head separated from his shoulders because he'd refused to wire Nepos a congratulatory dispatch on the occasion of the praetorian prefect's illegal ascendency to the purple? Did a man's fate now hinge on such meaningless blandishments?

"Why so glum, my brother?" Valentinian had turned away from the coolness of the open window and was smiling at him.

Norbanus had decided against histrionics, as the procurator distrusted the sincerity of proud words. But then it burst out of him: "I will die before I'll see you dragged back to Rome! I will—!"

"You will continue to serve as you are. And I'm hardly being *dragged*." Valentinian's eyes darted in warning toward the locked door—on its far side stood two praetorians of a maniple sent to Judaea by Nepos for "the good procurator's protection." The governor lowered his voice. "With me gone from Judaea, your continued presence here becomes all the more valuable toward the maintenance of the peace."

"But if Hostilius enforces this idiotic decree, there will be war!"

"That is what you must try to avert. And how can you do so if you wind up in a Mamertine cell with me?" Valentinian glanced away, and Norbanus realized that for the first time the procurator was revealing what he truly thought would become of him. "Now, if we find the noble lord regent's decree too formidable to simply shunt aside, perhaps we can chip away at it a little. Will you please take dictation for a wireless dispatch?"

"Of course, sir." Norbanus reached for the wax tablet kit on the long marble table at which he sat slope-shouldered.

"*To Decimus Antonius Nepos . . .*" Valentinian twirled his right hand in a purposely redundant gesture. "Add all those abominable honorifics he's ascribed to himself. And then: *Sire, let me assure you that Judaea*—Wait, make that *all of Judaea applauds your extraordinary efforts to salvage the African harvests to the benefit of the entire Empire.*" He rolled his eyes at his own unaccustomed floridity. "*At any other time a levy of one hundred thousand Jewish laborers would present no problem to the efficient administration of the department of Judaea. However, as I have advised the proconsul in Antiochia, all available manpower will soon be required to harvest the crops of the Plain of Sharon and the experimental farms of Idumea, the latter a project dear to the interests of the noble Gracchi gens. While appreciative of the emergency in Africa, may I implore you that the Judaean levy be reduced, temporarily at least, to fifty thousand men?*"

Now suddenly, after weeks of most encouraging improvement, the child had started vomiting again.

While a slave held a bowl up to Quintus' pale lips, the physician collapsed into a chair in the corner of the bedchamber.

What could he say to his noble mistress, Claudia? How could he explain away the wild delusions the boy had suffered all evening? Why had Quintus called out again and again for Germanicus Agricola to save him from Helios and Victoria, who were apparently storming about the room on the fringes of his frenzied nightmare? What explanation could he come up with to ward off yet another of Claudia's rages? The woman had actually chased him from her apartments with a dagger during Quintus' last bout.

"Hyperion of the Healing Gaze," he wailed to the high, shadowy ceiling, "what afflicts my charge?!"

Naturally, after finding the child's symptoms inconsistent with any disease he knew, the physician had suspected poisoning.

But by what agency?

Made desperate by the knowledge that Quintus' untimely death might spell his own, he had started ingesting and imbibing everything the boy did—but with absolutely no ill effect, not even the slightest rumble of indigestion, while Quintus' health continued to deteriorate, punctuated by remissions lasting only long enough to raise false hopes on the Palatine that the *imperator designatus* might recover.

He had begged for other doctors to be brought in on the case, secretly hoping that this might mitigate any blame on him should the boy indeed die. But Claudia would hear none of it, hissing with the fires of dementia in her eyes how she feared that some nameless enemy of hers *inside* the palace would plant an assassin among the visiting physicians. An assassin against whom? Her or the child? The physician had feared to ask. Like Caesar Augustus, she had stopped eating everything except figs she picked with her own hands from the imperial gardens; this diet had at first improved her figure, but lately she seemed more gaunt than thin, and her grin was absolutely skeletal.

"The lord regent requires you!" a martial voice now barked from the portal.

The physician bolted to his feet, muttering to the praetorian, "Yes, yes—immediately."

Quintus lifted his pallid face an inch off his pillow and whispered something to the slave, who relayed the child's barely audible words to the doctor: "He desires water, sir."

"He'll only bring it up again. . . ." Then, frowning, the physician relented: "Let him have a few sips."

The slave reached for the child's favorite cup, an ornate galena vessel embossed with Cupid and Psyche in gleaming prance, and the physician followed the praetorian out into the corridor.

"What does the lord regent want?" he asked, trying not to sound too anxious.

The guardsman ignored his question.

Whatever the physician had expected, it was not to pass through Antonius Nepos' vestibule and suddenly come face to face with a man dangling on tethers from the ceiling, his bloody toes almost touching the floor. Stripped naked, he was being flayed by two butchers from the praetorian kitchen in the household.

"Come in, come in," the lord regent said, almost jovially, "you're blocking the lamplight." He waved for the physician to take the couch beside him. "Make yourself comfortable. I need your professional opinion on something."

Stunned, the physician sank into the cushions.

The eyes of the victim were fixed on him, shining from a skinless face that was the gelatinous yellow of paraffin.

"What . . . what does the noble lord regent desire to know?"

"Well, we've been at this fellow for the better part of an hour—and he hasn't screamed once."

"He has made no sound whatsoever?"

"Oh, when first cut he made a sound rather like he was sucking his spittle back through his clenched teeth. But not once in all this time—which must seem an eternity to him—has he let go with a hearty bellow. I'm curious why."

Flabbergasted not that such cruelty occurred in Rome but that it was being so brazenly conducted in the imperial palace, the physician could think of nothing to say for a moment. Then, his voice breathy, he asked, "Is he a Pict?"

"Does it matter?"

"Only in that different races have different capacities for pain, sire."

"Oh, really?"

"Yes, Numidians have virtually none. Picts have enormous tolerance for it, particularly if angered."

"Yes, I believe that's true. So you're certain this fellow's a Pict?"

"I didn't say that, Lord Regent."

"Well, is he from northern Britannia or not?"

"I . . . I suspect him to be either a Pict or perhaps a German, although most Germans are brown-haired, not blond or redheaded as is commonly believed."

"Which is it, then?" Nepos persisted, as if stimulated by this inane but hideous conversation. "Is he Pict or German?"

"Well, sire, he is quite tall, and few Picts are tall. But his hair is red . . . unless the color comes from his blood."

"Oh no, it was red when he first stood before me. Perhaps it would help you if I laid out all the facts."

"Please," the physician rasped.

"This fellow is indeed German, a member in good standing of the Cherusci tribe. In better days for him, he served this very household as a praetorian guardsman. But lately he has kept a wineshop called the Red Cape. Is this information helping?"

Forcing back the taste of bile in his mouth, the physician nodded.

"Wait—I may have just answered my own inquiry. Do you suppose he's so intoxicated he feels no pain?" Nepos chuckled with a hint of self-deprecation. "I've been in that state myself from time to time. A whore in Gaul ran a stylus through my leg and I didn't know I was pierced until I felt a wetness of blood. What do you think, healer? Is this fellow too deep in his cups to feel anything?"

He realized from the lord regent's throaty chuckle that the man was himself close to the condition he'd just described, but amazingly his speech wasn't sloppy. "I can't tell, sire, without examining him."

"Then do so, man. I want this thing settled tonight."

The expressionless butchers stepped aside, and the physician approached the German, who greeted him with a defiant grin. His eyes seemed as lucid and clear as one could expect of a man being tortured to death. And he did not smell of drink. He stank of his own blood. "I don't believe this man to be drunk, Lord Regent."

"Oh, the demons. Do you suppose my carvers here are botching the job?"

"Sire?"

"You're a doctor," Nepos said with sudden irritation, "aren't you?"

"Certainly."

"Then find a place that gets a rise out of this long-skulled brute."

"But I—"

"Do it, healer!"

He held out his tremulous palm, and one of the butchers slapped the blood-slippery haft of a knife into it. But then he hesitated.

"What are you waiting for?" Nepos growled.

"I . . . I'm seeking out one of the common membranous investments, Lord Regent."

For some reason his answer amused Nepos, and the man laughed. "Do you find this diversion barbarous?"

"No, sire," he lied.

"Excellent, because this is the effort of a keenly civilized mind, an intelligence striving to maintain its balance in the face of barbarian outrages against me . . . against Rome. . . ." Nepos paused to drink; wine dribbled down the front of his tunic. "Do you have any idea what's going on along the German frontier these days?"

"Trouble, Lord Regent?"

"Trouble indeed. I just got word—this raffish King Rolf lured two entire cohorts of the Sixth Victrix into that dark and trackless wilderness of his and"—Nepos' eyes began smarting, but the physician sensed that the moisture in them arose more from the humiliation of defeat than sorrow at the deaths of two thousand legionaries—"and slaughtered them to the man."

The physician struggled to sound indignant: "Then these Germans must be punished and swiftly too!"

"Indeed, healer, that was my first impulse. Noble Claudia's too. We even planned to invade. We still do, eventually. But however much we long to massacre these tribesmen, to burn the villages of the Wald and salt the earth on which they stand—well, there are urgencies greater than Germania. Rome must eat. The ruler of a hungry Rome is not ruler for long. So now do you understand why I must blunt my appetite for vengeance against the long-skulled vermin in this way?"

"I believe I do, Lord Regent."

"Good." Nepos gestured with his cup. "Then hop up on one of those stools there and be at the big fellow. I want to hear him sing."

"Another matter first, sire—if you please."

"I don't please."

"It is most urgent."

"*What!*"

"Young Quintus worsens again."

Nepos glared at him, then rested his wrinkled brow onto his fist. "Why didn't you tell me right away?"

"Well, noble Lord Regent," the physician stammered, "I . . . I . . . I was—"

"Does my wife know?"

"No, the symptoms came on only since supper."

"Then you must do me a favor."

"Anything, sire."

"She is made more distraught by the boy's illness than you or I will ever know. And I fear bad news heaped on bad news like this will affect her own frail health."

Surprise more than concern widened the physician's eyes. "Is the good lady ill now as well?"

"No, no—it's just that she isn't the picture of robust health she appears to be. Enough said." With a restless flick of his fingers, Nepos turned the subject back to the boy. "You may consider your reportorial duties fulfilled if you notify me of any changes in Quintus' condition. Leave my wife in the peace of ignorance. What can she do anyway except torment herself?"

"But, sire—I'm afraid . . ." He could find no way to put his greatest terror into words: that Claudia would have him murdered if Quintus perished, and she might even order a slow and horrible death like this wretched German's if he withheld news about the boy's decline.

"You're afraid of what, healer? That my wife will do away with you if the gods take our beloved son from us?"

After a moment, he nodded.

"Well then, have your ministrations been the best possible?"

"Of course, sire! The most modern and carefully considered!"

"Lower your girlish voice. I have yet to meet a physician who was not either openly or privately a pederast. Is that what's ailing the boy?"

"No!"

"Shut up!" Again, Nepos gulped wine. "Good Mars, you sound to be in greater agony than this fine barbarian. And he's been half-flayed! Do you want to join him?!"

"Pardons, Lord Regent." The physician fell to his knees, then realized too late that he had knelt in a pool of the German's blood. Mixed in with the red liquid were strips of hairy skin, the sight of which made him want to retch.

Nepos lowered his voice, but it seemed no less menacing. "I will promise you this, healer—if you continue to treat our beloved son as diligently as you have these past weeks, and *if* you report only to me, thus sparing my wife unnecessary anxiety, I'll see to it you're given an ample retirement and safe-conduct out of Rome . . . should Quintus leave us. What do you say to that?"

It took only an instant for him to see that with Quintus fading by the hour this was his only chance to survive Claudia's inevitable wrath. And he now suspected that the former praetorian prefect, famous for his ruthlessness, would somehow survive both his wife and adopted son. "Thank you, sire." Ignoring the blood, he bowed deeply, his brow blotched crimson when he had straightened up again. "How can I ever express my gratitude?"

Once more, Nepos' mood had turned jocular. "Why, jump up there, man, and turn this old sausage into a canary!"

Steeling himself against the accusation in the German's eyes, the physician mounted the stool and poised the tip of the blade at the base of the man's neck. He tried not to think of the vow he had taken long ago to use his arts only for the healing of his fellow man. The adherents of Hippocrates had known nothing of medicine on the Palatine when they composed their famous oath in his honor.

Expertly, he punctured the exposed muscle and found the nerve.

The German roared like a wounded bear.

"That's it. That's what I've wanted to hear!" Nepos cried. "Louder now!"

The physician was growing dizzy, but as ordered he again touched the blade to the nerve.

This time, instead of crying out wordlessly, the German seethed: "By the grace of Donar, by the rage of his thunder—I be avenged by Rolf of the Marcomanni! I leave this body but come back with the Army of the Fur—!"

Hoping that Nepos wouldn't notice, the physician plunged deeper on the third thrust, all the way into the spinal cord, and the German slumped dead.

Nepos' smile dimmed. "What happened?"

"His heart failed, sire."

"He's still twitching. Throw some water on him."

"He is dead."

"Are you sure?"

"Positive." The physician stepped down off the stool, feeling both disgusted with himself and relieved that it was over.

"Well, no matter," Nepos said blithely, then turned to his guards. "Bring in another German. And throw these imposters into the Mamertine. Butchers, eh? They couldn't skin an apple. My wife's healer will do the cutting. He has a nice touch with steel, what?"

Mara held Germanicus back by the arm as Dathan and Shammai crept down a flight of stone stairs to what seemed through the darkness to be a small reservoir. This was confirmed in the same moment when the men could be heard quietly sloshing through water and Mara whispered, "The Pool of Siloam, our only way into Jerusalem without encountering the legionaries or the temple police. It is true of guards everywhere—they look outward and never inward."

While Germanicus gave no indication that he still intended to follow Dathan and Shammai, Mara continued to clutch his arm, tenderly almost.

"I have no objection to stealing inside this fortified city," he said with his lips almost touching her ear. "I've found the journey from Masada stimulating—to say the least. However, why couldn't this God-respecter of yours have met us outside Jerusalem someplace?"

"Impossible."

Germanicus was dissatisfied with her answer. Where were these strange Jews ultimately leading him? It didn't seem likely they would shepherd him halfway across the eastern empire to their secret refuge, only to betray him to the imperial wolves in Jerusalem. But neither had he expected the proconsul of Achaea, Gessius Fadus, to turn him over to the praetorian guard.

At their last rest stop before approaching the city, while squatting in a mottle of rare shade in the Judaean wilderness, he had asked Mara, "May I assume that a God-respecter is some sort of novice to your faith?"

She wrinkled her nose at the Latin word. "What is a novice?"

"A convert . . . a proselyte."

"Oh, no—although a God-respecter does most all the things a proselyte does. He gives alms to the poor, prays thrice daily. He worships the Lord of Heaven with the fullness of his heart."

"But wait now—he must have certain reservations about this Lord of yours if he elects not to convert, correct?"

"Not at all."

"Then the distinction escapes me."

Once again, her husky laugh made him smile. "How simply must I put it, Germanicus Julius?"

"Very simply. Remember—I'm an obdurate pagan."

"Well then, a God-respecter has done everything to honor the Lord except . . ." She teased him with a pause.

"Except what?"

"Submit to circumcision."

Reflexively, Germanicus had drawn his knees together. If one thing could be said for the Jovian pantheon, its gods were too preoccupied with their own sexual members to be much concerned with the condition of those of mere mortals.

Now, either Dathan or Shammai whistled softly from below, and Mara, who still hadn't let go of Germanicus' arm, began leading him down the steep stairs toward the pool.

"The first part of the way is clear," she whispered.

Germanicus didn't have to remind himself that the four of them had left their *pili* concealed in the Valley of the Kidron, and—as far as he knew—the three Jews were each armed only with a curved dagger known in Latin as the *sica*. During the worst episode of unrest in ancient Judaea, Jewish assassins had earned their name, the Sicarii, from their grim affection for this weapon. He now only hoped that these Perushim were as talented with it as their forebears, for he himself had nothing with which to defend himself.

Mara and he stepped off the bottom of the flight into knee-deep water. It felt almost cold in comparison to the heavy air of the summer night.

Dathan was waiting crouched at the mouth to a tunnel. "Shammai has gone on ahead. Follow, quickly."

The vague light at the arched opening receded to their backs and, when they rounded a bend, vanished entirely, leaving them in absolute darkness.

Ever cautious, Dathan led them another hundred paces down the meandering tunnel before switching on his *electricus* torch. "Stop," he grunted.

The torch beam danced ahead, cutting palely through the mist hanging in the long, snaking channel.

Germanicus couldn't catch sight of Shammai's imposing hulk. The only sound was that of water dripping off the ceiling into the stream, whose shallow flow they had been walking against in a northerly direction. Not particularly familiar with Jerusalem, never having served with any of the Syrian-commanded legions, he nevertheless sensed that this passageway was taking them under the lower city. He surmised that from this point Herod's Palace, the traditional home of the priests of the Sanhedrin, and the posh, jasmine-scented wards of the upper city, lay to the northwest.

"Follow," Dathan finally said.

"Who does he expect to encounter down here?" Germanicus asked Mara.

"No one—unless we have been betrayed."

Oddly enough, it somewhat quieted his own suspicions to learn that the Perushim also feared perfidy.

The tunnel bearing the stream veered off toward the east. However, Dathan turned up a dry adit that branched off the main passageway to the north. This dusty pipe terminated in a round iron hatch, and he motioned for Germanicus to help him force it. It took the combined strength of both men to push it open far enough for their threesome to slip past.

"Thank Jupiter, Shammai didn't have to come this way," Germanicus huffed as they strained to close it.

"But he did—and shut this again to leave no sign of his passing."

Behind the hatch was a curtain of water issuing from an overhead grate.

"The outlet of the aqueduct from Solomon's pools," Mara explained, nudging Germanicus to keep up with her father, who was hurrying down a badly decayed wooden catwalk. This ramp was suspended on rusty cables above a frothing cascade designed to aerate the water before it plunged into a large cistern. As soon as they stepped off the rocking and groaning catwalk, Mara crept over to the edge of the reservoir, where Dathan was already kneeling with his hands braced atop his thighs.

Both father and daughter were peering up through a circular opening in the low ceiling.

Joining them, Germanicus noticed a pair of sandals on the limestone floor. They were still warm to the touch.

He too then gazed up the masonry tube at whose far end stars flickered. But more amazing than seeing stars from this depth, was to realize that midway up this unlikely access to the surface a man was spread-eagled, supporting himself only by pressing his hands and bare feet against the casing stones.

Suddenly, he let go with his right hand—only to place it higher on the wall. Then he did the same with his left foot, his left hand and finally his right.

In this tortuous manner Shammai gradually ascended to the top.

Germanicus chuckled under his breath. "Even in the most vigorous days of my youth—I would have found that impossible."

"I know," Mara said in such a way it made him search out her expression in the darkness.

Shammai lowered a large canvas bucket to Dathan, who stepped inside but then looped the rope around his ankle to take as much of his weight as possible off the rotten-looking fabric.

Shammai windlassed him to the surface, the bucket trickling from a dozen leaks as it rose by fits and starts.

Within minutes, all four of them were standing under starlight, and Germanicus found himself in a courtyard enclosed by colon-naded porticoes set within massive walls. Beyond a low inner enclosure soared the Great Temple, its gold and white marble resplendent in the light of its bracketed torches.

Quickly, Dathan motioned them away from the well, and they took off at a trot toward the northwest corner of the compound.

Suddenly, Germanicus halted.

Several strides ahead, Mara noticed that he had fallen behind. She came back for him. "We must not linger here!" she whispered. "The temple police are making their rounds and will soon come this way again!"

Still, he refused to budge as he stared up at the Fortress of Antonia.

All at once it made terrible sense: These Perushim had deferred their greed this long in order to hand him over to a *specific* Roman, perhaps even Antonius Nepos himself. That way they wouldn't have to split their reward with any middlemen.

"What is it, Germanicus Julius!"

He thought for an instant he could glimpse the treachery in her eyes. Or was it only dismay because of the delay he was causing them? "Why didn't you and your father just let me die in Troy?"

Dathan was turning back now too, having sent Shammai ahead to keep watch for the roving patrol of temple police.

"What are you saying?" Mara asked, seizing him by a fold of his cloak, trying to pull him forward.

But he resisted. "I'm saying it was pitiless of you to drag me all this distance when you could have betrayed me to the imperial authorities in Anatolia."

"Please! Do you want all of us to die on a cross?"

"What is it?" Dathan hissed.

"He refuses to go on!"

The anxiousness in their faces made Germanicus begin to doubt his own suspicions, but he decided that Dathan and Mara could never be given a stronger imperative to tell him the truth. "Do you intend to deliver me to the fortress?"

"Yes," Dathan said matter-of-factly.

"Then what is this about?"

Mara clutched his hands in hers. "I gave you a bronze arrowhead," she said emphatically.

"What—?"

"I told you to keep it—so if ever you doubted me again, as you did that morning I went walking outside Ilium, you would know I was telling the truth. I am telling the truth now when I say no harm will come to you this night—but only if you do as we ask. Do you still have that projectile?"

Germanicus vacillated for a long moment, waiting for either father or daughter to resort to a dagger to get him moving again. That would clearly reveal their treachery. However, when the seconds passed and their hands failed to go for their weapons, he was tempted to show Mara that he now wore the arrowhead on a string around his neck, as a symbol of his fragile but growing faith not in God, but in her. Instead, he simply nodded that he would follow.

They hurried across the rest of the courtyard to a staircase that breached the northwest intersection of two porticoes and gave access to a door in the steep wall of the Antonia.

As they started up the stone steps, Germanicus saw that this portal was guarded by a legionary, although the torches had been extinguished.

Astonishingly, Shammai was standing beside the Roman soldier, whispering to him.

The legionary waved for the threesome to continue up the flight to him, but faster.

"I'm mad if I go along with this," Germanicus muttered, thinking no one had heard him.

But Mara said under her breath: "Yes, the Master of Heaven will pass over a thousand sane men, only to enlist a mad one in his service. His patience is spared endless questions that way."

The legionary wore one of the same decorations Germanicus was entitled to—the *corona muralis*, awarded to the first man to surmount the wall of an enemy bastion. And so it was all the more bewildering to hear this valiant soldier whisper, "Peace be with you."

"And with you, brother," Dathan said. "Is the corridor clear?"

"Only for the moment—come, and please pick up your feet."

However, Germanicus' bewilderment at this unexpectedly cordial welcome to the garrison was nothing compared to that of a minute later when he and his Perushim companions were conducted up into one of the towers. Awaiting them there in a small chamber were the procurator of Judaea and his adjutant, both in full regalia with silvered helmets and breastplates polished to flawless sheens.

The officers touched their right fists to their left shoulders in salute, then said quietly but fervently: "Hail Caesar!"

Germanicus gaped at the procurator, who was smiling with tears in his eyes. "Why, Aulus Valentinian—are you the God-respecter they've brought me to see!"

17

"I AM INDEED a God-respecter, Caesar," Aulus Valentinian said. "And Colonel Norbanus here is one as well."

Germanicus could only stare at the Roman general in silent disbelief, his unwavering patrician mettle telling him that every few years, if not sooner, officers on provincial tours should be posted back to the Italian peninsula lest they absorb the beliefs and customs of their native charges. Valentinian, he recalled obscurely, had been wasting away in Judaea for at least a decade, perhaps two—more than long enough for his memories of Rome to slowly unravel into a mental haze, for Jewish practices to begin to make visceral sense.

They had shared a year together at the Campus Martius as cadets, and although Valentinian had been a mere underclassman and the future Caesar on the strutting verge of his tribuneship, he had taken a liking to the lean boy with the dutiful manner and sensitive face. Young Aulus had been pious with a reserve appropriate to the descendant of one of the great clans of Rome; he, unlike so many others that year, had seemed immune to the religious hysteria introduced into the ranks by the Rekindled Cult of Mithras, the god of morning light. So, in recollection of that austere boy, Germanicus found it hard to believe that the grown man, who seemed even more austere, had embraced Judaism. Yet, here at last was someone of his own social class and occupation who might fully explain to him the purposes and machinations of these Jews, the people on whom he relied for his very survival.

"Aulus, might we have a few words in private?"

"Of course, Caesar." After urging Dathan, Mara, and Shammai to make themselves comfortable, Valentinian led Germanicus into his bedchamber. He must have anticipated Caesar's request, for at the foot of his sleeping couch were two chairs. They were separated by a tripod table, on which a metal urn of vinegar was warming over a chafing candle. Did he feel the awkward silence as keenly as Germanicus? His bony hand was trembling slightly as he proffered his former emperor a simple wooden bowl.

Germanicus savored the warm liquid. "Good Jupiter, that's nectar!"

Valentinian smiled. "The first cup you upperclassmen forced upon me in the mess at the Campus Martius—I thought it was urine."

"It probably was. Young men can be cruel."

"And old men as well. I have seen old men do terrible things in this country. Men who at first seemed wise and kind to me. It wasn't until I came out here that I understood Socrates' assertion . . ." He paused to take a sip.

"Which one, dear Aulus?"

"That philosophy is the study of death."

"Yes, well, serve in the eastern provinces long enough—they say—and you'll see every possible manner of death under the sun."

"True, sire."

He thought to tell him these royal forms of address were unnecessary, but then sensed that they were a reassurance, a comfort to Valentinian. He glanced around the stuffy chamber; it had a definite lived-in look about it, although only another legionary could have discerned this quality through the Spartan neatness. This governor was no clandestine voluptuary like Achaea's Gessius Fadus. "Do you spend most of your time here in Jerusalem?"

"Yes, I return to Caesarea only to endure the various delegations from Rome—guests who lack the self-control to enter this holy city. My house there is nothing more than a repository for the imperial standards, which must never be flown in Jerusalem."

"By whose order?"

"The Jews, of course." Again he smiled, but sheepishly this time. "I must confess, I was at the point of despair when Dathan's messenger suddenly arrived this morning."

"You in despair, my friend?"

"I am inclined toward it from time to time."

"I too," Germanicus said softly. "What news did Dathan's man bring you?" he then asked carefully, unsure which slant on the universe Valentinian now held—the Roman or the Jewish.

"That Germanicus Agricola was alive and under God's protection, that he needed to see his empire with new eyes."

"I no longer have an empire, dear Aulus. I have this simple cloak and a tired body dented by scars from wars whose necessity I no longer understand. And had Dathan and Mara not found me when they did—well, I'd probably be dead by now."

The procurator frowned. "You have something more valuable than an empire."

"And that?"

"*Gravitas.*" The concept was old Roman and defied strict definition, but the look in Valentinian's eyes convinced him that the man was thinking of all its nuances: weight, severity, seriousness, dignity, influence, even vehemence and violence. "Do I dare ask something, Caesar?"

"Of course, anything."

"Are you a God-respecter as well?"

"What makes you think so?"

"Well, Dathan brings you . . . and he has smuggled other respecters into my presence."

"No, I'm not."

Valentinian fought to hide his disappointment. "But why then are you among the Perushim?"

"We have a mutual friend who arranged this refuge for me."

"I see . . ." The procurator brightened again. "Well, it gladdened Norbanus and me you weren't drowned in Corinthus. An answer from God to our entreaties . . ."

Then both men fell silent, and it seemed Valentinian was fully expecting Germanicus' next question: "*Why*, dear Aulus?"

"I wasn't sure myself for the longest time. The confusion nearly deranged me. But I have always considered myself to be an honest man—"

"Indeed, along with Gnaeus Salvidienus, one of the most honest I've ever known."

"Yes, poor Gnaeus . . . an unjust end to a noble life." Valentinian glanced at the only window in the chamber, which was shut against the faint coolness of the night. "Come—before we suffocate, let's sit on the sill. . . ." He clicked off the *electricus* fixture and pushed back the panes with his fingertips. The temple lay agleam below, two separate patrols of its police visible in the gloom of the courtyards. "Beautiful, isn't it?" he asked in a hush.

"Yes. I suppose it even outshines Ephesus' reconstruction of the Temple of Artemis. I'd forgotten how splendid it is." He made no comment on the chockablock refineries, the Judaean terminus

of the Mesopotamian Artery, clanging and spewing white vapors
from the heights above the Kidron Valley. And the mount to the
immediate east of the temple, which on his last visit eleven years
before had been tufted dark green with olive groves, was now
covered with tenements. However, he found something disarm-
ingly boyish about perching beside Valentinian on the window
ledge, dangling his sandals out over the dark drop-off. Perhaps, in
this way, the man had intended to revive the familiarity they'd
once shared, and indeed Germanicus felt at ease to be in genuinely
Roman company once again. "And now—tell me what honest
Aulus had to admit to himself."

"That he did not have the courage to live without hope and
joy," he said simply. "Do you have any idea what joylessness is
truly like?"

Tapping his heels against the smooth stone wall of the tower,
Germanicus said nothing.

"Joylessness in the midst of rampant venality and injustice—
which one is compelled by an oath to serve?" Valentinian shook
his head. "No, Caesar, a life without worthy purposes turns the
heart into a Mamertine cell. And, in truth, I had but one
alternative to becoming a God-respecter—falling on my sword."

With a sudden and unfathomable sense of shame, Germanicus
recalled his own willingness to die this way only a few weeks
before. Valentinian fell silent after so frank an admission, and
both men listened to the breeze moan around the edges of the
tower. Germanicus asked himself how he truly felt about his
fellow Roman's partial conversion. Confused and vaguely disappointed, he supposed. And now Valentinian, like Mara, was
turning to him as if he were the definitive answer to his prayers.
"I'm a Julian who's had the purple ripped off his back,"
Germanicus said quietly. "I haven't a single legionary under my
banner. A sesterce to my name. A future worth planning. How can
I possibly be God's reply to your entreaties?"

"I have no idea."

Germanicus laughed. "Say what now, my friend?"

"I have no idea how you can help us here in Judaea." Yet
Valentinian didn't sound deterred in the least; in fact, a suggestion
of whimsy had crept into his voice: "But something will come of
your safe arrival in the East. Otherwise, you would have drowned
in that canal, as Antonius Nepos still believes."

"Then the *syllogismos* would be—*every life has a divine
purpose; I am alive; therefore I am fulfilling a purpose*?"

"Exactly—and I must remember that. Look what a Jewish sentiment wed to a Greek education can produce!" Sobering again, Valentinian gazed down at the temple. "I've been recalled to Rome, you know."

"No, I didn't." Germanicus clasped the man's shoulder; under Nepos' rule, recall meant the same as execution. "When must you depart?"

"As soon as the new procurator arrives in Caesarea—a day or two at the most, depending on how seriously he partakes of Antiochia's carnal pleasures."

"Who is he?"

"Hostilius."

"Never heard of him."

"He changed his name. It was Mucianus, I believe."

"Good Jupiter, you can't possibly mean Claudia Nero's arbiter of etiquette, Maximus Mucianus!"

"The selfsame."

"That mean-spirited fop would crucify his own mother for using the wrong fork. And what does he know about governing a prickly department like Judaea? He's spent his entire life staggering around inside the Palatine, primping the capes of praetorians!"

"That's not the worst of it. The recent civil war in Aegyptus has all but cut off the flow of grain to Rome. Nepos has ordered the immediate impressment of three hundred thousand laborers to harvest and transport the crop."

"What's your levy?"

"One hundred thousand, although I just begged a reduction to fifty thousand."

Having once been an eastern procurator himself, Germanicus quickly realized what this would do to the Judaean economy—and political stability as well. "What—?" Suddenly, his hand flew to the side of his head and began rubbing as if trying to extinguish the flash fire of pain there.

"Caesar," Valentinian asked, "are you all right?"

"Yes, quite. An old wound singing for a little attention." The pain subsided as quickly as it had come, and he felt no worse for it other than a little breathlessness. "What will the Sanhedrin do about the levy?"

"I fear to think."

"Which makes me ask, Aulus—where do you stand in this discord between the Sadducees and the Pharisees?"

"I'm something of a peacemaker, although my natural sympathies are more with the Perushim than their more worldly Jerusalem cousins."

Germanicus could think of no diplomatic way to frame his next question: "You didn't order the punitive raid on the village of En-Gedi, did you?"

"Oh, no. That happened two years before I arrived out here. Terrible business. It's taken all my cunning to prevent a repeat of that carnage on Masada."

"Then the Sadducees know about the redoubt there?"

"Absolutely—although if I told Dathan that, I'd be betraying a Sadducee confidence. But rest assured, either Norbanus or I would forewarn him if the temple police marched east. And I'd never permit the Sixth Ferrata to join in such a venture."

"But you will be gone soon, Aulus Valentinian. And I know this so-called Hostilius well enough to say he'll fill the levy with enthusiasm."

"Yes, unless . . ." Valentinian hesitated.

"Unless what?"

"The Sixth declares for you, reaffirms the authority of your imperium. I know the lads would do this in a blink. Nine of the ten cohorts are God-respecting, and we can count on the Jewish *auxilia* to join us as well. By recent accounts, the Third Gallica and Fourth Scythica in Syria are fed up with the lord regent and his powdered harlot."

"What does that give us then?"

"Well, three infantry legions and that many auxiliaries."

"To take on all the power of Rome?"

"At least we could carve greater Syria out of the Empire's backside. We could create a God-respecting imperium in your name here."

Valentinian's eyes were so lustrous with hope, Germanicus had to force himself to say: "No, dear Aulus. I've seen too many men die in my cause. And to what end? Another two thousand years of Julian emperors? It was a new republic I always wanted. That was my father's dream, too. But it can never be, especially now, and I won't try to nourish a futile enterprise with blood. I see nothing but disaster if I march against Nepos. Three infantry legions against ten times that many armored ones?"

Visibly, the procurator sank into himself—his last hopes had been demolished. But true to his Roman upbringing, he said, "I apologize, Caesar. I should not have presumed upon your intentions."

"You did nothing of the sort. You're in a nest of cockleburs, and I don't blame you for trying to fight your way out of it. But try to understand—I can't inflame these eastern legionaries with promises of a better world, only to lead them to slaughter the first time Nepos confronts them." Germanicus lifted his bearded chin toward the starlit variegations of the Judaean wilderness in the distant east. "Have you and Norbanus considered coming out to Lake Asphaltitis before Mucianus shows up? While safety there might be temporary, so's everything else in this life."

"No, but I thank you for asking. I think it wrong to postpone whatever God means for me." He rose a bit stiffly and began moving slowly back into his chamber. "Any minute now, the praetorians the lord regent so generously provided me might be returning from the errand I sent them on. You and the others must leave now or wait until tomorrow night."

"Very well." Germanicus swung his legs over the sill. "We'll be off."

But Valentinian stayed him with a hand. "If by the consent of God you change your mind, will you dispatch a runner to me right away?"

Germanicus smiled. "Yes, Aulus . . . in the unlikely event I change my mind." With his hand on the doorlatch, he asked, "By chance, have you heard news about my adopted son, Quintus?"

"No, Caesar. I'm sorry. I am no longer privy to reports from the Palatine."

While the dawn light was still glancing coolly across the parched wilderness, the three Perushim kept turning to fasten their curiosity on him: What had transpired between Valentinian and him? What things had been agreed to? What things contested? Germanicus was too exhausted to offer explanations, and eventually the Jews withdrew into their own thoughts.

Slowly, the shadows shrank back under the rocks, into the deep and divaricating gullies of a land that appeared never to repair itself, each dusty wrinkle a scar older than the nameless, mounded cities of Mesopotamia. The world became sun, a brutality of light that blared from all directions inward. Even the earth beneath his sandals had erupted into fire, and he trod on flames that wrapped around his bare legs like serpents.

"A moment . . . Dathan . . . Mara . . ." Pausing to catch

his breath, he shaded his eyes with a quivering hand and craned his neck to gape at a distant smudge. "What is that there?"

No one answered. There followed no sound except the faint roar given off by the feverish land.

Finally, the object wavered into focus: a hawk trapped by an updraft against the white-hot sky. But the great bird suddenly ignited and tumbled away in a cascade of sparks and kindled feathers.

"What—?"

Once again, the spectacular ache drew his fingers to the side of his head. He could feel the gristly edges of the sword cut he'd received at Agri Dagi. A sensation of warm, flowing moisture made him gasp: Was he bleeding afresh after all this time?

He cried out for Mara.

But the three Perushim had vanished into the conflagration.

He reeled and fell, kept falling until the fires burned black.

Colonel Norbanus was not surprised when the rail-galley from Antiochia skirled with locked brakes into Tyropoeon Station, and the better part of a praetorian cohort—perhaps as many as one thousand guardsmen—alighted from the cars and formed ranks on the sun-bright platform. They shook the dust out of their capes, fluffed up the Attic crests on their helmets, stole last-minute sips of water from their canteens.

With less than a maniple of Sixth Ferrata legionaries arrayed to his back, Norbanus realized that he was at a disadvantage right from the beginning of his relationship with the new procurator. But Valentinian had encouraged him to cooperate with his new commander as much as his conscience would permit, and secretly gloating that the Sixth Legion and its auxiliaries outnumbered these imperial coxcombs ten-to-one was not in that spirit of cooperation. For better or for worse, the guard and legions were supposed to be one force—all Roman in spirit.

A praetorian centurion marched self-importantly up to Norbanus. "Where's a sand-galley for the procurator?"

Norbanus glared at him—he was famous for the severity that could suddenly come into his eyes. "Has the guard adopted a new policy in regards to military courtesy?"

The centurion came close to blanching, but then recovered his cockiness and gave a languid salute. "*Pardons*, Colonel—may I inquire as to the procuratorial sand-galley so we might proceed to the Fortress of Antonia?"

"Impossible."

"*Sir*?" The centurion had now hooked a thumb in his sword belt.

"Is this your first time to Jerusalem, centurion?"

"Yes, thank the gods. Is it always this bloody hot?"

"Nearly so, except in winter when it's bloody cold. However, my point is that the streets of this city are narrow. Many of them are arcaded in the eastern fashion. So I've ordered a small lorry to convey the procurator through the Garden Gate to the garrison."

"A lorry?" The centurion chortled mirthlessly, then bawled at an astounded Norbanus: "Procurator Hostilius is not a turnip on his way to market!"

"*Oh?*" The colonel realized the danger he'd put himself in as soon as the word escaped his tight lips.

But he had been incensed for the first time in years.

The sun was but a breath away, so close to him only a quarter of its curvature could be traced with his smarting eyes. Along the rim of this bow, garlands of fire exploded and arced outward, only to bend down again into the ferment that had spawned them.

"What fearful beauty," he murmured.

"Germanicus Julius?" someone said from afar, someone female.

But he ignored the voice, despised it as the most inopportune distraction he had ever known, for the sun seemed to be rotating, revealing suggestions of features on a countenance he could not yet fully apprehend. Was that fiery ridge there the cut of some dreadful brow? Was that spire of flame a nose?

And then he saw the eyes.

They were both awful and glorious, fire opals as big as worlds, and he realized even then that he would never stop feeling their heat on his flesh, a burn that would never scab over. "Who whispers so?" It was sifting from deep within the eyes, where the shadows of men flitted:

"If all things which partook of life were to die, and after they were dead stayed in the form of death and did not come to life again, all would at last die, and nothing would be alive—what other result could there be? For if the living spring from any other

*things, and they too perish, must not all things at last be
swallowed up in death, my dear Cebes?"*

*"There is no escape, Socrates, and to me your argument seems
to be absolutely true."*

*"Yes, Cebes, it is and must be so. I am confident that there truly
is such a thing as living again, and that the living vault from the
dead, and that the souls of the dead are in existence, and that the
noble souls have a better portion than the evil. . . ."*

The whispering faded. The eyes dimmed and blackened.

Later, when a coolness touched him to the accompaniment of
dripping noises, when he sensed that he was recumbent and safe,
he croaked: "I have seen the face . . ."

"No, that is not so," the female voice insisted. "Only Mosheh
has seen the face."

"What's the row here?" Hostilius asked, floating down from his
ornate rail-galley car with the assistance of two slaves, Cretan
boys with heads topped by glistening black ringlets.

Norbanus could not believe it: the new procurator was wearing
cothurni, buskins laced to the knee, worn only by actors portray-
ing soldiers in tragedies. And, as if this affectation were not
enough, he had either rouged or pinched his depilated cheeks to
give them the high color that many fancied indicative of noble
breeding. He crossed his thin arms over his breastplate, but after
only a few moments in the sun found the metal too hot for
comfort.

The colonel had to dig deep into his reserves of discipline to
salute this mockery of a Roman soldier. "Kaeso Norbanus,
Procurator."

Ignoring the colonel, Hostilius turned to the praetorian centurion, revealing a nose that seemed all the more beakish by being
offset by a feminine mouth: "Where's my sand-galley?"

"This oaf didn't order one to the station."

"How then am I to proceed to my fortress?"

"By lorry—he says."

Hostilius shrieked. "What! A lorry?"

Norbanus caught his legionaries smirking sideways at one
another—and shot them a warning with his eyes.

"Procurator," he said when Hostilius had finally stopped
making noises as if he'd just been lanced through the bowels, "I
have already explained—it isn't possible for such a large craft to

negotiate the streets of this old city. More accurately, they are lanes—"

"What's this here?" Hostilius was tapping a maroon-painted fingernail against Norbanus' well-worn breastplate.

"I don't understand, sir."

"What's this unslightly iridescence in the silver-plating of your cuirass?"

"It's what comes of marching under this desert sun for fourteen years."

"Oh." Hostilius arched a carefully plucked eyebrow. "I suppose that's a comment on my newness here."

"Procurator, please—"

"Enough, enough," Hostilius said with a flutter of his gaudy fingers. "Please bring me the procuratorial sand-galley or I won't be held responsible for my temper."

Stone-faced, Norbanus turned on his heels and relayed the order to one of his tribunes, who dashed off, rolling his eyes.

"Stand easy," the colonel whispered so only his own troops could hear. As ridiculous a human being as he was, Hostilius could still order decimation, the execution of every tenth man drawn by lots—and Norbanus would not be able to stop him.

Then a glint of gold in the corner of his eye spun him around: an imperial standard.

Were Hostilius' praetorians actually preparing to carry it inside Jerusalem? Norbanus had his answer when they marched the eagle to what would be the van of the formation when the guardsmen right-faced and moved out. It would be an outrage to the Jewish populace beyond belief.

The colonel could no longer contain himself. "Mucianus!" he called out, hailing the procurator by his rightful name. "If that gilt bird passes into the city, you break a covenant as old as the Empire itself!"

"Arrest that man," a yawning Hostilius said to his centurion as the sand-galley clattered up to the platform.

The late Caesar Fabius visited him, clad in flames from head to toe. He reclined beside him as if on a grassy hillside of their youth.

"What do you want?" Germanicus growled, suddenly realizing that he had never liked his cousin but had always been obliged to defer to him.

"Only a word."

"Make it brief. I'm burning up and don't want your voice to be the last ever ringing in my ears."

"Very well then, here's the long and short of your failure, my little Germanicus," Fabius said pleasantly, his hair—locks of orange fire—tossed by a searing blast too terrible to be called wind. "See, you relied on that timeworn vision of ancient Latin nobles, prosperous farmers of moderate habits and pious ways, with the ashes of wronged Troy still dusting their broad shoulders, to restructure the world. Well—" The dead emperor paused to give a sultry chuckle. "—there never were such men. So how can there be such heroes in this age reeking of petrol?"

"There are such men."

"Name one."

"Aulus Valentinian."

"Decent enough sort, it would seem. But give my praetorians ten minutes to interrogate him and you'll find this fellow isn't as noble as he seems. Trust me. I lasted more than twenty years on the Palatine before that viper of a wife did me in. And you, my little Germanicus? Why, you didn't make it to the second anniversary of your imperium. Now what does that tell you?"

"It's easy to lose something you want with only half your heart. . . ." He tried to shift his tender head, but lay statue-still again when a thunderstroke of pain threatened to erase Fabius' insolent and fiery visage. All at once, he didn't want to be rid of his genius cousin; he had an enormous question for him. "You were always cleverer than I . . ."

"Indeed, my star-crossed cousin."

"How then would *you* restore the Republic?"

"I never wanted to restore such idiocy and confusion."

"But say that you did . . ."

"Hypothetically, then?"

"Yes."

"Hmmm . . . an interesting proposition, especially given your present dire circumstances." Fabius mused for several moments, the fist propped beneath his chin beginning to warp as if his countenance were the hottest part of his being. The skin suddenly trickled down his arm like melted wax, but then he took his hand away from his face and stopped dissolving.

"Manumission," he said abruptly—as if the single word settled the matter.

"What do you mean?"

"Just what I said—declare universal manumission. Whether you like it or not, the first order of business in restoring the Republic has to be the overthrow of Antonius Nepos and Claudia Nero. The imperial machine runs on slavery. How can they cope with a slave revolt instigated by the last legal emperor?"

"I don't know," Germanicus murmured, "it seems an extreme measure."

"Why, that's it! Bloody manumission!" Fabius, as usual, was taking glee from the brilliance of one of his own ideas. "Flood the peninsula with an army of runaways. They might even organize under arms by their own volition. It happened before with that Spartacus bully, yes?" He sobered. "What's wrong?"

"I don't know if I'm prepared to do that."

"Then prepare a grave for yourself, my little Germanicus."

"What is the meaning of this!" Valentinian shouted when his replacement arrived at the steps to the Antonia in a lorry bedecked with an imperial standard. Then he saw that Norbanus had been relieved of his sword, his hands bound behind him.

"Do you have any idea what that emblem will do to the peace here!"

Tightly flanked by his praetorians, Hostilius swept past Valentinian, scoffing over his shoulder as he continued on into the shadowy interior of the fortress: "Arrest Aulus Valentinian on the lord regent's orders." A moment later, his loud harrumph echoed out of the depths of the stone garrison: "That will teach him what a levy means!"

Two guardsmen pinned Valentinian's arms to his back, then tied his wrists together with a latchet. His *gladius*, which had been his father's and grandfather's ceremonial sword as well, was yanked out of its scabbard and reduced to two shards of junk by a blow against a granite pedestal, which in deference to Jewish sensibilities had never supported a statue.

Then the former procurator was soundly cuffed across the jaw.

One of the legionaries manning the portal started to intervene, but a praetorian lofted his *pilum* and shot him dead.

When the shock of seeing one of his men executed in cold blood had worn off, Valentinian realized that Norbanus was at his side, his face bleeding. "Did they strike you as well, my dear Norbanus?"

"No, General—I was knocked down when the new procurator tried to jam his sand-galley through the Garden Gate."

Although his heart was heavier than he could ever recall, Valentinian could not help but laugh. After a moment of bewilderment, the colonel glimpsed the desperate humor in what he himself had just said, and he laughed too. Together, they giggled like schoolboys until the praetorians threatened them with their niter pieces.

In the silence that followed, Valentinian could hear the first riotous cries rising in Hebrew and Aramaic above the city.

"Into Your hands," he whispered. The laughter had given him courage just when he feared that he had none left. And he would not die alone, for Kaeso Norbanus marched beside him down into the lowest depths of the Antonia. That was a comfort.

Germanicus awoke with wisps of gray cloud in his eyes. They were running up and down like the stripes on a zebra's neck.

He realized he was lying on his side, sprawled upon a pallet, with his right hand dangling out of the light bedding, his knuckles brushing the gritty earth. With effort, he sat upright, a wave of dizziness nearly flopping him back down again.

Mara was sleeping on a legion-issue blanket at his feet. Framed by the curvature of her shoulder and hip was Lake Asphaltitis, dappled by cloud shadow. Behind him lay the entrance to a cave, the early morning light scarcely penetrating it.

Masada, then.

She opened an eye.

"How did I make it here?" he asked, his voice cracking from dryness.

"Shammai carried you on his back."

"Is there some—?"

"Beside you."

He reached for the waterskin and drank directly from its neck. "No beverage sweeter after abstinence."

"That is true."

He scrutinized her face so intently he expected her to look away. But she didn't. "I have always feared that a man and his soul go out like a candle flame—with no hand to rekindle either his flesh or his spirit. Is this so?"

"No," she said, adamantly, "the spirit survives. It is everything."

"Then why do you assign such importance to the rite of circumcision?"

"God gave it to Abraham. On His part, He promised to take care of Abraham and the generations of his seed—if man would submit to circumcision as a sign of fealty to the Lord."

Rising, he tested his bad leg with a few halting steps.

"Do you think this fever was from the scorpion bite?" she asked.

"No, not this one."

"Then from the wound whose scar I felt through your hair?"

"Perhaps." He braced himself, expecting to swoon, but his consciousness withstood the dizziness. "I wish to be left alone until sundown. Then send your father to me. At that time I will tell him the things I intend to do."

She clasped her hands together and squeezed shut her eyes.

"I summoned you all here," Hostilius said brittlely, "to put a stop to this. . . ." A fluid sweep of his arm took in the Hippodrome, which was in flames, its plume of smoke wafting eastward and dimming the morning sun; the Hasmonean Palace, which in the last few minutes had also been set afire; and the shops along the road to Galilee that catered to a Roman clientele, which were now being looted for a second time since dawn—despite the periodic, savage sweeps of the praetorian guard to disperse the first signs of any gathering crowd. "Now get to it."

Sword-toting guardsmen had herded seventy members of the Sanhedrin onto a corner of the roof of the Fortress of Antonia. From there, they could see the first centurion of the Sixth Ferrata, a known God-respecter, being crucified from the wireless tower. Trying to ignore this gruesome sight, the chief priest was objecting to the procurator: "Lord Hostilius, I cannot do that."

"*What!*"

It was unnerving, the womanish shriek of this daft Roman governor. The chief priest found himself almost missing the old one, despite Valentinian's obvious partisanship in behalf of the heretical Perushim. Straining to keep the fear out of his voice, he went on, "Only you, noble Procurator, can put an end to this unrest."

"If you mean crucify the whole bloody town, I'll do it!"

"I did not mean that, sire. I was suggesting that the cause of this violence is the aquiline standard you brought into the city. When it is removed, this disturbance will subside."

Hostilius turned back to the parapets overlooking the city and began sucking on one of his large rings.

The holy man known as the "father of the house of judgment," the chief priest's right-hand man, whispered to him, "I have the most peculiar feeling that this is not truly happening."

"I too, my friend."

Hostilius twirled around, index fingers of both hands extended as if he'd just lit upon an excellent idea. "I am seeking a solitary decisive man. Is there not one such man among you Sadducee rabble?"

Resolutely, the priests, elders, and scribes of the Sanhedrin remained silent.

"Well then," the procurator said with sham sadness, "we must commence a process of elimination until one of you realizes his modesty to be false." With a sly wink, he beckoned a centurion. "Toss the chief priest over the side."

Even as two praetorians manhandled him toward the wall, the chief priest could not believe that Hostilius would carry out this outrageous order. He could see his temple police assembled below in the north courtyard, gaping up wild-eyed.

And then, as the guardsmen began swinging him between them as if he were a sack of lentils, the chief priest heard what he had fully expected.

"Wait!" Hostilius cried.

The chief priest began breathing again.

"Remove that exquisite cuirass before you pitch him over!"

His golden breastplate in which twelve stones were set, each representing a tribe of Israel, was ripped from his epaulets, and the chief priest was once again rocked back and forth between the sneering praetorians.

He fixed his eyes on the temple, the strand of smoke escaping from the altar of burnt offering. He did not believe in a life following this one, nor did he resent this divine condition even now as the sweaty hands of the guardsmen released him and the cries of the Sanhedrin faded behind him.

He blacked out a second before his body struck the roof of the portico and rolled into the courtyard.

"It is sundown," Dathan said to Germanicus, who was gazing at the dense blue haze clinging to the lake below.

Dathan suddenly noticed that his daughter was lingering in the background, looking as anxious as he did. "Go!" he barked.

"No," Germanicus said, "Mara should hear what I have to say as well. . . ." He gathered his thoughts in the moment it took her to race to his side. "Dathan—can you get a message to Aulus Valentinian?"

"Perhaps. But Jerusalem is in revolt, and both Valentinian and Norbanus have been arrested by the new procurator."

"No, no," Germanicus groaned. "What happened?"

"Hostilius brought an imperial standard into the city. Valentinian and his adjutant resisted this desecration. I have not heard any word of their executions, so there is still reason to hope."

"What has the Sixth Ferrata done?"

"I am not sure. Hostilius has a praetorian cohort under his command. Reports are sketchy, but I believe the temple police and two, maybe three cohorts of the Sixth are investing the Fortress of Antonia. . . ." Without apparent satisfaction, Dathan said, "Earlier today, the guard threw the Sanhedrin off the roof of the garrison. All seventy members. I care nothing for *Zedukim,* but they died like Jews."

Quickly setting aside his shock and disgust, Germanicus took stock of these new developments as military variables, then said, "Dispatch a runner to Valentinian or, failing that, the commander of the legionaries fighting Hostilius. Tell him that I, Germanicus Julius Agricola, will accept the *sacramentum dicere* of his God-fearing legion and Jewish *auxilia* on three conditions. . . ."

Gravely, Dathan nodded that he was taking note of all this.

"First, I will serve in the capacity of dictator, not emperor. By this ancient office I mean a magistrate with absolute authority who will hold such power only for a term of six months. By then, this campaign will be decided one way or another."

"Why do you decline the imperium?"

"Because it no longer exists," Germanicus said. "As of this moment, the Republic is *restored*. My second condition—the Sadducee temple police will take no further reprisals against the Pharisees. And you Perushim must not harass the *Zedukim.*"

"This will never work."

"It is my condition."

Dathan sighed. "Then we will try. But it probably will not work."

"Finally, as dictator, I declare a state of universal manumission." Germanicus realized that Mara had fallen to her knees. "What is it, woman?"

"The Lord who delivered us out of Aegyptian bondage now guides your hand to free the rest of mankind!"

Even Dathan seemed deeply moved. "Truly, your fever was God-inspired. This is something we have long awaited!"

Germanicus was on the verge of saying that his relapse probably had more to do with his old head wound and the heat, and that he had been persuaded to outlaw slavery on the advice of a familiar Roman ghost rather than the Jewish Lord—but he held his tongue. From this time on, he would try not to smother with endless qualms the mote of faith he sensed within himself. It would be hard enough to take and then hold Jerusalem without embroiling himself in self-doubt. It was probably impossible.

"Now, send that message," he said to Dathan with an energy in his voice that had been too long absent, "and find me a good Greek map of the city."

CODEX III
GLAESEA

18

"Bestir . . ." THE CHILD suddenly whispered.

The physician glanced up from the pile of scrolls he had unfurled across the table. Then, exhaling deeply, he shoved these flaking catalogues of useless treatments aside and studied the delirious boy.

How long had he been sequestered with this pale and ailing bit of flesh? A month? Two? A century perhaps? His own health was beginning to fail, if only from the constant anxiety.

Quintus was staring between his translucent-looking feet as if someone dear to him were standing at the end of his sleeping couch. A smile flickered on and off his lips as his frail voice soughed: *"Bestir yourself . . ."*

Rising from his chair, the physician relit the bronze censer hanging from the ceiling, and once again cleansing sulfur fumes filled the chamber. "What is it, my little rabbit?"

"Bestir yourself . . ." Quintus bared his teeth in a grin that seemed skull-like, so shrunken were the tissues of his small face. He had begun to greatly resemble his mother, who was now only slightly less emaciated due to her poisoning phobia.

"What are you saying—?"

"Bestir yourself, call up the Zephyrs, take to your wings and glide. . . ." Then, as the last syllable rattled out of his throat, all the animation in his face, his entire being, was arrested.

The physician began weeping—not for the child, whom he had surrendered to death some time ago, but for himself.

Reaching up, he cupped his palms over the censer and extinguished the jaundiced glow within.

Antonius Nepos stood at a distance, ringed by his guardsmen and in the company of his praetorian prefect, while Claudia Nero answered a wail of trumpets by mounting the funeral bier. Unsteady on her feet, she was assisted up the wooden steps by two Vestal Virgins, which he thought to be something of an affectation and a breach of the traditional forms. But he had decided to let her farewell her son however she pleased.

Surprisingly, she had taken the news dry-eyed, but then turned and, in that reptilian hiss of a voice she'd recently acquired, ordered her personal bodyguards to strangle her physician. Nepos didn't object to this, despite the promises he had made to the unfortunate man. The healer's execution would certainly prevent his being questioned should the Senate at some future time convene an inquest into the death of the *imperator designatus*.

Custom dictated that Claudia draw the veil off Quintus' face and open his eyes so he might glimpse the bliss awaiting him beyond the River Styx. Yet, after a long hesitation that started the patricians murmuring, she had one of the Vestals do this for her.

"Your wife endures nobly," Saturninus whispered to Nepos.

Of course, he really meant the shrew was showing an utter lack of nobility. It was the only thing Nepos admired about his flinty-eyed praetorian prefect: the deadpan fashion in which he could be insincere.

"Yes, I expected her to take this much worse. But I quite honestly believe she had tired of the child."

"Indeed?"

"This is between us, of course."

"Of course, my lord."

"Any dispatches from Antiochia?"

Saturninus smiled, so Nepos knew at once that bad news was on the way. Suddenly he didn't care for the man's disingenuousness as much as he had the moment before. He allayed his annoyance by reminding himself he would have Saturninus executed for treason in six months—not that he had any suspicion of disloyalty. Yet, as a former praetorian prefect who had undermined the very imperium he'd been sworn to protect, Nepos intended to nip in the bud the most likely source of any plot against him. From then on, he planned to rotate his prefects on the equinoxes, or thereabouts.

"I fear," Saturninus said at last, "another cohort of the Third Gallica deserted the encircled city last night and joined Germanicus' forces."

This report from Syria brought a tightness to Nepos' throat, although he reminded himself that any alarm at this point was premature. So far, the resurrected Germanicus—who supposedly

had been affirmed dictator rather than emperor by the Sixth
Ferrata in the interests of restoring some jumbled notion of a
republic that was part Roman and part Jewish—had met only
eastern legions on the field of battle. In a week, ten days at most,
Nepos would drive eastward with a consular army, twenty
thousand crack troops of two Italian and two Iberian legions with
five hundred sand-galleys raising the dust in their van. That
armored host would make short work of Germanicus Agricola's
last gasp at a republic. But now, Nepos was not about to let
Saturninus off the hook: "I thought you told me the Third Gallica
was solid."

The prefect continued to smile, obviously not seeing Claudia
sob as she clutched the delicate alabaster urn that would soon
contain the ashes of her son. "Five of its cohorts are extraordi-
narily solid, sire."

"That's not what you said."

"Well, I don't recall precisely—"

"You told me the *Third* was solidly behind me. You didn't split
hairs when we first discussed this."

"We must be mindful that in Judaea and Syria we are talking
about legionaries who in the course of years have acquired
Oriental sympathies and attitudes. However, I humbly apologize
if I inadvertently gave a false impression of this fluid situation."

"Your apologies are becoming tiresome."

"Sire?"

"When my wife recommended Hostilius for the procuratorship,
you added your voice to hers and told me he would be able to
control the Sanhedrin and the Sixth Ferrata with a single cohort of
guardsmen. And then you apologized when he couldn't."

"Well—"

"You told me the Fourth Sythica would quickmarch from
Antiochia to rescue Hostilius and his surviving force holed up in
the Fortress of Antonia. And then you apologized when the bloody
Fourth arrived a week later than planned—only to join Germanicus' siege of the Jerusalem garrison instead of breaking it!" In
deference to the occasion, Nepos had not raised his voice, but his
eyes were incensed.

And while Saturninus' smile had flattened considerably, he
persisted in wearing it. "If I have erred these past weeks, my lord,
it is because I have counseled against overreaction. Please
appreciate my rationale—the Senate must not perceive you in a

desperate light. But now, in another matter, I recommend bold-ness."

"What are you trying to say?" Nepos asked, seeing that Claudia was finally being helped down off the bier. Good Venus, but she was showing her age—all the more reason for him to continue his campaign to win the affections of the sixteen-year-old daughter of one of the richest and most exalted patrician families. What a perfect, porcelain-white vessel this young lovely was for two of his admitted appetites: lust and greed.

"I'm saying, sire, that Germanicus' promise of manumission is having a more serious effect on agricultural production and the general efficiency of the Empire than we first imagined. The number of runaways in September was five times the norm, and some large farms in the south of the peninsula are completely idle for want of field hands. Needless to say, with an offensive against Germanicus the Jew in the offing, we cannot afford to spare any more legionaries to round up slaves."

"Out with it, man—what do you propose?"

"I suggest we apply a military form of discipline to this domestic labor crisis."

"You mean decimation, then?"

"If you please. One slave in ten dies so nine others are well-warned."

Nepos considered the proposition, briefly. Most slave owners were now so terrified by the prospect of a servile war on the scale of the one ignited by Spartacus, they probably wouldn't balk at the ten per cent loss of property the measure would necessarily entail. "Do it."

"Very good, sire."

Nepos noted that his prefect had stopped calling him *Lord Regent* but had yet to call him *Emperor*, even in private. In the coming hours, as Quintus' ashes slowly cooled in the pit beneath the petrol-soaked bier, punctilious negotiations would have to be completed with key senators and generals before Nepos could be addressed as *imperator*. The title *Caesar*, of course, carried with it a specific familial connotation, and Nepos knew he could never presume to graft his own common ancestral branch onto the lofty tree that had sprouted—semenlessly, he might add—from the divine loins of Gaius Julius Caesar and his adopted son, Augustus. He would assiduously avoid any such displays of hubris in his first obsequious relations as emperor with the Conscript Fathers. Later, when he had the porcine old fools under his thumb, he would do what he bloody well pleased, even declare himself a two-phallused son of Mars if it struck his fancy.

At last, the torchbearers approached and lit the edges of the bier, which thanks to the petrol was swiftly engulfed.

Over the crackling of the flames Claudia keened. She wept and peed with about the same degree of emotion. He resolved not to remain for the rest of her caterwauling. "Come, Saturninus, I can hear the same concert in any alleyway of Subura." Wheeling, he nearly bumped breastplates with one of his praetorians, a red-bearded youth who begged forgiveness with a devout salute.

Nepos couldn't believe his eyes. "Are you German?"

"Aye, Lord Regent."

He glared at his prefect. "What's the meaning of this!"

"Sire?"

"A *German* among my own retinue! Post him somewhere away from Rome! Must I be reminded in my own household what these savages are doing to my northern empire! Are you all trying to drive me mad?"

He had scarcely calmed down when, three hours later, an unexpectedly polite invitation came from Claudia to join her in her apartments. Arriving late to imply that he had no intention of being manipulated by any show of sorrow, he found her dressing chamber, on the outer wall of the palace, chilly—she had opened the windows to the first rain of autumn, and the brazier set beside her couch was doing little to warm the wet breeze that was blowing back the curtains.

She was drunk, but for once didn't grimace as she caught sight of him.

He decided to remain civil—for the time being. He took a cup from a tray held by a slave, then dismissed the girl with a sideward glance toward the door as he reclined on a couch musty with stale perfume.

"I love the rain," Claudia said tonelessly. "Don't you, Decimus Antonius?"

"I'm afraid not—spent too many years shivering in it on campaign." Unseen, he dropped a tiny slip of poison-reactive paper into his cup. The lichen dye turned no adverse color, so he drank.

"Well, I love rain." And then she said with the same lack of expression: "I knew we couldn't kill him. I knew he didn't drown in Corinthus. You see, the gods protect him, my husband. We would need their support and an army of demons to put Germanicus Agricola in his tomb."

"I *have* such a army, woman." Swirling the wine in his cup, Nepos told himself to slow down; lately, he was drinking nearly as much as she, and now especially he needed a clear head.

"When do you depart?" she asked.

"Soon." For an instant, her eyes had seemed lucid, and he wondered why. "No later than the ides."

"By sea?"

"No, although my consular army will go by ship to Cilicia. But I intend to travel to Tarsus by rail-galley. Please keep that quiet. I want to surprise each of our governors and legion commanders along the way. See whose delight at my arrival is genuine and whose isn't."

"You think of everything, don't you?"

Wondering if this might be another clumsy accusation concerning Quintus, he tried to control a surge of exasperation with her—and lost: "What is that supposed to mean!"

Astonishingly, she didn't flare back at him. Instead, her smile trembled apart from a sob she finally brought under control. "Nothing . . . only that I rely on brave Decimus Antonius to bring me back the head of our son's murderer."

Nepos couldn't fathom the connection she was making between the boy's death and Germanicus, but felt reassured that the former emperor, and not he, was now the focus of her wrath. Where her muddle-headedness served his ends, he would offer no objection. He even tried to look consoling as he said, "I will do that, Claudia. I will make Germanicus Agricola suffer for all the anguish he has caused us." Rising from his couch, he tossed off the last of his wine. "Now, with your permission, my love, I'd like to mourn alone. Two griefs combined on a night such as this is more than either of us can bear."

In the dark vestibule that separated Claudia's dressing chamber from the vast rotunda in which she warehoused her clothing, Saturninus listened to Antonius Nepos take his leave. His lordship had obviously intended to keep something from his loyal praetorian prefect: that he would go by land and not sea, as all Rome believed, to the East.

Smiling, the prefect strolled out into Claudia's presence. He pretended to ignore the difficulty she was having in holding down a belch.

"Well?" she finally asked, knocking over the wine jar she'd been reaching for.

"Very good, my Empress. I rather thought he was holding back the truth from me. More and more he lies to me. And in that I glimpse my peril."

"Will you do it on the rail-galley, then?"

"Me personally? Oh, I'm afraid not. That wouldn't do now, would it? The empress's future consort cutting her husband's throat?"

"Whatever," she said, crossly, "I want him dead." But then just as quickly as it had appeared, her irritation toward him vanished, and she gave him a look she probably imagined to be seductive.

Without an instant's hesitation, he responded to this cue, even though boys were his decided preference over matrons. "You put unseemly thoughts in my head when you glance at me that way."

"Unseemly? How?"

"Need I explain?"

She was grinning now, sloe-eyed. "Yes."

"Well, I feel unworthy contemplating my own pleasure on so sorrowful a day."

Her eyes moistened, but only for a moment. "Then you must consider my pleasure, Saturninus—the supreme pleasure of accepting the seed that will become another son. Your son, my handsome love." She lay back down.

And the prefect went to her.

"This be my reward?" the guardsman asked himself as he slogged up the path through a grove of acorn oaks dripping with rain. "To run beside vermin?"

He was following the very crest of the Appeninus on his flight north. And, although he lacked helmet, cape, and short sword, the runaway slaves clogging this remote path immediately recognized him to be a praetorian and crashed through the undergrowth to be away from him. Yet, when he showed no interest in capturing them, some of the bolder men crept out of concealment, shivering in their threadbare tunics, and tried to pelt him with stones. They would stop only when the young, red-bearded German charged toward them a few paces, flashing his dagger.

"Be off or die!" he would rage at this filthy rabble, this malnourished horde of Abyssinians, Scandians, Nubians, Mauretanians, and only Donar knew what else. Eventually, he kept his blade fisted as warning to all who would trifle with him. But this did nothing to stop the catcalls rising from the copses along the muddy trail: "We're off to Germanicus, you bloody red cape! Death to Nepos and his whore!"

"Aye," the German agreed, but not so that the muck-clad vermin might have the satisfaction of hearing. Had the Empire gone mad, that dim-witted drudges who'd once flopped prone at the mere sight of a praetorian were now deriding one with all the gutter Latin they could think of?

A coarse voice floated down from a misty outcropping: "We'll send you to Charon with your manhood in your mouth! You and Nepos!"

Aye, the German thought as he kicked the mud off his *caligae* on the base of a leaning snag, then doubled his pace for fear of ambush, *there was the true blame for all this—Decimus Antonius Nepos.*

What ever had possessed him to throw in his lot with the prefect? Fear, he supposed—fear that Germanicus' republic would do away with the guard forever. But now what did that matter? He was finished with Nepos' praetorians, for he had no doubt that had he submitted to transfer to Hibernia, the garrison commander there would have greeted him by ordering his skull cleaved from pate to neck, the current preference over an old-fashioned lopping. Nepos was becoming notorious for this kind of arm's length treachery, but the young German hated the lord regent even more for what he had done to the owner of the Red Cape, a former praetorian himself—as if that meant anything to the likes of Nepos. The old man, as raw and hoary as a winter's dawn, nonetheless had always been good for a gratis quaff or a few sesterces to ease the loins across the Tiber, what if a long-skulled lad was down on his luck, or just homesick for the Wald.

Seven *coronas* for valor, two of these actions directly resulting in laurel-wreathed dispatches being sent to the Emperor—that is what the old man had heaped upon himself during his fighting days. And how did Nepos reward him for such enduring honor? Skinned him alive, then tossed his flayed corpse down the Tiber steps to be borne away on the yellow, rain-swollen tide.

Nepos did not know it yet, but he would pay for what he had

done to the owner of the Red Cape. The young German would hazard this journey and then an uncertain welcome to the Wald in order to make sure of that.

More slaves scattered in front of him. They were like lemmings on the run. All these surly slaves.

19

TIME AND AGAIN, afield and in palace, on rail-galley clacking across the Anatolian wastes and trireme folding open the gray waters of the Atlanticus, he had listened to Germanicus Agricola carp about his "loneliness in the midst of many." Never once had Rolf doubted the existence of such an affliction, for Caesar would not broach a thing unless it was as real as stone. But he himself had never experienced it until lately. Now he was surrounded every waking hour by his *thegans* and their sons, but felt utterly alone, bereft of any counsel wiser than his own, abandoned by the god-friend to fail for reasons he might grasp only in the instant of his destruction. It was nearly as powerful as the desire between man and woman: his sudden longing to seek out a strong and sympathetic mind with which he might discuss this strangely disturbing report from Rome.

He could think of only one such mind.

"Stay," he said to his thanes, who nevertheless began to follow with their swords clanking and cloaks rustling until he turned and glared at them.

The recent rains, earlier than usual by a month, had greened the fringes of the quags with a final burgeoning of cress, meadowsweet, and scouring reed. And those women not clustered on a flat boulder above the village to grind acorns were down in the fens with their wicker baskets. There he found Glaesea fishing long strands of cress out of the murky water. She was almost obscured by a brindle haze that hinted of the abiding chill soon to come.

"Glaesea."

She seemed bewildered and then pleased to see him, although she scanned the shadowy edge of the forest for his ever-present thanes.

"They be dismissed for a while," Rolf said, as if reading her thoughts. Then he added a bit awkwardly: "I come for your counsel."

She used some dry sedges to wipe the mud off her hands. "Are you troubled, my *Herzog*?"

He began to shrug off the question, but then gave up any pretense and said, "Aye, more than many be aware."

"Tell me then . . ." She half smiled, and it was all he could do not to embrace her, to find solace for his confusion in her warm grasp. "What is it?"

"Germanicus be *alive*."

Her eyes narrowed. "Are you certain? There have been so many rumors."

"A praetorian, a Marcoman like us, come home last night. Fresh from Antonius Nepos' service." Absently, he nodded toward the east. "It be true—Caesar lives. He be at the head of the Sixth Legion Ferrata and some Judaean rebels what attack Antiochia. The city, it be ready to fall to him."

"But isn't that the very thing you hoped for?"

"Aye, but too late now, Glaesea. All too late."

"Why?"

He wanted to explain to her that after his brutal raids on the garrisons ringing the Wald, bad blood would exist eternally between Rome and himself; even the legionaries who would harbor no grudge against Germans would remember Rolf of the Marcomanni with vengeance in their hearts; that his slow and agonizing death—certain now in his own mind—would be toasted in the wineshops of the ultimately triumphant Empire. But he could not string together the words to complete so dizzying a thought, let alone defend it against Glaesea's insightful questions, so instead he said, "Germanicus be different."

"What do you mean?"

"Just that."

"No, there must be more to it than *just that*."

"He be a convert to the Jews!" His haggard eyes gazed off into the mist. He didn't understand his own vehemence. Never had he felt any antagonism toward Judaeans; he'd even befriended one in his days of Anatolian service, and then mourned Aaron when the rebels slaughtered him and his family during a raid on a settlement for retired legionaries. Perhaps these strong feelings had more to do with Germanicus than with the Jews. He had always seemed the very bedrock of Roman virtue, and there was much to admire about Roman ways. Rolf clung to that view even here in the

Palatine-despising Wald. But why now had Germanicus abandoned his Romanness in favor of Jewish customs? What was the cause of this irresolution? Had the East proved a spiritual trap for one more stolid Roman? For it was said in the ranks that with time both Judaean religion and women become more attractive.

"And Rolf . . . ?" She hesitated.

He glanced back at her, hawklike. "Aye?"

"And Rolf has not changed at all since he said farewell to Germanicus Julius?"

Sealing his lips against angry words, he looked downward. There was a pugmark in the soft mud of the bank. Wolf. A good omen, and this somehow softened his temper again. He was desperate for favorable omens. "You, woman, be bristling with truths." Still, there had been enough bite in her voice for him to then add: "And I ask if Glaesea be with Mena, such be the salt of her tongue." He spoke of the Roman menstrual goddess.

She smiled again. "No, I am not consorting with Mena."

He met her gaze briefly, then looked away before she could see how her quiet reply had warmed his face. He had not meant to draw such words out of her, although they had given him a feeling that might have soared within him had it not been weighed down by shame. Segestias' waxen face was never far beyond her bare right shoulder.

"I think Rolf is troubled because this news reminds him how he stands between two worlds—one Roman, one German. He stands alone."

"Aye!" he exclaimed, astonished that his quandary could be summed up so simply.

"Rolf is as fierce a Marcoman warrior as any not yet enrolled in the Army of the Furious. Fiercer even than Estammic, whom he slew and now mourns as his brother." Then she spoke more breathily: "Fiercer than Segestias, who was a good man and a good thane, but not a great man and certainly not a king. This fierceness of spirit would give Rolf contentment—but for what he knows. A great man sees both sides of all matters. So much so, he has no contentment. And Rolf knows that a Germania outside the Empire will sooner or later break down again into the tribes. Into quarrels and much killing among kinsmen. He knows that for the sake of his own people some kind of peace will have to be made with Rome. These are the things troubling my *herzog*." Then she went back to gathering cress, draining the soggy green clumps in her basket.

He sat for a long while with his arms clasped around his doubled legs, saying nothing, watching her. Then finally he asked, "What be my true path, Glaesea?"

She laughed. "I am a woman."

"A woman full of the god-friend."

"Is that why you break your own vow and see me once again?"

Again he fell silent so long she went back to her task. When he broke this silence his voice was a murmur: "What be my true path?"

She just shook her head.

"What be my way with Caesar?" He shut his eyes. "Young Quintus be dead. Germanicus, he be mad with grief, I think. What be my words to a man so heavy with sorrow?"

"The grief is his concern," she said stubbornly.

"Then what be *my* concern, woman?"

"You should do those things that are good for both Germanicus and you—but only until you have a chance to meet with him and discover your differences. Then you must do what is good for Germania, for you are our king and we rely on your first loyalty to rest with us."

Then she hefted her basket onto her hip and hurried up the slope toward the forest, leaving him to stare off across the fens.

Hours later he was still sitting there, the darkness closing around him, when he suddenly whispered, "Nauportus Pass . . . there I be of service to us both."

Then he shouted for his lords to gather around him.

Ahead of Germanicus, over the glow of the fire and then forty miles beyond the quicksilvered expanse of the twilit gulf, lay Tarsus.

There, as he had it on reliable authority from the Perushim merchants of the city, the better part of a consular army had already disembarked from its transport galleys and was presently organizing itself behind the armored centuries. These swarms of sand-galleys would spearhead the drive against the motley force that marched westward under a peculiar standard: a golden Roman eagle carefully sheathed from the light of the sun by a Jewish *tallith*.

And that strange horde, consisting of three eastern legions and their *auxilia*, had no chance of defeating the imperial army led by Antonius Nepos it would soon face. None whatever.

No one knew this better than Germanicus Agricola, who, as so often in the past when on the eve of calamity, was composing a letter. It was to his adopted son. He sat close enough to the flames to make use of their light, but just outside their ambit of heat, which otherwise would have softened the wax of his tablets. His face had been chafed ruddy by weeks of autumnal winds; and, as he grasped his stylus, his eyes seemed especially thoughtful under their brim of sun-bleached eyebrows.

> *Kalends of October*
> *MMDCCXLI Anno Urbis Conditae*
> *Issus, Eastern Cilicia*
> *Republic of Rome*

My beloved Quintus,
   Once again I find myself encamped on some site of ancient adversity—and confronted with a modern urgency.
   Tomorrow, the day after at the latest, I must confront an enemy I cannot possibly vanquish. He has twenty thousand war-hardened troops; I have a convocation of garrison soldiers, their native auxiliaries, more runaway slaves than I can feed, and a sprinkling of Judaean rebels who are more adept at ambuscade than pitched battle. He has over two hundred sand-galleys; I can lay claim to nine whose vintage would be commendable if they were amphoraè *of wine rather than armored craft. He has enough* ballistae *to make the sky roar continuously, while I have virtually none.*
   However, in defense of the enthusiasm of my followers, I must confess that Alexander of Macedon, on the eve of struggle with Darius in this very coastal valley, had little more cause for cheer than I. Yet, by the time the sun had next set on Issus, more than one hundred thousand Persians but scarcely a thousand Macedonians lay lifeless across the ground on which I now repose. It is hard to believe that this sand was once sheened with blood, and harder to believe that soon it shall be so red-soaked again.
   I miss you beyond calculation, and pray that those around you have not poisoned your sweet mind against me. . . .

Frowning at his own lack of restraint, he rubbed out the last line with his thumb.
He prepared to start the paragraph again, this time more in

keeping with reason and proportion than his desperation to preserve the boy's love for him in the face of the outrages Claudia was most likely ascribing to the Julian scoundrel and his Jewish minions. Of course, even should he find some way to dispatch this missive to Rome, it would never arrive in Quintus' hands; Antonius Nepos and Claudia would see to that.

Through the transparent flames, he could see Mara smiling; for once, her eyes seemed subdued—perhaps the prospect of death had softened them. "Do you wish for more vinegar?"

"Please."

Rising from the sandy ground, she stretched, then carried the urn around the fire to him.

He gently caught her wrist when she had finished pouring. In two days they would both be dead—along with Dathan, Shammai, Valentinian, Norbanus, and thousands of others as well. Surely she knew this as well as he, yet her manner had betrayed no fear these past days of waiting. "You're a brave woman," he said with an odd smile.

She looked dismayed for an instant, but then nodded as if appreciative. After sweeping the fall of her dark hair behind her shoulders, she withdrew to the far side of the flames again.

Oh Quintus, you may rightfully ask: How can I lead tens of thousands into the certainty of defeat? Perhaps it is some aberration of honor, the longing for a dignified death no true Roman can deny. Or perhaps I find myself in the position of a Teuton king who cannot be surpassed in courage on the field of battle by the least of his followers. Indeed, these legionaries and respecters of the Jewish Lord enrolled in the Sixth Legion Ferrata, the Fourth Scythica, and Third Gallica; these auxiliaries and temple police, so outraged by the desecration of Jerusalem and Procurator Hostilius' murder of their entire high priesthood, they have largely put aside their internecine feuds to join me in the restoration of the Republic; these Perushim outlanders, men and women of remarkable resilience; even the slaves who have trod across half the Empire to enlist in our cause—all have shown impeccable courage on our march thus far, especially during the siege of Antiochia, which fell on your birthday. Did you receive the marmot you asked for?

Again, Germanicus thumbed out a line. Then he peered down the slope to the next closest fire, that of Valentinian's camp.

And, if I must catalogue my reasons for going ahead with this unlikely campaign, I admit that there is a protective aura surrounding this enterprise, which cannot be denied. Aulus Valentinian and Kaeso Norbanus, men of strength and high purpose, seemed irrevocably doomed when Tullus Hostilius, better known to us as that court buffoon Mucianus, ordered the execution of the former procurator and his adjutant in the moments before he himself took his own life. The praetorians tasked with this order decided to spare Valentinian and Norbanus with the aim of bartering the lives of the two God-respecters for their own. I did fully honor this exchange even though these were the very guardsmen who betrayed me, for I had been rereading Plato and was reminded that happiest are those who practice the civil and social virtues which are called temperance and justice. Now, for five sesterces, who was Plato quoting in this regard?

"Any word of your father's return?" he asked Mara, who shook her head.

Dathan and Shammai had left camp at dawn, hoping to steal through the defenses ringing Tarsus to ascertain Nepos' plans, if the lord regent was actually in command of the expeditionary army. So far, no one had seen him in the East.

Germanicus went back to his tablets.

As to this business of my God-respecting, I am certain much has been made of it in the capital, but please assume little of what you have heard to be the truth. I have not converted to the faith of the Jews, nor do I harbor any such intention at this time. However, I find much in this religion that would be beneficial to the maintenance of our new republic, for I believe that free men are also self-constrained men. As to God, my devotion is a joyless one if only because mine is a nature steeped in sadness, but if He does indeed direct our destinies, as all those about me claim, I suspect that I have been given a somber one and must therefore trust in the necessity that makes this so. . . .

gaze shifted back and forth across the darkened slope.
re approaching from below, although he could see no

You must understand that none of this is easy for me. . . .

Once again, he obliterated a line.

My greatest frustration has been the persistence of many in addressing me as Caesar. They seem to be of the ancient opinion aut Caesar aut nullus—*either a Caesar or nobody, in case you have lapsed in your high Latin lessons during my absence. Still, whether I am Caesar or not, and whatever becomes of us, you must trust that you remain my son, the object of my foremost devotion and . . .*

Dathan was standing at the edge of the firelight. Behind him was Shammai, wrenching the muzzle of his *pilum* with his hands.

Germanicus shot to this feet. "At last."

But the two Perushim seemed reluctant to speak and continued to stare at the Roman as if it were he and not they who bore urgent news. For once, Dathan's eyes did not flash with temper when Germanicus ordered him in an impatient tone of voice: "Tell me what you saw."

Dathan accepted a cup of water from Mara, then slowly came the rest of the way around the fire. "Antonius Nepos has not yet arrived in Tarsus."

"Who then is in command?"

"A triumvirate of generals."

"And their names?"

Dathan told him, then added: "If this army has any weaknesses at all, it is the dissension among its commanders. There is disagreement whether or not to mount the attack against us now, or wait for Nepos, who is still in Rome. Two cohorts are already on their way toward us. They are advancing cautiously, hoping the others will join them. But I suppose even these two cohorts alone will give us enormous trouble."

"What's keeping Nepos?"

Dathan's glance went to Mara, then back to Germanicus. "Perhaps he is consoling his wife."

"What's happened?"

Dathan's reply came like mingled echoes: "Your adopted son is dead . . . I do not know the cause . . . I am sorry, Germanicus Julius."

His eyes were drawn into the flames, but he remained expressionless. After a long moment, he pitched the tablets into the fire.

The rivulets of wax drizzled off the sandalwood panels and onto the coals.

North of Ravenna, the imperial rail-galley emerged from under the oppressive bank of low clouds that had obfuscated the landscape since Flortentia. A splendid autumn light, soft with gold, lay over Cisalpine Gaul, and Antonius Nepos found himself smiling in the privacy of his extravagantly appointed car—one, thank Mars, without the ubiquitous and tinny-looking bas-relief of ancient Julio-Claudians on the commode screen. Nothing but original Greek works decorating the bulkheads and lead-plated outer walls.

As the long string of cars rounded a sharp bend, he had a glimpse of the foremost *ballista* car, its huge siege weapon rampant. The topside deck seemed to have sprouted fluttering red wings—the capes of his praetorians perched there, keeping themselves entertained by popping their *pili* at runaway slaves unfortunate enough to be following the artery toward the un-Romanized far north.

Nepos chuckled to himself as one such wastrel, sprinting across an open field for the cover of a wooded ridge, suddenly clutched his side. Reeling, he tumbled into the ripened spelt. Nepos was surprised the farmer hadn't posted guards around his holding: with the breadbasket eastern provinces in disarray, grain was nearly worth its weight in gold.

He shouted for more wine.

When no servant rushed to answer the summons, he bellowed, "Colonel!"

Saturninus' adjutant sprang from his cubicle station at the opposite end of the car. The praetorian prefect himself had remained in Rome—a recurring ailment he'd picked up in the Novo Provinces, so he claimed—and would follow as soon as recovered. *"Imperator?"*

Antonius Nepos had taken the plunge from lord regent to emperor—and his detractors had not found the courage to utter a peep in protest. "Where is my manservant?"

"You dismissed him for the afternoon, sire. You said he could now make up for the sleep he lost to last night's preparations for the journey."

Nepos could not recall having said any such thing. But it was of no matter. The warm light streaming in through the windows was making him drowsy. He waved the colonel away and closed his eyes. After a while, he dreamed of a good and distant time when all adversity would be behind him and he would be sincerely loved, a robust old man the entire world adored and would lament when he was eventually gone. He dreamed of his funeral procession, which was inordinately grand. But the long train of grieving soldiers and citizens, of bands and exotic animals, of mumbling priest and Vestals, somehow saddened him too.

The light touch of a hand on his shoulder startled him awake. "What—!"

"Forgive me, sire," the colonel said, "but you didn't stir to the sound of my voice."

Recovering himself, Nepos turned on his sweat-soaked couch to have a look outside. It was dark, abysmally dark. Why, lately, did he perspire so in his sleep? Was it the wine? "Where are we?"

"Twenty miles beyond Patavium, sire."

"Ah." Long ago, in laying out the route of the Great Artery around the Adriaticum, Caesar Fabius had curved the line away from the sea and up into the Julian Alps in order to prevent the more ornate rail-galleys in the Empire from being raided by Dalmatian pirates, whose courage and resolve weakened with each step they took inland.

"The last signal banner we passed was raised, sire."

Nepos yawned, feeling heavy and dull from his vinous sleep. "Can't you get through with our wireless?"

"No. The mountains." The man had scudding eyes, which gave Nepos pause for a moment.

Beside each signal banner was a slate board on which a brief portion of the urgent message was sometimes chalked. "Was there anything on the board?"

"Yes, *Imperator*. A single word. A name."

"Well, out with it."

"Gaia . . . that was all."

Again, Nepos turned toward the darkness, but this time so that the colonel wouldn't see the worry in his eyes. Gaia was a code name taken from the traditional feminine *nomen* used in the wedding vow; he had instructed his young patrician lovely to use it if she ever found herself in peril. Had Claudia found out about her? All at once, he was filled with rage for the harlot and bitterly regretted not having arranged her assassination in his absence.

What better time to do away with one's wife than when one is out of the capital, fighting Germanicus the Jew and his Judaean rabble? Claudia's murder could then be blamed on Rome's Jewish population—a marvelous idea he would not forget.

The colonel broke the extended silence: "Instructions, sire?"

"I know no one of that name. Are you sure the operators read the slate correctly?"

"I have no reason to doubt them."

"Whatever—we'll have to wait until the next station, which I believe is many miles ahead."

"Pardon me, sire, but I believe there's a small garrison just around this mountain. Surely we can use the wireless facilities there."

"Then make the stop," Nepos said distractedly.

"Very good—I'll give the word to the operators."

He lay back. Who knew of his designs to win the hand of this rich young maiden? Only Saturninus, who was also privy to the Gaia code. Nepos had revealed it to him in the event she might need the ready protection of the guard. *But what advantage would my own praetorian prefect . . . ?*

Then Nepos sniggered. The blindness had suddenly left his eyes. Had not he himself been another emperor's prefect? And hadn't he realized vaulting advantage in supplanting that undeniably fair man? Saturninus was simply trying to beat his master to the same fate Nepos had intended for him. Understandable enough. Even admirable for its spirit of initiative.

The rail-galley was slowing as the colonel returned and saluted. "Does the Emperor desire a full or light guard to escort him to the wireless tower?"

"What do you think?"

The officer was taken aback. "Well . . . I don't know. It would depend . . ."

"On what? The nature of the reception awaiting me?"

"Sire?"

"You know full well who Gaia is, don't you?"

The colonel's face hardened, but he said nothing. Then, as he apparently came to the decision that he would have to take the entire responsibility for this matter and his hand gravitated toward the hilt of his short sword, Nepos reached under his couch and came up with the cut-down, multishafted *pilum* he now took everywhere with him. He loosed a three-shot burst that caved in the colonel's chest. It sent him flailing against the windows, painting the glazing with his gore before he fell lifeless against the wine-dispensing urn.

The next praetorian to enter the car came with sword drawn, and that was reason enough for Nepos to kill him as well.

The third guardsman to burst through the pneumatic door immediately understood that the loyalty of the retinue was at issue and wisely showed his palms to the Emperor. "My lord—I have no part in this!"

"No part in what?" Nepos asked severely, his forefinger within a fraction of an inch of letting go with another round.

"I . . . I'm not sure. But two traitors are dead and I knew nothing of their intentions!"

Nepos relaxed his grip on his stout *pilum*, but only slightly as he clicked his eyes toward the guardsman sprawled in the aisle. "Who other than this fool kept the company of Saturninus' adjutant?"

The reply came without hesitation: "The centurion Cordus."

"Is that all?"

"I swear!"

"Then catch Cordus unawares—and bring me his head."

Bowing like a slave, the guardsman backed out of the car.

Rushing to the lever on the bulkhead, Nepos put out the *electricus* lamps, then opened a window and squatted beside the breezy opening, watching the garrison lights slide into view over the sights of his *pilum*. His heart was trip-hammering and his mouth was quite dry, but he felt in fine control of himself. This sort of business had always been his bailiwick, not the machinations conducted behind palace curtains.

The guardsman came back a few minutes later, looming uncertainly at the edge of the darkness. He was clasping a severed head before him. "*Imperator?*"

"Stand where you are." Nepos was tempted to switch the lamps back on—to see the expression on Cordus' face—but decided against it in the interest of his own safety. Behind the guardsman stood a half dozen or so of his fellows, each trying to get a word in edgeways that he was completely loyal to the new emperor and had no idea what insanity had possessed their late colonel.

"Shut up, the lot of you—and listen!" Nepos shouted, seeing from the corner of his eye the first shafts of the station-platform colonnade flicker past. "Assassins are awaiting me here. Kill them. Kill them all—or I shall consider you against me!"

The praetorians began alighting from the rail-galley even before it had come to a full stop, charging across the platform and through the garrison portal.

Nepos wiped his face with his forearm.

And then a rattle of *pili* fire assured him that his "Gaia" was most likely in perfect health, and that Saturninus had used her code name only as a ruse to get Nepos away from his well-protected rail-galley and inside the garrison.

He laughed to himself.

Ten minutes later, his victorious guardsmen thronged his car, lofting the bloody hearts of their fellow praetorians who'd had the stupidity to back Saturninus—a grisly practice learned in the war against the Aztecae. They were wildly chanting the name of Antonius Nepos. But he scarcely heard them. He was listening to an operator explain that the first opportunity to turn the rail-galley around would come at the great revolving table in the yards at Nauportus. Before that lay the high pass of the same name.

Nepos had decided to return to Rome. It had become necessary to deal with Saturninus and Claudia before Germanicus. He had every expectation of burying them, then being on his way east again within forty-eight hours.

20

"Pasa . . ."

THE FIRST RAIN of the wet season had come to the Anatolian coast.
Below, the pinpricks of flame marking the campfires of his army
blurred to orange smudges, then vanished entirely behind the
curtain of water that splashed the rocky ground he climbed.

"Pasa . . ." the voice kept whispering from above.

He continued in pursuit of it, but the susurration seemed no less
distant after each leg of his ascent. He began to wonder if it was
within or without his agony, a figment of sorrow better left
ignored. Or perhaps it was only the voice of the wind.

"Pasa . . ."

Twice he slipped in the mud of a ravine—and thought how
much better to lie there and eventually dissolve into the ooze from
which Mara maintained all mankind had sprung. He ached for her
comfort, but had not wanted her to see him sob.

"Pasa . . . my brother . . . Inshallah . . ."

He began stumbling upward again—toward the voice and as far
away from the encampment as possible.

The moon began to penetrate the clouds, and through this
diffuse light he could make out the shapes of the hills, their gullies
and outcrops. On one such knob of stone a man was dancing in
silhouette—not with joyous abandon, as the men of this country
were known to do in fits of religious exaltation; but slowly, reeling
with his long arms outstretched in an inexorable slowness.

"Pasa," he whispered, his voice no less eerie for being close
by.

As on the occasion of their first meeting years before, Germanicus was taken by the Great *Zaim's* luxuriant white beard. It hung
down to his chest and now seemed luminous. His coarse woolen
habit appeared to be doing a better job of keeping out the cold rain

than Germanicus' cloak, for unlike the Roman, the Anatolian holy man was not shivering. He went on with his languid dance.

"Is it your grief that makes you slump so, *Pasa*?"

He had no answer.

"You must learn to keep moving through your grief. Otherwise it will have you."

"Then you mourn Khalid as bitterly as I do Quintus?"

"More so, my brother. You have those who caused his death to hate. Hatred is a fine antidote to sorrow. I entrusted Khalid's life to Allah, so I must take only obedience from his loss."

"But your son died in my service. You have me to despise."

The *Zaim's* eyes were flashing each time he twirled about. "Do not think so highly of yourself."

Then Germanicus realized what the *Zaim*, a man who inexplicably could see distant things, had just said. "*Who* caused Quintus's death?" he asked.

"You know better than I. You know the name of this devil, I have only glimpsed his face in a vision."

"Yes . . . yes! And how like the way of things—that he will go unpunished!"

"There is no way of *things*. I thought you would have learned that by now. Have the Perushim so lost the light that they now believe the One who shall one day turn the sky to molten brass and the mountains to tufts of wool—that this selfsame One is a *thing*, as the gods of Rome are things of marble and gold?"

Germanicus wrapped himself tighter in his sopping cloak. "I don't know . . . I just don't know."

"You *know*, Germanicus Agricola."

"Don't you weary of that spinning?"

"Yes. But if I stop right now, I fear my heart will drop through the center of me. It was hard enough to let go of Khalid, whose cheeks I still long to kiss, whose words I listen for in every silence. I no longer care for silence."

And from those words Germanicus understood that the holy man was partaking of Quintus' loss as if it were his own. "Thank you, my friend. It was a long ways to come from Agri Dagi."

He nodded serenely. "It is a longer ways to the gates of Rome. The two cohorts that left Tarsus have stopped, but only so the others can catch up with them. This will happen within the hour—my deepest ear is filled with the rumble of sand-galleys even now. Then this great force will advance again, united. What do you plan for the morrow?"

"To lead an army to the banks of the Styx. From there, Charon will take command."

"And if this disaster does not come to pass?"

"Well, at the very least I will have to rethink how the entire universe is directed. I will then put my faith in shadows, in blotches on the sun, in what old men with cast eyes mutter—"

"Good." The *Zaim* laughed. "It is for these words I journeyed from the Purple Village."

"Wait," Germanicus asked hopefully, "do you mean you've come to combine your warriors with mine?"

"Has my Greek grown so rusty you take such nonsense from my words?"

"I only—"

"No, *Pasa*. I see no need to fight beside you tomorrow."

"Why not?" And when the *Zaim* hesitated, Germanicus prodded: "Then, you, too, envision nothing but a slaughter?"

"I see you with much sadness, but with a few consolations to keep you moving forward. One of these consolations is priceless beyond measure. That is all I see. . . ."

When no words followed after several moments, Germanicus peered up: The holy man was gone.

The gray-headed German was not only well into his seventh decade, he suffered from a more specific infirmity as well. He was stone-deaf from the thousands of explosions that had broken against his ears during his years as a legionary-sapper with the Sixth Victrix. A metal fragment from one such detonation had caught him at the corner of the mouth, ripping his cheek nearly to the ear lobe and leaving him with a permanently snide expression that did not suit his amiable disposition; for he had hiked with the others the two hundred Roman miles from the Wald to this high pass in the Julian Alps in three and a half days—and done so without a mutter of complaint.

Still, his *herzog* had to tap him on the shoulder to get his attention as he straddled the rails atop the Great Artery, feeling the hum of the river of oil as if rushed toward the distant capital and its Tiber-side refineries. Rome's jugular.

The *herzog* was making impatient motions with his hands in the strong moonlight—too stark a glow for business such as this, but the king had made it clear that no other night was possible.

Antonius Nepos might never again venture through the Nauportus Col.

"A few minutes more," the old man said tonelessly, sensing what Rolf was asking about. Other than a faint buzz in his jaw and in the plates of his skull, he had not been able to hear his own voice in such a long time the lilt had gone out of it.

Through the soles of his bare feet he could feel the vibrations of the approaching rail-galley. But it was still far off, and the murmuring of the oil was much more pronounced than these faint resonances. He was braiding wires deep within the shadows of the Lebanese cedar trestles. He no longer needed to see to do such work. In the course of many years the tips of his fingers had sprouted eyes keener than those planted in his head. He was careful to avoid the *impulsus* wire stretched taut along the space between the trestles and the crown of the pipe, crackling with messages being passed back and forth between Rome and the far-flung outposts of the Empire. A careless brush with one of its *electricus* surges would reduce his king and him to a pretty powder flash. Not a bad way to go, if one were given the choice. But one never was. Death always had its own terms.

Rolf touched him again, and the old man whispered without looking up, "No worry, my lord. This galley be miles off and coming slow. Heavy laden. Many *ballista* cars, this galley. My *herzog* be sure he desire to snatch this serpent by its tail?" He chuckled, but then went on in a sober voice: "Go to your thanes. . . ." The raiding party was made up of all the nobles and their sons—to have left one behind would have been the same as insulting him. "I be ready by the time you get there."

A moment later he looked up and saw Rolf striding down the steep trace flanking this curved section of artery—toward where his noblemen were lying in wait. In all the miles between Italia and Parthia there was no steeper grade, not even those in the mountains of Agri Dagi could compare. And this was why the *herzog* had chosen the pass at Nauportus for his ambush. It was not enough to simply stop an armored imperial rail-galley; any gaggle of rebellious lads could simply crash a boulder or two into the pipeline, splintering the trestles, mangling the rails and maybe igniting an oil fire in the bargain. But then what would this sad lot have on its hands—even if it was fortunate enough to destroy the eagle-prowed van-car in a squall of its own steam? Only a mile-long iron fortress, bristling with *ballistae*, Greek firers, and a thousand praetorians to sortie from the cars, riddling with *pili* hornets all who dared so much as twitch.

No, the old man mused, agreeing with his Donar-touched king, that was not the way to deal with an imperial rail-galley.

Antonius Nepos let no guardsman enter his personal car. He continued to hold even the closest members of his retinue at bay with his stocky, many-barreled *pilum*, shouting orders down the aisle to them. He sent a tribune to the wireless car to order the mile-diameter revolving table in Nauportus readied for their arrival; the engine that turned the colossal device was seldom up to the task and had to be reinforced with the muscle power of several thousand slaves. *And good Mars,* he asked himself with a start, *were there even a hundred slaves left in a city that close to the northern frontier?*

The tribune returned to the car portal, his face drawn. "I'm sorry, *Imperator*. The wireless operator cannot get through. Mountain interference."

"No matter," Nepos said agreeably enough, for he had just changed his mind. Perhaps Saturninus and Claudia had posted a few conspirators in Nauportus as well in case the prefect's adjutant failed in his assassination attempt, as he indeed had. Saturninus was a careful man and would certainly have allowed for contingencies. It occurred to Nepos with a clammy kind of anger that he faced a series of cutthroats between here and his army at Tarsus. Of course, the one thing his dear wife and loyal praetorian prefect would not expect him to do was to wheel around his rail-galley at Nauportus and return to Rome. But what if one of their henchmen remained aboard and could get a message off to Nauportus or even Rome? Nepos could not let that happen.

"Tribune," he called.

"Sire!"

"Go back to the wireless car. Destroy the mechanism and slay the operator."

The tribune's jaw dropped. "*Lord Nepos?*"

He drew a bead on the man's breastplate. Its thickness was no match for *pili* shot. "Do as I say!"

The tribune raced for the wireless car.

It was a distraction Rolf had not anticipated.

While he hid beside his thanes, listening to the rail-galley lumber up the foot of the long grade, he suddenly began expe-

riencing her in everything around him. One of the *idisi*. A fatal
loveliness. He glimpsed her gown in the aura of the moon; her
slender uplifted arms in the autumn-bare limbs of the beeches; her
searching eyes in the amber forelamps of the van-car. And finally,
in an all-confirming instant, he heard the rustling of her wings in
the whish of his own cloak as he rose up briefly, to make sure none
of his warriors could be seen by the sharp-eyed praetorians who
would be riding in the eagle-prow.

"Aye, Swan Maiden," he then whispered so none but she could
hear him, for it would unnerve his *thegans* to learn that their king
had just been visited by an *idisus*, "and if this be my final battle,
I go down as a roar—as thunder, as stormy surf and Vesuvius in
blow."

She noted his acquiescence with a crosscurrent of breezes, one
smelling of the dank autumn leaves pasted to the rocks and the
other of the oily-exhalation from the rail-galley, which was now
clattering past him. The lungweed coals of the topside praetorians
were pecking the darkness with red.

He found himself smiling, although he was also gritting his
teeth as he waited for the blast.

It was a sad thing to die, of course. But by first light there
would be no Roman and no Marcoman within him to quarrel.
There would be no Rolf, only a transparency of him set against the
clouds. He would take to the sky, ride at full tilt with the Army of
the Furious.

He had once heard from a German legionary who'd nearly died
in battle against the Hibernians that it was pleasant to be visited by
an *idisus*. The man had not lied. Her appearance was sweet,
especially to a king weary of his office.

The old sapper crouched on a rock shelf above the artery, with
a stripped wire end in each hand. He had no fear of being peppered
with debris. It would not be much of an explosion.

And he had rigged himself two chances. But only two.

The rail-galley was now making the ground tremble, yet it still
amazed him that he could hear nothing of its rumbly progress, the
jets of steam erupting from the big petcocks as the great van-car
topped the incline and the operators fell upon their man-sized
levers to ease the pressure in the boilers.

He drew a long breath as he watched the overshot prow glide
past the first charge. He ignored the wash of the forelamps, which

was illuminating him, and then the first reports of *pili* fire being directed at him.

Exhaling, he clicked the wires together.

The detonation rocked the van-car, but only enough to jerk the helmets of the praetorian lookouts down over their brows and spoil their aim. Smoke puffed out from under the car, but the old man realized at once that the force of the blast had missed the pneumatic coupling by an arm's length.

Scrambling several yards to the side on his arthritic knees, he picked up a second set of wires as if they were traces, then waited as if oblivious to the praetorian rounds sparking on the granite slope around him, and finally connected the exposed ends.

This time there was fire, but a squiggle was all. Had he desired fire, there would have been plenty. However, what he had intended was for the niter powder to expend its fury on the coupling. This it had done, severing the van from the rest of the cars behind it.

At first nothing extraordinary happened. The rail-galley continued up the long climbing curve as if it were still of one strand. But then the van pulled ahead of the *ballista* car immediately behind it, and the headless rail-galley slowed to a stop before it could peak the summit. Its propulsion car, suddenly freed of its ponderous burden, sped on toward Nauportus, even though the operators were laying on the brakes, which the old man imagined to be screaking as they grated for a grip on the rails.

For a split second, the cars were perfectly suspended between ascent and descent. It was uncanny—how long that moment went on. But then, just as the praetorians were lofting their *pili* to have a volley at the old sapper, who was hobbling now for better cover, the rail-galley began to slide backwards.

Some of the guardsmen in a few of the cars had the presence of mind to set the brakes, for the old man could see their locked wheels showering the trestles with sparks, but these haphazard measures could never hold such weight in place.

So far, the rail-galley's speed was little more than what a schoolboy could run, but no one had thought to leap off the top decks.

Then the old sapper was hit. Although he felt no pain, he knew he had been hit because he was suddenly down on all fours. It had happened to him twice before, once in the Novo Provinces and another time in Mauretania. He waited for the numbness to work its way up from his bent leg; the agony would come later, hopefully when he was within reach of a horn of *met*. He would never mend from a wound this late in his life. Nevertheless he chortled to himself. He hadn't wanted to walk all the way back to the Wald.

He rolled on his side so he could track the helpless coasting of the rail-galley. Now the cars were skimming back down the rails so fast no man dared jump.

With a lurch, the first car in line, the last previous to the explosion, left the artery at the widest extent of the curve and plunged over the edge of the slope. Then, the midsection of the rail-galley buckled and began folding in on itself, and the old man regretted not being able to hear the crumpling of metal as the tangle of cars pitched over the precipice, spewing caped praetorians up into the moonlight as if they were houseflies.

"Ach!" he cried.

He felt a concussion in the hollowness of his chest, then surmised that one of the *ballistae* had discharged on impact with the gorge bottom. The shell exploded not far from an overturned car, its fiery blizzard of fragments massacring the guardsmen who were crawling out of the shattered windows.

"Ach!"

And when the silence finally came, all that could be recognized of the imperial rail-galley were its twin forelamps, jutting up out of the dust pall.

The old sapper saw Rolf move first toward the wreckage.

Antonius Nepos lowered his *pilum* slightly. The rail-galley was slowing as if it were suddenly bereft of its locomotion. In that moment he visualized some brushy barricade thrown across the Great Artery and a swarm of half-naked barbarians preparing to hurl themselves against the massed arms of his guardsmen. Then he realized that the muffled sound he'd just heard and largely ignored had been an explosion, although it scarcely jostled his car as it rippled down the length of the segmented vehicle.

Momentarily, all motion ceased, leaving him with the illusion that he was floating. He thought to hurry forward and inquire as to the reason behind this halt, but then it occurred to him that this might be another trick of the conspirators, a means of luring him out of his private car so he might be overwhelmed and murdered.

He remained where he squatted, clutching his *pilum*. "What is this?" he demanded.

No one answered.

Astonishingly, the rail-galley began to glide backwards, yet there was no indication that the van-car was pushing it in that direction.

Glancing out the window, he saw a black latticework of tree branches slip past at great speed, then ever faster, so swiftly they soon blurred to a streak of haze against the moon—although an ear-splitting skirl told him that the overworked brakes of a number of cars were being thrown into full lock.

Then a hard jounce flattened him against the deck, splitting his lower lip and filling his mouth with the sharp taste of blood. He had dropped his niter piece somewhere. He had heard it clatter against the corrugated iron plates.

The *electricus* lamps bumped twice and winked out. Yet, in the rectangles of moonlight laid out in the aisle by the windows he could see the corpse of Saturninus' adjutant slide like a sack of wheat down a ramp. Beginning to roll, turning into a flail of slack limbs, the colonel swept past him and thudded against the bulkhead. The other dead guardsman had been snagged at the foot by a couch bracket and was dangling upside down with his cape in swirly flux around his arms.

Then the car reared.

As he plummeted, Nepos cradled his head in his arms.

Lofting his sword, Rolf cried: "Follow!"

His lords hesitated, not for lack of courage but out of confusion. How could anyone have survived the buffeting taken by the twisted cars, which now more resembled a labyrinth of scrap metal than an armored rail-galley? Several cars were afire, and the screams of those trapped within were the only signs of life.

But Rolf knew better. He wheeled to bawl at his *thegans*: "Follow or live in shame!" He loosened a *baritus* that echoed again and again in the confines of the pass. His war cry was enough to start them trotting toward the wreckage. And then the first volley of praetorian *pili* set them charging, adding their own bellicose cries to the crackling of the flames. The Marcomans leaped through the broken windows into the darkened and shapeless cars, crawling over the dead and the dying to press the surviving guardsmen—who fought viciously, knowing what capture by the Germans would mean: slavery, if not torture and execution.

Somehow, a *ballista* car had landed smoking but upright, and now a squad of praetorians was managing to crank the huge rifled piece skyward, a massive column soaring up against the palely banded horizon.

Knowing what would follow, Rolf dived beneath a scrap of armored plating, shouting for his lords to do the same.

The *ballista* thumped—a concussion more felt than heard. Two heartbeats later, the sky lit up like phosphorous. This was followed by a lethal hail all about. It rattled on the ruined metal, snicked on the rocks of the slope until, suddenly, its startling fury was spent.

Metal fragments had been sprinkled throughout the col and were now glowing like embers.

Rising, Rolf scowled.

Those of his thanes not quick enough to seek shelter were heaped across the face of the declivity. Others more fortunate were already dealing with the *ballista* crew. A captured Greek firer was shuttled forward from the Marcoman reserve, and within a few seconds the praetorians were wreathed in flames, spinning headlong off the top deck of the car, one by one, at the conclusion of their strangely silent death dances.

Turning completely around, he surveyed the scene.

Having been one himself, he thought of praetorians as *cluster soldiers*, for they tended to cluster around the person of the emperor or, if made to fight like ordinary legionaries, around their commanding officer. Wherever the resistance was the stiffest, that is where Antonius Nepos would be. And the standard drill would be to remove him as quickly as possible from his own car, to strip him of his imperial vestments, and uniform him as a common guardsmen until the danger had passed.

Perhaps he was already dead, but Rolf didn't believe so.

It would take more than a tumbling rail-galley to kill this traitor.

"*Imperator?* Sire?"

Nepos stirred, but had to wipe the blood out of his eyes before he could bring the tribune's face into focus.

"Are you hurt, sire?"

His underlip was throbbing. "What's happened?"

"Ambushed." The young officer was half crouched. "We've been ambushed by Germans."

"Oh, the demons you say . . ." It wasn't possible—not this

far from the Wald. So perhaps Saturninus and Claudia had dressed some of their confederates as Teutons, knowing how Nepos despised them. Had this masquerade been intended as an artistic flourish to the attack? Or had his prefect and wife hoped to throw the blame on the barbarians should their venture at Nauportus Pass fail?

Groggily, he tried to come to his feet, but became so dizzy he had to accept the tribune's help.

The officer no sooner stood fully erect than he was knocked against the bent bulkhead of the car, down which he slowly slid, his eyes mystified. He had been hit in the side of the head. He died before his buttocks touched the deck.

Nepos himself made sure to stay low as he hunted in the darkness among the splintered couches and dining tables for his *pilum*. It was nowhere to be found. Nor could he locate his sword, and for some reason—perhaps the man had feared an accusation of treachery in the moments after Nepos had killed the colonel—the tribune's scabbard was empty.

He settled for a long and jagged sliver of aluminum, which he ripped from the burst roof of the car. The piece was so sharp it opened his palm, but he ignored the wet stab of pain.

He figured his best chances lay away from the rail-galley, away from the ambushers and even his own guardsmen, any one of whom might be more Saturninus' man than his own. He needed time in which to tend his wounds, recover his strength and think of what to do next. In fact, he would slay any praetorian who showed his face. No use taking chances.

One end of the car was completely collapsed, and the portal at the other was shut off by a wall of stony earth. Stumbling through the detritus of his fine appointments, he came to a window, once square but now crushed into a triangle. Taking a few deep breaths, he folded himself over the sill and dropped outside, heavily. His fall was cushioned by the body of a slave, one from his own household, who made a belchlike sound as his lungs were compressed by Nepos' knees. The servant had suffered a broken neck, and Nepos thought in passing that he himself was alive and this poor wretch dead if only because the gods took a hand in such matters; he thought this without any special sense of gratitude. The gods preserved those most like themselves. It was only natural.

He started plodding up toward the south ridge, which unlike the north slope was cloaked by moon shadow. The skirmish was confused enough for him to trust that he might not be noticed, as long as he kept to the tangles of debris.

But then a man in a crude cloak stepped directly in front of him, his hands clasping what Nepos imagined to be a dagger.

Instinctively, Nepos slashed at him with the aluminum sliver, catching him in the throat.

Gurgling, the man twisted as he fell, revealing a portable Greek firer hitched to his back. "Thievish bastards—our own equipment!" Nepos had it off him before the German's eyelids had ceased fluttering—for he was indeed a sausage, blood-red beard and hulking frame.

This explained everything: Claudia Nero had conspired with the abominable Germans from the beginning to weaken her husband's position so she could make her own thrust for the imperium. *The pustular bitch!* he railed inwardly, adjusting the nozzle to maximum reach. *Wait until the Senate hears about this! They'll tie her in a sack with a snake, a pig, and a cock—and dump her in the Tiber long before I can close my hands around her gullet!*

He strapped the firer over his shoulders, then continued up the slope at a run. Dispatching the German in so personal a way had invigorated him.

Rolf could make no sense of the praetorian defense. For once, it seemed helter-skelter. Did that mean Nepos was dead and each guardsman was only fighting for his own survival? One such panic-ridden soldier sprinted blindly toward Rolf's sword—and was promptly felled by it.

"Where be this eel?" Rolf muttered, widening his search, sensing that a vain man like Antonius Nepos would want to save himself from such a pointless fray as this.

He studied the lay of the col, the interplay of moonlight and shadow off the opposing slopes, then started up the dark side of the depression. The son of one of his thanes stood at the breach in the Great Artery caused by the careening rail-galley, watching a river of oil burble over the rocks. He glanced up and, like most men in their first battle, insisted on relating something of no consequence, some nonsense about all the praetorian food being ruined by the oil.

Rolf calmed him a bit by clenching his shoulder, then asked, "What of Antonius Nepos?"

"No one has seen him, *Herzog.*"

"Tell your father I be on the heights seeking this man."

"Do you wish him and my uncles to follow?"

Rolf scrutinized the pitchy woods above. "Aye, maybe—if they be with no more Romans to kill." He started off again, thinking momentarily to turn back and borrow the lad's *pilum*, but then deciding against it.

Within a short distance, he found signs that someone was hurrying through the trees before him—deeply indented tracks in the ground, and here and there a broken sprig of fir dangling from the bough.

"Aye," he whispered, doubling his pace, "vanity and cowardice be the father and mother of foot-speed."

Then, labored breathing sounded a short distance ahead.

Rolf halted and peered through the darkness.

A man was bracing himself between two trunks, trying to catch his breath. The silvered portions of his elaborate uniform were glinting in the moonlight.

Turning to face Rolf, he appeared to be without a niter piece, which gave the German the confidence to say: "Hail and farewell, Prefect Nepos."

"Who are you?"

"Rolf of the Marcomanni. Rolf, centurion to Germanicus Julius Agricola."

After a pause, Nepos gave out with a phlegmy chuckle. "Oh, yes. It's been a while, what? And aren't you a long ways from that sty you call the Wald?"

"I be willing to loan you my sword."

"Why?"

"To fall on it—in the Roman fashion."

"Why should Roman fashions matter to you, Rolf of the Marcomanni?"

"They do," he said, angry now, "especially the oath what a guardsman takes to his emperor."

"Well, my dear fellow, putting the issue of the *sacramentum* aside, I have no intention of falling on anyone's sword, particularly yours. Germanicus is not worthy of the purple if only because he was not strong enough to hold on to it. I, on the other hand, will do anything to retain the imperium. . . ." And with that, he reached behind him for the nozzle and clipped it to the tank of the Greek firer.

"No!" Rolf roared, hoisting his sword and barreling forward. But the gush of flame met him before he could reach Nepos, and the flood of orange swelled to envelop the world. Somehow, he whipped a corner of his cloak over his face, but the wool erupted and dripped off his forearm in greasy-looking tatters. The air was being sucked out of his lungs with such ferocity he thought they were collapsing like a ruptured billows. Still, he kept hurling himself toward Nepos, ignoring the tongues of fire that had rooted themselves to his arms. There were Marcoman voices nearby, but he knew he was beyond help. He only prayed that he would not be completely consumed in the few remaining feet to Nepos, who was already cowering, amazed that the wall of flame he'd sprayed on the German had not stopped him dead in his tracks.

Rolf swung frantically, then closed his eyes, grateful that he still had eyelids to close. He was also grateful to the god-friend for what he believed had been his last sight: Decimus Antonius Nepos' severed head rolling off a shoulder.

EPILOGUE

DRAGONS, CLOUDS AND cranes. These were the designs carved into the sandalwood screen separating him from the Xing emperor. Tora sensed flickers of movement through the graceful little apertures in the barrier, but dared not look directly upon the throned figure. It surprised him that, unlike all other courtiers in the imperial presence, he had not been instructed to prostrate himself on the coarse straw mat spread across the floor, with his face shunted and his eyelids pinched tight.

Perhaps the Emperor wanted to see his expressions as he told of his life among the Romans. *Hai*, he thought, *that is it. He wants to read my eyes and compare their various glints to my words.*

But did this extraordinary permission to remain on his knees also mean that the Xing emperor knew of his service rendered to Caesar during the seige of Tenochtitlan, which had led to the surrender of the Aztecae, close allies to the Xing? And would a swordsman appear at any moment to amuse the royal personage with a beheading? It did not seem likely for reasons of propriety, but Tora did not know this Master of the Restored Forbidden City as well as he had known his aged father.

"Tora," a minister said, for the Emperor would never deign to speak directly to him. In the man's cultured voice was that irritating blend of disdain and benevolence the Xing reserved for discourse with their Nihonian vassals: "You are to satisfy our curiosity about the kingdom of Rome"—it was not possible in the Xing mentality that an empire other than theirs existed anywhere in the world—"and its king. Firstly, what is his name?"

"Germanicus Julius Agricola."

His voice barely audible, the Emperor tried to pronounce it, but failed miserably.

"Tell us, Tora, how you came to know him. For this you have already admitted."

He did so over the next hour. He held back nothing about his own willingness to serve the Roman state, but ended his report at a point well before Germanicus' overthrow. Yet it seemed that the Xing had other sources of information, for the minister then asked, "But is it not true that this king has been deposed?"

Tora hesitated. If he related the absolute truth of Germanicus' circumstances, would war between the Romans and the Xing result? "No, please tell his Highness that this is not so. The Roman king has devised a stratagem to better understand his people. Secretly, he has put the captain of his imperial guard in temporary command while he wanders his domain disguised as a mendicant. But he retains all his power and will fully exercise it again when he has learned what he seeks."

"Which is?"

"Why men prize safety over freedom. And why men who sing his praises and fawn over him also mean him harm."

The silence grew so lengthy, Tora became certain he was doomed. But then the minister said, "Rise and come back tomorrow at the same hour."

He awoke. He knew not when. He knew not where.

But the moon was down and dawn was ruddling the east. He was not enrolled in the Army of the Furious, for the men carrying the litter on which he lay were far from disembodied. They were his own lords. And then there was the agonizing pain to remind him that he was not yet dead; he silently begged Donar to relieve him of the hideously scorched body he now lifted his head to appraise; he prayed for the *idisi* to wing down and let him know that relief was at hand. He listened for the rustling of wings.

"Your face was spared, my *Herzog*," someone said hopefully.

Rolf had to catch a groan in his throat. For the first time in his life he did not trust that his courage would last.

"We slew them to the last red cape," another voice reported. "And then used the *ballista* shells what to blast apart five miles of the artery. Nothing will roll east for a long while, my king."

"Finish me," he rasped.

The same man went on prattling about the job they had done on Nepos' praetorians. A complete massacre. But such things no longer mattered.

Again Rolf raised his head. "I beg thee. Free me unto the Army of the Disembodied. I be done with this body."

Suddenly, the litter was set upon the ground. He quickly shut his eyes, knowing that an exchange of glances at this moment would make his men balk. He waited, wondering if he would hear the blast before he felt the *pili* round. It did not seem likely.

But the silence lengthened. "Please, my lords. Be swift and earn my thanks."

"Nay," a new voice said. This man's features were lost in the glare of the risen sun. "We must take him to Glaesea's hut. She be familiar with poultices what molt the skin and grow another. Save him for Glaesea's touch."

Then the litter was lofted and jostled forward again.

Rolf yearned to argue, to change their minds, but he had to clench his teeth to keep from crying out.

Some time later, just before the god-friend's merciful blackness descended upon him, it occurred to him that the voice suggesting Glaesea's nursing had belonged to his late cousin Segestias.

Before Germanicus lay an empty plain. But along a ridge dimly seen in the west dust was being raised. Only a double line of sand-galleys could churn up such a dense pall. Since dawn the sea had been sending stiff breezes ashore, and anything that moved across the distant land sent brown plumes far into the air. As was peculiar to this country, the east side of the Gulf of Issus had been drenched by last night's rain, while the far shore remained parched.

Two hours—no more. And then Antonius Nepos' armored cohorts would be upon him.

The sun was already warm, although the tallith affixed to its eagle standard was snapping in a cool breeze. He gazed at the half-moon of phalanxes arrayed to his back; most of his men were dug-in, readying the pathetic weapons with which they would attempt to halt the speeding sand-galleys. A hundred slaves had volunteered to hide in covered pits out on the plain, crouching in darkness, waiting with crude Greek firebombs in their hands for the earth to start shaking.

Once again, he had sent Dathan and Shammai forward to track Nepos' advance, for surely the man had now arrived in the East; his entire consular army was on the move. Germanicus clasped his hands behind him and waited.

"The dust dissipates," Aulus Valentinian said when the sun was halfway to its zenith.

"So it would seem," Germanicus said. But he took no cheer from this observation, even when the pall grew thinner and thinner and eventually vanished altogether. It probably meant only that Nepos was outflanking him in a sweep to the north.

Germanicus would do precisely this if it were his gambit. Tomorrow, or even as early as tonight, he might well find himself under attack from the direction of the Caesarea Germanicia, a flyspeck of a garrison town named in honor of his ancient kinsman, Caligula's worthy father. Germanicus Julius Caesar had died soon after thirty, he mused, and he himself had lived a good deal longer than that. He had lived well too, loved three women and been given a valorous son—so there was no reason for him to begrudge the god who had spared him from suicide at Troy's ruin only to deliver him into the jaws of five hundred sand-galleys; for this was a more honorable way to perish, falling beside men like Valentinian, Norbanus, and Dathan; dying within sight of the fearless Mara. She was now smiling at him. *Yes, given time, I might have loved four estimable women.*

A hand fell upon his shoulder.

He spun around to face Dathan, who with Shammai had wisely circumvented the skittish battle line and entered the camp from the east. "We should march west again," he said offhandedly. "We can advance to the ridge over there."

"The battle will be brief enough without our being caught on the open plain."

"There will be no battle. Their army withdraws."

"But why?"

"Antonius Nepos is dead." Dathan almost smiled.

"What?"

"He was slain last night. I know nothing more about it than this. Except there is a rumor that this army and two others have been recalled to Rome."

"Another attempted overthrow then. What of Claudia Nero?"

"As far as I know, she lives."

His expression stunned, Germanicus turned to Valentinian, who had said something. "I'm sorry, dear Aulus, I did not hear you. . . ."

The general's own amazement showed in his eyes as a slight moisture. "Shall I give the order to march, Caesar?"

Germanicus nodded.

Soon after, trumpets blared and the standard was trotted to the front. Slaves approached from their ambush holes, confused; legionaries adjusted their packs and shouldered their heavy *pili*; the temple police prayed briefly and then scurried to their place in the advance, giving a wide berth to the Perushim rebels who glared at their hurried passing.

Finally, the first centurion of the Sixth Ferrata bawled the order, and a great stamping of sandals sounded across the muddy plain.

However, two figures failed to move with the others.

Mara stood transfixed. She was staring down at Germanicus Agricola.

Caesar had knelt.